Praise for *[illegible]*

"A winding, non-linear story that offers glimpses of history intertwined in a [illegible] abundant lens of human strengths and frailties."

—Dr. Sally Z. Hare, Coastal Carolina University Distinguished Professor Emerita; author of *The ElderGarten: A Field Guide to the Journey of a Lifetime*

"Ron Daise is an American griot. In this novel, Daise welcomes us into his village and, with his words, feeds our imagination and spirit. His voice connects our past with the present and helps us to get a glimpse of what our future might look like. This modern-day Gullah tale reflects the experiences of many Americans; in fact, it creates a bridge from the Lowcountry of South Carolina to the world."

—Alison Mc Letchie, Assistant Professor, Department of Social Sciences, South Carolina State University

"Ron Daise is a superb storyteller. When he speaks about 'the hag' and when you see the Gullah language written out, know that he writes of his heritage and was a member of the team that translated the language for the *Gullah Bible*. *Raptors in the Ricelands* affords readers an unforgettable journey with the customs and lifestyles of the Gullah community, which are shared with communities of the African Diaspora around the globe."

—Vanessa D. Thaxton-Ward, PhD, Director, Hampton University Museum

"Ron Daise's story offers a much-needed reminder of the voices of the Gullah Geechee ancestors that propel modern intimacy and pride of the Gullah Geechee in their land, culture, heritage, and language."

—Jessica R. Berry, PhD, CCC-SLP, Gullah Geechee Educational Consultant & Author

"*Raptors in the Ricelands* captures the music of the Gullah Geechee language and the dance of human interactions. Daise offers wisdom both grand and small, from secrets that cross oceans and centuries to the Edisto Islander cure for hiccups. Whether you are a beenyah, comeyah, or something in between, this book will leave you a richer and wiser person."

—Adam Knight Gilbert, Professor of Musicology [and comeyah], University of Southern California

"Ron Daise's exceptional storytelling skillfully immerses readers in the vibrant world of the Gullah Geechee community, unveiling its rich tapestry of culture, language, faith, spirituality, and the essence of Lowcountry living. As a Gullah Girl, my heart and soul resonated deeply with the narratives, and each story vividly transported me to its setting. Daise's work left me eagerly thirsting for more."

—Rev. DeMett Eva Jenkins, Director of Education and Engagement for Faith Based Communities, International African American Museum

"The many characters in this fictional story seem familiar and fully realized as Daise expertly shows the reader the connectivity between their lives, their Gullah culture, and the valuable 'Carolina Gold' rice. Equally important in this book are the teachings of Marcus Garvey Jr., and the reminder that humanity can only move forward when we unselfishly commit to helping those most in need."

—Eric Crawford, author of *Gullah Spirituals: The Sound of Freedom and Protest in the South Carolina Sea Islands*

RAPTORS IN THE RICELANDS

Ron Daise

RON DAISE

BELLE ISLE BOOKS
www.belleislebooks.com

ISBN: 978-1-958754-82-5
Library of Congress Control Number: 2023924355

Designed by Alexandra Littlehales
Project managed by Jenny DeBell

Printed in the United States of America

Published by
Belle Isle Books (an imprint of Brandylane Publishers, Inc.)
5 S. 1st Street
Richmond, Virginia 23219

BELLE ISLE BOOKS
www.belleislebooks.com

belleislebooks.com | brandylanepublishers.com

Dedication

To the memories of my beloved sister, Irene Daise Hicks, whose acts of love and philanthropy were unconditional, and Frances Grimes, PhD, my professor of African American Literature at Hampton Institute, I dedicate this book.

Acknowledgments

I sincerely thank the following individuals and organizations for encouragement, inspiration, and editing: Natalie Daise, Sara Makeba Daise, Simeon Othello Daise, Annette Gay Fowler, and "the coordinators," friends, and former Brookgreen Gardens staff members, Viki Richardson, Joyce Cirino, and Stephanie Atkinson.

This project is funded in part by the South Carolina Arts Commission, which receives support from the National Endowment for the Arts. This project also is funded in part by a generous award from the John and Susan Bennett Memorial Arts Fund of The Coastal Community Foundation of South Carolina.

Additionally, I thank Brookgreen Gardens for project financial support, and the following for project development and cultural resource information: Brandylane Publishers, Inc., particularly Jennifer DeBell, editor and project manager, and Mary-Peyton Crook, proofreader; Gwen Carson, Stanley C. Daise, Barbara Edwards, Johnny A. and Lynne B. Ford, Ray Funnye, Geechee Experience (Akua Page and Chris Cato), Veronica Gerald, Michael Glover, Ardell Greene, Vanessa Greene, Zenobia Harper, Vernell J. Heyward and Annie Ruth Smalls, Calvin B. Johnson, Lauren and Al Joseph, Ramona LaRoche, PhD, staff and students of the Athenaeum Press, and the Joyner Institute for Gullah and African Diaspora Studies; Vera Daise Thornton, Georgetta West, Steve Williams, Laurin Thomas Wilson, Sr.; and Coastal Carolina University for contributions to the "Seen, Heard, Esteemed: Living History Narratives of Georgetown County, SC" Audio Tour at Brookgreen Gardens, Murrells Inlet, SC.

A people without the knowledge of their past history, origin and culture is like a tree without roots.

—*Marcus Garvey*

Table of Contents

Author's Note

The setting for *Raptors in the Ricelands* is a fictional Gullah Geechee community of former rice plantations along the Waccamaw Neck in Georgetown County, SC. Plantation communities include Massaville, formally organized as Owners Town, a township off the Pee Dee and Black Rivers that was so populated with trees that plantation owners vacationed there during the summer heat. The enslaved workers of the original settler, Phillip Maurisina, creolized the pronunciation of his surname to "Mausna" and then "Maursa." Eventually, the enslaved population and their descendants began to regard the township as Mausaville. It is located west of the City of Georgetown and by waterways is near Darcatia Plantation, also owned by Phillip Maurisina, which extends from the Waccamaw River to US Highway 17 en route to Myrtle Beach.

The names and actions of characters are fictional and do not reflect any individuals or families of Georgetown, SC.

Preface

One hundred enslaved Africans were brought to the South Carolina Lowcountry by Spaniards in the summer of 1526. From then to 1867, Africans primarily from the Rice and Windward Coasts were enslaved and brought to produce rice, cotton, and indigo for southern plantation owners. Half of the rice grown in this country during the 1700s was produced in the 45,000 acres of ricelands in Georgetown County, SC, and imported on ships to European markets. Its savory taste was enjoyed by many. And the living culture of its African laborers and their descendants contributes continually to American heritage and Black American history. Rice production was laborious and almost year-round. It began in February and March. Trunkminders drained the rice fields, and male enslaved workers mended leaks in the dikes constructed around the fields which were caused by tree roots or the alligators that hibernated throughout the winter months. They burned the remnants of the past year's rice plants and leveled and softened the ground for planting. Oxen or mules were used to plow the fields by mid-April.

Females planted and harvested. Young girls would coat each rice seed with mud and drop it into the gumbo, so the seeds wouldn't float to the top after the fields were flooded. Walking through the fields in groups of three, one African woman, or their Gullah Geechee descendant, would dig a hole with a pointed stick. The second would drop a seed in the hole, and the third would cover the seed with soil, using her foot.

Rice fields were flooded and then drained four times, beginning in May. The sprout flow was allowed to stand on the fields for about one week until the seeds started to grow. The stretch flow allowed the growing rice plants to stretch for the sunlight through the six inches of water and killed the weed seeds. The long flow covered the rice completely and remained in the fields for about three days, killing any insects that might eat the rice plants. When the long flow was drained about mid-June, enslaved workers returned to labor in the fields for about thirty days.

The final and most important flood was the layby flow or harvest flow. It occurred when the rice stalks were about three feet high, and the harvest flow or flood was about three feet deep. It supported the tall stalks of rice so they wouldn't break as the seeds grew and became heavy. The layby flood was maintained for months, became stagnant and smelly, and bred mosquitoes. It was drained from the fields in September in time for the harvest, which continued through November.

Rice was harvested by hand, using sharp tools called rice hooks. Rice stalks were bundled together in sheaves, loaded on flatboats, and brought to the plantation yard for threshing. Women would beat the sheaves with long wooden sticks, knocking the rice off the stalks. They then gathered up all the seeds and pounded them with heavy handmade mortars and pestles to remove the bran from the rice. The grains were winnowed in large round "fanner" sweetgrass baskets. The hulls, or chaff, would fly away in the air, while the white grains of rice would fall back in the basket. Its savory taste was enjoyed by many.

Raptors loomed in the ricelands. Some with feathers, some with hands. Some signaled their approach with calls and screeches. Some were silent, yet alarming, and sometimes awe-inspiring shadows heralded them. Each raptor-type benefited the land and community, seeding the ecosystem with nutrients from their carnage or gifting mankind with grains of philanthropy. Some of the human species belied good intentions for the improvement of community and race, and sometimes politics or religion. Intentions, like talons, however, sometimes are deadly.

Cast of Characters

Vernon Russell Porcher, business commuter from Edisto Island, South Carolina

Wineglass Family

Chadwick Wineglass, of Georgetown, South Carolina, husband of Florence Tucker Wineglass

Florence Tucker Wineglass, Chadwick's wife

King Solomon Wineglass, Chadwick's father

Bernice Syndab Wineglass, Chadwick's mother

Blessing Celeste Wineglass, Chadwick and Florence Wineglass's daughter

Tucker Family

Adam Tucker, of Mausaville Plantation, Florence's father

Coralee Chaplin Tucker, Florence's mother

Emanuel Tucker, Florence's paternal grandfather

Blessing Tucker, Florence's paternal grandmother

Jasmine, Gardenia, Camellia, Andrew, and Thomas Tucker, Florence's paternal aunts and uncles

Community Members

(beenyahs)

The Right Reverend Jericho Bessellieu, Presiding Bishop of the 23rd District of the African Methodist Episcopal Church

William Dunkin, local root doctor

Gregory Dunkin, William's son

Melvin Marshel, husband of Thelma Thunderbolt Marshel

Abraham Marshel, Melvin's father

Precious Marshel, Melvin's mother

Rinda Middleton, of Darcatia Plantation, Emanuel Tucker's lover

Absalom Middleton, Rinda and Emanuel's first child

Easter Lillie Middleton, Rinda and Emanuel's second child

Sophronia Middleton, Easter's cousin

Carrie Middleton, Sophronia Middleton's daughter and Rinda Middleton's cousin

Eloise Nesbit, church mother

Mobo Night, a runaway slave from Darcatia Plantation: Eloise Nesbit's granduncle, and Sybil Thunderbolt' s great grandfather

Laverne Grice, a businesswoman and abused wife

Medicus Grice, Laverne Grice's husband

Gary Windley, an adult son who has returned home to care for his dying mother.

Eboni Manigault, a college student

Barry Gilliard, teenage son of Kendra and Raymond Gilliard
Otis Doyle, business investor

Bob Brittman, Chadwick Wineglass's high school classmate

(comeyahs)

Rev. Timothy Thunderbolt, twin brother of Thelma Thunderbolt Marshel, and son of Janie and Henry Leroy Thunderbolt of Seneca, South Carolina.

Thelma Thunderbolt Marshel, wife of Melvin Marshel, twin sister of Timothy Thunderbolt, and daughter of Janie and Henry Leroy Thunderbolt of Seneca, South Carolina.

Sibyl Thunderbolt of Columbus, OH, wife of Timothy Thunderbolt, and great granddaughter of Mobo Night and Nokomis Night, a Chippewa woman of Columbus, Ohio.

Historical Characters

Marcus Mosiah Garvey, Jamaican-born political activist, publisher, journalist, entrepreneur, and orator.

Renty Tucker, enslaved master carpenter of Plowden C.J. Weston, Hagley Plantation, Georgetown, SC, and builder of St. Mary's Chapel.

The Honorable Joseph Hayne Rainey, of Georgetown, the first Black person to serve in the U.S. House of Representatives.

The Honorable John Bolts, of Plantersville, SC, one of seven Black legislators in 1898.

Joshua John Ward, of Georgetown County, SC, is known as the largest American slaveholder, dubbed "the king of the rice planters". In 1850 he held 1,092 enslaved Africans on five plantations along the Waccamaw Neck.

Historical Geography, Events, and Organizations

Brookgreen Gardens, America's premier sculpture garden established on four former rice plantations, Murrells Inlet, SC

Brush Harbor Church, oldest African American church in Oconee County, SC

United Daughters of the Confederacy, formerly called National Association of the Daughters of the Confederacy, established in 1894 Edisto Island, SC, one of seventy-nine Sea Islands that comprise the federal Gullah Geechee Cultural Heritage Corridor

Freewoods Farm, the only African-American historical living museum in the United States, in the Burgess Community of Myrtle Beach, started in 1865

Friendfield Plantation, the land upon which former First Lady Michelle Obama's great-great-grandfather, Jim Robinson, and his descendants were enslaved, located along the Sampit River

Front Street, the business district of Georgetown, and site where tradition holds that a slave auction block and holding station were located during the 1800s

Gullah Geechee Cultural Heritage Corridor, which spans the Atlantic coast from Wilmington, North Carolina through South Carolina and Georgia to St. Augustine, FL, established in 2006 to promote the living culture of an African American people who are descendants of enslaved West Africans

Plantersville Plantation, one of several former rice plantations located in Georgetown County, SC, in which the PeeDee and Black Rivers converge

Harborwalk, walkway along the Sampit River in downtown Georgetown, SC

Black, Great Pee Dee, Little Pee Dee, North Santee, Sampit, and Waccamaw Rivers, a confluence of rivers into Georgetown County, SC that made freshwater tidal rice production possible

Howard Elementary and Howard High Schools, two (former) predominantly Black public schools of Georgetown County, established in 1908 on the original site of Georgetown Colored Academy, which was established in 1866 by nine formerly enslaved Georgetonians

The Atlantic Coast Lumber Company (ACL) of Georgetown, SC

The Divine Nine Fraternities & Sororities

The launch of **White supremacy** in Fort Mill, SC

The Monument to the Rt. Excellent Marcus Garvey, Kingston, Jamaica

The Orangeburg Massacre, Orangeburg, SC, February 8, 1968

The Reconstruction Era, the period from 1865 to 1877 during which Congress aimed to reorganize and readmit the Southern states into the Union following the Civl War and to determine the legal status of African Americans in a nonslave society

The Rice Museum, located in the Front Street business district of Georgetown, SC; houses the permanent collection of dioramas, maps, paintings, artifacts, and other exhibits that tell the history of rice cultivation in Georgetown Count

The unearthing of human bones in a slave graveyard at a construction site in **Hagley Plantation**, Georgetown, SC, 2007

The Universal Negro Improvement Society, organization founded by Marcus Garvey, its first President-General

Planting

Breaking the Ground

Their relationships with others, though starting innocently enough, would generally unravel from platonic and harmonious to unsettling. Like bobolinks in a rice field prospecting rice plants for their own self-interest, the couple would strip individuals of the vital kernels of friendship and self-fulfillment. Under the guise of helping, they lured the unsuspecting after chance sightings at church gatherings or after overheard conversations in restaurants and at recreational outings. Some responded with resentment, feeling somehow "hooked." Others, who were snared and numbed by the couple's unsuspecting sinkers, relaxed and waited expectantly to be pulled up and out of harm's way.

Vernon Russell Porcher, seeing the majestic and at times ominous shadows of large wings circling in flight overhead, wondered about their meaning. A weekly commuting businessman from Edisto Island, South Carolina, he was yet unlearned about the nuances of Georgetown County Gullah Geechee signs and wonders—about how the past shaped the present and future of individual Georgetonians, and about who was friend or foe.

2000s

Porcher began to have misgivings about the Wineglass couple early on. His first three encounters with them prompted a nervous tic in his neck. Unknowingly, he'd sat in the pew behind them following a drop-in at a Wednesday night prayer service visit. Overcome with a desire to sit still and meditate as he drove home from work, he pulled into the parking lot of the first church he saw. He heard uplifting music when gatherers entered, and he soon followed. The charismatic pastor at Walking Up the King's Highway, an interdenominational church group in Georgetown's Olde District community, asked for all visitors to stand and for members to greet them "with a love that transcends any kind of love that a weary traveler will need to journey up the King's Highway to heaven!"

The lone visitor, Porcher was weary that evening, burdened with thoughts about an impending personal financial crisis. His wife Mignon's car engine had died and needed to be rebuilt. Two of her car's tires had been replaced just the week prior. As a self-employed worker whose husband was commuting on weekends, she was without transportation for family or business. And Porcher's travel expenses for to-ing and fro-ing each week had stretched all discretionary funds to nonexistence.

The congregants' palpable compassion, the choir's vibrant praise and worship music, and the pastor's message that God's prosperity was abundant and overflowing to all who believed refreshed him. His parched soul absorbed the energy, the light about him. The atmosphere renewed his confidence. Without identifying any particulars about his family's financial circumstances, he stood and testified. He voiced awareness that the God who owned the cattle on a thousand hills would surely spare one hefty but metaphorical bull or heifer for him to steer to market or butcher for sustenance.

As Porcher tightly held the back of the red upholstered church pew, the Wineglasses, in the pew two rows in front of him, in one accord raised their hands upward, turned their ears toward his voice, locked eyes with each other, and slowly nodded their heads up and down. Their actions made no meaningful impact on Porcher, yet he replayed them in his mind months later and felt the chill of suspicion. He exited promptly after benediction but with a burning desire to return to this house of worship soon.

The following Wednesday evening, Porcher arrived late to worship. He sat near the entrance. The Wineglasses, seated on the opposite side of the center aisle, in unison turned their heads, smiled, and nodded as though they had been awaiting him, and then returned their gaze to the pulpit. Eventually, the pastor called them by name to advance to the front for communal prayer, announcing that a relative of Chadwick Wineglass had recently died.

Remembering the barrage of bereavement expenses for food, travel, and funerary costs following recent family deaths, Porcher expressed condolences to Chadwick as he departed. Chadwick stood apart from everyone, with his hands in the pockets of his olive-green cargo pants. Florence huddled in a group of women nearby.

Porcher approached him and handed Chadwick twenty-five dollars in cash, stating, "I know what it's like in times like these, man, believe me." The two men shook hands, and Porcher walked to the parking lot.

The third encounter at the end of the weekly prayer service a month later presented the probability of a beginning friendship. "Hey-y-y!" Chadwick called out to Porcher as he walked to his ocean blue Impala sedan, "you come in and flow out like a riptide. What's your rush?"

Porcher spoke into his phone, "Hey, Honey, let me call you back, okay?" then turned and greeted him. As Chadwick stepped closer, his broad smile revealed a space between his two top front teeth. It caught Porcher's attention, but he chose not to rely on what his cultural training intimated about its meaning. That the gap spoke about his character. That the individual was a storyteller, and that speaking the truth may not be an absolute for him. Truth for storytellers, Porcher had learned, sometimes is framed by their best interests or misguided judgements.

"Well, it's not like I know anyone here," Porcher answered. "Chadwick, right?" He nodded. "Hi, I'm Russell. Vernon Russell Porcher."

"Where you from, Russell? Who your people?"

"I'm only here during the week," Porcher replied. "I work in the realty office at Debordieu Colony Beach Club and commute home to Edisto Island on the weekends—'til my family joins me, that is. So, I stop in here when I can for a spiritual tune-up midweek. You know . . . well, maybe you don't . . . but living on the road can wear you out!"

"What I know is this, Vernon Russell . . . I mean, Russell—" Chadwick answered, "—you gotta talk to people to get to know them."

"Yeah, you're right. You see, I'm always in a hurry to leave when service ends each Wednesday cause it's my kids' bedtime." Facing

Chadwick, Porcher leaned back on his car's closed front door. "Telling them, 'night-night' is a ritual I'm gonna continue with, like things were before I started the job here four months ago," he explained. "That way, when my family is together again full-time after this school year ends, after our house sells, the circle will be unbroken.

"And, well, even though this is my third mid-week prayer service here, each time I visit, I still get invitations to stop in for Sunday service. And each time, I've said, 'Thanks, but I travel home on weekends.' So, it's not like I don't talk. It's more like when I talk, others here don't seem to listen."

Chadwick, nodding politely, said, "Do say, my brotha. Do say." He extended his hand to deliver what he'd been holding. "Tell you what. Here's my business card. Give me a call, Russell Porcher. Let's meet for lunch some time. My treat."

Opening his car door, Porcher reached inside and handed Chadwick his card in exchange before driving away. Abiding by an unwritten code of manly ethics that swirled in his head until that moment, Porcher had been determined to live a friendless existence on this side of his Georgetown commute. The code's dictates were this: Single women look favorably and in hopes of connectivity at unattached men whose wife or significant other is nowhere to be seen. Married men suspect infidelity by unattached men who align themselves with their spouses. Married women attach concerns of no-good to unattached men who spend time with their spouses. And most married men above thirty-something ascribe homosexuality to unattached men who want to connect with them.

Maybe, winds of change are stirring, Porcher thought. The lure had been tossed, and he, with reasoning based on limited knowledge of this community, its stories, or its personal entanglements, hadn't found it foreboding.

1980s

None of the nuns at Healer of the Land Catholic School had ever mentioned the name Marcus Garvey during Chadwick's elementary through junior high school studies. Yet Garvey's words began to anchor him years later. And the wishes and expressions of his middle-class parents, King Solomon and Bernice Syndab Wineglass, though at times understood through the lens of a child, had also shaped him. They wanted their three children never to be saddled with being labeled as Geechee or Gullah or any other moniker identifying them as ordinarily Colored, Negro, or Black. No, he and his siblings were to be standard bearers for their people. Almost daily, their parents imparted to them: "If a task is once begun, never leave until it's done. Be the labor great or small, do it well or not at all!"

"You ever hear White people saying, 'dis' for 'this'?" his mother would drill him after overhearing him converse with neighborhood children. "They sound so backwards. 'Dis' is not a word. It's a prefix. So don't use it. And dis-continue using it if you ever do! And say 'you,' please, not 'oona' or 'hoona.'" Shaking her head, she added, "And if I ever hear you or your siblings say, 'ainty' or 'ennit' for 'isn't that so', I will end your conversation before it causes the end of me!"

As Georgetown County Clerk of Court, Mr. Wineglass conversed each day at the dinner table about neighbors, church members, or community leaders who had defied the law and tainted presumed levels of integrity. "If you find yourself in jail, I'll help you out once," he'd advise. "So, live right! Once a fool, you're not a fool. Twice a fool, you a jackass. And if you continue on that hell-bent highway to rob, kill, lie, abuse, or drink yourself into hell, you'll be on your own . . . on the other side of this front door. Mark my word!"

Soon after graduation from Georgetown's Joseph Hayne Rainey High School, Chadwick was compelled to make his parents proud. He embarked upon becoming an entrepreneurial tour-de-force to show his Lowcountry South Carolina community that with a dream and a made-up mind anyone could "accomplish what you will." He aimed to be an exemplar of attaining financial independence—not back in Africa, but in the country of his birth—to show his schoolmates who had scoffed at his drive, his personality, his tenacity, and sense of self-sufficiency, that they, too, could excel if they self-actualized the thought, "Up, you mighty race!"

The words of Chadwick's mantras floated into his consciousness across generations, across continents, across racial barriers. They linked with lessons learned that had been whispered into his youthful ears but that should have been tossed out or at least questioned.

He launched Wineglass French Drain Installation with the awareness that with the burgeoning tourist market in nearby Horry County, real estate development would boom, demanding home and business construction. And the foundations of buildings and the surrounding pavements that had to be built atop wetlands and flood zones would require draining water away. His business idea was noteworthy. His diction and charm presented him as trustworthy. And his work ethic, character, and business acumen ushered in success. In time, he began to model the life of Jamaican political activist, publisher, journalist, orator, and entrepreneur, Marcus Mosiah Garvey, Jr. He had learned about the man during his honeymoon. And the haunting echo of his father's voice exhorting, "Be like God and help people, Son. And let God be your only friend!" remained a hallmark of Chadwick's development.

Late 1990s

Dalton Lachicotte of Georgetown, Chadwick's first client, had been so enamored with his French drain installation at his bed and breakfast inn that he'd recommended him to fellow investor, Otis Doyle. Chadwick's insistence not to use substandard materials even though this would've tripled his profit ratio caught Doyle's attention. Intrigued, the elder businessman began to shower Chadwick with nuggets of old-money wisdom. References of bankers. Recommendations of types of accounts that continue to accrue interest upon interest. Suggestions of affiliating with organizational boards in order to network, listen, and learn. The ultimate goal of being concerned with long-term profit margins over immediate family or community interests. In his naivete, Chadwick began to accept Doyle's advice without question, not realizing he was casting pearls before swine—never considering that Doyle one day would trample them underfoot and then turn to tear Chadwick's integrity to pieces.

Chadwick met the girl of his dreams during daily travels to a three-month construction site at the developing Carolina Gold Resort in Myrtle Beach. He drove to Calabash by the Sea for a quick lunch break from Carolina Gold Resort and eyed her through an open door to the kitchen as he walked to his booth. Over the counter, she handed plates to a waiter. She looked up, saw his intent and admiring gaze as he sat at his table, blinked, smiled politely, then returned to preparing plates.

Chadwick found himself smitten by the tall, smooth-skinned, walnut-brown beauty. He interpreted Florence Tucker's response to his admiring glances as meaning, *This is the smile, the look, the wink that I've intended only for the man I will marry and raise a family with. Uh huh!* He peered at her over the top of his menu, asked the waiter for her name and if she was single, and ate with utmost delight the food that he'd been informed she'd prepared.

He nodded at her as he left the restaurant and then returned for lunch daily for two weeks, asking each time to be seated at the same vantage in front of the Calabash kitchen door. On the second day, he requested to speak with the cook. When she met him at his table, they exchanged names, and he asked her to join him for a weekend date. Romance budded. They learned each other's likes, dislikes, familial connections, and peculiarities. Their shared laughter, tears, and intentions began molding them into one. And after six rapidly unfolding and love-filled months, Chadwick and Florence were wed. At his insistence, Florence left Calabash to prepare scrumptious meals and desserts for him and him only. Until, of course, the hoped-for and blessed day arrived when the newlyweds would find they had "a bun in de oven" and, as said in Gullah Geechee lingo, "had begun making feet for socks."

The eldest of eight, Florence had begun cooking for her family at age six, helping to raise her six stair-step siblings. Her four-pronged bridal dowry—cooking, cleaning, organizing, and helping—pleased her husband, who was steeled with commitment to be their sole provider. He wanted to ensure that her present and future never mirrored her past, growing up in one of the small, still-standing, still-used slave cabins on Brown Pelican Plantation. No, he would give her the world!

Calabash by the Sea employer Gregory Dunkin was not sad to see Florence step away from the throne of Calabash chefdom. Ever since the tall, muscular Chadwick Wineglass had sauntered into the restaurant, and even before he'd asked questions about Florence, Gregory had intuited many things about them. He had read Wineglass's aura, peeked at his palms, and noted a shift of energy in the atmosphere. The eldest son of an eldest son of yet another eldest son who was the root doctor of Mausaville, Gregory also knew that Florence, if she held onto the truths of her past, was about to step into her purpose.

Coating the Rice Seeds

Late 1990s

The Wineglasses honeymooned on a four-day cruise to Jamaica, an unexpected wedding gift from a member of the Gardens at River Bend Board of Trustees. Chadwick had only recently and reluctantly agreed to serve on the organization's board. Enamored with his honesty and community affiliations, Chadwick's newfound benefactor, Otis Doyle, had bankrolled both the cruise and Chadwick's two-year financial obligations to the board. He'd hoped his investment would pave the way for other African Americans of Georgetown County to explore, utilize, and experience the site of Lowcountry botanical wonders. The Gardens at River Bend was laid out in the shape of a stalk of Carolina Gold rice, and much like nearby Brookgreen Gardens, was established on grounds where a large enslaved workforce had once labored and lived. While Chadwick felt grateful and favored by the largess of Doyle's kindness, Florence felt wary.

The luxury cruise followed a simple churchyard wedding below the oaks near the Sampit River at Friendfield A.M.E. Church. In addition to the bride and groom, the wedding party only included the maid of honor, best man, and flower girl. But the immediate family members: extended family members of aunts, uncles, and first to twenty-fourth cousins; neighbors, coworkers, and friends from Mausaville, Georgetown and beyond filled the grounds with about four hundred. And although only the wedding party and immediate relatives could be seated in the church fellowship hall, no one left the wedding reception hungry. The repast, like a church picnic, was homemade by family cooks who'd joyfully been stirring pots for a week.

Chadwick and Florence, on their first trip beyond Georgetown County and outside the United States, marveled at the similarities of the Jamaican people with their own family and community members: the faces, the speech, the movements, the behaviors, the foods.

"Weh yaw seh?" street venders called out to them whenever they caught the couple's eyes as they passed and glanced at their merchandise. The Wineglasses quickly realized the meaning of the Jamaican Patwa greeting by the sincere and inviting brilliance of the speakers' eyes and smiles.

"Well!" and "Great!" Chadwick responded, while Florence eased into a "back-home" context. "Doin!" she'd call out, or "We doin!"

The Jamaicans recognized their cultural continuity, realizing that each of their ancestors had been on the same boat hundreds of years ago but had gotten off at a different "poht," or port. In turn, the scenes on the horizon—live oak, cedar, palmetto palm, and Jamaican dogwood trees, and boatmen casting nets and hauling fish—reminded Florence and Chadwick of their Sea Island homeland.

Small handicrafts of portraits, dancers, and animals intricately carved from ebony, mahogany, and baobab attracted their attention. Caressing one he'd picked up at the table of a short, thin-bodied Jamaican man whose complexion mirrored his wife's, Chadwick asked Florence, "Don't these remind you of the walking sticks and sugar cane pipes Old Man Forster whittles on his front porch?" She nodded in agreement.

Raucous laughter and conversation at a nearby vendor's booth piqued their interest, and they moved closer to listen. Amused, they poked elbows in each other's sides. The familiarity of the speaker's intonations tickled them. And although they found some words and expressions new, the vocal interplay they overheard was as familiar as a dish of red rice.

"Whappen when ya Cousin L.O.L. come home last week, Lottie?" a squat brown woman asked her friend who'd left her nearby booth to chat. "Ya been way tree day. Tree day! Dis Market ain de same when ya stay way! No talk fa make me dead wid laugh!" She paused to pull her colorful bandana down slightly on each temple.

"Him light up de sky when him cross ya doorway, I know."

"Hmpf," Lottie responded. Her large, round brown eyes deadpanned as her friend watched.

"Noooo?" Myrtle asked with incredulity.

"Him come home ta Jamaica, yeah. But him stay way from Trench Town. Tell we ta wisit him at de Jamaica Pegasus Hotel. Say de business conference him been tend ain lef em no time fa come see we. Him ain step oba no famlee threshold. It a shame, a disgrace!"

"Not Leaf of Life Campbell!" Myrtle whispered. She raised her hands over her lips, widened her eyes, and shook her head in disbelief. "No! L.O.L.? A turncoat?"

Lottie placed a hand on each hip and straightened her back before answering. "An him say, 'Don't call me no Leaf of Life or L.O.L. no mo.' Say him ansa ta de name Wilberforce, Wilberforce Campbell. Say dat what him 'colleagues' call him."

"Oh, shame! Shame an a disgrace!" Myrtle snapped. "Him betta rememba de story how him get dat name. Him mama breat been short short when de contraction start fa come wit him. So, Miss Sukey, de midwife, been brew de Leaf of Life plant and been gib huh de tea ta drink fa ease-ease huh burden. An when de time come fa she ta gone in, huh breathin been deep an scrong, deep an scrong, til she fusbon pop out huh womb. Him betta not fagit dat!"

"An me an him aunts and uncles been make all de tings him lob fa nyam," Lottie stated with tension marking her face. "Conch stew, Escovitch fish, curry goat, jerk chicken, rice and peas, corn pie, steamed cabbage, sweet potato pie, and cinnamon baked plantains. Him ain been home in tree years. Tree years, now! But if him nyam any a dese tings in Jamaica, him nyam em at dat drat Jamaica Pegasus Hotel Restaurant! An ain none of it got de lob him famlee been stir in we pot. No. No. No."

"Tell de trute, girl, wha lef oba?" She pursed her lips with imagined succulence as her mouth began to water. "If ya ain bring me none today, I gon folla ya home an seddown at de welcome table."

Myrtle paused to collect her thoughts, then added, "Well, I still lob em . . . fa true, but . . ." Their conversation stopped abruptly as each turned and became aware that their voices had held the Wineglasses' rapt attention.

"Wha yah deh pon?" meaning "How are you doing?" Myrtle asked with dryness to her tone, caught off guard by their presence.

The light in both her and Lottie's eyes had dimmed. They peered at the couple, but a wall of emotion lay behind their gazes. Florence and Chadwick could decipher the meaning, *What are you up to?* But the women's tone was filled with rancor, not lightheartedness. What they could not decipher was if the women were upset at their eavesdropping, perturbed that their personal conversations may have waylaid sales, or confounded about the Saga of L.O.L., also once known as Leaf of Life.

Embarrassed, the newlyweds lowered their heads and examined the collection of fabrics and handmade jewelry in Myrtle's booth. Florence oohed and aahed nervously and tried on some pieces, but the merchants' tension never eased. Speaking with her eyes only, she persuaded Chadwick to purchase a few colorful cloths, and they then moved on.

Young boys, six- to eight-years-old, shirtless, wearing short pants and sandals, ran up to them whenever they turned a corner. "Dolla fa bracelet," they hawked. "Pretty earrings fa lady. Two fa dolla." Teen girls pulled trays from their heads to offer their goods with outstretched hands. Purple Jamaican fruit star apple. Ginger candy, ginger cake, and ginger biscuits. Fruits. Purple Jamaican fruit star apple. Brown Stinking Toe Fruit. And green whole guavas with a few halved pieces, showing their succulent pink interior. After the Wineglasses selected their snacks, the girls deftly hoisted the trays back atop their hands to exchange currency.

Workers, young and old, were everywhere. Despite their own humble Sea Island beginnings, Florence was saddened by the impoverishment they witnessed.

"At least back in Mausaville, families can farm the land or fish or start a business other than toting baskets on their heads all day long," she stated as they walked back to where the cruise line was docked.

"Tote?" Chadwick asked. "I know I didn't hear you say, 'tote.' They were 'carrying' baskets on their heads, honey. 'Carrying.' If my mother heard you say that, she would try to get this marriage annulled immediately!" Her look mirrored surprise and indignation. Sensing that his joke had not been received well, he countered, "I'm joking, Wife. I'm just joking."

When her face softened, he added, "Come here, Florence Tucker Wineglass. Tonight, I'm going to 'carry' you over the threshold to the stateroom of our wedding bed one more time. I've been 'toting' lots of joy that I'm going to excite you with again and again!"

He reached into his pocket and pulled out jewelry he'd picked up secretly from merchant Myrtle's booth at the market when he'd separated briefly from his wife. Florence shrieked at the sight of the handmade emerald necklace and bracelet.

"Tote me, baby; tote me! I'm all yours!"

Strolling hand in hand on the beach in the morning, Chadwick thought about their conversation the night before.

"The thing about 'us'—back in Georgetown and here in Jamaica—is we always have to start at the bottom." He'd begun a light discussion in between several sessions of romance, eroticism, and rest. "Even if we have a good business idea, banks won't give us the same advantage as they give 'them.' And we don't have 'money that comes from money.' Our parents work and work but have nothing or little to pass on to their children. Maybe some are lucky enough to have relatives who leave them with a ten-thousand-dollar life policy."

He'd moved, fully unclothed, to the ottoman at the foot of the bed and looked back at his bride lovingly. She'd eyed his broad shoulders and bare back and made a sweeping gaze to the full glory of his engorged frontal view.

"But that's just enough to put people in the ground," Florence had said. As she sat up in the bed, the white sheets slid slowly down over her walnut brown breasts and revealed aroused chocolate nipples.

"You got that right! But you know what?" Chadwick had asked, enamored at the vision of her as she tilted her head back to listen to him. He'd paused to ogle, but also to ensure he had her undivided attention. "I want us to be able to do something to help others," he continued. "You know, like Otis Doyle, who gave us this honeymoon trip. Now, his family has money from way-y-y back."

Florence eyed her husband with a questioning look. "I hear he's a distant relative of Joshua John Ward," she said. "'The king of the rice planters.' Isn't that what they called Ward?"

Chadwick continued as though he'd been uninterrupted. "And

the planters made it off the backs of the thousands who grew that backbreaking Carolina Gold rice for them. I want to grow Wineglass French Drain Installation to be able to help 'us.'"

"Think big, Chadwick Wineglass. Think big!" she'd responded, smiling, and not wanting to deflect his enthusiasm. "If you've got a vision, we won't perish."

By and by, their "business talk" segued again to "body business." Unashamed and together. Up and down. In and out. Over and over. Spirit intermixed and connected with spirit. Again and again. No talk, no rush. Relax, release. Heart to heart. Skin to skin. Spouse to spouse.

Later, during an afternoon tour of Kingston, they came upon the Monument to the Rt. Excellent Marcus Garvey. The site changed the course of their lives from that moment onward.

A bronze bust of a suited man with penetrating eyes sat perched atop a ledge that was set at the center of two cascading stone walls. It overlooked a burial vault, made from terrazzo and inset with marble. A grave marker read:

Marcus Mosiah Garvey
Jamaica's First National Hero
1887 - 1940

The site filled them with the hushed reverence they felt whenever they visited the graves of their ancestors. *Who had this man been?* they wondered. *Why is he so nobly honored?*

A volunteer from the St. Ann Parish Library handed them each a flyer that had a picture of Garvey, an excerpt of one of his speeches, and the library's address. The elder motioned for them to follow him to the shade of a nearby rosewood tree to answer their questions. Standing in front of the rosewood, he was almost camouflaged in stature and complexion against its elongated trunk and tree bark. His tan straw hat, white eyes, white teeth, and strident voice made him stand out.

"Oh, Marcus Garvey was born right here in St. Ann's Bay," the docent said with pride. "He came from humble beginnings, but he became known around the world! He lived in America for a while, and in England, and he became a great writer and orator."

"I never heard of him before now," Chadwick said, shaking his head. Florence echoed his words and movements.

The six-foot, two-inch, medium-built man pushed his eyeglasses onto his oval face. With a white handkerchief, he wiped away the perspiration that had caused them to slip forward. His gold, small-hoop earrings glistened in the sunlight. "Garvey believed, 'I shall teach the Black man to see beauty in himself,'" he explained. "And millions learned from this lesson. 'Up, you mighty race,' he would exhort. 'You can accomplish what you will!'"

The Wineglasses learned that Garvey's body had been brought back to Jamaica from England, where he had died, and was re-interred at the monument, in a vault that lay in the center of a black star. This was the symbol Garvey used among his enterprises, one of which was the Black Star Line Shipping Company.

Intrigued, the couple left the monument with minds abuzz. At a nearby restaurant, they reflected on the flyers each had received.

Florence's read:

> "For three hundred years the Negroes of America have given their life blood to make the Republic the first among the nations of the world, and all along this time there has never been even one year of justice but, on the contrary, a continuous round of oppression. At one time it was slavery, at another time lynching and burning...this is a crime against humanity; it is a crime against the laws of the Nation, it is a crime against Nature, and a crime against the God of all mankind."
>
> Marcus Mosiah Garvey
> (Hill ED. MG Paper, Vol. 1, 213)

Chadwick's flyer read:

> "Gradually we are approaching the time when the Negro peoples of the world will have either to consciously, through our own organization, go forward to the point of destiny laid out by ourselves or must sit quiescently and see the more of economic serfdom, to be ultimately crushed by the grinding mill of exploitation and be exterminated by the strong wind of prejudice."
>
> "The Negro's Place in World Reorganization"
> (Philosophy and Opinions, 34)

Husband and wife sat sober in thought at their restaurant booth until their order arrived. The aroma of their plates of Jamaican Run Down revived their senses. Tantalizing scents of seafood, coconut milk, tomato, onions, garlic, and other aromatic seasonings made their bellies, their bodies, their hands, and their heads begin to dance. Not knowing what to expect, Florence was surprised to find that this fish stew was similar to many a family meal she had prepared since childhood. Chadwick savored the crumbly, soft, run-down consistency of the mackerel in its coconut broth but wished it had been flounder. And though they enjoyed the dumplings, they both commented, "We need this dish with rice if we come here again. Good God, is it good!"

With their appetites satiated, their thoughts returned to their late-night conversations and afternoon outing. They sat amidst a sea of guests speaking mostly Patwa but many other languages, wearing colorful Rasta hats while sporting dreads and showcasing myriad styles of braids, twists, and Sisterlocks. The couple re-read their flyers and exchanged them as they sipped on red Jamaican sorrel drink. Their glasses clanged with ice cubes.

"So, Chadwick, you think we should follow Garvey's lead and start our own organization or business to help the people of Georgetown?" Florence asked.

"Yes, Honey," he said. "I think we should. I think we can." They looked into each other's eyes and clasped hands across the table.

"Well, think big, Baby. Think big!" Florence whispered. And then, Chadwick witnessed an explosion of enlightenment in his wife's eyes. "That's it!" she said with excitement.

"What, Florence? What are you talking about?"

"We should call it 'Think BIG'. No, just 'BIG'. No, no, no. Let's see, let's see . . . 'B.I.G.' That's a homerun, there, Chadwick. 'B.I.G.'—for 'Benefactors in Generosity.'"

"I like it!" Chadwick agreed. "Let's do it. Soon as we got back home. We're a team, Florence Tucker Wineglass. We're a team. Fa true!"

Dropping the Seeds into the Gumbo Soil

2000s

Eleven months following their return home, a collision of unexpected events began to impair Florence's newlywed bliss. Emotional stress became dead weight within her. Caretaker weightiness reshaped and redefined her. She became Woman. Wife. Daughter. Sister. Friend. Granddaughter. A-maybe-one-day-mother. Community member. And custodian of all.

To care for everyone was her responsibility, she reasoned. Because she had been born with a womb . . . could sense everyone's needs . . . knew what needed to be done . . . could provide . . . was expected to provide . . . had to provide.

Florence Tucker Wineglass became the seed dropped in the rice field whose responsibility was to make more seeds. And to ensure that all other seeds flourished.

Florence's mother, Coralee Tucker, died on her drive home from work at the McFarlands Elementary School Cafeteria, hit broadside by a drunk driver. Her tragic death eclipsed the conversation Coralee had been meaning to have with her husband that evening about the conversation she'd overheard that day among other cafeteria workers. They'd gossiped about her father-in-law, Emanuel, having been seen some time ago hiding in the shadows at a double family funeral in a nearby community. About how the dead four-year-old had never been seen outside the Darcatia community. That it was said the child had been the spitting image of

Emanuel Tucker. The workers' whispered chatter stopped abruptly when they realized Coralee had been listening, and they averted their eyes when they spoke to her.

"Up, you mighty race" became Chadwick's mantra as he worked in the face of family sadness.

Overcome with grief, Florence's father, Adam Tucker, wondered how he would continue to provide family care. His village, however, responded before he could begin to fret. His widowed father, Emanuel Tucker, who still lived in his own home on the family compound, moved into his son's home to help care for his younger grandchildren. He got them off to school each morning. Helped to tuck them in at night. And Florence pledged to prepare their dinners weekly, bringing them to the Tucker house in refrigerator dishes marked for each day. This arrangement worked well for two weeks, until Emanuel contracted vertigo.

Despite their own complicated emotions from a failed pregnancy, the Wineglasses brought Emanuel Tucker to their two-bedroom modular home for temporary care. Looking or turning to the right made the elder Tucker regurgitate. He could steady himself to walk only with a cane. And at times he needed to crawl to get to the bathroom.

Day in and out, Chadwick grew his business, returned home to cherish his bride, and mapped out plans to implement the dream they had envisioned in Jamaica. *You can accomplish what you will*, Chadwick would think, completing the quote of Garvey's words. In the waiting room before his annual dental appointment, he read a quote in *Black Enterprise* magazine that inspired and challenged him. Founder and publisher Earl G. Graves, Sr. had written: "Money makes people listen. When you have it, then you have something others want and need. When you don't, you become invisible." *I want people to see me!* Chadwick reasoned to himself. With polished teeth and a made-up mind, he left his appointment determined to effect a change.

To keep themselves mindful of their honeymoon bliss and discoveries, Florence began making weekly or bi-weekly visits to the Georgetown County Public Library to find out more information about Marcus Mosiah Garvey. On her first visit, she checked out a copy of *Black Moses: The Story of Marcus Garvey and the Universal Negro Improvement Association,* by E. David

Cronon, with a foreword by John Hope Franklin. She imparted snippets of information about the Jamaican hero to Chadwick during suppertime and evening conversations. That he'd sowed seeds of new Black pride and determination; that he'd been attacked by the Black intelligentsia and ridiculed by the White press; that he'd developed the Universal Negro Improvement Association (UNIA), in just four years, which went on to become the largest and most powerful all-Black organization that America had ever seen.

Always attentive, Chadwick listened to her stories, relishing the memory of their visit to the Jamaican monument and their business decisions made afterward.

"What you say?" he'd asked with an openmouthed follow-up when Florence informed him about Garvey's organizational philosophy.

She explained that in Jamaica, Garvey had joined the National Club, which fought against privilege and British colonial control over his homeland.

"Listen," she added, "an organ of that political group was named 'Our Own.' He poured abundant energy into it. Garvey said, 'I trust that you will so live today as to realize that you are masters of your own destiny, masters of your fate; if there is anything you want in this world, it is for you to strike out with confidence and faith in self and reach for it.' This is what we can do with B.I.G., Chadwick! We can help our people here in Georgetown to become masters of their own destinies. To get freed from debt in some small way and then move on to greater things."

The couple rose from the dinner table and embraced. With arms around each other's waists, they pulled apart from their chests up, winked at each other, and then pecked the other's lips like love birds.

In Florence's continued library visits, she uncovered more information about Marcus Garvey on microfilm and through inter-library loans. She marveled at pictures of him wearing a purple and gold uniform and a Napoleonic bicorn hat with feathered plumes. She learned that his presence, oratory, and writings evoked pageantry and inspired many throughout the world.

To inspire her husband's greatness, she left handwritten gems of wisdom where he'd find them as a surprise—excerpts of Garvey's speeches or information about him. In his shirt pocket for the next workday. Rolled inside a sock in his dresser drawer. Taped to the steering wheel. Always with a lipstick print of her kiss below the words, "Think B.I.G., my Darling! I love you!!!"

Widowed some three years before he was relocated with his granddaughter Florence, Emanuel Tucker had begun to lose all sense of order after Coralee's sudden death. Both Florence and Chadwick noticed a change to the flow of energy in their home upon Emanuel's arrival. Framed pictures or art dropped from their wiring on the walls. Water pressure at the kitchen sink, in the bathroom, and for the washing machine began constricting more and more. Cabinet doors unhinged. The family's ease of conversation wilted. It was as though a vapor of untruthfulness had been released, and disorder and confusion were its result.

Throughout Emanuel Tucker's stay with Florence and Chadwick, as she more fully embodied caretaking, Florence's sense of order about her own marriage began to derail. Grief from the recent loss of her mother combined with postpartum depression following the additional loss of her first child didn't help.

Emanuel, during candid recollections of what Florence presumed had been memories about matrimonial bliss, often called the name of another woman—not the name Blessing, his deceased wife of forty-five years.

"When Rinda been hol up the baby, it been look just like me!" he whispered with pride.

"Rinda?" Florence asked. "Who's that? Are you talking about when you first saw Daddy?" Family members always marveled that Emanuel Tucker must've spat Adam out. The son was the spitting image of his father.

"Oh, yeah . . . yeah!" Emanuel fumbled to answer, realizing that he'd vocalized a memory that had been buried within him for some time. "That's what I meant to say."

A few days later, he voiced another zinger. Thinking he was alone in the room, he said, "Wear the red dress, Rinda. Don't listen to people who say, 'Black women can't wear red.' You make red sizzle. Um-hmm!"

"Who you talking to, Granddad?" Florence asked quietly.

His head snapped to attention at the sound of her voice. "Oh, nothing, Florence," he said unconvincingly. "I was just thinking of a conversation I'd had with your Grandma Blessing." He paused, then asked, "Would you please bring me a glass of tea?"

Returning from the kitchen, Florence wanted to pour the iced refreshment of Southern hospitality onto his crotch—to see if it helped him to synchronize his recollections with his ramblings. Was he mindlessly professing to have stepped out on his wife? Her grandmother? And on more than one occasion? She knew a red dress had never draped a hanger in her grandmother's closet. He had forbidden her from wearing anything with that vibrant color in it. Had convinced her that wearing red made other men look at her with wicked intentions. Had accused her of harboring a sinful streak of flirtatiousness if she ever spoke admiringly of another woman's red outfit! Instead of confronting him, Florence decided to stay within earshot of his babbling confessions as much as possible. To listen. To learn.

Within a month, the education she'd gained left her embittered. She'd pieced together that Emanuel had lived a secretive life that seemingly no other Tucker family member knew about. In fact, he had created another family with this "Rinda" woman. She and their one son and one daughter had lived on nearby Darcatia Plantation, a fisherman's one-hour boat ride from Mausaville, across the Pee Dee and Waccamaw Rivers. And if Florence had not been steadfast in soaking in all that she overheard without blurting a question or judgment, she would have remained among the great cloud of Tucker family members who were ignorant of their patriarch's infidelity.

Hmpf, she thought to herself. *All his late night and early morning fishing expeditions . . . all those stories told at family gatherings about his delayed returns home . . . but always with an abundant catch. Why, on most occasions, those were nothing more than just jaunts for hauling in more than nets full of shad or buckets full of clams or oysters! He had caught lots, more than just fish . . . because he was a double-dipper. Maybe Grandma Blessing is spooking him now from the other side!*

As she looked at her grandfather through the open doorway to the den, she remained silent, cat-like. Her body stiffened. Her left hand rested on her hip, and her right hand cupped her shaking head. Her lips soured as contention veiled her gaze and recollections. *I hope Grandma Blessing is sending a hag to ride him at night,* she internalized, and spoke her thoughts of him in the third person. *He keeps mouthing things off cause he can't sleep. Hah! That's why. The wicked, old hag is tormenting him. Good for em!* She didn't say a mumbling word about her new awareness to no one other than her husband.

"Oi-ee," Chadwick responded. "You tell Adam?"

"No, I can't tell Daddy that! It'd kill him," Florence stated. "And the rest of the family, too. And . . . and . . . the church members and his fellow deacons would nail him on a cross."

Florence thought about an incident from her childhood that had pained her father. He had taught his children the importance of remembering each family member's "born day." Explaining a proverb, he'd say, "'By crawling a child learns to stand.' And each year that you stand taller, on each birthday, you should be celebrated. Celebrations are like rain. They make God's gifts, his plantings, grow bigger and better!"

But one year, for some unknown reason, Adam had forgotten his wife Coralee's birthday. When he came home from work, Florence had baked her mom a birthday cake, Coralee had cooked dinner, and all had awaited what surprise Adam had arranged. Each birthday, every year, had a surprise! But not that one. He'd forgotten. She'd learned years later that this had occurred during a time of great personal and financial stress. Her father's job as a coffee distributor was being threatened by younger, White staff members who argued that Adam had been hired only to fulfill the company's minority quota, despite his being the top sales agent for four quarters straight, and despite his being punctual, courteous, and present each workday. And even though her mom had been understanding about his birthday misstep, he'd never forgiven himself.

"I should've stopped on the drive home and pulled up some wildflowers to give you . . . something . . . anything!" Florence had overheard her father on numerous occasions berating himself about his inaction. And she recalled her mother's ever-constant, soothingly quiet response: "Oh, Adam Tucker, every day with you by my side is all the celebration I want, all the love I need!"

It was as though he'd felt he had been unfaithful on a precious promise, a commitment to which his children had been witnesses. So, for Adam to learn about his father's indiscretion, Florence reasoned, would've left him undone. Would've sparked within him an ember of anger about his father's hypocrisy that could blaze into rage. A rage that could rend and not repair. That could scorch relationships during a time of grieving. *No, I cannot tell him,* caretaker Florence told herself. *Not now. Maybe not at all.* That she knew about it, and now Chadwick knew about it, was all that would be needed!

"What about this Rinda?" Chadwick asked. "Her children are your uncle and aunt. How old are they?"

"I think the boy was born sometime after Aunt Jasmine and Aunt Gardenia."

"So, he started fishing in waters away from home when your grandma was expecting your dad?"

"Yeah, I think that's right. One time, just the other day, he blurted out names—in chronological order, I guess. I listened to two names in the roll call that I'd never heard mentioned before—Absalom and Lillie. 'Absalom' came after Adam. And 'Lillie' came after Uncle Andrew and Uncle Thomas, and before Aunt Camellia. I thought my grandparents had six Tucker children, Chadwick. But, no, no, no . . . he had eight!"

"And this Absalom and Lillie, if they have any children, they are your first cousins."

"If they don't know anything about me, I don't want to know anything about them," Florence reeled. "Now, if what Granddaddy said is true, that bastard-Uncle Absalom and Daddy must look like twins!"

"Well, well, well. Now, as far as I know, there aren't any 'yard children' in the Wineglass family line. But what I know about other families that have 'house children' who are born to a marriage and 'yard children,' who are not, is that when Emanuel dies, everything he did in the dark will come to the light. If the sun don't shine through before then, daylight will shine, shine, shine, and everyone will see, see, see when people parade around the casket for the last viewing."

Two-and-a-half years to the date after Emanuel Tucker moved in with the Wineglasses, sorrows and excitements arose. Not only had the couple weathered the storm of their first unsuccessful childbirth and just learned that they were expecting again, but Florence's grandfather also joined his ancestors and was buried on the peaceful grounds at Friendfield A.M.E. Church. He had died alone. At his own home. Unexpectedly. Mysteriously. But the mystery would unravel over time.

Late 1990s

Timothy Thunderbolt learned too late not to ask God for patience. He had not known to be thankful that an all-powerful God would equip a totally surrendered believer with the capacity to handle any situation. Had he realized this, his prayer on his twin sister Thelma's wedding day would not have become a self-fulfilling prophecy in building his character. His answered prayer stretched and increased his patience and faith to an almost unbearable hilt.

The Thunderbolt twins grew up in Seneca, South Carolina and did just about everything together until college. At that time, their lives diverged. Thelma studied library and information science at an HBCU in Augusta, Georgia, and fell in love, while Timothy transferred, pursuing religious studies first in Charlotte, NC, and later in Atlanta, GA. Whereas intolerance and narrow-mindedness became takeaways of his schooling, tolerance and open-mindedness, particularly about her love interest, became hers. Years later, Thelma's betrothal burdened her brother. He'd learned that the religious beliefs of many Gullah people bordered on witchcraft and paganism, and her husband-to-be was Gullah Geechee. So, he prayed for patience to accept her decision.

In divine response, an administrator at the Interdenominational Theological Center in Atlanta, GA, where Timothy had pursued his Master of Divinity degree, recommended him for the pastorate at Low Bottom Community Church in Georgetown, SC—a Lowcountry community of Geechee religious and spiritual beliefs that he'd heard about and found unsettling. And which, he discovered later, was near his soon-to-be brother-in-law's homeplace.

The Low Bottom Community Church elders and congregation

approved Timothy Thunderbolt from among three candidates, and he and Sibyl, his wife of seven months, journeyed from Atlanta to begin his first pastorate. The only counsel he offered her before their move was the words, "We've got to stay prayerful, Sibyl! Down there, they talk funny, wear colorful clothes, and have strange beliefs about God. I hear that some even talk about a local conjure man called Dr. Buzzard. If that ain't the Devil, I don't know what is!"

Only after relocating did Reverend Thunderbolt more fully discuss with his wife his misgivings about the community to which he'd been sent. Gathered in their rental home, he said, "The story is that this Dr. Buzzard was a successor, but the original root doctor had lived in a simple cabin tucked away in the marsh grass on a distant island."

"Don't you be pulling my leg, Tee!" Sibyl said. Seated at the kitchen table, she looked up at him as he stood in front of the refrigerator. Her eyes declared, *You're just trying to impress me with what a great storyteller you are . . . .*

"No, no," he exclaimed. "I'm not pulling your leg. I'll put my hand on a Bible. This is something I've really heard." He pantomimed laying his left hand on an imagined, outstretched Bible and raised his right hand before continuing.

"They say that those who wanted to see him had to go down to the creek shore," he whispered. "There, they would see a boat, a rowboat with two oars just a-resting there as though down in some lonesome valley." He spoke a little louder. "Then, they had to call his name three times . . . Dr. Buzzard! . . . Dr. Buzzard! . . . Dr. Buzzard! . . . then wait." His volume increased with the statement, "Now, they should've been calling on the Lord!"

"Preach it, Pastor Thunderbolt!" Sibyl responded, chuckling.

"Well, do you know what some people say would happen then?" Timothy asked.

Sibyl shook her head three times in unbelief. Timothy's body convulsed, his right foot began stomping on the kitchen floor, and he flailed his left hand in the air.

"They say, they say . . . that three buzzards—not one, not two, but three buzzards, by and by—would come flying over the water. Two buzzards would land, one on each oar. The third buzzard would sit in the boat looking at you until you had sense enough to push the boat into the water and jump in—"

"Oh, Tee, this is too much! Too much!" Sibyl tittered. "You know God doesn't like this."

"Well, well, well . . . I'm only telling you what I've heard," he explained. "The two buzzards rowed the boat to the other side of the creek. And the third buzzard flew overhead . . . directing all, when the boat landed, to Dr. Buzzard's front door!"

"Timothy Thunderbolt, I don't know why you felt you had to tell me this story," Sibyl said, standing to look at him eye-to-eye. She placed a hand lovingly on his shoulders and continued. "That's some story, but South Carolina is your home, and you've never shared such a tall tale before." She blinked her almond-shaped eyes. "I love it each time we visit your parents in Seneca."

"Well, I'm from the upstate, Sibyl, baby," he'd answered. "Down in the Lowcountry, things are quite different. The air is different. The water, the animals, the trees, and, yes, the people. But with the Lord on our side, the two of us, you and me, will survive any storm. Any circumstance. Any stumbling block the Devil puts in our way!

"Now, more than anywhere else in this country, church people down here in the Lowcountry sing some spirituals. And if they sing any other type of church song—hymns, anthems, gospel—they will put a beat to it, a polyrhythmic handclap with a 1-2-3, 1-2-3-rhythm that'll sound just like they're singing a spiritual. You wait. You'll see. And sometimes, I believe, that rhythmic beat calls down spirits . . . ."

Her husband's bravado assured Sybil. Her love and admiration of him bolstered her. But her introduction to the South Carolina Lowcountry boggled her mind. The heat and humidity deviated from her Columbus, Ohio birthplace. The keen awareness that people had of everyone else's business contrasted with the friendly but somewhat distanced neighborliness she'd become accustomed to in Atlanta. And the speech ways, body language, dark skin tones, and African-like features of the church and community members clashed with her sense of self. Making her always feel, she realized, like Dorothy and Toto when they had landed in Oz; that she, too, was no longer home—not in Atlanta, Georgia or her hometown of Columbus, Ohio.

And the Geechee women were not Munchkins. No, they were

full-figured, with thick arms, legs, thighs, and bosoms, while she was petite, small-boned, and with a fair complexion. They walked erect and unbowed. Without shame. As though their bodies, their spirits, and the world around them were one. The heritage of Sibyl's dark-black, straight hair was rooted in the Chippewa tribe of her great-grandmother, Nokomis, whose name meant "daughter of the moon." The common denominators were her firm, round buttocks and full, broad nose—hand-me-downs of her African great-grandfather, Mobo Night, about whom she knew only snippets of information that had been handed down for four generations.

He'd been a runaway from a cruel slave master somewhere in the South. From a place near the "big wata" that reminded him of his African homeland. The master had been so cruel that after he'd fled, Mobo adopted the new surname, Night. Speaking in an African language and with almost unintelligible English when he reached Ohio, he'd said that "Masna" was mean and that he was from what had sounded like "dah-cahnt-sha." From generation to generation and through reasoning and storytelling, the recollection became lore: that Mobo had said he was from the "dark continent," his African homeland where only dark-skinned people lived; that he had described the land from which he'd fled as a place where the trees looked like the village elders who were watching him from their stools perched on the limbs of trees; and that it had been a place where ancestral spirits whispered to him on midnight-dark and full-moon-bright nights, "Use ya wings. Fly way. Fly way, Mobo, fly way! Rememba wa ya fus name mean. E mean 'freedom.' So, fly way, Mobo. Fly way. Fly way by de light ob de moon!"

Covering the Hole with a Foot

1960s through 1980s

The Thunderbolt twins were born in the South Carolina upcountry. Near the city of Seneca in Oconee County, in the foothills of the Blue Ridge Mountains. Their grandfather had been a gandy dancer, laying the railways that made the town's economy boom. Their father had worked as a railroad porter, and their mother had washed and ironed White people's clothes. Desiring their children to live a better life, Timothy and Thelma's parents paid their way to attend Paine College, an HBCU in Augusta, Georgia.

While Thelma had felt at home at Paine College, Timothy, sensing a calling to preach, had transferred during the second semester of freshman year to Johnson C. Smith University in Charlotte, NC. He'd hoped his sister would join him, but during their discussions, he'd seen the raised furrow of her eyebrows and had known he'd be transferring alone. No longer living under the watchful eye of her twin brother, Thelma soon met a male friend whose camaraderie she enjoyed. She and Mausaville's Melvin Marshel met during auditions for the college's theatrical production of "Purlie Victorious." Both were cast.

The musical took Broadway by storm in 1970, and during the 1978 college production, Thelma and Melvin starred in the roles originally played by Ruby Dee and Ossie Davis. They both felt victorious as their friendship blossomed into love during the two-week rehearsal and two-week run. Thelma loved Melvin's Georgetown accent, his charm, his intellect. Melvin was enamored with Thelma's independent spirit, joy of life, conversation, and beauty.

In the play, Purlie Victorious returns to his shabby cabin to reacquire the local church and to ring the freedom bell. The play's themes of racial bigotry, Southern White privilege, and a community that is unwilling to change would foreshadow Melvin and Thelma's lives. They grew together, they graduated, and, in time, they wed. But, little by little, before the wedding and afterward, the things that had enthralled each about the other began to perturb them. And they settled into rushed professional and marital lives without learning how to argue or how to address issues that disturbed and annoyed them in ways that would benefit them both. The church in the play is saved, services are held, and the freedom bell rings when the characters learn to trust each other and work together. Melvin and Thelma would have to learn to do the same.

Growing

Sprout Flow

2000s

"I choose Laverne Grice as the ember you should ignite with possibilities," Florence recalled her husband saying to her. They were beginning the second phase of their secretive fiduciary tryst. But the word that once filled them both with a sense of mission, purpose, and joie de vivre now seared an indelible pain in her heart. *What about Laverne speaks to something Chadwick admires and that he wants me to take on? she wondered.*

Following their honeymoon, Chadwick and Florence had established a loose set of rules for their meager philanthropic gifts. They contributed a ten-percent tithe to their church and doled out an additional ten percent, without fanfare, to those in need. On a monthly basis, fatherless children, widows, community members who were sick-and-shut in, college students, and youths who excelled in sports or scholastics would receive an unexpected and anonymous gift of twenty-five, fifty, seventy-five, or one hundred dollars.

They tweaked more intense ground rules during a meeting-of-minds amid a period of sexual tension during their third year of marriage. It flared up following the extended visit of aged family member Emanuel Tucker, Chadwick's insistence to take on multiple part-time jobs to waylay financial obligations, and Florence's emotional departure to Planet Caretaker. Chadwick, over-exhausted, longed for a show of affection in thanks for all he was doing. Florence's physical desire only simmered. She was frustrated. She wanted to contribute by returning to work but felt saddled by Chadwick's insistence on the ever-continuing stay of her grandfather.

The Wineglasses brainstormed and established a fiduciary menage-a-trois, in which they would identify themselves as igniters and those they chose to assist as *embers*. This philanthropical twist turned them on! At a time when they craved adventure, they used tension, interaction, and pleasure to lubricate the connections of their entanglement.

As foreplay and to tantalize each other with jealousy about the choices of their selections, Florence would select the males Chadwick would interact with financially, and Chadwick, the females that Florence would fund. Accordingly, they agreed their contacts would not misconstrue any sexual impropriety on their parts. When a contact was identified, each igniter would proclaim, "I choose (name of community member) as the *ember* you should ignite with possibilities." And then the fun would intensify.

The spouse, not the *igniter*, would determine the amount of money to be contributed to the *ember*, based on their judgment of the *ember's* personal needs or the emotional intelligence they hoped the igniter would gain from the interaction. Monies could be dispersed only by the igniter—in whatever timeframe, frequency, and amounts that he or she desired.

Because the couple's intimate desires were not being met, voyeurism would be the goal of their extramarital monetary arrangements. The marital partner would monitor each related transaction, conversation, and response.

The crescendo of their pecuniary eroticism would climax with the awareness that they had fulfilled another's release of all or some financial burden and had birthed within them new possibilities of financial freedom. There would be no need for Georgetonian riceland residents to return to Africa, as Marcus Garvey had once promoted. And anonymous Black philanthropy would provide a win-win for the funders, and for those who were funded.

Above all, however, once the agreed-upon allotment of monies had been distributed, Chadwick and Florence would terminate each transactional, relational, and emotional affair and await their mate's selection of a new *ember* for them to ignite.

No one would be hurt, they reasoned. They'd learn about their neighbors while helping to lift them up one bootstrap at a time. And Chadwick and Florence could watch each other's personal growth along the way! Neither spouse smoked or consumed alcohol, but they foresaw that at the conclusion of each "affair," they would intertwine in each other's arms, panting and gasping with delight.

The process of flooding and draining, as in a rice field, needs intricate monitoring to ensure perfection. For the Wineglasses, the cultivation of their love, the flooding and draining of marital emotions, was tumultuous. The expectant parents received shocking news about their first pregnancy during a visit to Florence's ob-gyn during the beginning of the second trimester, a few weeks before Emanuel began living with them. The couple learned that the embryo had died.

"Oh, Chadwick, baby, I am so, so sorry," she'd lamented softly after they'd left the doctor's office. Until that moment, words, sounds, breath had been dammed inside her chest. Her diaphragm had frozen. Her trachea had stiffened and congealed. She'd blacked out in her husband's arms, and he'd nestled her lovingly, soothingly in his embrace until he was convinced they could rise and walk.

In her shocked stupor, she'd contemplated what she could have done to bring about this horror, this damnation. Should she have not hung laundry on the clothesline, as her mother-in-law Bernice had advised? Had raising her arms over her head strangled the fetus, causing the umbilical cord to wrap around the embryo's neck? Had not breaking her habit of crossing her legs, as she'd done out of a sense of modesty since puberty, suffocated the baby? Maybe, just maybe, when she and Chadwick had walked barefoot on the grass in the brisk evening air, exalting in their newfound pregnancy, coldness had entered her bloodstream from the bottom of her feet and had caused an infection to invade her womb. "It was all my fault, all my fault," she sighed to Chadwick. "Why had this happened? Why?"

Chadwick seated her in the black Ford pickup, fastened her seat belt, and closed her door. The news hurt but did not paralyze him. Dazed, he walked around his recent second-hand purchase—made because its shiny color, he believed, screamed success. He slumped sluggishly below the steering wheel. Then, only then, did Chadwick inhale deeply and release slowly and audibly. He clasped his right hand in his wife's left, and she placed her right hand on top. Together, they cried.

"I'm so sorry!" Florence repeated her lament.

"It's okay, dear. It's not your fault. God has another plan. Don't know what it is right now. But we'll see. We'll see."

"I love you, Chad. I want to give you the family, the dreams you're always talking about."

"I know, Flo. I know." He paused, then added, "You know what?" She looked into his eyes, knowing from rote what his reply would be, but needing desperately to hear it. "Love you too!"

They drove home to Black Duck Road, hands still clasped. Her mind, however, continued to ponder superstitious beliefs. Had she looked too long at roadkill during her travels? Had such a sight marked her unborn child and made Death come a-knocking at its door? Had the miscarriage been brought on because of her husband? Had he laid his hat on their bed, killed a bee that entered their house, or exited their home through a different door than the one he'd entered, bringing bad luck to their family?

It was during another period of emotional upheaval that Chadwick determined plans for achieving fault-proof success. Also, during this period, they each selected the first *ember* for their spouse.

A year later, after the stillbirth of their second child, the flooding of the Wineglasses's marriage left it in a stagnant pool of salt water, drained almost completely of the vital freshwater needed for its continued thriving. It followed the obstetrician's prognosis that Florence's uterus would never nurture an embryo throughout live birth, and that the fibroid tumors in her fallopian tubes, cervix, and ovaries would never support another healthy pregnancy.

Weary, worried, and convinced that this humiliation could not have resulted from any transgression of her own, Florence wondered what secretive activities of darkness within her or her husband's families may have led them through the floodgate to some generational curse. Was it because of some untold history regarding their fathers, mothers, uncles, or aunts?

It's Granddaddy Emanuel, that lyin Emanuel Tucker! she reasoned, when the thought resonated. *All his cavortin an rompin roun with this Rinda woman, that's the thing that has wounded my womb. Oh, no. Oh, no! What he's not gonna do is stay up here in my house! Not with what I now know about him . . . .*

Florence, the story keeper of the Tucker Family, felt bamboozled that this saga was one that she had known nothing about. But her consolation came from knowing that this secret rested only with her and Chadwick. She convinced herself that perilous forces had piggybacked onto her and her husband's trip to the baby market—that this alliance was reaching across time, causing her and Chadwick to cry, "Wee, wee, wee!" about any chances at parenthood. If a friend or stranger had delivered her a divine revelation or prophesy, if she had procured a crystal ball or a tarot card reading (that is, if she had been so inclined to secure one), then, perhaps, she would have been enlightened about the murmurings Chadwick was listening to from Otis Doyle, a name that she remembered with a bitter aftertaste from her honeymoon! It was he who had gifted them their honeymoon cruise to Jamaica and had wanted to share his business acumen with her husband.

"Do the things that are necessary for your family over the long haul," Doyle had shared with Chadwick soon after they'd become associates. "Set monetary goals and meet them, upping the amounts incrementally. What your family doesn't know will not harm them. But with what you save and invest, you will assure them the rewards of all you've worked for."

In a more recent lunch meeting at Calabash by the Sea, Doyle had imparted more monetary wisdom to Chadwick that would've incensed his bride. A portly man with jowls who stood five-feet eight-inches tall, Doyle had to sit about two feet from the table because of his robust belly. Although Chadwick felt comfortable about their acquaintance, he was always taken aback by the piercing gaze of Doyle's blue eyes and the redness of his thick, wrinkly neck. It was three hues darker than his complexion elsewhere, and the remaining blond strands atop Doyle's head also had a hair-raising effect on Chadwick. Doyle's features reminded Chadwick of photos he'd seen in *Ebony* and *Life* magazines of Klansmen at rallies and lynchings, and policemen holding fire hoses and German shepherds by the collar as they clubbed Black men, women, and children. But he suspended that suspicion with thoughts of Doyle's generosity toward him and his wife, of his not noticing any untoward behavior, and of what he could learn from Doyle to assist others.

Doyle wore a tightly fitting light pink seersucker suit, for which the jacket would never button, and a white shirt, for which the top two buttons would never close. Always affable in Chadwick's presence, he centered his conversations on business opportunities and plans. Chadwick found favor in acknowledging that the man was well respected in the community and beyond: a member of the Saints of Waccamaw Neck Church on Kings River Road and the American Legion, Pawleys Island.

"So, Wineglass," Doyle said, as he looked around from table to table, "a restaurant like the business plan I've been telling you about. Have you taken time to think about it?"

Chadwick was slow to respond. He nibbled on the cornbread that had been delivered as an appetizer, then wiped his mouth with the paper napkin. "Yes, I've been thinking about it, Mr. Doyle," he answered. He always added a handle to Doyle's name in deference to Doyle's seniority of thirty-some years.

"Well, investors are needed. Owner Laurin Carpenter is beginning to come around to what I've been telling him."

A buxom waitress with frizzy blonde and black-braid extensions and a round mole on her right cheek interrupted their conversation with the arrival of their meals.

"'Scuse me, gennamen," she said, smiling, and set plates before each. "Wan mo fa drink? Mo tea? Coffee?" Awaiting an answer, she added, "Enjoy ya food, den. Dis de bestes time fa git yah. Ten minnit mo and dis place been ga fullup! Ef ya come den, ya been gon haffa wait een a long line fa nyam een yah!"

Chadwick watched Doyle's eyes twinkle with amusement after the waitress said the word "nyam" and listened as she continued talking.

"Now, de bus git me yah late taday," she said, "but I glad glad ta git yah an ta git ya table. Lemme know ef ya need anyting." She turned and walked to another table. Her strong Gullah speech amused Doyle but offended Wineglass.

"Nyam een yah . . ." Doyle repeated her words with derision. "Hm. Hmmm." He spoke while looking only at his plate. "Now you know and I know, because we're beenyahs, that 'nyam' means eat . . . in some strange African language, that is." He chuckled and then stuffed five fried okra pieces into his mouth, one after another. "Nyam, nyam, nyam . . . ." He watched Chadwick eyeing him as he spoke, then said, "Well, tourists don't know that." He chomped three times. "And they'll eat it up!"

Why can't she say, "this" and not "dis," "more" and not "mo," and "will be filled" and not "ga fullup"? Chadwick wondered. He knew his mother would have rubbed her temples to relieve tension for not having corrected her grammar instantly and would have scowled in indignation.

Doyle's plate was a carboholic's paradise. Not only fried okra but fried catfish, rice and gravy, and bread pudding filled his plate. Chadwick had ordered Chicken Bog, a house salad, green beans, and no dessert. He remembered meals he'd ordered when Florence was the head cook there, and how he'd been trained to eat during childhood and as a husband. Doyle looked at his plate askance.

"That Lowcountry talk, you know, that Gullah gibberish, and the sweetgrass baskets, and this good food are things tourists come here for in droves," Doyle said after swallowing a mouthful of rice and gravy. "Now, each year my family takes a cruise to the Bahamas and visits Kingston, Jamaica, and other islands. You ever been there?"

"Yes, I have," Chadwick answered with a surprised grin. "Remember, that's where you had Florence and me visit on our honeymoon cruise." He found it strange that Doyle had forgotten.

"That's great. That's great!" Doyle said. "Now, did you see all the poverty? All the bad living conditions? Things are bad almost everywhere over there." He squeezed the lemon wedge in his glass against the side with his spoon, stirred with three quick whisks, and then sipped on his iced tea. "This is a great opportunity to help those people. At least some of them. And God smiles on all who can help 'the least of those'! You know that, don't you, Wineglass?"

Chadwick nodded his head, still unsure of where Doyle's talk was leading.

"Did you hear how the way they talk in Jamaica is just like the dialect of you people here in Georgetown?" Doyle continued. "People there look like they could be y'all first cousins!" The comparison tickled him as he chewed a mouthful of catfish and okra until his chuckle made him spew drops of spittle that landed midway on the table. He quickly wiped his lips with the back of his right hand. A moment later, however, he dabbed his lips with his napkin when he noticed Chadwick's stare of dismay, and then he continued speaking.

"If we bring Jamaicans to Myrtle Beach, about fifty to one hundred and fifty over time, the money that they make here . . . much more than they're making down there . . . would help them to send money back home to their families. And their labor would be cheaper for restaurant owners like Carpenter here at Calabash by the Sea. It would be a win-win for everybody!

"If investors can construct or find a residential facility nearby for this workforce, then restaurant owners won't have to wait on workers who are always late to work from traveling as far away as Kingstree and Hemingway in Williamsburg County, or Andrews in Georgetown County, or McClellanville in North Charleston County.

"Now, either you're in on this or you're not, Wineglass! Investors are laying their cards down on the table. You've got just two more weeks to let me know. Two weeks, now. That is, unless others step up to the plate before you do."

They parted with a handshake and a promise to get together again soon. On his drive back to work, Chadwick peeped at his wife's love-note quote à la Marcus Garvey that now lay on the passenger seat. It read, "You at this time can only be destroyed by yourselves, from within and not from without. You have reached the point where the victory is to be won from within and can only be lost from within."

Trying to justify Doyle's proposal, Chadwick rekindled his displeasure of his waitress's speech, demeanor, and admission about being late to her job. *Had she said that in hopes of influencing a larger tip?* he wondered. *She should've gotten there at least fifteen minutes before clock-in time.* That's how his parents raised him! *She should have just done her job. And done it well. And was her rambling conversation an attempt to disguise the feeling of defeat of having to dance daily with poverty and not always being able or ready to catch the bus to success? Jamaicans would sound about the same and would just say, "Yes, ma'am," "No, ma'am," or "Yes, suh," "No, suh," would smile and serve, smile and serve—and would not play the let-me-make-you-think-you-know-me but I-know-you-don't-really-want-to-know-nothing-about-me tourist shuffle. Perhaps Doyle's idea was worth the investment . . . .*

Florence's first selected *ember* for her husband to illuminate with possibilities had been an elderly man whose mobile home had burned following the use of a space heater during a Lowcountry descent to temperatures below twenty degrees. The newspaper account of his destitution in a nearby trailer park reminded her of memories in their first post-wedding home. The astute handyman, Chadwick had checked and rechecked all wiring and extension cords on the day before Halloween each year. And he made sure the windows were covered with plastic and the doorways were sealed with insulation linings, so that no accidental haints or haunts could blow incendiary sparks their way.

Aware from the neighborhood grapevine that Patrick Forster's only living daughter would arrive in two days to relocate him with her in Camden, New Jersey, Chadwick tracked him down at the home of one of his cousins.

"Mr. Forster," he said when he'd parked and met him in the yard, "I just want to give you something to help you out, as best as I can. I know this can in no way replace all that you've lost, and I'm sorry to know that the outcome of your loss means that the beauty of Mausaville is some place you must leave. But as a community elder, you've got to know that others have seen the light that you've shed along the way."

The elder Forster, hobbling with one of the few handmade walking sticks that had survived the house fire, was moved to receive a visit from Chadwick Wineglass. He stood tall and smiled. Both hands gripped the carved handle of the cypress cane. It braced him, planted into the ground between his two legs. The embedded green eyes of the deer head he'd crafted stared at Chadwick in the same tone-of-voice as the brown-eyed crafter. The attached drift-wood deer antlers dignified the cane with the same air of nobility that the gray-haired and bearded Forster bore.

"Well, son, none but de Lawd can splain!" he said as he extended his right hand to shake Chadwick's. He, like numerous others, had seen the light that Chadwick had been casting since childhood. As the twenty-something Chadwick now stood before him, his mind drifted back to the Easter Sunday School program when the then seven-year-old Wineglass's gifting had been revealed.

Forster knew from hearing stories retold how Chadwick's mother had drilled her son for the recitation of his "Easter piece." He remembered watching Bernice silently mouth her son's every word from her perch in the pews as Chadwick had delivered his lines onstage. With aplomb! But what had stood out in church members' minds was not his memory and elocution of a recitation that was geared for a twelve-year-old. What had made church leaders testify that "de Lawd done laid His hands on him" were the comments he made about the piece following the church service.

The recitation had been:

Roman guards made Christ haul the cross
Up, up Golgotha's hill.
They'd whipped and scourged and spat on Him --
The scriptures to fulfill.

But when they saw him struggling
Under the heavy weight,
They gave the cross to Simon.
He did not hesitate.

So, when your burdens seem too great,
Let this lesson be your guide --
When black Simon bore the cross of Christ,
He eased his suffering before He died.

Christ hung his head on Calvary
And died on that cruel tree.
But when He rose on Easter morn,
He gave us victory!

Chadwick had received thunderous applause for his fluid delivery, without pause or hesitation. Older women had removed their flowered hats and flailed them in the air with their left hands. Elders and deacons, Forster included, had stood, and with eyes fixed on the pulpit, had swayed their shoulders to the right and then back, and then to the left and back, during the youngster's final four lines. When Chadwick had concluded with "He gave us victory!" they had simultaneously bowed their heads and shouted, "Yassuh!" They'd raised their right arms to heaven and had whisked the palms of their outstretched right hands in an upward motion to the left as though they'd been hailing the presence of God Almighty.

Chadwick's Sunday School classmates had smiled and clapped their hands with contagious excitement. Some twelve-year-olds, however, had smirked among themselves and darted their eyes at each other, annoyed that his presentation had outshined their own luster. Or lack thereof.

After the service, church members expressed, "Well done!" to all exiting youths in the church foyer. The head deacon had stopped Chadwick as he was leaving with his parents and siblings. "Young man, young man," he'd said, while planting a white Fedora with a light blue hat band onto his balding pate. It complemented his white spats and double-breasted white pinstripe suit and matching blue tie and jacket pocket square. "That was a good recitation today! A good recitation! Now, can you tell me, please, what was the most important part of it?"

All ears had inclined to hear the youngster's reply, expecting to hear him say that Christ had arisen on Easter Day. But he'd surprised them. "Well," Chadwick had begun, looking into the eyes of his mother and then his father, "I think . . . that Simon, Black Simon . . . is a good person to remember."

"And why is that?" the deacon had asked, looking at others with a sense of amazement.

"Because Simon . . . he saw that Jesus was in trouble. And he tried to help him. He could've told the guards, you know, 'No!'—

and walked away. But he took that cross on his own shoulders. People need to help people. Especially when they see they're in need."

Forster remembered how Chadwick's parents had beamed and how the Pastor and others had begun prophesying, "He's got the gift! The gift of helps, brothers and sisters! We've got to watch this one. Gotta pray for him on this journey!"

And now, an older Chadwick Wineglass was visiting Forster in a time of need. He watched and listened as though he was having an out-of-body experience. Chadwick pressed six hundred dollars in six, doubly folded one-hundred-dollar bills into the palm of Forster's right hand as they shook goodbye. The cash was folded in half, then folded again. "No need to tell a soul about this, now," he whispered. "Just go in peace. Go in love." He didn't look back as he walked away, and his truck departed quickly, before Forster had the opportunity to count the amount of his gift.

Before he arrived home, Chadwick had established a game plan for successive *embers*. He first would offer suggestions about how money could be utilized to improve their financial success. Instead of presuming that others would know how best to manage their finances after he and Florence had lessened one of their debts, Chadwick reasoned that words of financial wisdom would complement the potential monetary deposits that he subsequently would bestow upon them.

Florence's selection of Patrick Forster as her husband's first *ember* had been made to encourage him to realize that Black Georgetonians had not forgotten their family members whom they'd left behind. That they assisted them financially from afar, as well as from nearby. And many would gladly relocate their aging relatives with them. Unless, of course, the elders could maintain their care themselves or, like Mr. Forster, were determined to spend their golden years in the community where they'd been born and where their ancestors were buried.

"I know he was happy to see you!" Florence told Chadwick upon his return home. "When's his daughter arriving?"

"Oh, he was happy all right. And his relatives are gonna be

happy too, I'm sure. His daughter Lizzie flies in the day after tomorrow, and they'll be gone the day after. Now, when his relatives find out how much we contributed, they'll start hinting and asking and making up their minds that we oughta help them out too. You know, to get whatever things they want but don't need. Or can get for themselves if they just discipline themselves. And, you know, whispering that we dikty, you know, uppity, or think we're White."

"Did you give him the full amount today? Or will you see him again when Lizzie's here?"

"Oh, I gave him the whole thing. You can check him off my *ember* list and find me a new one when you ready."

Chadwick's smugness made Florence wonder if he'd learned anything new about himself. She'd hoped he would've spent more time investing in the elder man's interests and concerns, connecting with him on a more personal level. She'd learned about Lizzie's marriage to a West Indian during her last visit south. And through the grapevine, she'd heard that they'd recently given birth to a boy. She remembered that Lizzie's husband's hands looked as thick, and his heart seemed as large, as her father Patrick's. That he, too, enjoyed wood carving. Had Chadwick allowed himself to see the past and the future with Mr. Forster, and not just the present? If so, she reasoned, perhaps his service as a Benefactor in Generosity would've made him less concerned about freeing the man from financial debt. More concerned about showering him with love and respect. More aware that Forster's departure from Georgetown could fulfill the Circle of Life. That he could pass on his whittling knife to his grandson. That it perhaps wouldn't eventually and solely become just a memorial resting and rusting atop his grave.

As he'd been taught by his father, Dr. Buzzard, Gregory Dunkin always prayed before entering a graveyard. On the dirt road leading into Mourning Dove Cemetery in Mausaville, he paused, looked east then west, and then closed his eyes. His presence there had resulted from a visit by Florence Wineglass.

"God, bless this house and keep the soul," he stated softly. "Please, I ask permission to come into this house." He opened his eyes and looked about in the afternoon light. Sensing no objections to his request, he concluded in quietness, "God, bless this house and keep the soul."

Gregory was searching for periwinkle plants and knew they'd be growing atop the slave graves from the 1800s. Buried below the ones with grave markers were the remains of a few of the more than one hundred thousand enslaved West Africans who'd toiled in rice fields of the twenty-four Mausaville plantations. This burial practice had most probably been creolized. Although the planters commonly had their laborers decorate family graves of plantation owners with the "flower of death," the practice followed European lore of weaving periwinkle vines into the headbands of dead children or criminals being led to their executions. To honor their own ancestors, however, the Africans also seeded the graves of their loved ones with this ground cover. The ebullient burst of periwinkle blue in the graveyard each April and May served as a reminder of the large and foreboding waterway that separated them from their homeland. On the other side of the Atlantic Ocean, over which many had been transported, was the preferred reconnection site with kindred souls, atop soil that had not been drenched with tears, bloodshed, and sweat because of inhumanity, injustice, and oppression.

Four leaves of periwinkle blue would be needed for Gregory to resolve the request Florence Wineglass had made of him. He pulled a small bottle of Crown Royal Peach Whiskey from his pocket and poured a stream of brown liquid onto the ground.

When the large black Chevy Tahoe had rolled into his driveway late one evening, he'd peered with curiosity from behind half-closed draperies in his meeting room to see who was visiting. The driver parked below the street nightlight in his rural neighborhood, keeping the engine running awhile and the park lights illuminated. The brilliance of the truck's polish and its upkeep indicated high maintenance. Its tinted windows shielded the transparency of its driver. Gregory lit a blue candle to resonate calmness and waited.

He was used to their arrival under the cover of night: the affluent, the everyday citizen, the churched, the unchurched, the been-yahs and comeyahs from far and near (those who were born here, the natives; and those who had come here, the transplants), the young, the old, people of all genders, races, and nationalities—but he'd never, *never* expected to see his former co-worker, Florence Tucker Wineglass, walk from her vehicle to his doorway.

"Why, Florence, you're the only chef I've ever missed down at Calabash!" he greeted her. "Girl, you are irreplaceable." Florence raised her eyebrows and smiled in acknowledgement but stood before him subdued and skittish, glancing slightly in either direction or back to her SUV.

"May I come in, please?" she asked softly. She noticed two small flowerpots on the porch railing. The peculiar plants within had long, pointed, thorny green leaves that spiraled up, out, down, left, and right, like serpents. She looked away quickly, glad to hear Gregory's response.

"Why, yes, yes. Please forgive me. I'm just so surprised to see you!"

On the horizon in the evening sky, Gregory saw flashes of heat lightning. Although the humidity was borderline oppressive, he knew that the summer storm they signaled was too far away to elicit fear. Calamitous memories of pelting rain, piercing lightning bolts, and pounding thunderclaps, however, hid just around the corner, but Florence's arrival and presence on his front porch only evoked his curiosity.

Gregory's mind wrestled with the conundrum of church people. Their unbending, one-track, cause-and-response rationalizations about how the Spirit of God works. Their wounding words hurled at others with such self-assurance that they were single-edged swords. The twisted thoughts they wrapped around themselves with self-righteous splendor—as though their accusations in no way reflected their own sullied behavior.

Gregory's eyes shuttered momentarily, unseen by Florence as she looked back at her Tahoe. The pain he'd buried since his father's funeral began to transform the heat lightning from moments earlier into an ominous recollection of rain, lightning, and thunder that could've changed all who'd witnessed it into pillars of salt.

Gregory moved aside as Florence entered, then quietly shut and locked the door. "How yo family dem?" he asked as they walked toward the candlelit living room. "Make yourself comfortable over here, please." He pointed to the beige sofa, comfortably cushioned and accented with pillows showing vibrant, colorful flowers. "Now, to what do I owe the honor of this visit?"

Quickly and quietly, she requested his services to confirm if Chadwick in any way, directly or indirectly, was plotting her grandfather's demise. She'd become fearful that Chadwick would not answer truthfully if she asked him directly. And that he would become distrustful of her for inquiring.

She offered no explanation yet could not halt her own reasoning. First, she remembered the strangeness of hearing her husband singing as he was packing Emanuel up to transport him back to his own home. Chadwick, she knew, hardly ever sang. And when he did, the tune he emitted should not be heard by anyone!

The second puzzling memory had to do, again, with music. She and Chadwick and her grandfather had listened recently to a gospel song playing on the local Christian radio station, WHHN for W-His Holy Name. They had been riding home without speaking to one another following their meeting with an insurance agent. The lyrics to the chorus were: "Jesus, when you died, you gave us the victory! /Jesus, when you died, you gave us the victory!"

Third, she later recalled that before Chadwick and Emanuel had walked to the Tahoe, Emanuel had asked him, "Son, you sho bout all dis, now?" and Chadwick had nodded his head solemnly.

Fourth and most troubling was her vague remembrance of the new lyrics she thought she'd heard Chadwick mouthing softly as he'd walked back to the house, leaving Emanuel in the passenger seat. She thought she'd heard, "Emanuel, when you die, you'll give us the victory! Emanuel, when you die, you'll give us the victory!"

As she'd waited for Chadwick at the front door, holding her grandfather's last box of personal items, he'd been surprised to see the look of astonishment on her face when he'd climbed the last step. And when she'd asked him what words he'd just been singing, he'd grabbed the box, given her a wily smile, kissed her on her forehead, and said, "Oh, nothing . . . I'll drop this load off, then come right back to pick you up so we can help him get settled in."

As the Tahoe drove away, her grandmother Blessing's words had echoed in her mind. "When you lie, you steal. When you steal, you cheat. And when you cheat, you kill."

And here she was at Gregory Dunkin's doorstep.

My services? Gregory snickered to himself before a stream of unspoken thoughts expressed in the singsong tongue of his Mausaville ancestors flooded his mind. *Some say, "root," some say "hoodoo," some say "black magic" or "conja." But she spectful. She say "services." Eh, Lawd, I only work wit plants. Plants made by Gawd. People eat em and drink em, make perfumes and colognes wit em, and even sniff em or cut em down. Me ain know why dey git scared up bout wa I do wit em. I jes make medicine wa heal de mine, de bohdy, an de soul. An de same Gawd wa make dem an de plants de One wa guide me, long wid de ancestas, fa know which ones fa use.*

Unashamed of the melodic litany that had rambled in his mind, he realized that if it had been expressed to a comeyah, he would've code-switched and stated: "Some say 'root,' some say 'black magic' or 'conjure.' But she's respectful. She says 'services.' Eh, Lord, I only work with plants. Plants made by God. People eat them and drink them, make perfumes and colognes with them, and even sniff them or cut them down. I don't know why they're scared about what I do with them. I just make medicine that heals the mind, the body, and the soul. And the same God who made them and the plants they come from is the One who guides me, along with the ancestors, to know which ones to use."

To Florence, he stated. "Tell me more."

He listened and agreed to assist. Florence rose quietly. Suspecting that Gregory's wife, Earthaline, and their three children were sequestered in other rooms of the home to avoid his frequent late-night business interactions, she asked him to extend greetings to them, then left. Stealthily, she returned to 496 Black Duck Road.

That had become their address when she found herself caught up in an interconnected swirl of business dealings that Chadwick conjured and then convinced her to agree with. He'd pondered if the time was ripe to move to a larger home soon after he'd learned about their second pregnancy.

She, however, felt they should wait awhile before making such a major change. That they should breathe. That she, if not they, needed to "stand the storm" as she'd heard her Grandma Blessing sing, because if they paused, "it won't be long," and they would then have the stamina to "anchor by and by." But Florence's mind, body, and spirit were too weary to live out the words of the old spiritual and wail objections. She allowed Chadwick's plans to become their plans, even though she didn't agree with them. She convinced herself to stay supportive, and that his ideas for stabilizing their welfare had their best interest in mind.

They'd left their modular home and advanced to a more bedrock Georgetown community on the other side of the tracks from Black Duck Road. They both were pleased with the new neighborhood and the home's appointments and its curb appeal. But it had been the number of the address that had sold Chadwick, she remembered. He'd said that 496 was a perfect number. That is, it was the sum of its divisors, excluding 496 itself. Because of this fascination with numbers, he'd believed the address would ensure it to be a perfect home, from which they could conduct a perfect plan to uplift their race. To ensure the success of this new venture he'd maintained the black pickup for work, purchased the black Tahoe for leisure, and planned to rent their modular home as income-producing property.

As Florence drove home from her visit to Gregory, Chadwick's song, his love of numbers, his plans for their wellbeing that seemed to disregard her input, and his probable lying became a horde of ricebirds devouring each grain of her peace of mind.

Thirteen months earlier

When the hearse and funeral motorcade had pulled up to Mt. Moriah Missionary Baptist Church, darkness momentarily had come over the land. The sun had begun to peek from behind an opaque cloud only when the last family member, Gregory Dunkin, emerged from the shiny, black limousine. Remarks from friends and four family members had recalled William Dunkin's church and civic service and his gift of helpfulness. He alone had funded the church's Bibles and hymnals. He alone annually sponsored Mausaville's Wild Hogs Baseball Team's uniforms. And it was he alone who had driven selflessly to SC State College to rescue his cousin and two other Georgetown students during the night of the Orangeburg Massacre.

The nerve-wracked young adults had filled him in on the details of the melee during the two-hour, late Thursday night return journey. Dunkin had heard only snatches of information about the incident during the evening's world news TV broadcast. He was certain that their eyewitness accounts were more truthful. Over time, the event became recognized as one of the most violent but least recognized markers of the Civil Rights Movement.

Late 1960s

The teens apprised William Dunkin that the student standoff with local law enforcement officials had begun three days earlier. Coeds from SC State College and Claflin University had visited the All-Star Bowling Lanes to protest its Whites-only policy. Owner Harry K. Floyd, however, refused them entry, maintaining that because his business was private property, it was exempt from the Civil Rights Act of 1964 and other segregation laws. The protesters left peacefully.

Having two institutions of higher education in a small town resulted in producing a small community that was rife with Black intelligentsia, many of whom had joined the Civil Rights Movement to rout out racism in every village, hamlet, and town. The next night, a larger group of unarmed students visited the bowling alley. But they were met by police equipped with fire hoses to keep their protesting at bay. Students taunted officers, lit matches, and during the skirmish a plate glass window at the bowling alley was broken. To teach them a lesson, police pummeled students with billy clubs. Fifteen students were arrested, at least ten students and one officer were injured, and a feeling of rage gripped the Black community.

Come Thursday, South Carolina-born civil rights activist Cleveland Sellers along with about two hundred protesters, including the three from Georgetown, gathered on the SC State campus to decry the local bowling alley's ban on Blacks, and racial segregation at all privately-owned businesses. They started a large bonfire near the campus entrance. Through the flames, they eyed National Guardsmen who had been deployed to quell a potential riot and the police who had been armed with shotguns and buckshot used for hunting large game.

State Law Enforcement Division Chief Pete Strom ordered the fire be put out, after students had taunted law enforcement with words, rocks, and other objects. A police officer was struck in the face with an unidentified hurled object as the fire was extinguished, and mayhem ensued.

In the darkness, claiming to have heard gunshots, police opened fire on the protesters, and students scurried to safety. Three casualties resulted. Freshman Samuel Ephesians Hammond, Jr., eighteen, was shot in the back. Fellow student, eighteen-year-old Henry Ezekiel Smith, was shot three times. And seventeen-year-old high school student Delano Herman Middleton, whose mother worked at SC State and who had attended nearby Orangeburg-Wilkinson High, was shot seven times. Bullets slugged them in their backs, their buttocks, their sides, and their feet. At least twenty-eight protesters were shot and wounded as Black gatherers fled. Sellers was shot in the armpit, arrested for "inciting to riot," and sentenced to one year of hard labor.

"Mr. Sellers didn't incite no riot," the Georgetown students confided to Dunkin. "He wasn't agitating. He was just helping us to know that we have rights."

"Some people are like buzzards," Dunkin said. "They see the life and beauty in others. But they don't understand it, and then they get scared. So, they pick and pluck and poke their talons into those who help others see their worth—to devour their beauty, their glow, 'til they're fit to be buried. That's what's being done to Sellers and the students who got shot. But remember, children, what has been buried ain always dead." He paused, then continued. "In fact, some people try to bury me 'cause I know plants. Well, the roots of every plant is the thing than nurtures it! Let your roots grow down, even when others try to bury you. When you blossom, your seeds, your leaves, your stems will make the world a better place!"

2000s

Because of William Dunkin's generosity in retrieving their children from the Orangeburg massacre, the students' parents hadn't missed their 11 p.m. to 7 a.m. "graveyard" or 7 a.m. to 3 p.m. "dawn" work shifts at Georgetown Steel Company. And he hadn't required any payment for gas or travel.

Yet the visiting pastor from the Low Bottom Community Church in Big Dam had felt called to slight William Dunkins's memory. The family had not requested his participation in the service, and his name was not on the program. However, in the style of Gullah-down-home-church-funerary practice, Reverend Timothy Thunderbolt had been invited by the officiating pastor to sit on the dais, among clergy, male and female, who had known the deceased or not. And the officiating pastor, in a spirit of clerical unity, had called on Thunderbolt, the one preacher with bombastic oratorical skill, to give the prayer following the readings of the Old and New Testament scriptures.

With the mention of Thunderbolt's name and the sight of him rising from the auxiliary metal chair and walking to the pulpit, Gregory had sensed a tempest beginning to rage. He'd looked to the left and to the right and glanced quickly behind him. Others had seemed oblivious to the oncoming buffeting winds. But Gregory knew what others did not know, and within him, peace. was. not. still.

"Almighty and everlasting Heavenly Father," Thunderbolt had begun his supplication, "the supreme being who made both heaven and earth. Lord, you are our Alpha, Omega, the beginning and the end. Lord, we give thanks today that if we rise on the wings of dawn, if we settle on the far side of the sea, even there your hand will guide us. Even there your right hand will hold us fast.

"Hold us fast, we ask, Gracious God. Hold us fast in moments like this one today, dear Lord, a day for which we are assembled together. Moments when, when our loved ones are with us no more. When, when our hearts are saddened and familiar footsteps and laughs and voices have been hushed. When, when a family member like William Dunkin, a community member, a husband, a son, a lover, a friend, has navigated the journey from the womb to the tomb . . . that we find that we need just a closer walk with Thee."

Like Anansi, Thunderbolt with his rhythmic opening had spun and cast a web. Church members and officers had landed in it and had begun responding with "Yes, Lord," "Um-hmm," and "Grant it, Jesus, if you please." Thunderbolt then began to lure them in. Regaling them with love and sounds of unity, he prayed for peace, comfort, and strength for the Dunkin family, for all to recognize the faithfulness of God and to look to Him alone for the desires of their hearts.

It was at this moment, in his mind's eye, that Gregory had seen a vision of his father looking into the face of a woman who felt that she'd been rebuffed by him, who seemed distraught that he could offer no assistance to her plea. Moments after, as Gregory sat on the front pew, he had heard his father whisper the woman's name into his ear: Thelma Thunderbolt Marshel. It was she—the person whom he now remembered as the one his father had anonymously confided to him when he'd begun to mentor Gregory—who was the only client that he'd refused to service—ever! And she, Gregory now intuitively recognized, was Pastor Thunderbolt's sister.

Rev. Timothy Thunderbolt's declamation pivoted from one who was connected with God to one who knew that his words, though shrouded with love, could damn those who had hurt one who was close to him. His awareness fueled the conclusion to his prayer. And in its delivery, he accented some words like sprays of Mace.

"And, Lord, let us remember that even when others speak well about us," he paused so that listeners could consider the remarks that recently had been made, "not *one* of us is *better than* Jesus Christ. He *alone* bore our stripes and *by Him* we are healed. And no one, *no one* who engages in *idolatry* and *witchcraft*, hatred, *discord*, jealousy, fits of rage, *selfish ambition*, dissensions, factions *shall inherit the kingdom of God*.

"So, help us, right now, Good Shepherd, to know, that we know, that we know, that we know, that we've got a *home* up in a-*that kingdom*. And *that* is *good news*! Amen. Amen. A-men."

The only good news that had resonated within Gregory was that this stealthy firebrand had stopped his railing. Because Thunderbolt's pokes at his father were based on ignorance. Because the gnashing of teeth that Thunderbolt had intimated his father was now experiencing was based on beliefs that had been birthed in Africa. Beliefs that in this country had been paired with Christianity. That allowed people to not be passive victims of circumstance or fate when others offended, threatened, or harmed them. Beliefs that teemed with idolatry or witchcraft, according to many, but to others commingled with love and reverence of the true God. Who was not a blue-eyed, blonde-haired God. And because selfish ambition had never been a part of his father's genetic makeup. William Dunkin provided a supernatural service only for those who requested it.

Gregory had not been aware of the other funeral attendees' recoil at Thunderbolt's prayer-sermon, particularly at its condemnatory close. His mind had drifted away. Away from the service. Away from the anguish, the grieving, the sadness. To a space of knitting together the why's and what's in Thunderbolt's life that had climaxed with such caustic eulogistic banter.

Gregory's mind floated back within him only after the family had processed to the church graveyard. There, in the sunlight, amidst the tree branches, he had felt like himself again. And there, following his father's visitation, Gregory received a better understanding of his father, the work his father had left for him to do, and the resistance by many to the sincere and authentic spirituality of his work. When he saw Thunderbolt glance at him as the casket was readied to be lowered into the grave, Gregory was at peace that the pastor had not succumbed to the destiny of Lot's wife and been transformed into a pillar of salt.

Stretch Flow

Laverne Grice began to doubt the intentions of her unsolicited benefactor. Yet the weekly invitations to lunch, the refusals to allow her to pay—even for her own meals, and the opportunities to clear her mind of thoughts about burdensome daily office politics or her abysmal marriage, initially fulfilled her desire for peace, support, and hope. Lately, however, she felt as though she was being grilled about her course of action and set up to make an imminent decision. *How had this friendship, this sisterhood begun?* she wondered, as recollections paraded across her mind.

"Girl, you are wearing that dress!" a tall, walnut brown fellow shopper had said as they browsed racks of dress shoes in Dillard's. "Where did you find that?"

Appreciative of the sisterly compliment, Laverne paused and looked up to make sure it was she being addressed. "Oh, this?" she replied as she stood erect, brought her heeled feet together on the floor, and continued shoe-shopping. "It's an Aurora Jones. At Chico's. The sale continues through the weekend. I picked up some handbags and summer scarves too."

The social banter continued before they went separate ways. But it picked up again when they somehow saw each other at the makeup counter. Smiling with picture-perfect pleasantness, Florence asked to sample the same fragrances as she and Laverne made idle chit-chat about perfumes. She even purchased a shade of Mac foundation, the same brand that Laverne called out to the department clerk.

Laverne grabbed the hook. Before parting, they exchanged

names, phone numbers, and an agreement to "do lunch" soon.

To her surprise, Florence called two weeks later to schedule a lunch date. They met at Savory & Scrumptious Deli the following Thursday for a salad, soup, and sandwich. Florence wore her recently acquired Aurora Jones wrap dress and thanked her lunchmate for steering her in the right direction.

Laverne leaned forward as she sipped iced tea to inquire about Florence's line of work. She'd acquired nothing about her on LinkedIn and learned through the indirect answers she was given that Florence was a professional non-profit organizational volunteer. That is, she did not work outside of home or at a home business. Her husband provided the sole household income.

Hmmm, she reasoned to herself. *I've never met an African American woman of this socio-economic stature. And here one is, right in front of me. In Georgetown, SC. I sure hope she doesn't think we live in the same bubble. And I can't front about this, either.* Instead, she conversed about her job at Regions Bank.

"Here I am, having worked through the ranks to commercial banking compliance administrator over the past two decades, and there are these upstarts, straight out of undergraduate school, who think they can rival me."

Florence raised her left hand from her lap, flipped it palm-side up on the table, and asked, "The . . ." She stroked from palm to fingertips twice with her right hand, then completed the inquiry with her head tilted downward to the left and eyes raised upward to the right. ". . . ones?"

"You know it. If I'm lying, I'm flying," Laverne laughed. "And as you can see, I sure don't have any wings. It's those ones who think that having their granddads or daddies or mommies or uncles or aunts call anywhere in the world on their behalf will make the Earth rotate backwards on its axis."

They laughed. They bonded. They enjoyed each other's company. Letting her guard fall, Laverne wiped the right side of her top lip too brusquely with her napkin. The action exposed a deep bruise that seemed to extend to the cheekbone, below the covering foundation.

Florence's eyes widened in alarm before she attempted to avert her gaze elsewhere.

"Hmm, they make the best chicken salad here," she stated

matter-of-factly, staring at her plate. "The 'wow' is the walnuts and the grapes."

Embarrassed, Laverne replied in a deadpan tone, "I'm so sorry about this, but, um, it's not as bad as it looks. I fell off my bike yesterday evening. An unleashed dog dashed across the street, right in front of me. I think today it must look worse than I feel."

"I don't know why some people unleash their dogs when they're not in their own yards," Florence stated. "Make sure you see a doctor about that, now, if it starts to get irritated. No need to get an infection from any makeup."

"Thanks, I think it'll be all right."

"Well, this has been a treat! Let me take care of the bill."

Laverne reached for her pocketbook. "No, no, I—"

"Not a cent!" Florence interjected. "Let's plan to do this again real soon."

They stepped outside the restaurant and parted ways amicably in the parking lot. Florence had revealed no motive about their encounter. And Laverne had been denied any awareness that Florence's husband, Chadwick, sat on the same nonprofit board with someone who worked at the same company as her husband, Medicus. Or that Chadwick, for some reason, had intuited somehow and informed his wife that a turbulent storm was raging in the Grice marriage.

Little by little, Florence learned more and more about Medicus Grice's abusive relationship with his wife Laverne during their bi-weekly lunch outings. One time, she saw Laverne flinch when she'd accidentally rested her chin onto her hand. Another time, Laverne's makeup smeared below her left eye when she laughed to tears at a joke Florence shared.

Two hillbillies sitting at a restaurant saw a distressed guest who apparently had begun choking after she'd been served some lamb stew. The woman began pounding the table with both hands, then stood up and began clutching her throat and grunting. Everyone looked at her in panic.

The two hillbillies rushed over as the woman's complexion began to turn pale and she appeared ready to collapse. Sensing what the problem was, Hillbilly #1 told her, "Don't worry, I got this!" He then stood behind her, raised her dress to her waist, lowered her panties, and with his tongue licked her left cheek and then her right. The woman, appalled at the spectacle to which she was center stage, began to convulse and with a yelp, coughed up the dislodged piece of mutton to the far end of the restaurant.

"I'd heard about this before, but I ain't never seen anybody do it!" Hillbilly #2 told his pal.

"I ain't seen it or done it before either. But that 'Hine Lick' is something they should teach you in CPR class."

"The sight wasn't pretty!" Florence concluded. And neither was the sight before her. And always, always, whenever Florence asked about her husband, Laverne's body language stiffened, and she'd quickly navigate to another topic. And with Florence's determined insistence on paying for the check at each encounter, Laverne decided to enjoy the opportunity of not having to explain her frivolous lunch expenses to her husband.

At each outing, Laverne answered a call from her husband, informing him where she was and with whom and when she'd be leaving. During their third month of lunching, Florence felt emboldened to confront the elephant in the room. Laverne had entered the Feast on This restaurant wearing a shoulder cuff.

"I love my husband," Florence confided quietly after they'd dined. "I do! I don't know how I'd live without him. But if Chadwick Wineglass ever laid his hands on me . . ." She looked away and then directly at Laverne. "I would have to find a way to make a change. To get some help for him. To get some help for myself. "I mean, I don't know what you're going through. But I can see that you're going through something. I have not said anything to anyone. But woman to woman, what are you going to do?"

Shocked speechless, Laverne waited until Florence's tempest of words had stopped swirling around her.

"Thanks so much for your kindness," she replied. "I'm not sure what you're talking about, but . . . I'm okay. Really!"

Laverne dropped her napkin onto her plate, began gathering her purse, and signaled to their server.

"Check, please," Laverne said when she caught her eye.

"Oh, I've got this!" Florence stated. "My treat, please!"

Laverne looked about but not at her and did not say a word.

"Thank you," she smiled, snatching the bill before Florence's quick reach to appropriate it. "I don't mind at all, Florence," she said politely. "And thank you so much for your concern. It's always good to meet and talk and laugh." She glanced at her smartphone. "Oops, I almost forgot. I've got to run. I've got a 1:15 p.m. appointment back at the office."

"You pick the restaurant in two weeks, okay?" Florence asked. She realized that her four-hundred-dollar *ember* allotment had not yet been fully transacted.

Laverne smiled but never answered. Nodding her head and eyes downward, she froze her gaze momentarily, then turned and walked away.

As she watched Laverne's retreat, Florence recalled hearing family stories told by adults who thought no children were near enough to hear. Had they been aware of her silent eavesdropping, the tapestry of her "Tucker Family Story Quilt" may never have reached the fullness, the patchwork of tales, truths, and twists that she had pieced together. As the keeper of secrets, she knew about her Aunt Camellia's physical and emotional abuse and follow-up visits to her sisters, Gardenia and Jasmine, for reprieve, for recovery. Florence knew her aunts never understood why Camellia had wrongly linked her life with a comeyah. Her family knew not who his people were, what his past revealed, and to whom he could be held accountable.

Florence could rattle off how Charlie had "done sandied his candy an full em up wit de dut," that is, how he'd made the mistake of allowing his lollipop to drop from his mouth and into the dirt. Had its sandiness made it inedible by being too encrusted to rinse off?

Charlie's lollipop mishandling had occurred after a weekend reign of reckless mistreatment: when he'd doused his and Camellia's laundry with bleach because his work clothes hadn't been cleaned to his satisfaction, then ordered her to purchase a new wardrobe for each of them, from her next paycheck. Because of her obliviousness about household responsibilities, he had locked her in their bedroom closet for six hours—to make her understand that she "was nothing and nobody" without him. Then he'd held a loaded pistol to her temple when he'd released her—to ensure she never inform her family members about their personal business. And had dislocated her left shoulder during a ruckus—for frying chicken instead of pork chops for their Sunday after-church supper.

According to Florence's recollection, her Aunt Camellia's brothers at this point had grown tired of Charlie's reckless mistreatment of their sister. They'd reasoned that, as Florence had rattled off in Geechee sing-song cadence, because Charlie had accidentally dropped his succulent lollipop onto the ground and because it was now sandied, it could no longer be enjoyed, that it, like Charlie, had to be tossed.

Florence, story keeper Florence, remembered the no-longer-shared utterances about how Charlie, after Camellia's brothers, Adam and Thomas, had tracked him down, had mysteriously disappeared! Was never seen or heard from again. How they had driven him, bruised, bloodied, and blindfolded, with duct tape across his lips, inside the large trunk of Thomas's raven black Ford Thunderbird to the border of South Carolina and Georgia. He lay next to a suitcase stuffed with his bleached belongings. How he was threatened, in no uncertain terms, to never, ever return to the state or to Georgetown County. Ordered to sever any association with Camellia or any member of her family. Or he would live a final night like Daniel in the lion's den . . . without the presence of the angel of God. And that they themselves would be the marauding and ravaging lions!

She remembered hearing how the home, car, bills, everything, had been in Charlie's name only, and how the debt he'd amassed had left Camellia destitute. How many of Florence's younger relatives knew only about Aunt Camellia's second and more adored husband, Uncle Jack, and how older relatives had expunged Charlie from their memories and their mouths.

Yet she, Florence Tucker Wineglass, knew the truth, the whole truth, and nothing but the truth from her family eavesdropping. And because of the many family truths she held onto, she knew that her own name would be included on every personal piece of property that she and Chadwick owned. That they would be partners, co-collaborators, in all business dealings.

And as she watched Laverne walk away, she knew that as a Benefactor in Generosity she needed to do more than dole out a balance of four hundred dollars.

Two days before his grandfather-in-law moved to their modular unit, Chadwick wiped away a lone tear that slid down his left cheek. Halting the dismantling of what was to have been the crib of his first born, a son, he inhaled deep breaths. His eyes looked around with the innocence of an infant and then locked in on the smiling face of a bright yellow polliwog named Binyah Binyah that was painted on the changing table his parents had given them. He knew that they and his siblings were longing to witness the day-to-day changes of the newest Wineglass.

"A newborn is a reminder of a fresh new start for hope, for dreams, for laughter," his mother Bernice had said. "Now, they will stink from time to time, but just wash them and smile with them. The scent of newness will bounce back in no time!"

"You can't stay at this pity party too long, Chadwick!" he alerted himself. "Get this stuff done, then check on your wife. You know what needs to be done. So, do it."

One by one, he carried all the baby furnishings out and brought in what he'd rescued at the Salvation Army. A double bed frame, mattress, box spring, chest of drawers, and floor-length mirror. He nibbled on a fingertip after each action. Despite his nervous assault on his hands, he considered it an honor to take in one of his wife's elders. Throughout his childhood, he'd watched his father, King Solomon Wineglass, give to those in need throughout the community whatever he had. Food, cash, a place to stay, the shirt on his back. You name it. And now Chadwick wanted to pay this familial generosity forward.

"Now, if you give—give and don't expect nothing in return!" King had advised his brood. "God'll bless you. Those who you give to don't have to repay you. If they want to, just tell em they have to give you back *everything*. Just the way they received it. And if they can do that, they probably didn't need what you gave em in the first place." His father's verbal haunting continued. "Don't hold onto it long, though. A blessing is a blessing. So, if you get anything back, just pass it on to someone else who needs it."

And what a blessing his parents had provided for him and Florence! As a testament to what people could do if they managed their money well and stayed out of trouble with the law, they'd paid the down payment for the previously owned modular home that the couple had purchased as newlyweds.

Still dressed in her floral nightgown, Florence peaked into the second bedroom as she walked slowly from her bedroom to the kitchen.

"Oh, Chadwick Wineglass, you're a keeper!" she said after sizing up all he'd accomplished. "When did you do all this? I would've helped if you'd called me . . . ."

"*Help* me?" Chadwick stood up after sliding the bottom draw into the chest. "Did you say, '*help*' me?" He hugged his wife and planted a loving kiss first on each eyelid and then on her lips. "You help me best by resting and getting your strength back. Mama left some breakfast for you on the table. Let's go see what's what."

He scooted behind her and put his arms around her waist, and they sauntered lockstep into the kitchen. A glass of orange juice sat on a placemat next to a folded napkin with silverware, and a plate lay below a glass pot top. After Florence sat, Chadwick lifted the pot top with aplomb. Whiffs of grits, bacon, scrambled eggs, and a blueberry muffin wafted about them. It was the same meal he'd enjoyed earlier, before he began his labor of bedroom renovation, but the unleashed aromas refreshed him. Since their return home from the doctor's office, Bernice had arrived early each morning to prepare their breakfasts. She returned in the late mornings to sit with Florence and provide her lunch, and then readied their dinner before rejoining King and her other children.

"Now, Florence, Honey, call me if you need anything, please," Chadwick said after cleaning away her dishes. "I'll be at a site in Murrells Inlet this morning and then at another one in Pawleys Island this afternoon. Mama should be back here soon."

She watched from the porch as he stepped into his pickup truck, looked her way, and winked. Sadness flooded her thoughts because her gifts of cooking, cleaning, caring, and indulging his intimate desires could not be extended or appreciated. Knowing she needed rest, she blew him a kiss and returned to bed.

Porcher's first connection with Chadwick following his impromptu invitation to lunch occurred on his drive to work. He recalled answering the ringing iPhone as he crossed the Waccamaw River Bridge. With the radio blasting the closing lines of "When You Believe," he listened, spellbound, to the blended vocal artistry of powerhouses Whitney Houston and Mariah Carey. Hearing, "Hey, there, Boss Man," he smiled when he recognized Chadwick's distinct Georgetown voice.

"Good morning, Chadwick," he said. "How's it going?"

"I'm doin," Chadwick replied.

"'Doin?' did you say? Doing what?"

"Doin, Russell, doin . . . That's not something they say in Edisto?"

"No, Chadwick. Uh-uh. What's it mean?"

"'Everything is everything.' I tell you, I forgot. You're a comeyah. I've got to teach you some things about your new home. Anyway, I'll be at a work site in Pawleys Island on Thursday. Wanna grab lunch if you're free? We can decide on a time and a place later—hold on. Excuse me. I've got to take this business call. I'll be right back—"

Chadwick switched his call before Porcher could respond, leaving him to stare at the phone in disbelief. A nanosecond before ending the call with a swift push of his right thumb, he heard Chadwick's voice on the other end.

"Russell . . . Russell, I'm so sorry. Thanks for holding."

"Uh huh," Porcher answered. A light irritation had begun to settle at the nape of his neck on the right shoulder.

"That was a potential client I've been waiting to hear from for three weeks."

"Next time—"

"I know, I know. Next time, I won't leave you on hold. So, is Thursday a good day to plan for?"

Porcher agreed—with reservations. As he drove into Debordieu Colony, the shadow of the wingspan of a large raptor crossed the roadway before him.

He learned about the telephone deportment of the self-employed during their Thursday lunch and relaxed his reservation about their initial phone conversation. Following the hostess to the table where Chadwick was seated, he smiled as Chadwick pulled the phone from his ear momentarily, mouthed, "Just a minute more," and motioned for him to be seated. In fact, Chadwick maintained his headset plugged into one ear throughout lunch, paused to answer each call and listen momentarily, and informed the caller of a time frame in which to expect his return call.

"If they don't talk to someone, they'll call someone else," Chadwick informed him later. "If they talk to someone else, it's most probable I won't hear from them again. Until they reach out to find someone to repair the inferior work that my competitor did, that is."

"How oona do?" Porcher greeted Chadwick in Lowcountry fashion after his initial phone conversation ended and then waited to hear the unfamiliar follow up.

"I'm doin," Chadwick responded on cue. Porcher then informed him that a common Edisto response to the query about how someone was doing is, "I'm here!" or "I just in Mercy trus. I don't make no fuss!"

With the icebreaker of linguistic peculiarities behind them, their lunch conversation was enjoyable. They sparred about the ref's call of the past night's play that led to the Broncos win over the Green Bay Packers. They joked about each receiving a check-in call from their wives within two minutes of each other. Porcher laughed about missing his two kids, and Chadwick revealed that he was dealing with the second and still recent stillbirth.

Without words, the two communicated with averted glances followed by arched eyebrows their awareness of the number of restaurant patrons who seemed unnerved at the sight of two Black men dining together in a sea of whiteness. A hiccupping toddler at a nearby table began to cause a din. The vocal glitch became louder with each repetition. It was followed by pitiful sobs from the distressed child and nervous expressions of concern from the mother and her lunchmate. One picked the little boy up and patted his back. The other reached out with a cup of water to the panicking child. With a raucous, "AAAWRP!" water began to dribble from the boy's mouth, soaking his light-blue onesie. Conversations at other tables paused. A few mothers from other tables walked over to suggest remedies.

"Now, that situation would have been resolved quick-quick if it happened on Edisto," Porcher said.

"Yeah?" Chadwick asked. "How so?"

"Well, an Edisto mother or some Edisto Islander from the restaurant kitchen would've torn a piece of a brown paper bag, spat on it, and then slapped it on that boy's forehead. And the hiccupping would've stopped. Dead in its tracks!"

"That so?" Chadwick mused. "I never heard of that being done around here. But some people say if you comb your hair outdoors, a bird could get it and make a nest with it. And if that happens, you could get headaches. Headaches bad enough to give you a fit! Now, my mama says that it's just an old wives' tale. But that's what lots of people say can happen. Myself, now, I comb my hair inside my house."

Fully agreeing with this practice and understanding his attentiveness to his mother's counsel, Porcher said, "Me, I do *not* comb my hair outdoors. And, like you, I know better than to disagree with or disrespect my mama, my daddy, or any elder in the community. Or they would beat my boonky or put—"

Chadwick quickly joined in, "—de mout on you!"

No longer focused on the hiccupping tirade, they continued to compare common local practices.

"And when people get bad headaches, what's the best thing to do?" Porcher asked.

Chadwick rested his right elbow on the table and perched his head atop his closed fist. He snickered as he stated, "Wrap their heads up—"

"—in a leaf of collard greens!" Porcher rejoined for a combined finish.

They laughed so loudly that other guests turned away from the hiccups to focus on their chuckles.

Porcher started whispering, "Oops, I guess it's time—" and Chadwick concluded, "—for us brothas to get up out of here."

Chadwick footed the bill, as promised, but his philanthropic zeal did not rest. As they reached to shake hands before heading to their cars, he pulled Porcher in close. Clasping right hands tightly and embracing him with his left arm around his shoulder, he pushed something into Porcher's hand.

"Don't count this now," Chadwick said. "Just put it in your pocket. It's for that commute you make home on weekends. And I'm sorry, again, about making you hold for so long on the phone call. I'm back at a nearby worksite in about a month. Maybe we can catch up for lunch again. Okay?"

Back in his driver's seat, Porcher pulled from his pants pocket a wad of cash. Four one-hundred-dollar bills that had been folded in half, then folded again. The precise amount needed for a two-way commute home and back for four weeks!

Chadwick expected the prompt call a few minutes later. "It's a gift, Russell," he stated as he answered.

"Grea-a-a-t day, Chadwick! You don't have to do this. I can't accept this."

"But it's a gift. You didn't ask for it. If you don't want it, you can give it back. But you don't have to. It's yours. For your commute."

"Okay . . . well . . . thanks, man. I appreciate it," Porcher said. "I mean, I know exactly how this can be utilized."

"And what's this, 'Grea-a-a-t day' thing you just said? That's from Edisto, right?" Chadwick chuckled then added, "Maybe I'll see you at Bible study. Before you steal away to talk with your kids, that is. But hopefully, we can get together again in about a month. Okay? I'll call ya!"

Although Porcher missed the next two Bible studies, Chadwick's calls began in earnest. Often, multiple times a day. While he was traveling to work sites, Porcher guessed. Never after his workday ended, however. And almost always to pass along personal financial information or tidbits. Leading with testimonials or questions, the discourse and his insistence on paying for meals led Porcher to inquire point-blank, "Are you flirting with me?"

"I don't know what you're talking about," Chadwick responded, seeming somewhat flustered. "It's nothing like that, Russell."

After that, probing questions took a breather, and a brotherhood seemed to develop. Porcher no longer needed to respond to queries like, "Your wife is insured, right?" Or testimonials like, "I had to learn to save whatever I could. I collect pennies and change that lie around the house in a jar, and at year-end, deposit it." Or "How much credit card debt are you in? I hear some people are ten to thirty thousand in debt with their credit cards. Don't be too ashamed to say what it is now, Russell; you've got to be able to say the amount of debt that you're in so that if one day your circumstances change, you'll know exactly what's needed to get you to freedom."

They began checking in regularly about jobs, their marriages, their families, their health. Cracking on each other about personal idiosyncrasies—like saying "I'm doin!" as a greeting, or "Grea-a-a-t day!" as an exclamation. They introduced wives and kids during one of Mignon's weekend visits with Russell.

All seemed well until imposing shadows began to become evident on the horizon. During a dinner visit at the Wineglass home, Mignon asked how their friendship had begun. Reaching for a dessert plate of Florence's fragrant, lemony, buttery pound cake, Russell answered that Chadwick had invited him for lunch after they'd met at a Bible study that he'd stopped in on occasionally. But Chadwick's nonchalant rebuttal sent an uneasy chill down Russell's spine.

"Florence told me to reach out to him. That's how it began."

So, our "friendship" started because your wife told you to begin it? Porcher pondered silently. That was one of the most bizarre things he'd ever heard! Tension in his shoulder began to knock and announce, "I'm here."

Later that evening, Mignon rubbed her husband's tight neck and upper back muscles and listened to his disquiet about Chadwick's response. "You know, babe," she said, "maybe it's a guy thing. Some men find it difficult to talk about feelings, or just don't know how. Maybe him saying that Florence told him to befriend you was his 'guy' way of saying that she encouraged him to make friends with someone who he thought would have similar interests. What d'you think?"

"I don't know, baby. I just don't know," he responded. "Something just doesn't feel right . . . ." He smooched her left knee as he sat on the floor between her legs with his back to the bed. Then he lightly massaged her ankles, running both arms behind her legs and gently tapping the tops of her feet.

"See, that's what I mean. You're a feeling person. That's what I like about you." After a moment of silence, she added, "Well, they seem like a nice couple. But I just met them. It's good that you have someone to hang out with while you're up this way, but if anything about this friendship begins feeling too weird, just share it with me on our daily calls, or hold onto it until we see each other on the weekends."

"Thanks, Mignon," he said, before resting into her embrace and looking up and backward into her eyes. She felt his muscles tighten when Eldridge and Ethiopia bound into their bedroom through the open door. Each waved a fifty-dollar bill and exclaimed how "Aunt Flo" or "Uncle Chad" had pressed it into their hands before they left and had told them to get something special for themselves.

To calm her husband's percolating agitation that she was sure would have him snatch the money from their hands and say something that he might regret later, Mignon pressed her left arm lovingly but firmly around him and extended her right hand to the children.

"Why, that's a lot of money," she said, looking with love into their eyes. "Now, that's too much for you to hold onto. Did you say thank you? Well, Mommy and Daddy will think of the best thing to do with this, okay?

"Now, go on get ready for bed. We'll be in soon. We're going to visit—"

"—Freewoods Farm in the morning," they spoke together.

"That's what Daddy promised," Mignon finished.

"And a promise Daddy makes is a promise Daddy's gonna keep!" Russell said.

When the two were again alone, Porcher stood up and then sat beside Mignon on the bed. "See what I mean?" he asked. "What the—?

"Now, now, now, Vernon Russell Porcher," she interrupted. "It's a down-home Black people thing to call the friends of your parents 'aunts' or 'uncles.'"

"Yeah, yeah, yeah . . . and to dole out dollar bills or fives or tens—not a fifty-dollar bill. And a fifty-dollar bill times two is a hundred. And I told you he gave me four hundred the day he took me to lunch. Friendship is one thing, but making someone a charity case is another."

"Are they Georgetown billionaires?" Mignon asked. "Maybe they just got it like that?" After a while, though, she waffled. "I don't know . . . I don't know . . ." she said. "It does feel a little . . . *something.* Whenever people give you something, they usually want something in return. Keep your eyes open. And your ears. And your heart. But if they're Black Rockefellers, keep your hands open too. And bring the money home to me, baby!"

Momentarily, she added, "Now there *was* something about that pound cake."

"Yeah?"

"You know my daddy and his daddy bake pound cakes, right?"

"The best!" Russell chimed in, shaking his head as his shoulders danced up and down. "Pound cakes are a big part of our culture."

"Well, Daddy always said you can tell a lot about people by the cakes they bake. Her cake smelled good and looked good but tasted almost good. I think something was a-missing, and her face didn't flinch when she tasted it. Now for a baker to not acknowledge that a cake isn't her best or to not know that an ingredient is missing could mean that keeping things secret from others is a part of who she is. Or maybe who she wants others to believe they are. I'm just saying . . . ."

Porcher nodded and found during the next few weeks that Chadwick's mutterings and actions seemed to become cryptic. A forty-something Black man passed by their lunch booth when they met at Cousin Ann's Restaurant. He paused and looked at Chadwick as if waiting to be recognized.

"Hello," Porcher said, to initiate conversation. The stranger smiled at him, then returned to staring at Chadwick. "And how have you been, Mr. Wineglass?" he asked.

"I'm doin," Wineglass answered with more civility than cordiality. He looked up but never into the bystander's face. "Gary Windley, this is Russell Porcher. Russell, this is Gary Windley." That was their total conversation.

"Nice to meet you, Russell," Gary said, before moving on. "Chadwick Wineglass is one of the nicest people I know."

The scene was surreal. There was something peculiar about the shape of Gary's mouth, the inflection of his voice, his body language as he'd waited, and about Chadwick's definitive lack of interaction with him.

"What was that about, Boss Man?" Porcher asked. It hadn't been a freakish lover's spat, he reasoned. It was as though a friend, or an acquaintance, somehow had been dissed without receiving any prior acknowledgement.

"He's someone who's received something and is looking to see if he'll receive anything else," Chadwick stated. And then, he changed the subject. Completely.

Porcher paid for his own lunch that day. He would've paid for both, but Wineglass insisted that he did not have to and should not. Before they parted, Chadwick asked Russell to wait outside the restaurant while he got something out of his truck. Russell thought, *I hope he's figured out I'm going to decline anymore of his monthly financial charity!* But Chadwick returned with two plastic film cannisters.

"This is how I store the batteries I need for flashlights and my power tools," he said. "Here are some extra ones— Cs and Ds. You've got to keep your flashlights charged and ready to use, now, especially if you make late-night drives to Edisto. Good to see you today. You hold 'em down, Russell."

Florence's *ember* assignment for Chadwick prior to Russell Porcher had been for Gary Windley. She'd overheard a conversation that intrigued her while shopping down an aisle in the Piggly Wiggly store. The man who she'd later learn was Windley was being commended and consoled by an older woman.

"If you ain been deh, Gary," she'd said, "Bessie Windley been done gone on frum yah longtime ago. Tank Gawd ya come back yah fa hol e han an leh em kno e only chile ain fagit bout em. Ebrytime she been git sick, I tell em, Bessie, e coulda been wussa, ya know. An she keep on a goin on gen an gen til tings git wussa, fa true! De suga diabetis breng huh ta haffa deal wit de kidney-allasis. An den de cansa come an tek em on ta glory."

The woman stopped speaking as she cried and dropped her head into her hands. She then clasped her hands around his. "Gawd gon bless ya, son! I know e ain been easy fa lef ebryting—ya jawb, ya frens, ya home—an come back yah fa a lee while fa see bout ya mama. But Gawd gon bless ya, fa true!"

The scene reminded Florence of the hurdles she'd had to clear about changes in life plans when her grandfather had to move in with her and her new husband. To make ends meet, Chadwick had begun working two extra jobs. He cleaned office buildings on weeknights and served as a convenience store attendant on the Saturday graveyard shift twice a month. She'd hoped that assigning Gary Windley to Chadwick would help her husband to realize something, that the people whom they sponsored had goals. Goals that vitalized them even when their financial indebtedness seemed insurmountable. That just like Windley and others, they too needed to envision some goals, some personal, marital, and family joys to reach for other than increasing their income in order to help others.

It was the only aspiration Chadwick spoke to her about. As though he was justifying his time away from her side, her embrace, their bed. Thankful that he'd not balked at her decision to care for her grandfather, she offered to return to Calabash by the Sea, if only part time. But he would hear nothing of it, arguing that he was doing everything he could. That this sacrifice was for the best of everyone concerned. That it was only temporary, and they'd reap a harvest in a short while.

When her grandfather overcame his bout with vertigo three months later, she offered again to return to the workforce, but Chadwick maintained his decision. To her surprise and dismay, he even protested that Tucker should reside with them full time because of his age— because she could manage his time and care better than if he lived alone. That in addition, they should enroll him in a life insurance policy to cover his end-of-life debts. Debts that no other family member would likely be prepared for.

She agreed to the latter only following her insistence that Emanuel Tucker was physically capable of caring for himself. That she needed time away from her grandfather to deal with her newfound awareness of Tucker's marital infidelity. Chadwick concurred with her decision to have Tucker return to his own home nine months after his arrival, but only after learning that he and Florence were again expecting.

Long Flow

Late 1970s - 1990s

Thelma Thunderbolt, who had come to Gregory Dunkin's mind during his father's funeral service, wed Melvin Marshel, a Low-country Georgetown man, six months following their graduation from Paine College. Each was offered a promising job in Rock Hill, SC, Melvin as a policy analyst with the Social Security Administration and Thelma as archivist with the Winthrop University Library. With bachelor's degrees from a state institution of higher learning in what they envisioned was an evolving South, each was fearless not to self-identify as poet Maya Angelou's "caged bird." A bird who "stands on the grave of dreams." Whose "shadow shouts a nightmare scream." Whose "wings are clipped" and "feet are tied." No, they began their professional lives and readied for marriage in York County, the birthplace of one of the leaders of the 20th century Ku Klux Klan. Unlike the imagery of Angelou's caged bird, however, the couple somehow did not yet know how to open their throats to sing.

Music, however, infused their wedding ceremony and reception. The sanctuary of Cross Roads Baptist Church in Westminster, SC, was filled with orange and yellow autumn flowers. The Thunderbolt family's home church was the oldest African American church in Oconee County. Often called Brush Harbor Church, the original log structure was built in 1860 in what was then known as the Crossroads community.

"Cross Roads" aptly described the conjoining of the bride's and groom's families. Thelma's parents loved Melvin, though they regularly asked him to repeat whatever he said. Her twin brother Timothy, however, considered his own inability to discern his future brother-in-law's thoughts as alarming. Unless Melvin wanted his thoughts to be known, he remained quiet—a tradition followed by many people of African descent. Timothy regarded this trait as ungodly. In his theological studies, Timothy had learned that some sea island beliefs and practices were rooted in pagan West African religions. Melvin's looks and demeanor when he chose not to answer Timothy's questions, or thought he had done so, bewitched the pastor. He had argued with his twin sister to ensure that she and Melvin were equally yoked.

Classmates from around the country had joked with Timothy about the dangers of dating women from the coastal communities of South Carolina. About never eating their red rice. About how they entrapped men by mixing in drops of their menstrual flow. He worried that perhaps Melvin had engaged in some similar hoodoo black magic to ensnare his sister.

"Melvin loves God. He loves me, and we love being together," she had told him on several occasions.

Nevertheless, hours before the ceremony, Timothy, who was one of three groomsmen, confronted Melvin at the hotel where he and the Marshel family were staying.

"Hey dere!" Melvin's family members greeted him with smiles upon his arrival. "Soon time fa git dress, man. Whyso oona da tarry roun ya?"

"I'm looking for Melvin," he responded, after he'd deciphered their question about why he was tarrying there when it was time for the wedding party and attendees to get dressed.

"Ohhhh, de groom, huh?" an uncle asked. "Oona ain breng no bad nyews, ainty?" Overhearing the conversation, Melvin's parents walked over with a look of surprise on their faces.

"Oh, no sir. No, sir," Timothy said before shaking the uncle's hand. "I'm not bringing any bad news. And good morning, Mr. and Mrs. Marshel," he added after pivoting and hugging them. "So good to see you both."

"What breng ya way oba yah?" Mrs. Marshel asked. "Need some las minnit hep decaratin de reception hall?"

"Ya kno, ef ya need any hep wit anyting, we all right cha fa len a hepin han," Mr. Marshel added. "Mm-hmm! Soon we ga be one famlee. An we lob ya sista, fa true! Huh done cas a spell oba we boy. A good spell, now. A good good spell." Charmed with his revelation, the Marshels chuckled, entangled arms with each other, and watched Timothy's face as they awaited a reply.

Spells, rituals, and enchantments were the very concerns that Timothy wanted to discuss with Melvin. But, beguiled by the Gullah Geechee conversation and facial expressions, he could not admit this.

"Oh, I just want to give him some last-minute advice about how to keep my sister happy," he said, playing the devil's advocate. He clasped his hands before him. "—so this upcoming marriage will last a lifetime."

"Oh . . . I see, I see . . . well, Melbin, up een de room da git ready," Mr. Marshel said. "Numba fibe o seben." Timothy had become used to hearing substitute v's in the middle of words with b's and headed to room 507.

"Gone see em, chile," Mrs. Marshel added. "Dohn stay long, now. We haffa make it ta de chuch on time. Dah fa sho!"

The elders looked lovingly at Timothy as he walked away, then returned to mingle with family and friends. Unseen by them, however, Melvin's uncle tossed salt over his left shoulder minutes before the couple approached, to ensure that any evil thoughts that Timothy may have brought with him to the hotel about the upcoming marriage would become undone.

Upon hearing the knock, Melvin answered the door, holding a disposable razor blade in his right hand and with shaving cream over his moustache and beard.

"Melvin?" he said with surprise. "Come on in. Come on in. Ebryting alright?" He would've pronounced "everything" with the "th" but the alarm of seeing his future brother-in-law before him caused his inner-Gullah to defy any linguistic training. Timothy was pleased with Melvin's overall diction but found that the intonation of his speech was often peculiar. That his statements at times were delivered as questions, for example, and his questions at times were delivered as statements. Particularly if he was angered, agitated, or alarmed.

"Ya come fa tell me Thelma change e mine! Oh, no . . ." The

look of panic on his face made the whites of Melvin's eyes turn a hue brighter than the shaving cream. Melvin's dark brown irises blackened and canvassed Timothy's face. Left to right, right to left. Up and down, down and up.

"No. No, no, no," Timothy said. "That's not why I'm here." He put his right hand on Melvin's left shoulder. "Calm down, Melvin, calm down." He walked him over to the foot of the bed and they sat, making certain not to disturb the white tuxedo ensemble that was laid near the pillows. "Oh, I'm so sorry to make your blood pressure go up. I didn't think my showing up at your door would have such an effect."

Melvin heaved deeply, then began to take regular breaths before rising to lay the razor blade in the bathroom. "What you think, man?" he asked when he returned to the open doorway. "Now, you have to go gather some moss and bring it back to me. Mm-hmm! Does moss grow here in Seneca?"

Stumped, Melvin asked, "Moss? What's that? Why do I need to find some?" He stood and began pacing. "Can I get it at a drugstore? A department store?"

"Moss, Timothy! Moss. Ya cyan buy no moss at no sto!" With Timothy's surprise visit and Melvin's reunion with Lowcountry family members, any semblance of formal English from Melvin's lips had taken a pre-wedding holiday.

"What is it? Where do I get it?" Timothy questioned.

"Ya story, ainty?" Melvin implored, asking if Timothy was fibbing. "You ain know? Fa true?"

Timothy shook his head with sincerity. The rest of his body did not move. The sight made Melvin begin to chuckle, to heave with laughter. Forgetting the shaving cream, he placed both palms on his cheeks to compose himself, then quickly wiped his hands on the black athletic pants he was wearing. Shaking his head with incredulity, he began to speak with college-graduate aplomb.

"Moss grows on Sea Island trees," he explained. "It's gray, hangs from the branches, and looks like beards. People pinch some off and wear it in their shoes to lower their high blood pressure. Some women place it under their breasts or inside their bras. I've never tried it. But people swear it works. Your visit was about to make me a believer!"

After grabbing a towel and wiping his face, he sat again with

Timothy at the foot of the bed.

"So, what's this visit all about, brother man? You sure had me some kind of shook up!"

Timothy decided not to pursue his initial plan of counsel. So, into a sea of memories that teemed with lectures he'd heard and papers he'd written, he cast a rod and reeled in a thought about the importance of compromise.

"Well, you've probably heard this before," Timothy began, "but I felt it was important to share it with you before the two of you become one. . . ."

"Okay. Go ahead. Tell it," Melvin said.

"I don't know from experience . . . . I'm still a bachelor . . . but I've read that this blending-together-thing sometimes gets difficult. Husband and wife each come with their own set of thoughts and beliefs and fears about almost everything. Religious practices, who to seek advice from, how to resolve arguments and raise children, everything. And each may think that his way or her way is the right way. The only way. But to make things work for the long-haul, Melvin, I say this, 'Remember the art, the discipline, the ministry of compromise.' Maybe you don't know it yet, but Thelma can be pretty strong-willed. It's a Thunderbolt thing, I guess. Compromise is the avenue to not let minor things become major crises."

"Compromise, huh?" Melvin responded. "Well, I can live with that. Thanks, Timothy. Thanks for stopping by."

Timothy doubted that his compromise declaration would prove effective. After answering Melvin's query about his visit, he had prayed silently for patience to know how to address their future marital or family scenarios that could become rife with cultural discord. Groom and groomsman shook hands and gave each other a manly hug, with three pats on the back. In the hallway, Timothy yelled to Melvin standing at the door, "See you at the church. And don't be late. If I am, it's because I'm driving around searching for some . . . some . . . what you call it?'"

"Moss," Melvin hollered back. "If you see any, grab it off the tree, now. Not from off the ground, please. It could have redbugs. And I don't need to contend with redbug bites on my honeymoon!"

The two stained glass windows at the front of the church, the conical green spire atop it, and the four white columns upholding the porch added elegance and reverence to the building's simple architectural construction. Inside, Melvin and his groomsmen walked with the pastor to the pulpit. The bridesmaids, then flower girl and ring bearer, walked down the aisle. And when the pianist played a chord for attendees to stand, Thelma, veiled and dressed in a close-fitting white gown, stepped through the doorway of the single-story, white clapboard building. With jubilation, she walked with her father toward her groom as a soloist sang Natalie Cole's "Our Love." The piano keys and vocal strains soared within listening hearts and ears . . . .

I've got love on my mind
Love is always right on time
Love is you and love is me
Love is gonna set you free

As Timothy glanced at Thelma and Melvin, however, his mind's eye envisioned detrimental long-term results of their cultural differences. They saw sparks of love. He saw imprisonment, not freedom. Not bliss, but bondage.

Thelma glanced at her brother, smiling, and watched him smile in return. But sensing a familiar fraternal-twin inkling, she realized from a furrow above his eyebrows that he was not in full agreement with her marriage. She wondered why he hadn't shared with her any vision of discontent and instantly resolved that it was because he'd accepted that her choice in the matter was more important.

Immediately following their three-night honeymoon in Atlanta, GA, the Marshels returned to work under the watchful eyes of office supervisors whom they'd begun to regard more as overseers and taskmasters. Each had chafed at their requests for a two-week vacation for wedding preparation and honeymoon, even without pay, because they'd been employed for less than a year. So, the couple had wed on the Friday after Thanksgiving. Following the reception, they'd driven to their bridal suite at the Marriott Hotel in the Sweet Auburn District to begin matrimony with a weekend jaunt of Black-owned restaurants, nightclubs, and museums.

Had they realized the ire that their wedding inspired among their White colleagues, the title of the last song that they danced to with their wedding guests would've seemed like a prediction of things to come. And the joy and fellowship that they'd experienced with family members and close friends of the Divine Nine who'd attended Paine College would've been regarded as the shenanigans of thieves, addicts, and riffraff at backwoods juke joints.

Before jumping into Melvin's champagne gold Ford Fairlane with the words "Just Married" spray-painted on the rear window, Melvin had carried Thelma in his arms to their getaway-mobile after all had danced the "Do It" to the old-but-not-forgotten rhythms of Fontella Bass's soul-some hit, "Rescue Me."

Back at work, when Thelma approached the library break room, she overheard conversation that ended upon her entrance. "Yeah, it was probably a shotgun wedding," one woman snarked to another as they sipped coffee and shared a box of macaroons. "A pickaninny's probably on the way. Be here before nine months, I'm sure!" the other responded. At the abrupt stop of their tee-hees and snickers, Thelma passed them by without acknowledging their coarse discourse. She sat alone on the only green chair she could find to enjoy reading a magazine and nibbling from a package of jellybeans.

The voices of two White male co-workers floated into her hearing from an office across the hall in the early afternoon. "Today, they've got these high-powered jobs, but to me, Negroes were born to pick cotton and tobacco," one said with a deep southern drawl. "They don't need to involve themselves in business, the law, government, nothin'. Those were the good old days, when all they did was work in the fields. And sing their songs . . . ."

"That's God's plan," the other responded with the delivery of a Sunday school superintendent. "And we need to return to it. Now, they all goin' to college. Talkin' betta than White people. Thinkin' they betta than White people. It's gotta stop. It's an abomination."

Thelma tugged at her left ear lobe with her left thumb and forefinger and looked around the office to see if she alone had heard the conversation. Seeing no one else respond, she tapped her right foot nonstop to steel her nerves. She breathed in slowly to still her determination to walk to the doorway, stare into their faces, and emblaze them with fire from each eyeball. Fontella Bass's closing lyrics reverberated in her mind: *Rescue me/Rescue me/Mmm-hmmm, mmm-hmmm.* A moment later, she walked to the reference shelves to complete an assignment.

"What them letters mean on your car, Melvin?" one of his White coworkers had asked. The man and two others seemingly had been lounging in the men's room for a while when he'd entered. This surprised Melvin, because he'd seen his supervisor glancing at his watch as soon as Melvin walked away from his desk and entered the office hallway. And he'd looked at it again when he returned. Melvin felt certain that his times away from his desk were being tracked.

"What letters are you referring to?" Melvin responded with feigned ignorance. "Do you mean the letters on my license plate?"

"No, not them letters," an older, wiry looking man chimed in. "The three letters, symbols or whatnot on that bumper sticker of yours. I never seen nothing like that before."

"What's the colors on it mean?" the third inquirer asked. A drizzle of tobacco oozed from the left corner of his mouth, and Melvin noticed the round outline from a tin of Snuff in his shirt pocket. "That something from your church? Some kind of advertisement for 'a' chicken dinner or 'a' pork chop dinner?"

To Melvin, their leering looks began to appear sinister. They walked closer to him to listen, but he felt inclined to leave. Quickly!

"Oh-h-h-h, 'A Phi A,'" he answered. "Is that what you're talking about?" He paused to give them a professorial glance. "Alpha Phi Alpha is the fraternity I belong to. I joined while in college. Our colors are black and gold." Sensing that he'd answered each of their questions, he smiled politely, turned, and exited.

Chicken dinners?! he mouthed to himself with quiet disdain. *Oh, no, no, no . . . not today! Not today!* He made a quick about-face to inform them that Alpha Phi Alpha fraternity was the first successful historically Black Greek Letter Organization to gain intercollegiate status within the United States. That it had begun as a study and support group for African American males at Cornell

University because they had not seen other persons of color on campus for prolonged periods. That Black Greek Letter Organizations provided opportunities for inclusion for African Americans who were ostracized and banned from joining many social organizations at universities during the early 1900s.

"And my wife is an AKA," he continued, with a sullen stare like that of a college professor who was weary of students who had no knowledge of well-known facts. "That's for Alpha Kappa Alpha, the first Black Greek Letter sorority. It was founded at Howard University. You know that's in Washington, DC, right?"

His listeners shrugged their shoulders and made motions to walk away.

"Wait, wait, wait . . ." Melvin urged, stepping in front of the door to bar their retreat. "AKAs and A Phi A's are part of the National Pan-Hellenic Council . . . nine Black Greek Letter Organizations commonly referred to as 'The Divine Nine.' The symbol and colors on my car that you asked about means that I'm part of the Divine Nine . . . from an HBCU, which means 'Historically Black Colleges and Universities.'"

With a look of triumph, Melvin looked them each in the eye, then left, arriving back at his desk before his two white colleagues' slow return. And feeling like Maya Angelou's caged bird, he witnessed a peripheral viewing of his "restroom time" being checked off by his supervisor. He was unnerved about the ignorance and resistance of his associates. He knew history. Why didn't they?

Melvin thought of Thelma, his bride and Greek sister, whose colors were pink and green. He wondered how she'd respond this evening to today's office stressors, and what stressors of hers he'd learn about.

Just their drive to work and back home was exasperating. Before their wedding, Melvin had begun renting a home in Paradise, an African American community in Fort Mill, a twenty- to thirty-minute drive from their jobs. They each had been fortunate to board in rooms on a monthly basis, at family homes of a fraternity brother and a sorority sister in Rock Hill. Neither had known either family beforehand, but their Greek-letter network had procured them both lodging and a safety net.

Their new commute caused them to drive by the offensive Fort Mill street signs and venues, including Confederate Street, on which Confederate Park was situated; Booth Street, named in honor of President Abraham Lincoln's assassin; and Forrest Street. The latter was named for Nathan Bedford Forrest, the first Grand Wizard of the KKK. The park housed the "Faithful Slaves" monument, which was erected in 1895 to celebrate White supremacy, and to extoll the docility and loving kindness of a people who, according to its inscription and carvings, enjoyed slavery more than freedom.

To encourage, console, and support each other, Thelma and Melvin daily discussed their workplace botherations and, afterward, voiced suggestions or expletives as coping mechanisms.

"I believe my supervisor is a direct descendant of Mildred Lewis Rutherford," Thelma stated. Reclining on their green second-hand sofa and with her legs on her husband's lap, she sighed with relief as he massaged her feet and legs.

"Now, who was she?" Melvin asked.

"Well, she was one of the leaders of the United Daughters of the Confederacy," Thelma answered. "That dastardly group of White women who sought to rewrite the history of the Civil War, idealize White supremacy, and romanticize the Confederacy. Oh, the things I've read, the things I've seen in the Archives Department, Melvin! It'll make you scream, 'Well, I'll be John Brown!'"

"The White women did this? Not the White men?" Melvin inquired.

"Well, the White men wrote the laws: literacy requirements and property ownership to vote; poll taxes to disenfranchise voters during Reconstruction; Jim Crow laws to institutionalize racism. And they waged violence and destruction against Black business owners and legislators. But, make no mistake, make *no* mistake, they did all this while the White women cheered them on and dug trenches deep in the battlefields of people's minds and hearts. The White women erected monuments of Confederate soldiers throughout the country. They made sure public-school books spread false history. That states' rights and not slavery was the cause of the Civil War. That slaves were content and happy and benefited from the evil institution, and that Confederate soldiers were heroic, mythical figures worthy of being revered for defending the Southern way of life."

Rubbing her temples with both hands, Thelma felt a twinge in her neck. "Oh, honey," she screeched. "This so good, so good!

Would you please do my shoulders next?" Melvin moved to the corner where she had reclined, had her scooch down to where he sat, and to lie belly down with her head on his thighs. Her laments and her muscular spasms continued as he tried to relax her with prods of his fists and the pressure of his flattened palms to her neck and back.

"Today, I found a handwritten notebook of Daughters of the Confederacy quotations that was tucked away on the library shelf that I was assigned to work on," Thelma said softly. Her volume intensified as she continued. "I know it was that heifer, my supervisor, who left it there for me to find. I think she's trying to spook me to quit. But I got her number. I ain't going nowhere!"

Her muscles contorted as she reflected silently on the quotations she had read. "Honey, reach in my pocketbook, please," she said. "It's there on the floor on your side of the sofa."

Thelma lifted her head as Melvin turned and stretched his right hand down to the left and right to search for her purse.

"Thelma, Thelma," he said with exasperation when his fingers connected and he pulled the green leather bag up by the straps, "I know I've told you fifty 'leven times not to keep your bag on the floor. My mother says women who do that don't attract wealth. Or if they do, they can't hold onto it."

"Melvin, that's just another Geechee wife's tale," she said. "You and your Lowcountry people are full of them."

His eyes flattened, his facial muscles stiffened, and she knew her words had struck a nerve. If she didn't act quickly, she'd learned, her husband would shield all of his thoughts behind a glare of motionless eyes. And when he unleashed his contemplations, his eyelids would widen, the whites of his eyes would brighten, and he would spit out a rhythmic barrage of words in which *th*'s were pronounced as *d*'s, and *str*'s at the beginning of words would be pronounced as *skr*'s. Final consonants at the end of words would be silenced. And *-er* or *-or* word endings would be pronounced as *ah*.

To avoid the fright this behavior gave her, though she'd come to know she shouldn't be alarmed about it, she countered with softness, "But I'll try to remember . . . . Thank you, Melvin!"

She felt his body relax as she laid her head face up on his left thigh and stretched out on the sofa. Riffling through her purse, she pulled out a stack of folded papers of copied handwritten words. She read the first aloud.

"The work of the United Daughters of the Confederacy is not based on sentiment alone, as the records of our work will show. Our main objects are memorial, historical, benevolent, educational and social. We are building monuments of bronze and marble to our noble Confederate dead as an inspiration to future generations. We have built and assisted in building all over the South, monuments in the form of Soldiers Homes, Hospitals, Memorial Halls and Schools for the descendants of our Confederate soldiers, in whose veins flow pure Anglo-Saxon blood, who otherwise could not be educated.

—Mrs. I.W. Faison, President of the North Carolina, UDC 13th Annual Convention, 1909[1]

"What?" Melvin exclaimed. "Let me see this." He pulled the sheets of paper from her hands and read silently:

The old Confederate soldier looks down from the sky and laughs as he sees the principles for which he fought established, the great battle for the Constitution, State's rights, white supremacy, all the South has conquered.

—Mrs. Lucy Closs Parker, President of the Vance County chapter, North Carolina UDC, Third Annual N.C. Division Convention, 1899[2]

It is true, he [white men] had to fight his way with shackled hands during the awful reconstruction period; but wise men of the North understand why it was a necessity then. He [white men] were compelled to establish the political supremacy of the white man in the South. [Applause]. So too, the Ku Klux Klan was a necessity at that time, and there can come no reproach to the men of the South for resorting to that expedient.

—Mildred Lewis Rutherford, historian general for the national UDC, Washington, DC, 1912[3]

---

1 Greg Huffman, "The group behind Confederate monuments also built a memorial to the Klan," Google, last modified August 14,2021, https://www.facingsouth.org/2018/06/group-behind-confederate-monuments-also-built-memorial-klan., 4.

2 Huffman, "Confederate monuments," 4.

3 Huffman, "Confederate monuments," 7.

> *What was the condition of the Africans when brought to his country? Savage to the last degree, climbing coconut trees to get food, without thought of clothes to cover their bodies, and sometimes as cannibals, and all bowing down to fetishes -- sticks and stones -- as acts of worship.*
>
> —Mildred Lewis Rutherford,
> 1914 Address in Savannah, GA[4]

> *The North and the Freedman's Bureau was necessary to protect the negro. The South said that the Ku Klux Klan was necessary to protect the white woman. The trouble arose from interference on the part of scalawags and carpetbaggers in our midst and they were the ones to be dealt with first to keep the negros in their rightful place.*
>
> —Mildred Lewis Rutherford, 1915 Address to the
> UDC National Convention, San Francisco, CA[5]

"Thelma, you do not need to carry this venom around in your handbag," Melvin said. "And we can't keep it inside this house." A change in his speech began to emerge as he became more agitated. "Ima put dese in a Ziplock bag and leave em outside unda a rock til ya wanfa see em gain! Uh-uh-uh!"

Rising from her prone position, Thelma smooched her husband on his lips, and said, "Thank you, baby!" She did not, however, give him an opportunity to convey irritations from his workday. Her action launched the beginning of their marital demise. It marked the moment that they allowed stressors from outside their marriage to derail internal bonds they should've held onto dearly.

While her pains were being waylaid, she had experienced a "Rescue Me" epiphany. She'd conceptualized a three-pronged Family Plan of Action to achieve success in the racist York County community. Although she did not articulate it, she allowed it to resonate within her as though it had been vetted and had received spousal approval.

One, they would speak English so well, with such polish and perfection, that their coworkers and others would be ashamed to

4 Huffman, "Confederate monuments," 8.
5 Huffman, "Confederate monuments," 10.

doubt their intelligence. Two, they would emphasize appreciation of the arts, literature, and social constructs other than an agrarian lifestyle to validate their worthiness of acceptance. Finally, three, they would visit, or at least promise to visit, Melvin's family regularly to deter the family visiting them, which would result in utter embarrassment because of their bad speech, boisterous mannerisms, uncultivated demeanor, and peculiar ways.

She skipped into the kitchen to prepare dinner. After opening a large twenty-pound bag of rice that Melvin had insisted they buy, a recurring phenomenon began. As the rice began to steam in the pot, she developed a runny nose and stomachache and began sneezing and itching.

Lay by Flow

Late 1990s

Little by little, Sibyl began to shed resistance to the Lowcountry community—a perception her husband's stories had inclined her to adopt. However, inner proddings and sensibilities began to assure her that somehow, someway, she had come home to a place that had been awaiting her return. And that like Dorothy, had proclaimed while clicking her heels three times, "There's no place like home!"

Despite physical and cultural dissimilarities, the spirit within Sibyl communicated readily with the spirit within the women of Low Bottom Community Church. The church mother, Mrs. Eloise Nesbit, invited her within three months of her arrival to attend an urgent Tuesday meeting of elderly women. The noonday prayer service at her home would be for an important concern. As a rule, the council usually did not include younger women church members, but Miss Eloise found something "speritual, deep down speritual" about the church's new first lady. She hadn't felt so inclined about previous ones.

Sibyl, in turn, encouraged her to ask the ten other church women older than seventy to meet at the sanctuary instead, and to arrive a half hour early. To their surprise, Sibyl began the meeting with a foot washing ceremony. The women had woken that morning with their minds set on praying. Had hobbled into the church from their cars, rolling walkers with upside-down tennis balls on the rear legs, ambling with canes and walking sticks, or moving at a slow gait. They arrived steadfast to learn the concern that had made Eloise assemble them and to commence to pray without delay.

Sibyl greeted them with a hug in the church foyer, asked them to wait until all had arrived, and then directed the group to the fellowship hall. They heard a recording playing piano solos of old spirituals as they approached. When they reached the entrance and saw yellow wash tubs with white towels beside them on the floor in front of chairs arranged in a semicircle, the women were confounded. All but Eloise wondered if the meeting had been called concerning a false accusation about themselves.

"What's all this for?" a woman with a blue rinse in her hair asked after she had sat. She wore yellow pants and a white blouse and clutched a wadded paper towel in her right hand. Others looked to her and then at Sibyl, who was dressed as ordinarily as they. Sibyl pushed a plastic bench with her left foot to the center of the semicircle. Sitting, she looked up into their faces, took a deep breath, and said, "I give thanks to God for each of you and for every church member every day. Low Bottom Community Church called my husband to pastor. As his wife, my chief duty is to lift him up so that he can, in turn, keep every church member uplifted. But, as a daughter of God, I think it is important that I honor the church mothers in a special way. Mothers are way-makers. So, please, remove your sandals, your sneakers, your flats. Place your feet into the tub of water. Just relax and unsettle your minds." She looked to Eloise and continued, "At the appointed time, we'll lift our prayers to the throne of grace."

As the ladies quietly sang the verses to the instrumentation of "There Is a Balm in Gilead," "Standing in the Need of Prayer," and "Ev'ry Time I Feel the Spirit," Sibyl dried their feet. Aged. Blistered. Calloused. Imperfected with bunions and corns. Some with painted toenails. Some in need of clipping. Others discolored with fungi. Afterward, she cleared away the tubs and towels. When she returned, the women's hearts and minds were on a higher plane. She set another chair before the group, sat down, and asked the women on each end to move their chairs closer to hers to form a circle.

Eloise stared into space absentmindedly as she rocked slowly back and forth, back and forth in her metal chair. She closed her eyes and bowed her head for about six seconds. On the seventh count, her head lifted, her eyes opened, and rocking stopped. Voice soft and speaking with pauses, she began, "Fus ob all . . . A jes haffa say . . . Tank ya so, Sista Tundabolt. Tank ya frum de bottom ob me haart!" She looked to the other council members. "Dat been beautiful, ennit?" Each nodded or raised both hands upward before their faces. "Beautiful! E pit me mind een de right place fa why A ax ya fa come togedda dis day . . . A been hab a dream . . . a dream wa beenna gib me a troublin mind. An A wan we fa tech an gree so dis ting wa A been see een de dream . . . Gawd stop em frum comin bout."

"What you see, Eloise?" asked a woman in a red jogging suit. "You know your dreams are like the eyes of God on the sparrow. God watches them, and they always come true. Just the way you see them." She rested her left fist at the intersection of her right thigh and abdomen as she leaned forward. Her right arm flanked her right thigh.

"Tell it! Tell it, Eloise," the woman with the blue rinse said. She had transferred the paper towel to her left hand. "We gon take it fo de Lawd an ax em fa make a way!"

Sibyl looked at each face. She felt a charged tingling in the room. All eyes were set on Mother Eloise Nesbit. A widow, mother of twelve, grandmother of forty, great grandmother of seventy-four. A retired laundress and cleaner of White people's homes. Her face was unwrinkled, and folds were only now beginning to appear around her ninety-year-old, hickory nut-colored neck.

"Een my dream," she began, "de chuch been become de nyew slabe auction block. Jes lok de one wa beenna been een front ob de Rice Museum pon Front Skreet."

"No-o-o-o!" several women sighed. Others urged her to continue with expressions of, "Mm-mm-mm," and "God's gonna ease yo troublin mind."

"We men ob Gawd been de slabe masta dem," Eloise continued, "lashin dey whip an shoutin de wod ob Gawd frum dey mout whilst dey been stan een front ob de block! Dey beenna shout at chuch peepul. Chuch peepul wa been horrify ta fin deyseff pon de block. Cause dey beenna done tell de preacha dem ebryting bout wa dey see and wa dey feel, an wa dey dohn wanfa see and dohn wanfa feel . . . an de preacha dem ain been study tall bout wa dey been yeh. No, no, no. De preacha dem, dress up een dey fine-fine suit an shoes... some wit dey bishop robe on . . . jes beenna raise dey han one by one when de auctioneer holla out a higha numba . . . ."

Because Sibyl still struggled to understand Gullah Geechee speech, she allowed Eloise's brush strokes of melodic word pictures to paint meaning in her mind. In Mother Eloise's dream, the church became the new auction block. Just like the one that had been on Front Street, in front of the Rice Museum. She had seen nowadays preachers as the new slave drivers. They lashed whips by shouting the word of God from their mouths as they stood in front of the auction block. They shouted at church people who found themselves standing on the new auction block. The church people were horrified because they had told their pastors things they'd seen and experienced and what they hadn't seen and experienced. But no pastor had listened to them. Dressed in fine suits and shoes, each pastor had raised his hand as the auctioneer's bid amounts got higher and higher.

"Mother Eloise," Sibyl interrupted, "are you sure this dream was from God?"

"Well, as you've heard, every dream that Eloise has ever had has unfolded just as she's seen it," responded a council member, wearing a wig of straightened and re-curled hair. A retired high school English teacher, she looked at the pastor's wife with compassion, and added, "Tis so sweet to trust in Jesus."

Eloise continued, "De chuch peepul dem pon de auction block staart fa sniffle an cry, sniffle an cry. Cause de preacha dem ain been show dem no way ta freedom. Dey jes beenna haul way de ones dey buy. . . den dey cas em deyseff enta de fiery pit ob hell."

The church people on the auction block began to sniffle and cry, sniffle and cry, Sybil reasoned from what Eloise continued to describe, because the pastors didn't show them a way to freedom. They just hauled away the ones they bought and then cast them into the fiery pit of hell.

The eleven listeners sat mortified.

"Lawd, hab mussy," Eloise moaned. "Den A been see buzzard dem da swoop roun an roun oba de holin station wa beenna been nex do ta wheh de Rice Museum now da at. Dah same holin station wheh de Africans been git maarch to frum de ships wa been dock een de Georgetown Harba...Dah same holin station wheh some Africans git breng to from de pes house een Sullivan's Island... atta dey git haul off de slabe ship wa been dock een Chaaston. Dah same holin station wheh befo dey git deh, dey been git douse wit palm oil den git scrub wit dat ruff danby brush til dey skin da shine lokka de boots ob de buckra dem.

"Das wa dey done ta me peepul dem wa git breng ta Darcatia Plantation an ta Mausaville cross de wata. Me peepul wa A kno an me peepul wa run way, lok de African name Mobo, wa become jes anodda story bout 'many tousan gone' wa one time been lib pon all dese plantations roun yah!"

Hearing Eloise moan, Sibyl continued to paint understanding with the word pictures that Mother Eloise spoke. "Lord, have mercy, then I saw buzzards swoop around and around the holding station that had been next door to where the Rice Museum now stands. The same holding station where Africans were marched to from the slave ships docked in Georgetown Harbor. The same holding station where some Africans were brought to from the pest house in Sullivan's Island after they were hauled from slave ships in Charleston Harbor. That same holding station where, before they arrived, they were doused with palm oil and scrubbed with a rough danby brush until their skin glistened like the polished boots worn by White men.

"That's what they did to my people who were brought to Darcatia Plantation and to Maussaville, across the water," Eloise said. "My people who I know and my people who ran away, like the African named Mobo, who has become just another story about the many thousand gone, but who at one time lived on these many plantations around here."

Sibyl flinched upon hearing the name "Mobo" but remained silent, listening intently.

"Een de dream," Eloise continued, beginning to sob uncontrollably, "een de dream, de holin station been full up wit nyoung chuch peepul dem. We chullin. Some olda, but mostly teens an nyoung adults wa done los hope, wa dohn care no mo bout wa de preacha dem ga say or do ta em when de git maarch out ta stand deh pon de auction block. Cause dey tink de preacha dem done stop yeddy dem. Dey tink de preacha dem cyan hep dem fin no freedom. Dey tink de preacha dem jes wanfa cas dem eenta de firey pit ob hell."

Eloise began to sob uncontrollably, and Sibyl took note. The elder explained that in her dream, the holding station was filled with young church people—their children. Some older people but mostly teens and young adults who had lost hope, adults who didn't care anymore about what the preachers said to them when they were marched out to stand on the auction block because they thought the preachers had stopped listening to them. They thought the preachers couldn't help them find freedom and only wanted to cast them into the fiery pit of hell.

All gathered in the fellowship hall had begun to bawl about Eloise's dream. But one by one, each began to pray. Silently. Vocally. Two by two. Three by three. Or all together. Sometimes sing-song. Sometimes muttered. Seated. Standing. Holding hands. Raising hands in the air. Walking around with their hands akimbo. They continued for ninety minutes. Until they felt their pleas had been heard. Until they were assured that God's answers would come. Maybe not when they wanted them to, but right. on. time.

The ladies hugged each other before departing. They glorified and praised God for all the things they had heard and witnessed. Mother Eloise's panoramic and unsettling dream about present-day Black clergy acting like slave owners on plantations, and the sight of buzzards swooping around and around over a present-day holding station.

Sibyl treasured everything that had happened and pondered the experience. The dismay of Georgetown youths and adults who found themselves on an auction block, standing before pastors; the horror of seeing ministers who did not listen to or acknowledge the hurts and crises of their parishioners; their invalidation of their members' deep-rooted traumas that spanned generations as unworthy of acknowledgement, even as demented; their purchase of parishioners one by one; and their merciless castigation of them to hell.

At home, Timothy shared with Sibyl two events from his day, one that he considered as positive and the other as negative.

"People are beginning to say good things about me, to know I'm here," he said with excitement. He poured a glass of orange juice, kicked the refrigerator door closed, and joined his wife at the kitchen table.

"Yeah?" she asked with a smile before placing the magazine she'd been reading onto the table to give him her full attention.

"Yeah, I'd stopped for gas at a 7-Eleven on the outskirts of the city of Georgetown when a stranger pumping gas on the opposite side of the tank recognized and spoke to me. He'd been in a shiny black pickup truck hauling an enclosed black trailer, and I'd seen him watching me. Light blue lettering on the trailer sides boasted the name 'Wineglass French Drain Installation.' The image of water coursing through a drain in front of a building while a stick figure family looked on and smiled with satisfaction was an attention-grabber.

Before I finished pumping, he said, 'You're new around here, right?' When I nodded, he continued, 'You carry yourself like a reverend . . . you're about six-feet tall . . . and your tag says Georgia. You must be the new pastor at Low Bottom Community Church.'

"I told him, 'Yes,' and asked if he was a local. When he said, 'yes,' I asked him if he knew how the community got its name, to be conversational.

"'Well, we're called the Lowcountry because we're at sea level,' he said. 'And the Low Bottom section is the lowest area in the Big Dam community, which is next door to Big Dam Swamp. The water table in Low Bottom must just be two inches below the ground. When it rains, don't you wish your predecessor had built an ark in the church parking lot?' He chuckled then added, 'I didn't get to William Dunkin's funeral, but I hear you prayed a prayer that people will be talking about for some time!'"

"People around here see and know everything about everyone!" Sibyl said, shaking her head in amazement. "And who was he?"

"Well, he said his name was Chadwick Wineglass. He's self-employed and owns Wineglass French Drain Installation. Said he'd heard about my interest in developing low-income housing in the Low Bottom Community and said we should talk. If I had a good proposal, he said, he might be able to steer me to some investors. He passed me his business card and invited me to get in touch. Now, Sibyl, I haven't spoken about this idea to anyone since my second interview with the Pastor's search committee. Maybe this is a sign that God wants me to follow-up on this idea."

"Tee, maybe it's a sign that you need to think this idea through more thoroughly," Sibyl interjected. "Maybe church people have been talking about it because it's the last thing they're interested in doing. And maybe you need to investigate this-shiny-black-truck-driving Chadwick Wineglass. He could be a wolf in sheep's clothing." Sibyl paused. "Anything else interesting happened today?"

Timothy gulped the last bit of juice and set the glass down with a thud.

"Oh, yes, you should hear about this!" he said. "There's a teen in the church, a young male, who has been fainting, experiencing spells of some sort for the past year. I understand the Gilliard family has been having him treated at the Medical University of South Carolina, MUSC, down in Charleston. It all seemingly had been going well, until about the time of our arrival at the church, just before the new school year started. Since then, Barry has been relapsing. The parents have asked for prayer, and I'm to meet with them tomorrow. But here's the kicker. Now, I don't know, but I've been told that the young man has been seen in the company of a Gregory Dunkin."

"Gregory who? Who's he, Tee?" Sibyl queried.

"Well, he's the son of William Dunkin, the local root doctor. Barry and Gregory *do not* need to mix!"

Sibyl reached for her husband's hand across the table. As she watched his eyes move from left to right again and again in righteous indignation, she prayed silently for him, the Gilliard family, and the Dunkin father and son.

"Mother Eloise, I hope you don't mind my stopping by without an invitation," Sibyl stated as she walked from her car to the house. As she had parked her blue Buick in the shade below a live oak tree, she'd seen Eloise sitting inside the screened porch, cooling herself off with a hand fan.

Dressed in a sunshine-yellow sundress and wiping perspiration with a handcloth, the elder stood to unlatch the screen door for her guest. "Anytime, chile!" she said. "Anytime. Jes swat dem skeetas an noseeums way frum ya, fo ya come een, now!"

In the few steps from her parked car, Sibyl flinched from the annoying buzzing near her ears and the shadows from large mosquitoes. She wasn't familiar with the term "noseeum," but she readily understood its meaning. Smacking at bites on her legs, arms, and neck from teeny-tiny, blood-sucking gnats, she shimmied her body and swished her arms and then sat in a rocker beside Eloise.

"Now, wa breng ya roun yah, Miss Sibyl?" Eloise's smile revealed that she was receiving guests even though she was without her dentures.

"Oh, I'm trying to learn my way around the community," Sibyl responded. She looked around the porch and into the yard to avoid embarrassing the matriarch about her toothlessness. She reached into her pocketbook and pulled out a bag of Skittles. "I've seen you nibbling on these at times," she said, "so I hope you'll enjoy them."

"Mm-hmm!" Eloise said with a smile. "Oona too much. Too much! Now, when A put me teet back een, dis ga be good good. Mm-hmmm. . . ."

They rocked and chatted. Rocked and chatted and fanned.

"Mother Eloise, you mentioned some interesting names when you told us about your dream a few weeks ago," Sibyl said. "One of them is a family name, and I've never heard it said by anyone outside of my family."

"Wa name da dah, chile? Hep me memba."

"Mobo," Sibyl answered. "Mobo." She searched Eloise's face for some spark of recognition but observed only a slight widening of her eyes. "Well, Mobo Night is the name of my great grandfather. And if I understood you correctly, Mobo was the name of your grand uncle. Right?"

Eloise nodded her head slowly. "Das right," she answered. She placed both hands on her thighs, sat forward, and widened the space between her legs and feet, assuming a storyteller pose. "E come from Africa an e git breng ta Darcatia Plantation. Right up de road. Dah mean ole Massa Maurisina been make him an e sista, me grandma, slabe fa em pon e rice plantation. Mobo been a fiel han wa haffa chop down dem cypress tree een de swamp. Chop em down and drag em out. All ob em. Til de swamp git tun eenta a rice fiel. Oh, wa me peepul dem done been shru!

"But Mobo, dey tell me, Mobo run way one night ob de Harbes Moon. Dis befo A been bon. An no famlee memba ain neba see em gain. Nebanomo. Neba!" She shook her head again and again about the remorseful recollection.

After a long pause, Sibyl asked, "And the plantation is named 'Dar-ca-tia'? And the mean plantation owner's name was . . . what did you say?"

"Maurisina. Massa Maurisina."

"Oh, Mother Eloise," Sibyl sighed as tears began to course down her face.

"Wa, chile? Wa happen? Oona wan sompn col fa drink?"

"No . . . no, thank you . . ." Sibyl said and collected herself. "I think you and I, the two of us, are connected. Let me tell you my family story, please?" She waited as Eloise sat back in her rocker. "I'm a fourth-generation Night family member born in Columbus, Ohio. Columbus, Ohio, is where the African Mobo settled after he ran away."

"Oh, chile, oh, chile!" Eloise proclaimed, rocking more quickly than before. "A feel like deres a fiyah da bun, down een me bones. Oh-h-h-h-h! E been a-bun eba since A been lay eyes pon oona. Oh, great Gawd . . . grea-a-a-t Gawd! Go on. Tell me mo, tell me mo . . . ." She leaned forward and stopped rocking.

Sibyl retold the family story she'd heard since childhood. That her great-grandfather had been a runaway from a cruel slave master somewhere in the South. From a place near the "big wata" that reminded him of his African homeland. That the master had been so cruel to him that he'd fled, and Mobo had adopted the new surname, Night. That Mobo had spoken in an African language and with almost unintelligible English when he reached Ohio and had said that "Masna" was mean and that he was from what had sounded like "dahcahntsha." That from generation to generation and through reasoning and storytelling, the recollection had become documented that Mobo had said he was from the "dark continent"—his African homeland where only dark-skinned people lived. That he had described the land from which he'd fled as a place where the village elders seemed to be watching him from stools perched in the limbs of trees, and where ancestral spirits whispered to him on midnight-dark and full-moon-bright nights, "Use ya wings. Fly way! Fly way, Mobo, fly way! Rememba ya fus name. E mean 'freedom.' So, fly way, Mobo, fly way by de light ob de moon!"

Eloise stood. She placed her hands on the top of Sibyl's head then pushed the screen door open and walked into her yard. She glanced back at Sibyl. With her hands on her hip, she nodded her head up and down, then looked to the heavens with uplifted hands. She turned and walked below the live oak tree. Only then did Sibyl notice the beardlike moss hanging from the limbs. She began to imagine watchful elders sitting in the high crooks of the branches and on limbs that spiraled downward and rested on the ground.

When Eloise returned to her rocker on the porch, her first words were, "'Masna'? An 'Dah-cahnt-sha'? Dah wa Columbus, Ohio, peepul dem been tink him been say? No-no, no-no, him been tellem say him Massa Maurisina been mean! An dat him been frum Darcatia. Dar-ca-tia Plantation. Bless e soul. Bless e soul!" She pointed to the oak tree. "See dah moss deh, Sibyl? See dah moss?" She explained that the story handed down by their family on this side is that her grand uncle had told others beforehand that he'd heard voices in the moss hanging from the tree limbs, voices telling him to remember that Africans had come to this country with the ability to fly, and that he'd left on the night of a harvest moon.

Sibyl informed Eloise that Mobo had married her great-grandmother Nokomis, whose Chippewa name means "daughter of the moon."

"Well, grea-a-a-a-t day een de maw-w-w-w-nin!" Eloise proclaimed. "Huh lob fa him mussa shine bright as dat full moon dat night when him been yeh de woice dem wa tellem say, 'Fly way, Mobo. Fly way home.'"

Harvesting

Cutting Stalks with Rice Hooks

Mid-1960s

In part because they hadn't learned how to argue, little by little, Thelma began to alter Melvin. His speech, his childhood recollections, his beliefs that differed from hers—it all began to annoy her. So Thelma, personifying God in the words of "The Creation" by James Weldon Johnson, "like a mammy bending over her baby/ Kneeled down in the dust/Toiling over a lump of clay/Till he shaped it" shaped not Adam, but her husband "in [her] own image."

She reasoned she was helping Melvin develop into manhood. And he allowed it! She knew that he reasoned that being conciliatory would placate her need to be controlling and would empower her to walk in the tenderness of her femininity more fully. Still, she scoffed at his vain imagination!

She monitored and then prohibited visits to her husband's homeplace. She planned, for the time when they would become parents, to control their children's meetings with any cousins who favored the Mausaville behaviors and speech that she thought they should not model. She projected that without her intervention, their children would grow up too connected to their Lowcountry heritage. She hoped that Melvin one day would become detached from old friends, old beliefs, old recollections.

Then one day, in a moment of reckoning, Melvin realized, *I'm lonely. I am alone*. It occurred at a time when fertilization had begun but neither prospective parent was yet aware. During an intense moment when hormones were in flux, mutual irritations were at their zenith, and a conciliatory spirit had drifted away, he confronted Thelma. Her steeled response was, "If you want to go back to those backwoods people, go ahead. But I'm not going with you. And when we have kids, I'll make sure they don't go if I don't go."

Having grown slow to think for himself, Melvin realized that what becomes old will not become new—not ever again. He felt an urge to visit the footpaths of his youth, to commune with family he'd not interacted with on more than a casual level in years.

When he pleaded with Thelma to join him, to help detangle the vines that would choke their lifeline for years, she listened, but soon spoke over him. "Melvin, maybe later, but not now. None of the younger generation there remembers you, anyway. And they probably can't stand to hear what I always hear. Those old, ho-hum tales that everyone regurgitates each time I visit with you. You know, how your neighbor would call out, 'Ago-o-o' whenever she approached someone's house—now, why on Earth was she making some old African sound even though she wasn't born in slavery?

"Or where the old homestead's boundaries are—one was by the front of the scuppernong grape vine, right? Why anyone didn't think to put a marker there, I don't know. Besides, we are *not* relocating there!

"Or 'How your mama's potato salad was better than your Aunt Willie Dee's while your Aunt Willie Dee added this or that to her pot roast to make it outshine your mama's. Or how your daddy would eat the fish, the whole fish, and everything on the fish—leaving a small pile of chewed up fish bones on his plate.

"And here's the kicker," she continued, "who died, when they died, and what they died from, or the last flare-up Uncle Watermelon had from gout, and how he got that name because his mother had been feasting on watermelons all day when her water had broken. Who had an affair with whom, and whose child was the spitting image of some relative who'd shamed the family name . . . It's just the same stories, the same inane, tired old stories, year after year after year . . . and traveling from one relative's house to another's to hear the remix. The same song, with a different high note at each location."

At that moment, the part of Melvin's Mausaville past that Thelma had dreaded most came unleashed and revealed itself before her very eyes. Her abrasive litany had made him aware that his immediate relatives in Mausaville no longer reached out to or connected with him—that they responded to his phone calls only matter-of-factly. They no longer shared any back-home news. One day, he realized, they would pass along no blessings, no endearments to his children or his children's children. Because no one would know them!

He realized that he himself was allowing everything around him to become sinking sand. And in that enlightenment, Melvin arched his Gullah back, pulled himself out of the miry clay, and proclaimed in what sounded to Thelma like the force of a mighty wind, "Haul ass!"

Knocked to the ropes by surprise, Thelma determined to defend herself against any other sucker punch from Melvin. In her mind and with her words, she started shuffling with a Muhammed Ali two-step and began to counter with passive aggressive jabs.

"So, after just six years—four in college and two here in Rock Hill—you really want me to leave? Okay, then, I'll leave. If you think that's what is best for you, I'll leave!" Floating like a butterfly to the left, she added. "Now, I don't remember ever hearing you say that anything was wrong between us. Did you ever express this to me? No? Well, are you certain we shouldn't just live together under the same roof for a while? Until we can think our actions through more clearly?"

Stepping back then forward to sting like a bee, she added, "Now, what will our one-day children, or our grandchildren think about this moment, Melvin? You know I care about you, right? I do. And I want what's best for you."

Aware of her black widow spider tactics throughout the years, Melvin stayed silent but refused to get caught off-guard with her mind-numbing, nonstop litany of questions and statements. In the pit of his gut, a childhood rhyme began to gurgle. He hadn't thought about it since schoolyard and bus-ride fights. Whatever may have caused an argument between the two, male or female, whenever the offense was brought to their attention, a peacemaker would ask if either person cared that the other had been offended. In response, one of the disgruntled children would sneer, "I don't care!" And the other would retort with the words Melvin heard himself spewing from his lips to his wife, "Care?! Care don't get you nowhere. Care don't grow up. Care don't grow down. Care don't grow all around. Care . . . care . . . you think I care? I don't care!" And then a punch or smackdown would ensue.

To qualify his new attitude, Melvin glared at Thelma with flat eyes that were flatter than she had witnessed from him ever, reflecting expressions she'd seen in many of his relatives in Mausaville. Expressions that would manifest especially after she'd said something that, to be fair, she had thought later should never have parted her lips.

They turned their backs to each other, then Thelma walked to the bathroom, dropped to the floor, and hurled. Melvin walked to the guest bedroom to sleep that night.

This was the scene that eventually drove Thelma to seek William Dunkin's mojo services during their visit to Georgetown in the following two weeks—a planned visit during a strained period of marital reconciliation, but one without their awareness of the new life the couple had sparked.

After Dunkin informed her that there was nothing he could do, Thelma's persistent questions conjured up the same flat expression she'd witnessed in her husband. She could not read it. Could not decipher it.

"What? What do you mean there's nothing you can do for me?" she'd rallied. "If anyone can do something about someone from this back-in-time place, surely you can!" She looked at the natural environment around her with disdain and continued, "Do something. I can pay you for it. Do something!"

Had she been able to silence her utterings, to sit with her thoughts, to listen within herself, perhaps she would've assessed that she and her Gullah man's problems were for her and her Gullah man and the Spirit of the Ages—and not William Dunkin— to resolve.

Rinda Middleton's last vision of and connection with Emanuel Tucker had been from afar at their four-year-old son Absalom's burial. To mask their infidelity, she'd maintained and guarded their child's existence since birth; Absolom was known only within the confines of the Darcatia Plantation community. Although the boy's father's name was on his birth certificate, she made no mention of him to relatives, friends, or inquirers. They'd agreed they would unwrap their secret only when Emanuel left his wife, Blessing—whom Rinda learned about only when she informed Emanuel that she was pregnant with Absalom, and whom she'd come to understand he *would not leave* when she'd announced her second pregnancy and Emanuel had informed her quite emphatically.

Before that moment, they'd agreed that the unraveling of their clandestine affair would result only when others saw similar, almost identical Tucker family features in the parent and the child. Broad nose, slanted eyes, squared shoulders, long feet, walnut coloring. Absalom parroted all of these except for the lighter pecan coloring of his mother. Rinda kept her child close to home. When she left Darcatia, she covered Absolom's face. As he grew, she'd leave him with family members and quickly return.

She and Emanuel had met at dusk on the evening of a summertime full moon. Emanuel's bateau had run aground on a sandbar along the western end of Darcatia Plantation during a fishing expedition that had begun in the early afternoon. He'd wandered ashore to await the rising high tide, trekking through a bog of cypress knees. The eerie darkness from towering and interlocking cypress tree limbs slowed his movement. As he progressed, he heard singing and followed the song.

A raspy female voice sometimes shrieked and sometimes whispered. Accompanying handclapping pulsated to the rhythmic 1-2-3 sea island beat that had been heard during hush arbor and praise house worship since the days of slavery. It was the rhythm that ushered in a sense of freedom. Freedom from the troubles of the world. Freedom from the drudgery of day-to-day existence. Freedom to believe there was more joy somewhere.

As he neared the clearing, the singing and the hand clapping lulled his mind to stop fretting about a stranded boat. Or an expectant wife and two stairstep children. Or the need to return home quickly to a family who required his absolute attention minute after minute following a long day on the water. Or the rigor of having to row the boat ashore.

"Hallelujah!" he sang to himself once he cleared the bog. Then he saw a lone singer who was freeing her mind. Flailing her arms, thrusting her breasts, swaying her hips, pounding her feet onto the sand. She danced, cried, sang, wailed, and moaned.

"Kate bought de flouah
Frum C'Pat.
De powdah she use
Was de Rough on Rat
Fa man, she bake
De sweetes bread
She wounded two
An she kill Green daid.
Oh, de possum laugh.
Oh, de possum laugh.
E gonna lib a long time.
Oh, de possum laugh."

She repeated the song over and over again, laughing with raucous abandon on the lines, "Oh, de possum laugh. Oh, de possum laugh. E gonna lib a long time. Oh, de possum laugh."

Drawn in by Rinda's dance, her song, her bewitching beauty, Emanuel had no awareness of why she sang. Of how the song had inspired and ultimately freed her. He paid no attention to the moss billowing in the breeze, responding to every movement.

Since childhood, she'd been known as "Cracky Rinda" within the Darcatia community. Her physical strength, petulance, and pulchritude were formidable and beyond the natural realm. Her mind skipped time. She reasoned irrationally. Her head bobbed to voices and rhythms heard only between her two ears. And as soon as she had begun to smell her pee and her body had blossomed into womanhood, she chose to fancy only the men her Mama told her to stay away from.

"Haard haid make fa sof hiney," her mama said before she tossed her out of her home.

"You can bounce ya roun bahine back heh when ya ready fa do wa we tell hunnah fa do!" her daddy said. "Not befo. Not til!"

In defiance, sixteen-year-old Rinda took up with fifty-something-year-old Fred Cuttino, better known as "Danger Boy." His rap sheet was lengthy. Public drunkenness. Knock-down, drag-out brawls with whoever contested him. About anything! He was known for domestic abuse charges by numerous women who allowed him to overstay a weekend drunk. He had beamed one in the back of her head with the heel of his boot until her left eye detached and dangled and had to be carried in her hand until authorities were alerted. Another charge was lack of child support, issued by the wife of his youth who had borne him thirteen children and whom he saw afterward only on occasion.

Cracky Rinda only needed lodging. Danger Boy longed only for someone to cook for him, collect his mail, and cash his disability check. Now he was mostly toothless, riddled with diseases from a decadent lifestyle, and older than the rambunctious and turbulent young adult he'd been. Cast aside by his family, who'd long ago aborted any hope of him transforming, he languished in an isolated, rundown cabin deep in the woods, near the cypress bog—way back in Darcatia Plantation.

Cracky Rinda had wandered and wandered and in surprise, found the cabin. No one else had ever attempted. She'd agreed to keep him fed in exchange for room and board, although conditions were quite primitive. His abusive tongue, the kernel of wretchedness within him, was the one iniquity that his destitute life could not dispel. And it was the one thing that aggravated her.

Late one afternoon, she saw a half-filled mason jar of white lighting on the battered kitchen table. While she stood wondering in disbelief how he'd found the stash of corn liquor that she'd hidden following his last abusive/drunken revelry, Danger Boy tipped into the kitchen like a plat-eye behind her. Like the folkloric being that could shift-change and had at least one glowing eye as large as a plate. Drunken Danger Boy was scary!

"Mess wit my likka gen, chile, an dat de end a you!" he snarled.

She reeled around and eyed the switchblade in his hand.

"Oona tink ya pretty so! Enty?" he continued. "Umh-humh. Wen A cut ya face, de pretty ain ga be deh no mo. Heh, heh, heh!"

Unafraid, Rinda began staring trancelike at the crusty canker at the right corner of his lips. "Oh-h-h-h . . ." she whispered with feigned concern.

"Wa oona see?" Danger Boy asked with growing suspicion. "Wa oona da look at?"

"Dah so dah da ooze out pus . . . orange pus," she lied.

"Wa?" he replied, lifting his left hand halfway to his cheek. Snapping to attention with the least inebriated portion of his brain, he countered, "No pus orange. Ya cracky sef! Ya story! Ya story, an A ga cut de pretty an de lyin outta ya!"

He advanced and made a wide swing toward Rinda with the knife. She did not budge but saw the cast iron skillet on the stovetop in her peripheral vision. She maintained an intent gaze on his canker as his litany ensued.

"Oona so cracky ain nobody wancha. Ain no man wancha an oona ga daid widout hab no chirren. No chirren fa look at an laff at e cracy mudd . . . Cracky and dum . . . ya dum as a oysta!" His invectives became louder and meaner. "Ya fool up! Ya ma an ya pa ain wancha. Ya famlee ain wancha. Dah whyso ya find yasef down yah wit me . . . walkin roun listenin ta tings een ya haid wa nobody else can yeh. A ain wancha needa! Hide tings frum me? Me ownt tings, at dat? Ama cut de tiefin outta ya too!"

He moved forward then staggered backward, in a drunkard's two-step. Without flinching her eyes from the putrid infection on Danger Boy's face, Rinda reached back with her right hand, elongating her arm without altering her focus. She snatched the skillet and swung it with enough force to stun a sow or wild boar before slaughter. Danger Boy collapsed onto the floor. His canker and the hardwood communed.

As Danger Boy's insults festered within Rinda's thoughts throughout the night and she wondered about options for lodging, a playful tune settled in her conscience. It stimulated a plan of action. She recalled the meaning of the song lyrics. Kate, a jealous island woman, had fed her husband, Green, a cake laced with Rough on Rat, a rat poison. Her sweetbread killed him and wounded two others. The possum had laughed because Green, a hunter, had been a sure shot, and his death had ensured his own longevity.

Had Emanuel not been entranced with the sight of Rinda when he first saw her, and if he had been empowered to discern the words she was thinking as she sang, he would've taken e foot een e han, turned around, and hightailed away like a rabbit that frets the snare of entrapment. Rinda's unsung words revealed the actions she had taken as Danger Boy had lain crumpled on the cabin floor and during the few days afterward.

"Rinda bought de floah.
Dat is dat.
De powdah she use
Was de Rough on Rat
Fa man, she bake
De sweetes bread.
Danger Boy nyam em.
Now him daid.
Oh, Rinda laugh.
Oh, Rinda laugh.
Danger Boy gone.
Oh, Rinda laugh."

She'd begun her dance in the clearing moments after she'd hauled Danger Boy's body into the cypress swamp. The red eyes of four alligators and the gleaming dark brown eyes of three turkey buzzards grinned at her with thanksgiving and joy as she headed back to the cabin.

A fall breeze blew ragweed in Emanuel's direction, and he sneezed loudly and uncontrollably in response. Rinda froze and turned. He stiffened and tried to hide himself. Their eyes met. He saw arms he could flee to. She saw a father to not-yet-considered-or-conceived children. Lust, like a mist, seeped up from the soil and shackled them.

Daily, the moon waxed and waned, rose and fell. In the salt-infused Lowcountry air, for generations, one day has always been as a thousand years, and a thousand years as one day. Time is not linear. Today's happenstance occurred yesterday. And will occur tomorrow. Youths, elders, and ancestors, living and deceased, are a continuum. Sung with a sea island lilt and an African diasporic pulsation, their voices resound in the immortal words of a Gullah Geechee song, "We Been Comin a Long Time, Oh, Yes!"

Lessons learned are echoed. Indiscretions unacknowledged and unatoned for are repeated—in an infant's first breath and behavior, an elder's twitch and mannerism, an ancestor's whisper and intercession.

As mystical and timeless as moonbeams reflecting on a marsh front waterway, the setting where Rinda's and Emanuel's stars had aligned was the very site where she last saw her son Absalom alive. The lad who'd been conceived amidst the mist. In the bog. As the full moon loomed above—and then disappeared.

Just a few years afterward, Rinda's brother Michael had begged her to let him row Absalom in the bateau just a short distance on the Waccamaw River to see a school of dolphins up close. The squeaking, clicking, and diving sea mammals enchanted his nephew whenever he saw them from the coastline.

"Don't go too far. And bring him back safe, now!" she had warned, fully aware of Michael's expert boating skills. But neither ever returned.

Michael and Absalom had tossed minnows into the river to attract the school of three dolphins they'd seen about a mile away. The trio arrived with excitement. One dolphin barreled over the boat, spraying them with an unexpected splash of water when it landed. Another tipped them over when its tail passed below the boat. As Michael and Absalom thrashed about, all three nibbled on the remaining minnows that bobbed in the water. They whistled and attempted to help the Middletons with their bottle noses. But Michael caught a cramp in both legs, and Absalom could not swim.

When their bloated bodies emerged near Sandy Island three days later, their faces were no longer recognizable. Rinda waited for her child's father to show himself, to share their mutual sorrow and loss. But Emanuel, fearing a family and community comeuppance, stayed in the shadows.

"Wa e look like?" he'd asked his wife, Blessing, and his neighbors, with guarded concern when they spoke about hearing that the bodies had been found.

"Swimps an crab dem done bitem up!" was the universal response. "De Corana kno who dey da cause a when dey git drown. Dey gon check dey teet fa be sho!"

Suspecting that his secret was still only somewhat safe, Emanuel did not attend the joint funeral or wake but hid in the background behind mourners gathered at the St. Agnes Baptist Church graveyard. It was a warm September day. Rinda, pregnant again from a non-immaculate but unacknowledged conception, knew that all eyes were on the lookout to see who her lover-man could be. The netting on her black hat veiled her tear-drenched eyes. The symbolism of her black dress mirrored the sorrow of her heaving shoulders.

Two weeks later, the realization that Emanuel had not and would never show up to console her, prodded Rinda to leave Georgetown County for Harlem, New York, on a Greyhound bus. She did not return alive. But eighteen years later, her daughter Easter did.

2000s

Florence recalled catching herself giving her grandfather the side-eye from time to time while thinking about his overheard revelations, and nervously awaiting new ones. Her slanted eyes, squared shoulders, and walnut complexion mirrored those of her grandpa and dad. Her other features were passed down through her mother Coralee's lineage.

After Tucker's death, she resumed attempts to connect with Laverne. Her initial *ember* had sidestepped her since their lunch date at the Feast on This Restaurant. Calls, texts, and emails were not returned, and the full amount of Laverne's appropriation had not yet been doled out. Chadwick prompted her to mail the remaining four hundred dollars in an anonymous greeting card and to have someone else to address the envelope. He nagged her to officially terminate the ongoing arrangement and then await a new one. But Florence sensed a need to tarry. One morning, Laverne answered her call.

When they met for lunch that same afternoon, Florence was aghast at what she saw. Laverne, about ten pounds thinner, was not as polished as usual, and was wearing clothing that fit her loosely. Her sunshades hid her eyes but not the areas on her chin and cheek that were covered with copious makeup. And her spirit seemed broken.

She had called in sick to her job, she confided, and had considered it providential that Florence had reached out. She longed for someone to talk to but had considered Florence distrustful. Until the moment the caller ID revealed who was ringing, that is. Why Florence had become so interested in her and had always dispersed money never sat well with her, she admitted. When her phone rang that morning, however, her inner voice hadn't cautioned, "Don't answer! Why is she calling?" Instead, it had reasoned, "Why not? You're worthy of being cared for, valued!"

What Laverne disclosed during lunch left Florence's head spinning. Her husband Medicus's grandmother, an eighty-something Gullah woman with dementia, had been living with them for three months. Laverne found her behavior strange. She kept plastic bags filled with her own hair hanging from her bedroom doorknob. She insisted that a broom be kept near each exterior door of the house.

A native of Westwood, New Jersey, Laverne was relieved to learn from Florence the meaning of these local customs: that her mother-in-law feared getting headaches if birds somehow secured her hair and made nests with it, and that the old woman was ensuring that no hag or evil spirit entered the home where she now lived. But there was more.

Her grandmother-in-law, Hester Grice, could provide self-care but would spend about ninety minutes grooming herself and then dressing in new outfits, sometimes three times each day. Time and dates were only abstract thoughts to her. Each new hour could be breakfast time. And each new day could be the same as the day before. Or last week. Or last year.

Age had diminished Hester's sight and hearing but seemingly had increased her sense of smell. A constant aggravation for Laverne was to hear Hester's singsong, Stepin-Fetchit-sounding chant whenever something was cooked in the kitchen or even heated in the microwave:

"Sompn smell good, good, good
Een de neighbahood! Oh, my, my, my.
Ahm gonna seddown an nyam, nyam, nyam cause
Sompn smell good! Ummm. Hmmm."

The follow-up was the sight of addle-minded Hester, dressed in mismatched clothing, hobbling to the table with a cane that plopped the floor like a pegleg and making a statement that was as far from the truth as abstinence was from gluttony. "Someboddy ga gib me sompn fa eat? A ain hab nottin fa eat al-l-l day!" she'd say. "A mean al-l-l day!"

"It's like a knife in my head to see and hear her!" Laverne growled.

"Like she's a mumbling, shiftless, senior citizen fool. Straight from the Chitlin Circuit! And some young people today think talking the way she does is something to be proud of. Um, um, um."

Laverne had begun to hate returning home. In speech that sounded as though it emanated from a mouth filled with hot grits, Hester asked an overabundance of questions about people and places and names from her youth. Topics that neither Laverne nor her husband knew anything about. And in an off-key voice, she constantly sang old, old, old tunes that Medicus identified as common meter and long meter songs that she'd learned in a praise house during her long-ago youth. The tunes may have been meaningful and melodious to the singers Hester had heard, but they were mournful and mind-numbing to Laverne. And, still, there was more.

"She's become a looming presence in my home, Florence, sucking it dry of any peace, any contentment, any normalcy," Laverne said, as she stared mindlessly across the table. With her hands folded tightly in her lap, Laverne flitted her eyes like a banshee. Left, right, up, down. "Sometimes, I just want her to die!"

Medicus, who had been raised by his grandmother since age seven, was distraught about having to care for her and had become abusive of his wife. He'd lost his job about a month after Hester had been relocated with them. The nursing home where she had resided had been shut down by the SC Department of Health and Environmental Control for health violations, and Medicus did not have the surplus income or time or presence-of-mind to have her moved elsewhere.

"I'm so sorry," Florence said. In a low voice, she added, "Chadwick mentioned that Medicus was fired."

"I'm sure the grapevine has been buzzing about why," Laverne answered, breathing in deeply. She tapped her index finger three times on the table. "Well, he was caught watching porn on his office computer."

"Umpf!" Florence retorted and waited to hear more.

"He was stupid to do so at work. But I can't say I don't understand."

Florence squinted her eyes in disbelief.

"That woman, that Hester Grice, is a Witherer of Manhood. A Drier Upper of the Divine Feminine," Laverne said. She closed her eyes momentarily and remained still, as though she had breathed her last breath. She breathed in slowly and continued. "Life as we knew it had not been perfect before she arrived. But it went packing when her presence crossed our threshold. I keep bags of M&Ms around the house to offer her when she makes my head boil. It's not because she's so sweet. Um-Um. She's another kind of M&M. Mean and Manipulative. So, my offering is a take-it-and-shove-it kind of response. Who she is makes Medicus go batshit when he's around her. I think her presence brings on flashbacks of his childhood. And he was so glad to get out from under her controlling personality."

Medicus had begun putting his hands on Laverne's face whenever things about his grandmother agitated him. He refused to empty Hester's bedside commode during the day, even though he was at home and supposedly conducting online searches for jobs.

In a state of depression, he argued that there was no need to find employment anytime soon or to contribute to shared expenses, as Laverne's income could take care of finances. He called Laverne throughout the workday, checking on her whereabouts and accusing her of spending too much time and money with coworkers or friends.

He demanded that Laverne begin caregiver patrol as soon as she returned home from work each day. And he gaslighted her about having agreed to do so, so that he could unwind from the pressures of dealing with Hester during the day. Regardless, he left soon after Laverne arrived and returned home at a time his grandmother should be asleep.

"I'm slipping," Laverne said with remorse. "Things are falling between the cracks at work. I need my job. I need my mind. I need . . . peace."

Placing her hand on Laverne's across the table, Florence said, "Oh my God, Laverne! I don't know how you're holding on. What you need is help. You need support. Now, support is available for Hester's at-home care, I'm sure. For her dementia too. Support is available for Medicus and his childhood and man-without-a-job issues. But most important is to find support for you! Let me support you, please. Here—" She passed a note card with the telephone number for the National Domestic Violence Hotline across the table. "Call them. Please. You can call them right now if you like. Or you can call them at some point before we part ways today. But I'm here. I will be your support. You will get the help you need. I promise."

One of the three men Porcher saw conversing in the parking lot at Brandon's Barber Shop looked vaguely familiar. After parking in the farthest space from the shop, he jumped out of his car just as their talk seemed to be winding down. "What's up, gentlemen?" he asked and nodded as he passed them. All nodded politely in return. Two, with fresh haircuts, then headed to individual cars to depart, and the third, who like him had hair that needed professional help, turned and walked behind him to the door. When they got inside and sat, Porcher kept thinking, *Where do I know this guy from?*

The two sat in adjacent barber chairs. The familiar stranger's voice as he gave instructions for his haircut left Porcher pondering about his identity. Things crystallized, however, when Porcher's chair revolved and he saw the man's profile. The surreal scene at Cousin Ann's Restaurant came to mind as he noticed something peculiar about the shape of the man's mouth, but he didn't say anything. The man exited about five minutes before Porcher's haircut was complete.

"Have a great weekend, fellas!" Porcher said when he left.

Outside, he had a surprise. Standing propped against the driver's window of his own car and facing the barbershop door was the man from the barber shop, Gary Windley, seeming to be awaiting him.

"Hey," Porcher said with hesitation, intent to continue walking to his Impala.

"Hey," Gary shot back. "You're Russell Porcher, right?" he asked. When Porcher nodded, he continued. "I thought I recognized you when we greeted each other earlier."

"Same thing here. And you're Windley . . . Gary Windley? Did I get that right?"

"Homerun, Boss Man. Homerun. We met briefly at Cousin Ann's."

"Yeah, I remember."

"Well, I don't want to take up too much of your time, and I don't mean to upset you by minding your business, but if I could—"

Curious, Porcher stated, "Go on . . . ."

"I heard the barbers joking with you about being new to the area. I mean, I didn't think I knew you from Georgetown, but, anyway, your friend—"

"Who? Chadwick?"

"Yeah, he's a piece of work, enty?" Porcher's facial expression and hand gestures of confusion seemingly startled him. Stuttering, Windley continued, "Well . . . well, all I'm trying to say is . . . um . . . like Dr. Maya Angelou said, you know, 'When people show you who they are—'" He paused and waited. Porcher completed the statement with him, "'—believe them.'" They both chuckled.

"I don't understand," Porcher said.

"Again, I don't want to get in your business. So, I'll just ask questions that you don't have to answer if you don't want to. And then, if you want me to take things a step further, then I'll make a statement."

"Okay," Porcher said, curious.

"Has he asked you for personal financial information?" Pause. "Has he been giving you large amounts of unsolicited cash?" Pause. "Did you confide in him some large personal debt you're in?"

Porcher cocked his head from one side to another each time he recalled a coincidental memory: The Wineglass's reaction during his first visit to Walking Up the King's Highway Church, when he'd testified about an awareness of God's abundance. The conversation with Chadwick in the church parking lot, how he'd mentioned to Chadwick the difficulty of having a commuter job. And Chadwick's initial outlay of four folded one-hundred-dollar bills following their initial lunch, how it was the exact monthly gas expense amount. His eyes popped, and his right hand began to rub the back of his neck.

Seeing Porcher's response after each question, Windley continued. "Has he been acting like you're his closest confidante ever, contacting you like a robocall?" Windley watched his eyes. "Has he read you the riot act for calling him at home or on weekends?"

Noticing Porcher's calm and thinking that maybe he had not experienced this interaction, Windley explained. Mimicking Chadwick's voice, he said, "'Now, why are you calling me . . . at my home . . . at this hour of the day?' Or he won't answer and then might dial you back when the Missus Wineglass is nowhere around, I guess. Hmf!

"He wants something, Russell. Watch yourself. He's like a raptor, flying around looking for someone he can swoop down on and devour. The Missus got all his manliness locked up and satisfied, but between me and you, he might be doing some kind of freaky, monetary BDSM on the downlow. Anyway—" He looked at Porcher's wedding band and pointed to his unadorned ring finger with his right-hand pointer and added, "—you seem like an innocent family man who might not want to get caught up in any shenanigans."

"Um, ah, thanks for your candor, Gary. You didn't have to share any of this with me. That took some balls. Some courage."

He smiled and extended his arm to fist-bump.

"Are the two of you still in touch?" Porcher asked. "At Cousin Ann's, there seemed to be some breakdown of communication or some—"

"Oh, no, no, no! But I've remembered something he said on one of his many phone calls to me, when he'd switch over to take a business call and leave me waiting. He ever do that with you, Russell?" He searched Porcher's face and then continued. "Well, he said, as though he didn't think I was still connected, and he was talking to himself, 'I wonder how you'll act when I stop calling . . . .'

"I never confronted him about that overheard statement. But one day, well, he just stopped calling. And if he picked up when I would call—just to check-in—he'd answer *real* friendly, then cut the call short after only a few minutes, saying something like, 'Hey, let me get back with you. I got something I've got to take care of . . . I'll get right back to ya . . . right back . . .' Then, click!

"Well, after a few attempts to reach out to him, his 'get-right-back-to-ya' return call got to be two days later. Or seven. Or never. So, I don't dial his number no mo. No! Mo! And his number is blocked on my phone." He paused and looked at Porcher with unmasked concern before walking to his car. "Watch yourself, Russell Porcher!"

As Windley drove away, he rolled down his window and shouted the reminder, "Believe them!"

Porcher walked to his car, jumped in, and then turned onto Rice Field Drive, all the while rethinking the meaning of the harangue he'd received from Chadwick during their last phone conversation. When he'd picked up Porcher's call, Chadwick's tone had been somewhat distant, and it never warmed up to pleasant or friendly.

He'd spoken about his kids' extracurricular activities, but Chadwick never engaged. *Maybe he'd been grieving the miscarriage.*

Porcher had laughed about a ref's call during the past night's televised game, in which Chadwick's favorite team had played, but Chadwick replied dryly that he hadn't watched it. *Maybe he'd been exhausted from a tiring work schedule.*

Searching for something that would interest Chadwick, Porcher had asked about Florence and stated that Mignon had just learned that a first cousin had passed unexpectedly. Chadwick's response had revved up a bit, but in a most unusual manner. He'd launched into a monotone, nonstop diatribe about the burial of his older sister's husband, for whom Porcher had given him twenty-five dollars during their initial meeting at the Walking Up the King's Highway Bible Study. In a one-sided conversation, he'd rattled off a bullet list of frustrations. That cremations are less expensive than burials. That funeral home directors offer grieving families add-ons that are expensive but unnecessary. That his family members look to him as the Great Provider, as opposed to considering how they, or his in-law's family, would handle funeral obligations. That people should learn to not rely on him for things they should be able to do for themselves. And then, seemingly, he'd had enough of this conversation at that time because he suddenly said, "Listen, I got something I've got to take care of . . . I'll get right back to ya . . . right back . . ." Then click!

Maybe Gary Windley speaks the truth about Chadwick Wineglass! Porcher thought. *Maybe, you, Vernon Russell Porcher, should think about the things he's told you about himself and 'believe him'."*

Bundling the Rice Stalks in Sheaves

Timothy Thunderbolt wanted to believe in the everlasting endurance of his twin sister's marriage to a Lowcountry man but believed that Melvin's expressions about his cultural beliefs had revealed that the couple should not coexist.

He had no way of knowing that William Dunkin had seen two words burnished behind Thelma Thunderbolt Marshel's open eyes when he'd penetrated behind her gaze: *haul ass*. A few years into her marriage, Thelma had requested the root doctor's service—a concoction, a brew, a bag of mysterious, bad-smelling herbs or other ingredients—anything to make her husband Melvin's heart, mind, and spirit dovetail again with hers. Without this knowledge but with pastoral and brotherly love, Thunderbolt had prayed for her. Had anointed her from afar with oil. Had enlisted prayer warriors on her behalf. But, not understanding how his beloved sister had sown the wind, he knew no reason to accept that she was now reaping her own personally made whirlwind. The reactionary agreement that Timothy had solidified with others on her behalf would prove ineffective. It did not follow divine order. His agreements had not been sanctioned by the Holy Spirit to whom he had sent up sacrificial timber. Accordingly, his hopes of seeing Thelma showered with an outpouring of blessings for which he alone had done everything he could do to earn had never materialized in the timeframe he'd prayed for.

When he became aware that Thelma had met with root doctor, William Dunkin, Rev. Thunderbolt presumed that she'd aligned herself with darkness—that Dunkin had cast a spell over her, and that Satan's army was keeping Thelma and her husband separated from marital bliss. But unknown to Rev. Thunderbolt, William Dunkin had seen the two words masked behind her eyes and had known that this woman's battle was not one for which he could even suggest a conjuration or a homeopathic concoction to fix.

1980s

Each showered the other with the affections they found more desirable for themselves. As a result, the bickering became insufferable. When they visited Melvin's family, Thelma made certain to include herself in his every conversation and every interaction, looking to impart and receive words of affirmation. She loved quality time, but Melvin longed for moments of "alone time" with kin and his childhood crew.

Thelma noticed that although the Marshel family members were cordial, they'd begun to eye her with disapproval whenever she spoke about things she did not know, or whenever she appeared and lingered at times that a conversation with Melvin had begun without her. She detected his irritation at the way she addressed him.

"Mel!" she screamed with sharpness, thinking that her husband's attention span needed to be corralled. "God wants us to be one, and we should be one. In everything!" He slumped his head and did not argue. He wanted her to be happy.

When Melvin cooked a big pot of rice—and produced dinner—several days a week, he bristled with resentment as she retired to their bedroom. He longed for Thelma to demonstrate acts of service, like cooking his meals, even though she'd been diagnosed as having rice allergies.

"What Gullah man marries a woman who can't even cook rice!" began the hurtful insult Thelma overheard her husband expressing to someone during a phone call. "I won't do it, but even the devil beats his wife for scorching the rice." Following a loud chuckle, he had added, "Yeah . . . yeah, that's right. That's what people say happens when it's raining while the sun is shining. Well, no, man, my wife can't even scorch it . . . and rice cake tastes good, good . . . Mm-hmm!"

When she was certain the rice steam in the kitchen had dissipated, Thelma tiptoed from the bedroom and confronted Melvin from behind like an assassin. "Don't bad-talk me to your friends, Mel!" she warned. "Never, ever again!"

Alarmed, he pivoted his neck quickly at the sound of her voice as he sat at the table. When he saw her leering at him from the kitchen doorway, he dropped his fork and turned the chair around to face her. "I was just being jokey," he said.

"And if you even *think* of beating me, God *and* the Devil will be my witness . . . it won't be rice, but boiling hot grits will somehow find a way to sing 'Good morning, heartache' —just like Billie Holiday—to your bare back!"

"Thelma, I was just joking around. I know you can't be around rice while it's being cooked, but—"

"You know I'd cook for you more, Mel . . . but you want rice . . . not once, but three times a day! Twenty-one times a week. Nobody, *nobody* needs to eat that much rice!" Her voice softened. "I make you potatoes, fried corn, cornbread, macaroni and cheese, biscuits on Sunday morning. And I even learned how to make fried shrimp and gravy just like your mother. But you only want what you want. And you want . . . ah-h-h-h-h-h-h . . . *rice*! I never had to cook rice before I started cooking it for you, Mel, and do you really want me to wheeze, itch, and feel like I'm going to die just to give you what you want? What about what I want? I ask you all the time to come with me to lectures or meetings or stores . . . ."

Feeling attacked—and not understanding her love of quality time or words of affirmation—Melvin interrupted Thelma's expression with a rise from his chair and a retort: "And I ask you for more intimacy and for more opportunities to reach out and connect on a physical level," he snapped, "but all you want to do is talk about what you want and what you can do for others. Ways you can make your coworkers and my coworkers understand they're racists . . . I don't want to talk all the time about racists. No-o-o-o-o!"

She looked at him in disbelief. "If there's something you don't want to talk about, how would I know if you don't?"

"You give me time to talk?" he volleyed. "No, certainly not when there's something you want to talk about. If you'd free your mind, you could cuddle with me in the nighttime. Or just let me feel your hands on my shoulders and back in the mornings. But you stay wound up so tight and ready to talk, talk, talk that none of that is ever an option for you. And if I try to spoon you in bed at night, you squirm away fast, real fast. Like you think I'm some kind of crab ready to snap you with my claws!

"You want to talk. So, I let you talk. I don't butt in. Do I? No, I listen. Even when I have something to say—or, should I say, when you allow me a moment to speak what's on my mind—I say it real quick . . . real quick and then let you have center stage. That's what *you* love. And that's the love I make sure you get!"

"A-a-a-h-h-h!" Thelma screamed. "A-a-a-h-h-h! Shh! Hush!"

"Just like I just said." He grimaced. "I open my mouth, and you find a way to shut it up!" She looked at him as though he was an alien and saw him look at her in the same manner. *Another unresolved argument,* Thelma thought.

Melvin's unblinking eyes camouflaged his silent musing, *Why do we keep wounding each other? We can't keep doing this.*

Thelma felt shut down. She felt clueless about her husband's need for touch and acts of service. "Melvin, this argument, today's argument . . ." she said softly, following a deep sigh, "started after I overheard you speak badly about me because I can't be around rice that's being cooked."

"I'm sorry, Thelma," he said with a sheepish nod. "I was wrong. I won't do that again." Her probing silence urged him to think. "I love me some rice, girl. You know that . . . and I don't ask you to cook it. Just make yourself scarce when I do."

"But it's something you can live without, Melvin. Or something you can cut down on eating so regularly. I make sure other staples are available."

"But it's my heritage, Thelma. I don't know any Georgetown people who can do without it. Who would I be if I couldn't have my rice?"

Um-hmm, she thought, *you'd better think of who you'd be without me as your wife. . . I can't keep on living like this. I just can't!*

For years, their bickering continued. Among themselves. In front of others. Until the day they heard themselves mouthing the words of an old spiritual.

You don't know what the Lord done for me, done for me.
You don't know what the Lord done for me, done for me.

You don't know, you ain been there.
You don't know when and you don't know where.
You don't know what Lord done for me, done for me.

2000s

Barry heard voices. All the time. A din of voices. The unspoken thoughts of those around him. The sneers, the hateful comebacks, the hurtful accusations that others suspected were swirling around only within their own minds, Barry heard them all! The sometimes-unending clamor jarred his overwhelmed sensory system. When it was utterly, overly extended, the sixteen-year-old fainted.

The challenge had commenced in middle school. It subsided during summer break but returned with a vengeance when he began ninth grade, high school. He, his parents, friends, school nurses and psychologists, and medical doctors did not know what to do. Prescriptions dulled the noise but left him feeling lifeless and behaving dully. Although church members prayed for him and his family, Barry received their unspoken reproofs and pity as spittle and lashings inflicted upon him. He knew he had not willed this condition upon himself and began to feel hopeless that it would never end.

Following a late afternoon family meeting in the church office one weekday, Pastor Thunderbolt pulled the Gilliard parents aside to discuss their son's concerns privately. But Barry, though presumed to be out of hearing range, heard the conversation and empathically interpreted it.

"It may be a matter of spiritual warfare," Thunderbolt said. What Barry heard, however, was, *I think your son is demon-possessed.*

"Ultimately, prayer is the answer," Thunderbolt continued. "Do you pray as a family? Do you encourage Barry to inform you about what he's experiencing?"

The unspoken thoughts that Barry sensed, which made his eyes roll back in their sockets, were, *If you prayed right, this would not be happening! When he tells you about something he thinks others have said, but really have not said, just slay the child with some holy water or oil and the word of God. The things he says are not of God. They're of the Devil. So, let him talk, but do not listen.*

Thunderbolt's silent broadsides escalated within Barry's mind, in his being, and reverberated with earlier nonverbal onslaughts that he intuited from others at school. Teachers speaking, "I think you've got this, Barry . . ." but saying, *If you paid attention and stopped looking around at others, I wouldn't have to say this same thing over and over and over again! What's wrong with you?* Classmates whispering among themselves, "Do you think he's all right? He's getting that strange look in his eyes again. That must be difficult for him . . ." but shouting nonverbally, *My mama wants to know if what he's got is catchy. Maybe he's on drugs. You know, the mind snaps 'cause you've done something you shouldn't have, and so others will know the truth ain in you, then you fall out and froth at the mouth . . . .*

When Barry's parents and Pastor Thunderbolt went to call him back to the office, Barry had collapsed on the hallway bench. Alarmed but responding with muscle memory, his parents rushed to him, gently sat him up, and then sat on either side of him. Mr. Gilliard couched his son's head and shoulders in the crook of his left arm and moved his right palm in a circular motion over Barry's heart. His mom caressed his cheek down to his neck with several strokes on each side with her right hand and clutched her son's hands in her left. Each parent, in lockstep, began to whisper soothing words, looking intently at him, shutting everything and everyone else out, enclosing themselves in a bubble.

"Should I call 9-1-1?" Pastor Thunderbolt bellowed. Barry's father looked at him and shook his head before resuming his actions. Barry's mother, however, looked at the pastor and did not avert her gaze.

"Is there anything I can do?" Thunderbolt continued.

"Shhh!" she responded, as she continued looking at him while clasping her son's hands. She looked at her son and then back at Thunderbolt. "It seems you've done enough."

With a turn of Mr. Gilliard's head, Pastor Thunderbolt found himself caught in the crosshairs of both parents' defiant stares. He looked back and forth to each in befuddlement.

"Were you talking out loud but thinking something else?" Mr. Gilliard barked in a matter-of-fact timbre that did not invite a response.

"This is what happens to our son when that goes on," Mrs. Gilliard snarled.

"We listen to him, and we pray with him and for him," Mr. Gilliard added, as his son began to stir and regain consciousness.

"Thank you for . . . offering help," Mrs. Gilliard stated, as the family struggled to stand. "But—" She looked to her husband, whose care for their son calmed her to remain silent.

Not losing a beat, Mr. Gilliard completed her statement. "—We'll be going home now," he said calmly, "and will look for . . . a different kind of assistance . . . from a different kind of *care*giver."

Smarting from the sting of the Gilliards' stares and accusations, Pastor Thunderbolt felt not humbled, but ready for battle! He stormed back toward his office, mouthing Bible verses like riot gear, to assure himself that his outlook for handling their son's situation was the better option. To convince himself that any other outlook should not be tolerated.

The Spirit of the Lord is upon me, because he hath anointed me to preach the gospel to the gospel to the poor; he hath sent me to heal the brokenhearted, to preach deliverance to the captives . . .

Correct thy son, and he shall give thee rest; yea, he shall give delight unto thy soul.

There is a way which seemeth right unto a man, but the end thereof are the ways of death . . . .

He marched past his secretary's desk and into his office. She raised her head in bewilderment and rotated her head and office chair in slow motion to follow his movements. She rested two fingers of her right hand on her right cheek and sat back in dismay. Once he was inside, she returned her focus to the front, dropped the papers she'd been reviewing, and placed her palms on her desk to push herself up to stand to attend to whatever may be troubling him.

"Pastor . . . Pastor Thunderbolt . . ." she called softly. She picked up her glasses from her desktop and pressed them onto her face. He froze upon seeing her when she reached his doorway. He stretched his left palm toward her and began shaking his head.

She removed her glasses and held them in her left hand. Looking at him in silence, her eyes darted left and right, up and down, surveying him and his surroundings. She waited for what seemed an interminable period. When he spoke, she relaxed. Somewhat.

"Do you know anything about a man named Gregory Dunkin?" he asked.

"Well, he's a member of Mt. Moriah Missionary Baptist Church in Darcatia," she answered.

"Mm-hmm. And what kind of work does he do?"

She paused, thinking what and what not to say, then responded, "I believe he works at Calabash by the Sea."

"Is that so?" Thunderbolt said. "Tell you what . . . tomorrow, will you contact him, please?"

"Yes, sir!"

"Tell him I'd like to speak with him. Not at the restaurant, though. Schedule a meeting with him at . . . at the downtown Georgetown riverfront."

"Pastor, would you like any of the deacons to meet with you?" she probed.

"Oh, no. Just the two of us. That'll be fine."

"Are you sure, sir? You may not know, but . . ." she continued, peering above the glasses that she'd put back on.

He extended his left palm toward her again, and she stood down.

"It's been a long day of doing God's work, Sister Elizabeth," he said, as a benediction. "Thank you for everything you've helped with. Thank you for everything you'll help with when we meet again. I pray you'll have a safe journey home and a restful night."

At home, Pastor Thunderbolt remained undone. He greeted his wife but did not talk. Sibyl waited. He left most of his dinner untouched. Sibyl wondered. He paced. Sibyl watched. She prayed silently for peace and for understanding of how to be a blessing and how to offer encouragement. Soon, she saw a light.

"Tee," Sibyl said softly, as she rose from the white chair at the kitchen table, "come sit with me in the living room. In the quiet, on the sofa, maybe you'll unwind a little bit. I won't say a word. And you won't have to say a word. I'll just sit close by to keep you company, okay?"

Following her after nodding his head, Timothy flipped the switch to the bright, incandescent overhead kitchen lights. Sibyl turned on the living room lamps when she entered and sat on the cream-colored fabric sofa, close to her husband's armchair. Seconds after falling back into his seat, Timothy's emotional purging began.

"Can you believe it?" he commenced. "The Gilliards think I'm the cause of their son's fainting spell today at the church following my meeting with the family!" Sibyl's eyes expressed alarm, but her mouth remained silent. He continued. "I told them calmly that they were dealing with a spiritual matter and that prayer was the answer. That family prayer about this concern was important. What I made certain not to voice was that spirits, Satanic spirits, were loose within their son's mind. That if they prayed right, this would not be happening! That when Barry tells them about something he thinks others have said, but, really, have not said, they should slay him with some holy water or oil and the word of God. That the things he says are not of God. No, they're of the Devil. So, then, what they should do is just let him talk, but not listen to him.

"And when we left my office and found that the child had fainted, the parents just . . . turned on me. Like the herd of hogs that Jesus cast the evil spirits into from the demon-possessed man in the Gadarenes. You should've seen the disdain in their eyes.

"All the while, they started spouting off these words to the boy in a real low voice. And then they told me that *godly* help would no longer be needed. That they would look for 'a different *kind* of assistance . . . from a different *kind* of *care*giver.' I feel certain they were talking about that Gregory Dunkin. Hmpf, they were probably mouthing off incantations of some kind."

Spent, Timothy reclined into his chair and rested his arms on its arms. His head did not move, but his eyes darted left and right. Sibyl watched but said nothing until he asked, "So, what do you think about all this, Sibyl?" He breathed in, brought his hands together, and with interlocking fingers, turned to look at her.

"Why, that was some afternoon session!" she said. "No wonder you've been so agitated." Shrugging her shoulders, she asked, "Are you certain things occurred exactly as you've relayed them?"

He looked at her quizzically, then responded, "God is my witness! I asked Elizabeth to schedule a meeting with me and Mr. Dunkin. We need to have a talk, a confrontation. There's too much wholly-hoodoo and faux-gospel going on in some of these Low-country churches. And it's got to stop!"

"I see," Sibyl said after a few moments. With eyes remaining on her husband's face, she smiled at him and continued. "Well, I leave this meeting between you and God." She thought of a Native song from her youth and began humming softly and moving her head to the rhythm.

She reached for her husband's hand and whispered, "A Native proverb says, 'Bitterness gives ill health and wastes life. Gratefulness leads to good health and happy life.' Another says, 'We will be known forever by the tracks we leave.'"

Timothy tilted his head and raised his eyes. Sibyl explained, "Let us be grateful for Barry. It's a difficult time for the Gilliards. And maybe Gregory Dunkin offers some virtue that you aren't yet able to see. When we speak, our words must leave tracks that we will be known by forever."

Timothy Thunderbolt began hovering around the perimeter of the Georgetown Harborwalk thirty minutes before his scheduled meeting with Gregory Dunkin. He convinced himself that any tracks left behind from either party following their encounter would be coated with ashes. He felt assured that through him, and because of his zeal and his self-centered understanding of the mind of God, God would rain down fire. After all, he reasoned, he was a modern-day biblical prophet Elijah, and wicked Gregory would be consumed like the wet wood and bulls that were sacrificed on the altar at Mount Carmel. He walked the four-block area along the recently constructed Harborwalk several times, all the while envisioning Dunkin's spiritual and emotional plunder. During his walking and waiting, however, Timothy Thunderbolt did not ask for guidance on the miracle that he thought he was most well-versed about and most capable of manifesting.

He had gathered twelve river rocks, one for each of the tribes descended from David, built an altar in the name of the Lord, and placed it below the bench on which Gregory would sit when he arrived. Soon afterward, Gregory did indeed walk directly to the designated bench at the King Street entrance. It sat past the twenty-four-pound Naval Gun, facing the Harborwalk Fountain and backing the Kaminski House Museum. Timothy stood to greet him.

Pastor Thunderbolt extended his right hand to Gregory, shook, and said, "Thanks so much for meeting with me today, Mr. Dunkin."

"Oh, please call me Gregory, sir," the younger man interrupted.

"Okay . . . Gregory . . . thank you for agreeing to this informal meeting. Please . . . have a seat."

Gregory, dressed in khaki trousers and a blue, long-sleeved, buttoned shirt, plopped down. Moving his feet below the bench to erect his posture, his right heel almost capsized the hidden altar. He looked to the right. Attuned and attentive, he waited to learn about their meeting from the older church leader, who was dressed in a blue suit jacket and trousers and an unbuttoned tan shirt with no tie. This was the guest pastor whose funeral prayer had scourged the memory of Gregory's father.

"We've never met," Pastor Thunderbolt began, "but . . ."

"Oh, we *have* been in each other's presence before, sir," Gregory stated. Pastor Thunderbolt looked at him with suspicion, as if fearing an accusation of wrongdoing. "You were invited to pray at my father William Dunkin's funeral."

"Yes, I remember," Thunderbolt said. "I'm sorry for your loss. A father shapes the minds and hearts of his children. And memories of our fathers are long lasting."

"Yes, they are," Gregory responded while nodding his head. "Yes, they are."

Getting to the chase, Thunderbolt softly clasped his hands together before his chest and stated, "It's been brought to my attention that you have been offering counsel to one of my young church members."

"You must mean Barry Gilliard?" Seeing Thunderbolt nod in affirmation, Gregory continued, "Yes, his parents asked me to speak with him."

With his elbows resting on his thighs, Thunderbolt spread the fingers of his opened hands as he spoke. "Since coming to the Lowcountry, I've come to understand that some church members intermingle a lot of different religious beliefs with Christianity," he said. "So," channeling the spirit of Elijah as he spoke with Ahab, Thunderbolt continued, "if you don't mind, for my peace of mind about the members of my fold, do you waver between two opinions? Do you believe the Lord is God and that Jesus is his Son? Or do you hold other beliefs?"

The altar below Dunkin either was going to erupt or it would cause a lightning bolt to appear above him, Thunderbolt thought. He raised his head in jubilant expectation of a fiery display that would result from Gregory's confession of clutching to other beliefs.

"Yes, I do believe in the sovereignty of God and Jesus and the Holy Spirit," Gregory replied. "Do the intermingling with other religious beliefs among Christians that you're talking about include celebrating the birth of Christ on December twenty-fifth and hiding Easter eggs to celebrate the Resurrection?" Gregory knew that his question confounded the pastor. He watched him twist his head, flex his hands, and move his eyes to formulate a response. To cause the pastor's thoughts to tiptoe with caution before making a brash statement, Gregory added, "Or are you referring to a belief of some Lowcountry people that their ancestors watch over them? In the same way that some Christian people believe that the spirits of Elijah or the apostles or even Moses guides and directs them? I'm not sure what you're asking."

To center himself amidst the flurry of unexpected questions, Thunderbolt thought with assurance about the altar of river rocks below Gregory and stated a scripture verse. "'The Spirit of the Lord is upon me, because he hath anointed *me* to preach the gospel to the poor; he hath sent me to heal the brokenhearted, to preach deliverance to the *captives.*'"

"Sometimes, the *captives* aren't always the ones who don't think *exactly* like us or who don't behave *in the exact same ways* we do," Gregory said. "Don't you find that to be true in your ministry? The Spirit of God made us all different. Yet the slightest difference sometimes makes people, Christian people, suspicious. And sometimes . . . hateful."

Thunderbolt patted his right foot. He raised his upward right palm to Gregory to silence him and began to pontificate. "'There is a way which seemeth right unto a man, but the end thereof are the ways of death,'" he stated. "I cannot abide with having my church members influenced by root, or hoodoo, or black magic. And if your talks with Barry or his parents or anyone in this community falls under the Ruler of Darkness, I bind that spirit, in the name of Jesus, to leave you and be cast to roam over the waters that surround us!"

Gregory relaxed and waited to see the response on Thunderbolt's face when nothing about him changed. After a few moments, he spoke. "I suppose those words were . . . a—a holy incantation," he said without smugness, sarcasm, or humor. He looked around him, at himself, and at passersby. "Well, I hope it accomplished all that you had hoped. As for me, yes, I work with plants. Plants made by God. People eat them and drink them, make perfumes and colognes with them, and even sniff them or cut them down. I don't know why some people get scared about what I do with them.

"Some *root doctors* deal in *hoodoo*. They can put a *root* on someone for others. To hurt people's enemies or attract lovers. They can concoct a *mojo* with *goofa dus*—that's gopher or mole dust—or animal parts to work spells on people or ward off evil spirits. But me, I just make medicines that heal the mind, the body, and the soul. From things you can find in your own backyard or in the woods or in a field. And the same God who made the healing plants is the One who guides me, along with the ancestors, to know which ones to use.

"With the help of God, I don't bring harm to anyone. If you want to know more about my talks with Barry, please, feel free to ask."

Thunderbolt, battling with the thought that the two men somehow were on the same side of the fence, remembered his wife's words. *It's a difficult time for the Gilliards*, she had said. *And maybe Gregory Dunkin offers some virtue that you aren't yet able to see.*

He turned to Gregory and stated, "Barry fainted in the church office recently. When his parents sat with him as he was recovering, they began quietly saying some words to him that I somehow thought you must have encouraged them to recite. They looked only at him. At no one else around them. It was like they were—"

"Reciting *an incantation*?" Gregory asked with sarcasm.

Thunderbolt pursed his lips. "I was going to say it was like they were under some kind of spell."

"His parents were personalizing the fruit of the Spirit to him, to help *his* spirit to recover," Gregory said. "They selected words from Galatians 5:22-23—not from me. I told them to bathe him in words, in light, that would restore his sense of self. Because he was reacting to dark and violent thoughts of others about him. I think these are the words of their *incantation*, and they bounce them back-and-forth among themselves: "Beautiful are you, considerate and true, peaceful, patient, joyful, self-controlled, peaceful, patient, too. These are the gifts I view. I love you and the sweet spirit of your soul. Barry, we love you and the sweet spirit of your soul."[6]

After the last thought sunk in, Thunderbolt asked, "Would you mind walking with me?"

On the Harborwalk, their conversation deepened. And because they were in a small community, they had to pause their discussion on numerous occasions to greet persons they knew and met along the way. The most telltale and long-lasting effect, however, was that their presence together ignited an instantaneous rumor-mill buzz about the meaning of their late afternoon stroll and their topics of discussion.

"To which hospital in Charleston are the Gilliards taking their son?" Thunderbolt asked. "I can't remember the name they said. SCMU, I believe, but I hear it's pretty reputable."

"It's MUSC," Gregory corrected. "Medical University of South Carolina. I hear the doctors there are very helpful. I just find that many medical doctors don't always look for the root cause of a person's 'disease'."

"Or the spiritual cause," Thunderbolt interjected.

"Or the things that may be going on in a person's physical environment, the home, the community, the school or job, before they offer some prescription when there are natural medicines they can use that God has provided," Gregory continued.

To offer a more reverential point-of-view, Thunderbolt stopped walking. Lifting his right pointer before him for emphasis, he added, "And prayer is most important!" Somehow, though, he'd forgotten his lack of prayer before today's meeting.

Chadwick Wineglass began walking toward them. He'd seen them on the boardwalk after exiting from a restaurant. "Pastor, Gregory, good afternoon," he said. After everyone exchanged pleasantries, Chadwick first addressed Thunderbolt. "I've been waiting

6 Ronald Daise. 2001. "I Love You and the Sweet Spirit of Your Soul." Track 2 on *Sweet Surprises, Christ-Centered Inspirational Love Songs.* G.O.G. Enterprises, compact disc.

on your call, Pastor. I think there are some community members who will be interested in your project." To Gregory, he said, "Young Dunkin, how are things at Calabash? I'll be that way again sometime soon."

"Everything is everything," Gregory answered. "And how is the best cook in Georgetown County who you stole away from the Calabash kitchen?"

"I'll see Florence when I finish my evening cleaning job," Chadwick said. "I'll be sure to tell her you asked about her. How's the Gilliard boy? I hear you're helping him manage all he's going through. That's good."

Despite Chadwick's outward projection that all was going well, Gregory sensed a strain of sorrow, frustration, and worry as he walked away. As if he was undertaking matters on his own. Matters that should be shared with family and directed by a higher power. Unknown to anyone, Chadwick's conflicted thoughts as he walked away centered on his partnering with Otis Doyle.

Before the two continued along Harborwalk, Gregory told Thunderbolt with excitement, "See that?" He pointed to a plant with purple flowers and long pointed green leaves that was growing out of the gravel beside a concrete parking lot wheel stop. "That's a spiderwort. Tea made from boiling the roots can be used as a laxative, and a salve made from crushing the leaves can be used to ease the sting from an insect bite. When our meeting ends, I'm going to collect some of them to carry home."

"Yes, you did say you have a way with plants," Thunderbolt said. "You sound so excited! And just as some plants are for our nourishment, the word of God is also to be consumed daily. 'When your words came, I ate them; they were my joy and my heart's delight, for I bear your name, O Lord God Almighty.'"

"Jeremiah 15:16," Gregory said. "A great verse!"

Thunderbolt looked at Dunkin with surprise at his knowledge of scripture verses. He pointed to an orange flowering plant in a flowerpot on the porch of a business and asked, "And what's that one good for?"

"That's the Angel's Trumpet," Gregory answered. "Its beauty is mesmerizing. The blooms can be orange, yellow, pink, white, or peach."

"Angel's Trumpet," Thunderbolt beamed. "That's a name worth remembering. It must be used for healing a lot of things."

"Oh, no!" Gregory shot back. "The flowers pay homage to the name, but it should be looked at only and not touched. The whole plant is poisonous. Touching or eating it could bring on fever, muscle weakness, hallucinations, rapid pulse or even convulsions, coma, or even death."

Before Thunderbolt could comment, they walked up to Abraham and Precious Marshel, Melvin Marshel's parents, who were holding hands as they strolled Harborwalk.

"Well, well, well," Abraham said, "Ef e ain de one an only Timaty Tundabolt."

Precious spread her arms, and Thunderbolt advanced to hug her. "Son, ya come yah ta we town, an ya ain drop by fa see we yet," she said. "Wa dah bout?"

Thunderbolt listened, smiling at his growing understanding of Gullah Geechee speech. He'd become aware that "th's" at the beginning of words sometimes spoken as "t's." That "enty" or "ennit" meant "Isn't that so?" That "yeddy" meant "to hear or listen." And that "v's" at the beginning or words were sometimes substituted with "w's."

"Ya sista Telma an Melbin got a cute up lee gal now, ennit?" Abraham said with a glow on his face. "Ya see em yet?" Abraham eyed Thunderbolt up and down with a smile. "Man, we ain seen ya sense dey weddin day . . ." Timothy thought of his twin sister's wedding day, which he'd hoped would not happen.

"We yeddy yah marry a pretty ooman," Precious chimed in about Timothy's bride. "Breng em by de house. Ya famlee, ya know."

Turning their attention to Gregory, Precious said, "Hey, deh, son. How oona do?"

"I'm doin," Gregory answered. "Good afternoon, Mr. and Mrs. Marshel."

"Oh-h-h-h, A know who ya dah," Precious stated. "I can tell when A look at ya nose. Ya William Dunkin son, enty?"

"Yes, ma'am."

"An ya woice soun de same as ya daddy woice," Abraham said. "E beenna nice man, nice neighba. A saary e gone on." He shook Gregory's hand before leaving, and said, "Apple sho dyon fall faar frum de tree."

Thunderbolt felt a bit undone about the Marshels' observation that Gregory was very much a younger clone of his father. *In all their ways?* he wondered. *Was his and Gregory's conversation interesting because Gregory was a master of deception? Was he being spiritually blind not to discern this? Should he bolt and walk away?* He noticed people pointing in their direction and looking at them from a distance with rapt attention.

Undeterred by those who pointed and stared, Gregory continued their conversation. "When the Gilliards stop by my house," he said, "I always have them to drink some tea I've made from boiling lavender leaves. It relaxes them and calms their nerves." He noticed a suspicious expression spreading across Thunderbolt's face.

"So, do you find that starting your session with a plant-based product is the most effective thing to do?" Thunderbolt asked."

"I didn't say that," Gregory corrected. "Before the Gilliards arrive, before I boil any tea or light any candles, I ask God to guide me in what to say and do to help them." He stopped walking and braced his back on the Harborwalk beam that fronted the businesses. "Is your question, Pastor Thunderbolt, because you have some root magic paranoia?" Thunderbolt listened but did not respond. Gregory raised and quickly lowered his head to eye-level with Thunderbolt before continuing. "So, do you ask yourself questions like that before you drink peppermint tea or pop a Tums tablet for an upset stomach? You know, mint leaves grow in some Lowcountry yards, in places where water gathers . . . ."

To make room for passersby, Pastor Thunderbolt joined Gregory in leaning his back on the Harborwalk beam. The two looked at the Sampit River view for a few moments. Before moving on, Pastor Thunderbolt flinched as he lifted his left hand and gasped, "Ouch!" Upon inspection, he saw that a splinter had nicked his pinky. He pried it out with his right thumb and pointer.

"Now, if that nick had been deep and drawn blood," Gregory said, "applying aloe vera gel to it would heal the skin quickly. I've got two pots of healthy aloe vera plants on my front porch for instances like what just happened."

The two began walking again. In silence. As they neared the Harborwalk exit behind the Rice Museum, Gregory decided to continue speaking—whether Thunderbolt was listening or only pretending to.

"Sometimes, after praying, voices begin instructing me on what to do," Gregory said. "Maybe your comfort level would only allow you to understand me if I said, 'I begin to hear the voice of God.' But to be honest, the voices I hear don't sound like White televangelists. No, they sound like people I've known or would have wanted to know. And when I follow through on what the voices tell me, I am blessed. Not cursed. Blessed! That, to me, means the voices I hear come through God.

"Sometimes, people . . . teachers, classmates, friends . . . speak softly to Barry, but their thoughts are different from their words. And their thoughts shout at him. Sometimes, church members pray nice-sounding prayers over Barry, but he can hear the negative, unspoken thoughts they may have about him. Others can't hear the silent noise they make. But it builds and connects and then overwhelms Barry. It causes him to faint. And when others don't listen to him when he talks about what he's experiencing, his trauma is reinforced. The voices that I hear tell me to help him connect with his inner ancestral child."

From his peripheral vision, Gregory saw a look of panic in Thunderbolt's eyes. A foreboding look that registered as recoil for having overheard supernatural mumbo jumbo, which could condemn him to hell. Gregory continued talking.

"Maybe he's carrying the burden of an ancestor, way back from up to seven generations ago. An ancestor who wanted to be heard."

He noticed Thunderbolt roll his eyes, fold his hands, and begin mouthing unheard words.

"An ancestor who was snatched from his African village. Who had overheard the voices or thoughts of danger from nearby enslavers and had told the village elders. But the village elders hadn't listened . . . Maybe Barry is carrying the burden of an ancestor who was whipped mercilessly by a mean master for something he did not do. An enslaved male or female who took a whipping while tied chest-against-bark to a tree. Even though they yelled and cried for their innocence, they realized their utterances made no difference because the master only wanted to make an example of their suffering for others."

Thunderbolt stopped walking. Looking intently at Gregory's face and with eyes darting up and down, he raised his hand for the talking to end. "Why are you telling me this?" he asked. "You and Barry Gilliard are hearing voices? Maybe you need to take a trip to MUSC too!"

Nonplussed, Gregory stated calmly, "Why? I thought if you knew just what to pray for, you would find it helpful when you prayed. I'm just letting you know the burden Barry needs release from so that he can develop into who he was meant to become since the time of his birth! And in this community, with all the oppression and violence that took place in Darcatia, there's an abundance of those who need help in dealing with their inner ancestral child. They're in churches and outside the church walls. They are old and they are young. And they need to know what it is they're dealing with. And how to overcome it. Epigenetic trauma is passed on for as many as seven generations!"

Thunderbolt paused to reflect. With his face and body motionless, his eyes moved slowly, steadily in all directions. Nodding to affirm what he thought he'd grasped, he said, "Epigenetic trauma. That's what you said, right?"

"Uh huh," Gregory affirmed.

"I guess that's trauma that passed on through one's genes. That's a new one for me."

To his dismay, Thunderbolt began to hear a familiar soft, small voice within his inner man. Its message was concise: "Listen."

They left Harborwalk and moved toward Front Street. Shaking his head slowly, Thunderbolt placed his right palm on his forehead and brought it down in slow-motion over his eyes, nose, mouth, and chin. He nodded for Gregory to continue, breathed in, and listened. When talking commenced, Thunderbolt placed his left hand on the crown of his head and dragged it down to the nape of his neck, which he massaged gently.

"Many don't know about it," Gregory said. "But this community-wide trauma is a living wound in need of healing. Those who are in this kind of bondage aren't helped by listening to screaming and yelling Bible-thumpers who accuse them of being evil or vile because they are in pain. Or that they should act as though what they feel doesn't exist.

"They need to be able to give voice to what they are experiencing—without condemnation and with assurance that they are being understood. Their trauma is as real as the fingerprints of enslaved children that are etched throughout time in the bricks of buildings throughout this country. These are the bricks made on Southern brick plantations by six- to ten-year-old youths who were forced to produce them—in the heat of the day, straight from the foundry, day in and day out—instead of enjoying their childhoods.

"There are many in our congregations around here who long to be as visible to others as the finger marks are to those who are trained to look for them. They need to hear how they can apply life-affirming words to themselves, in their unique circumstances, and not feel pigeon-holed and judged as godless or worthless. And above all, they need to feel loved and appreciated. Not rebuked but loved."

When Timothy Thunderbolt finished his dinner of stewed turkey wings, mashed potatoes, broccoli and carrots, and dinner rolls, he shared with Sibyl the details of his adventurous meeting with Gregory Dunkin. He explained that his meeting with Gregory Dunkin had taken him on a journey unlike anything he had ever experienced.

"Well, Tee," she asked, "what occurred mostly in the way that you expected? And what thing was the most unimaginable?" She was happy that his intense sense of rage, confusion, and determination to affect a specific outcome had dissipated from the previous evening.

Although their round, white wooden table seated four and they were in their usual chairs across from each other, he pulled out the chair to his right by its top three rails and invited Sibyl to sit closer. He looked into her eyes when she sat and said, "Well, I expected him to show up, and he did!" He tapped "Ba-doom-boom" onto the tabletop with both hands and smiled. "So many things happened that I could not have imagined! One, I expected to see him consumed by a cloud of fire, but he wasn't. Two, I didn't imagine that he gives Christian counsel to the Gilliards. And now, three, if anyone had told me beforehand that the voice of God would tell me to listen to the son of a root doctor, I would've said, 'I doubt that that would happen.' But it did!"

Astonished, Sibyl placed her hands atop her husband's and asked, "And what did you hear when you listened?"

Timothy shared a detailed account of what he'd learned. About an inner ancestral child. About the cross-generational trauma that some Lowcountry residents have been dealing with because of violence and oppression experienced by family members since the Transatlantic Slave Trade. About how church leaders can best help members, particularly young members, to deal with their inner ancestral child.

He saw that his answer left his wife visibly shaken. She withdrew her hands from his and placed them on her neck and over her ears. She stared at him in disbelief, lifted her head and eyes to the ceiling, and began breathing heavily when her eyes returned to him.

"Sibyl, what's wrong, dear?" he asked. "What did I say? What can I do?" He leaned in to touch her forehead, and then placed both hands on her shoulders.

"What you heard was just like what happened in the dream that Mother Eloise had!" she said.

"What dream?" Timothy asked. "Tell it to me, please."

Sibyl sat back in her chair. Her husband listened.

"It was a week or so ago. I'd been invited to attend a call to prayer meeting of the elderly women's council. We prayed about the dream Mother Eloise had had. It was about youths at the church. She revealed that in her dream, the church had become a new slave auction block. Just like the one that had been in front of the Rice Museum on Front Street. In her dream, though, church leaders were the new slave masters who lashed their whips and shouted the words of God while they stood on the street in front of the auction block.

"She said the church leaders shouted at their members, who were horrified to find themselves on the block. The churchgoers were horrified because they had told the preachers about what they'd seen and felt and what they didn't want to see or feel. And the preachers hadn't listened to anything they said.

"Mother Eloise said the preachers in her dream were dressed in fine suits and shoes. Some wore robes. They all just raised their hands one by one when the auctioneer called out a higher number—until the highest bid was accepted. The church people on the auction block started sniffling and crying, sniffling and crying. Because the preachers didn't direct them to freedom. The preachers just hauled away the ones they had bought, and they themselves cast each purchased individual into the fiery pit of hell.

"And then a buzzard started swooping around and around over the holding station that was located next door to where the Rice

Museum now stands. This had been the holding station where Africans were marched from slave ships docked in the Georgetown Harbor. The same holding station where Africans were brought from the pest houses on Sullivan's Island after they had been hauled off slave ships that had docked in Charleston. The same holding station where, before they arrived, they were doused with palm oil and scrubbed with a rough Danby brush until their skin shined like the polished boots that White men wore.

"Her dream showed her these things that were done to people who were brought to Darcatia Plantation. But the holding station in her dream was filled with young church people. Our children. Some older, but mostly teens and young adults who have lost hope, who don't care anymore about what preachers say or do to them when they get marched out to stand on the new auction block. Because they think that preachers don't listen to them anymore. They think preachers can't help them find freedom. They think preachers just want to cast them into the fiery pit of hell.

"Tee, isn't her dream the same thing that you heard from Gregory Dunkin?"

Nodding his head, he said, "It's confirmation, Sibyl. Confirmation of what I was told to listen to!"

"God wants you to do something, Tee. Listen to God, pray hard. And don't tarry!"

2000s

Gregory's phone call summoned Florence to learn what had been revealed following his most recent visit to Mourning Dove Cemetery. Following the first meeting, he had set the four periwinkle leaves within his Bible. Each over a particular verse. Two from the Old Testament and two from the New:

Ezekiel 17:5-6 He took one of the seedlings of the land and put it in fertile soil. He planted it like a willow by abundant water, and it sprouted and became a low, spreading vine. Its branches turned toward him, but its roots remained under it. So it became a vine and produced branches and put out leafy boughs.

Ezekiel 47:12 Fruit trees of all kinds will grow on both banks of the river. Their leaves will not wither, nor will their fruit fail. Every month they will bear fruit, because the water from the sanctuary flows to them. Their fruit will serve for food and their leaves for healing.

Matthew 15:13 He replied, "Every plant that my heavenly Father has not planted will be pulled up by the roots.

James 1:11 For the sun rises with scorching heat and withers the plant; its blossom falls and its beauty is destroyed. In the same way, the rich will fade away even while they go about their business.

Pressing the covers closed, he prayed as the flame flickered on a pink candle, lit to channel emotional love and harmony:

Ancestors, guide the way
To the throne of Wisdom.
This I pray.
Holy Spirit, Lamb who was slain,
Lead me to Truth,
Though it brings Joy or Pain.

On separate sheets of parchment paper, he scribbled the initials of the individual being investigated and the individual who'd requested an otherworldly investigation. He used light blue ink for deep wisdom. "CW" for Chadwick Wineglass was placed below the Bible. "FTW" for Florence Tucker Wineglass was placed atop it. He waited several days for the reveal.

On day three, the leaves on the New Testament passages had decayed most, signifying they pertained to the individual being investigated. On day seven, the same leaves had decayed further and were removed. The remaining two leaves on the Old Testament passages, however, had maintained their vibrant color, signifying they pertained to the individual who'd requested the investigation.

Gregory fasted and meditated for a day to discern the meaning of each verse's application, sipping on ginseng and chamomile tea for grounding, strength, and tranquility. He felt guided on day eleven to bring the Bible, with the leaves still within the pages, to Mourning Dove Cemetery and await a sign. He felt no inclination to bring a container of alcohol, bottle or can.

He paused at the trunk of the large live oak that stood like a sentinel at the apex of the dirt road. The graves from the 1800s lay on the left, newer ones on the right. Looking east then west, before closing his eyes, he prayed.

"God, bless this house and keep the soul," he stated softly. "Please, I ask permission to come into this house." He opened his eyes and looked about in the early morning light. The tree limbs to the left began flailing rapidly, though he felt no fierce breeze. He decided not to enter. The grasses and bushes to the right soon began undulating as though the ground was shifting sand, yet he felt no tremors. When the vision of movement stopped, the sight he saw caused him to fall on his knees and give thanks. "God, bless this house and keep the soul," he proclaimed before racing toward an abundance of yellow flowers, wingstem, a wild herb. The petals billowed in a patch all around a stately lone palmetto tree. Its green fronds moved up and down like the wings of angels.

At once, Gregory's face changed, and his clothes became as bright as a flash of lighting. In the midst of the flowers, he saw looking directly at him one like a son of man, clothed with a long robe and with a sash around his chest. The hairs of his head were white, like white wool, like snow. His eyes were like a flame of fire, his feet were like burnished bronze, refined in a fire, and his voice was like the roar of many waters.

When this bronze being looked to the right, an ancestral spirit bearing a sheet of parchment with the letters CW glided from the cemetery section of old toward the wingstem patch. Two palmetto fronds popped off their branches and floated down from the tree. The being then looked to the left, and an ancestral spirit bearing a sheet of parchment with the letters FTW glided from the newer cemetery section toward the wingstem patch. It picked up the palmetto fronds and placed one on either side of the CW ancestral spirit's neck.

"If Chadwick Wineglass has in any way directly contributed to the physical harm or illness of his bride, Florence Tucker Wineglass, or to the demise of their unborn children," the FTW ancestral spirit stated, "then tie, palmetto, tie." In a moment, in the twinkling of an eye, the green fronds began to entwine around each other, furling together at the front and then the back of CW spirit's neck, as if to choke it. But it then released and unfurled.

The burnished bronze being then clapped its hands. In a voice of rushing waters, it spoke words to foreshadow actions that were beyond the veil of understanding, even for Gregory. "No one who practices deceit will dwell in my house," it said. "No one who speaks falsely will stand in my presence."

With eyes that focused on Gregory and then at the Bible in his hands, the being motioned with its right arm for him to advance. Gregory walked slowly and obediently toward the wingstem and placed the Bible into its hands. The being placed a giant key within the pages of the book, handed it to the FTW ancestral spirit, and nodded.

Looking away from the bronze being and into the eyes of the CW ancestral spirit, the FTW ancestral spirit held onto the handle of the giant key, with the pages of the Bible facing downward. "By St. Peter, by St. Paul, by the grace of the good Lord who made us all," the spirit stated with boldness, "if Chadwick Wineglass is plotting the death of Emanuel Tucker, I pray, Bible, you will turn and fall."

The Bible did not move. It did not flip over the key and fall to the ground. Its inertia heralded that the accusation was false. So, both ancestral spirits looked to the burnished bronze being, who in turn looked to Gregory.

"Take the wingstem. Learn the truth," it stated in a soft and gentle roar. "Children are a gift from the Lord." When it instructed, "Go!" Gregory turned away from the vision with haste, grabbed a handful of the yellow wild herbs, and left.

Loading Sheaves onto Flatboats

Before her home kit or gynecologist had confirmed the pregnancy, Florence knew precisely when her second conception had occurred. It was the Sunday morning after Chadwick had returned home from the graveyard shift at the convenience store with a bouquet of roses.

"Oh, honey, they are lovely!" she'd gushed when she saw them on the kitchen counter. She'd risen to get some water after hearing him showering before coming to bed. The gift of what she perceived as his thoughtfulness sent a refreshing surge of no-longer-stifled titillation coursing throughout her frame. Torched with unshackled sensuality, she disrobed, returned dreamily to her marriage bed, and awaited her husband with wanton desire.

Somehow, as they spooned and slumbered following their prolonged reacquaintance, her subconscious must've fired a synapse with the understanding that something was awry. She sat up in bed, not fully awake, snarled, "Gr-r-r!", and nipped him, full-toothed, on his chest.

"Ouch!" he said, rising on an elbow. "What you do that for?"

Florence did not hear him. As he looked in bewilderment and then settled back down, she thought about their bedroom behavior over the past few months, which she'd later find began soon after Emanuel Tucker, like a spider, had spun a silken web of dishonesty in their home.

In a series of connected dreams, she saw herself responding without spontaneity or urgency to her husband's sexual advances. She thwarted his attempts to arouse her. His touches seemed disassociated from the being she was below her skin. She perceived the undulation of his fingers, his thighs, his chest against her body not as a gift of sharing some loving feeling but only as actions to *do* her. Because a *good man* would physically satisfy his lover. She saw herself moan in feigned ecstasy. And she watched Chadwick, in appreciation, arise from their bed and bring her a bouquet of flowers. As he neared her, in her dream, what she noticed alarmed her. The flowers were drooping. The vase, stained. The gift was sullied.

Startled, she woke from her dream as the morning sun filtered through the closed bedroom curtains. Leaving Chadwick asleep, she walked to the kitchen to examine the bouquet that had altered her mindset and had left her with the faintest sense of life beginning *to make foot fa socks* within her innermost being. She removed a vase that had been given as a wedding gift from a lower cabinet, placed it on the countertop, then picked up the flowers to sniff and admire them. A note had been attached to the bouquet on the side that lay on the counter. Florence opened it slowly. Read it repeatedly. Then retreated speedily to her bedroom, bouquet in hand.

"Chadwick Wineglass!" she railed. "What is *this* you brought into *this* house?"

He awoke. Baffled. Blustered. Blindsided. "Huh?" he stumbled. "What's the matter, Flo? Why are you yelling at—" Sitting up, awakening, and beginning to focus on his surroundings, he saw the flowers first and then the look of the Grim Reaper on his wife's face.

"And *who* is Vermelle?" she snapped.

"Ver . . . who?" His reasoning returned when he saw Florence brandishing the notecard and the plastic card holder at him. "Oh-h-h, you saw the roses," he said, with affection. His eyes danced. "I thought you'd like them."

Her eyes hurled daggers. "These are *not* for *me* to like," she hissed. "They're for Vermelle. Who's Vermelle, Chadwick? Answer me! Who's Vermelle?"

"I don't know," he responded before beginning a bulleted explanation. "A man tossed me some flowers that he no longer wanted. I brought the flowers home to you. I put the flowers on the counter when I got home and came to take a shower. I meant to put the flowers in a vase when I finished my shower, but you had other plans for me when I walked out of the bathroom. I mean, hot damn! Thank you, ma'am!"

Baffled, he sat up in bed and eyed his wife with incredulity before continuing. "And now you're standing over me and yelling, 'Who's Vermelle?' I don't know any Vermelle! And, somehow, I'm beginning to think you don't like the flowers . . . but you always tell me roses are your favorite!"

While engaged in a heated cell phone conversation, a man had entered Chadwick's workplace to get change for the gas he'd pumped. Snippets of the conversation that Chadwick had overheard were: "Listen . . . I'm sorry . . . I know . . . Yep, baby, I was wrong. Uh huh . . . I'm on my way home now . . . I'll be there soon."

The man returned to his car before Chadwick had given him his change, so Chadwick followed him out. As he approached the passenger window, the befuddled and seemingly guilt-ridden customer slammed his cellphone onto the car seat and began to breathe rapidly as though in the throes of a heart attack.

"Hey, you forgot your change!" Chadwick had said, looking on with concern.

Turning toward him slowly, like one headed to the gallows, the man had reached for the cash, then promptly picked up the bouquet next to his phone and handed it to Chadwick in exchange.

"You know someone who likes roses?" he'd asked. "Here. Take them. The one I got these for . . . she don't want them. Not today. Not tomorrow. Not again. I messed up!"

Heading who knows where, he'd driven away, and Chadwick had returned with the flowers to the convenience store counter where he remained until quitting time.

Chadwick and Florence stared at each other and then looked away, perplexed.

Florence and Chadwick's lives had begun to mirror the lyrics of the slave song, "The Buzzard Lope." They'd persisted in providing for their *embers*, without reciprocity and without any continuation of communication or perceived friendship. The annulment would begin at a predetermined time, a time that those who were assisted were ignorant of. Those who'd bitten their lure, for whatever reason, soon began to feel like carrion. Though still alive, they felt as though the

Wineglasses had encircled them. Seen them. Hovered over them. Plucked at their eyes. Their organs. Had ruffled their Wineglass feathers and made their debtors flee. And, with their hunger satiated, the raptors had flown away. Far away.

As Chadwick prepared to shave before work one morning, he found a strange "encouragement quote by Marcus Garvey" that Florence had left taped to the bathroom mirror. It read, "I regard the Klan, the Anglo-Saxon clubs, and White American societies, as far as the Negro is concerned, as better friends of the race than all other groups of hypocritical whites put together." He returned to the bedroom to dress and sat down on the bed beside Florence.

"Morning, Chadwick, dear!" she whispered.

He leaned forward and kissed her forehead. Holding the love note, he said, "'Morning' backatcha!" As he noticed the note's signature salutation, a lipstick print of her kiss below the words, "Think B.I.G., my darling! I love you!!!", he chuckled then added, "This quote seems different from his others! What's the story behind it?"

Florence rolled on her side and placed her arm around his shoulder. "Well," she began, "I read that Garvey wanted his 'Back to Africa' movement to succeed so badly that he tried to get Klan support to achieve it!" Batting her eyes and rolling her head with neck-ti-tude, she left no doubt about her revulsion of the thought. "He flirted with them and their racist attitudes, thinking they both wanted the same thing!" She relaxed her voice, squeezed him tighter, and looked wide-eyed into his eyes. "I just wanted to remind you to 'Think B-I-G.' and not 'Think S-T-U-P-I-D'. What's your day like? You know mine. I'll be right here."

"Well, work today is in Hagley's Plantation and in Surfside. If I can, I'll squeeze in a lunch meeting with someone who's been waiting on a response from me."

"About a work offer?

"No, something else." He didn't want to expound, so he added, "We can talk about it some other time."

"O-kay. . . ."

She lay back down. He dressed. They kissed goodbye. Their normal workdays began.

Following a mundane workday with Wineglass French Drain Installation, Chadwick arrived at the office of Peregrine Investors, LLC, in Garden City a little before 7:00 p.m. to begin his ninety-minute part-time custodial shift. Following that shift, he serviced an adjacent office building for an additional ninety minutes. Accordingly, he amassed a combined fifteen hours of extra income each week.

Two late-working Peregrine workers walked to their cars before Chadwick stepped out of his black pickup. Their conversation intrigued him.

"Yeah, you heard that right, but don't quote me," the male worker said. "My client said that the construction crew that dug the pool site at their new mansion on Hagley's Plantation uncovered bones."

"Human bones?" the female worker inquired. "That can't be right!"

"Uh huh. Human bones," the male replied. "Could be slave bones. Hagley Plantation dates back before the Civil War, you know. But, like I said, you didn't hear any of this from me!"

The short, milk-chocolate-colored woman in a dark-blue pantsuit stopped near the trunk of her white Audi sedan. She brushed her hand across her shoulder-length weave and said, "I saw the house plans that he left in your office, Barrington. It's going to be fabulous! Will construction have to be put on hold? Will he have to move construction to another site?"

"Here's what I told him, Skylar," black-suited Barrington said before he opened the door to a red Corvette convertible. "I said, 'With all the money you've got tied up in this house, just pay those construction workers off not to say a word about those bones to nobody. No-bo-dy. If they found bones—and it's just pieces of bones, I hear—and if these are bones, slave bones at that, what ain't been dug up in more than two hundred years . . . who's gonna miss them?" He grabbed an Ole Miss Rebels baseball cap from his dashboard and fit it over his blond hair.

The two chuckled in conversation, started their ignitions, and drove away. Stupefied by what he'd overheard, Chadwick swept and polished floors, cleaned sinks and toilets, emptied trash cans, and returned home to rest. In the morning, he began another long workday. At his weekend part-time job at the 7-Eleven on the outskirts of Georgetown, he overheard chatter that synced with what the Peregrine workers had divulged.

"Take de money, boi," a chunky, twenty-something Black male said to another as he pulled a six-pack carton of Corona Extra from the refrigerator shelf. He muscled a bag of Dorito Nacho Cheese below his left arm and clasped a bag of Dorito Flamin' Hot Nachos in his left fingers.

"I ain know bout dat," his store partner answered. The rail-thin but muscular young adult with shoulder-length dreads set two bottles of AVA Grace red wine on the counter as he answered his friend in a hushed tone. "You ain spose ta mess wit de daid. Peepul say dey might wan me an de odd-as wa been dig at de pool site fa say we ain been see nottin!" As Chadwick cashed him out, his friend with the chips stood behind him and added, "Dey full up wit de Benjamins, boi! If dey offer some of em, take em. An, yeah, if dey come roun de hood, offering bank ta de ol mens sittin unda de tree fa say dey ain know nottin bout no slave graveyard wa been deh but dat dey know bout anodda slave grave yard wa been in Hagley, I'm a tell em, 'Take em. Take all de Benjamins.'"

Chadwick listened and took everything in.

"I dohn know . . . I dohn know . . ." the dreadlocked male said as they exited. "Daid peepul haunt ya ef ya ain do em right."

Chadwick shared with Florence the conversations he'd pieced together about deterred bones at Hagley Plantation as they cleaned the kitchen following Sunday morning breakfast.

"I hear people are offering hush money so that house construction plans at Hagley don't get pushed back or get pushed to another site," Chadwick said.

"What?" Florence responded. "I sure hope no one takes it!"

"Well, with a little money, more than they had before, people can do a lot of things they may have wanted to do," Chadwick said.

"And what good would that do?" Florence countered as she moved their plates to the sink. "If they have to lie to get it, no amount of money is worth it!" She looked at her husband with surprise for even suggesting that someone could harbor such a thought.

Chadwick placed the bottle of orange juice and the butter dish in the refrigerator. "From what I heard said at the store," he explained, "some are being asked to not say that human bones were uncovered. And some are being asked to say that there was a slave cemetery at another location in Hagley, far from where they supposedly were found." He paused and burst into song, "'Them bones, them bones gonna rise again!'"

Florence covered her ears with her hands and pulled her body into a knot in response to her husband's off-key singing. She made a sour-faced smile and began to fill the sink with water. When she poured in some red dishwasher detergent, a thought came to mind and her body froze. She turned slowly to Chadwick and said, "Now, if just a few bones were found, and not a lot, those bones could be from the Renty Tucker church graveyard."

"Renty who?" Chadwick asked.

Stumped at his ignorance, Florence replied, "Now Chadwick Wineglass, please don't tell me that you don't know anything about Renty Tucker!" She watched him shake his head. "We learned about Renty Tucker in fifth grade at Joseph Rainey Elementary School. What were the nuns teaching you elementary students at Healer of the Land Catholic School?"

She informed him that Renty Tucker, an enslaved worker owned by Plowden C.J. Weston of Hagley Plantation, had been born in the early 1830s and had become a highly skilled master carpenter. At Plowden's orders, he'd received training in England to build magnificent and intricately detailed buildings, and upon his return to Georgetown had built St. Mary's Chapel in 1859. Although it was celebrated as the most elaborate slave house of worship in the South, the eloquent building on Hagley's Weehawka Plantation was destroyed by fire in 1931. About 250 enslaved worshipers could be seated there and were favored with a tower, carved oak pews, double walls for coolness, stained-glass lancet windows, a clock, and chimes that the Westons had imported from England. The chapel site, however, was never marked, and the grave markers were bulldozed in the late 1970s for residential development.

"Those must be bones from the chapel graveyard," Florence said. "I can't understand people who have no respect for the dead. People just can't trample over a final resting place. It's sacred."

Their conversation made them remember the hushed reverence

they had felt when they'd visited the Monument to the Rt. Excellent Marcus Garvey during their honeymoon. Although Garvey died in England, his body had been returned to his homeland and laid to rest in a magnificent vault to be honored as Jamaica's first national hero.

"Those bones of slaves can't be sent back to Africa, but they have to be honored," Florence said with a tear spilling from her eye. "They weren't national heroes, but their lives made a difference. While they lived, they mattered. Though they're dead, their memories matter."

At his full-time job the following day, Chadwick learned the folly of his overheard conversations. The developer at Hagley Point had alerted and turned over the comingled remains to county administrators. The unearthing of human bones was not being silenced, and no hush money had been considered or exchanged.

Chadwick informed Florence when he returned home. Before he left to travel to his part-time weekday-evening job as a custodian, he also voiced concern for her criticism of his elementary school education. He informed her with great pride that the seed for Wineglass French Drain Installation had been planted at Healer of the Land Catholic School. He'd seen a picture of a Roman aqueduct, and Sister Kathleen had explained to him that they had been used long ago, from 312 B.C. to A.D. 226. Not, as he had expected, to transport automobiles like the Black River Bridge or the Waccamaw and Peedee bridges that he saw regularly, but to transfer water from a freshwater source, like a spring or a lake, to a faraway city.

"I know, like I've heard time and time again," Chadwick said, "that the Black teachers at Rainey Elementary who had taught before at all-Black schools like Howard Elementary and Howard High, kept the Black students informed about local and national Black history. "Like how Rainey, Georgetown's own who was born into slavery, was the first Black person to serve in the U.S. House of Representatives. How he made sure there were laws that provided public education for everyone."

"Yes, our teachers did!" Florence chimed in. "In Black history clubs, drama clubs, speech Clubs . . ."

"That's right, and that was good!" Chadwick interrupted. "But the moment that that teacher at Healer of the Land took with me had a life-changing effect. And I'm grateful for it. Later, in junior high, I wrote my first essay about aqueducts for Sister Seabrook's class, and that paved the way for every essay I've written since! I got an A+++, and I even remember my three choices for the topic sentence she helped me to develop. I wrote about how civilizations used this water that had been channeled from elsewhere for drinking, irrigation, and for public fountains and baths."

Florence responded with a bright smile and soft applause, "Good teachers do make the world a better place!"

But the conclusion of Chadwick's wind-up had not yet been reached. His exhilaration changed to exasperation as he continued. "I stayed interested in aqueducts even when I transferred to Rainey High School," he added. "For an assignment in business class, I did a business plan for a French drain installation company. It would only use pipes to channel water—not pipes and tunnels and canals and bridges like with aqueducts. But do you know what most of my classmates said about it?" Florence raised her eyes, and Chadwick frowned. "They huffed and hawed. Said this business plan was for a job that was no better than being a ditch-digger. And that our people had dug enough ditches when we had to work in the rice fields.

"The one White student in my class, Bob Brittman, was the only one to give me any positive feedback. He suggested that I needed to consider sources of revenue to finance the plan. And guess what he is now? The president of Rice Fields Regional Bank! I may not have known anything about Renty Tucker, but I've got my own business. And most of the kids who laughed at me are probably all working in some low-level service industry job somewhere."

Florence nodded her head in affirmation and asked him to stay put. She sped to her bedroom dresser drawer and rifled through her collection of pre-written love-note quotes from Marcus Garvey. Making a selection, she returned and kissed her husband and handed it to him before he left. It read, "'We are going to emancipate ourselves from mental slavery, for though others may free the body, none but ourselves can free the mind.' —Think B.I.G.! Florence"

Gary Windley had flashbacks of his attempt to repay Chadwick three hundred of the two thousand dollars he'd received and eventually used for his mother's cremation. They'd met soon after he'd returned home to care for his mother. Chadwick had gotten in touch and started meeting with him for lunch biweekly, leaving him with cash—four one-hundred-dollar bills folded in half and then in half again pushed into his hand when they shook to depart. Leery about receiving money from someone whom he still considered to be a stranger, Gary used some of the benevolent income to assist with living expenses during his leave-of-absence from work.

Scrambling not to become indebted to someone without a clear understanding of their reasons for helping, he'd spoken with Chadwick during one of their lunch meetings. "Here, let me give you back what I can of what you've given me," he'd said. "It's so kind of you, but I'll be all right."

Chadwick had continued eating his fish sandwich for several bites as Gary held an envelope of cash out to him over the table. After taking the envelope, he excused himself for a few minutes, and Gary watched him exit the restaurant and walk to his truck. They continued their meal with light conversation after he returned, but a shakedown-of-a-sort occurred after Chadwick had asked for and paid the check.

"I don't want to embarrass you or make you feel bad," Chadwick said in a business-like, matter-of-fact tone. "Don't be ashamed to take things that you need. There have been times I've needed things, and I've had to humble myself and take what has been given to me. You're out of work. Away from home. Taking care of your family. You need this."

Gary counted the money in the returned envelope when he got back to his mother's house. In addition to the now expected four hundred, there was an additional six hundred—double the amount he'd tried to repay. His first reaction was a feeling of being rebuffed. Several hours later, after reflecting on Chadwick's remarks, however, he called and left a message on Chadwick's voicemail: "Hey, Wineglass, thanks! I guess you're right. Glad to have you as a friend. Love you, man!"

Unknown to him, the transaction in the returned envelope had fulfilled the amount Florence had appropriated for her husband to dispense. Furthermore, Chadwick, troubled by the intent of the last line of Gary's voicemail message, particularly because of his feelings about the peculiarity of Gary's mouth—its shape as he spoke or when he looked at him—was relieved that their obligatory association, at last, had crossed the finish line. Florence also underwent misperceptions about her helpfulness, but she skirted being regarded as a predator and as a bondsman.

Chadwick had assigned her to a high school senior whose father had worked for him at a two-week jobsite. The father had boasted to the work crew that his daughter had turned her life around, overcoming the habit of always saying something negative about herself. And even more important, she'd received a small scholarship to an out-of-state HBCU. Chadwick had hoped that this *ember* would afford Florence the cache to become a role model of financial stewardship among other local high school females. He approved the dispersal of two thousand dollars over a one-year period.

After reading the list of scholarship announcements in the Georgetown Gazette, Florence arranged through the Joseph Rainey High School guidance counselor to meet with the student and her parents. She presented a five-hundred-dollar gift toward the girl's post-high school education, after learning that Eboni Manigault was the only graduate who'd be attending Hampton University, and after researching the school's mission. Thrilled, the Manigault parents encouraged their daughter to maintain communication with Florence T. Wineglass. They'd heard about the Wineglasses' generosity from several community members.

Eboni mailed Florence a thank you card within a week of receiving her gift. She telephoned her before departing in the fall and inquired if they could email. Florence promised to stay in touch throughout her freshman year. Shrewdly, she began to mail or CashApp Eboni small installments of fifty to two hundred dollars only when she'd received at least one email every two months and depending on an expressed financial need.

Eboni's emails began to reveal a descent to negativity, about which Florence was already aware. "I don't know why I thought I should come here," she'd write, or "I feel like such an imposter!" or "I can't learn this stuff," or "Everybody thinks I'm a nobody, a Geechee, a loser."

Florence would encourage her to respond with five affirmations about herself for each negative self-attribution she'd made. Eboni's initial reply encouraged her.

"I am young," she wrote. "I am beautiful. I am smart. I am loved by a woman who sees me for who I am, who sends me money, and says kind things about me and to me. Only with her love can I go on!"

Subsequent emails, however, began to worry Florence. Eboni began sharing confidences that she thought her parents would not understand or accept. She wanted to explore feelings that she'd refused to explore before. She said that she thought often about the way Ms. Florence had looked at and cared for her.

Florence sensed a shift in the teen's awareness of boundaries in her communications. She informed Eboni of the topics she would respond to, and offered suggestions of university officials she may wish to contact. To keep Eboni from spiraling to depression, Florence assured her that she would not share with her parents anything that she'd confided.

When email contact resumed the following month, Eboni's issues with boundaries had burgeoned. She asked what five things about her had attracted Florence to befriend her. If Florence considered herself a cougar. If she would visit her soon so that she could meet Eboni's professors. She wrote that she would love to stay with her at the hotel for the weekend visit. And if possible, she would love for Florence to travel alone.

Florence contacted several people at warp speed: her husband, her attorney, and Eboni's parents. Fearing the media sideshow of Florence being carted to jail on mistaken sex offender charges, the Wineglasses and their representative met with Eboni's parents to convey the email trail and transactions of money and to request that Eboni discontinue communication. In a show of support, Florence awarded the remaining eight hundred to the Manigault parents to ensure Eboni received needed psychological counseling as she completed her freshman year.

DeShante, another *ember* whom Chadwick had assigned to Florence, also almost tethered Florence to the penal system. Florence had befriended her to appropriate nine hundred dollars over three months to cover the cost of having a wheelchair ramp built onto her father's home; the man had suffered a diabetic leg amputation. DeShante, following one of Florence's gift installments, had used a portion of the money on another matter, not having been told that it was designated for a specific purpose. She needed a five-hundred-dollar bond for her sixteen-year-old son who was charged for simple possession, first offense. DeShante never informed her newfound friend about this, since their lunchtime conversations usually only concerned her father's care.

During the fourth month of their meeting, however, the son of one of DeShante's single-head-of-household friends also needed bond for a police charge. Believing Florence could be a rock in time of trouble, she called late one night to inquire about a loan or advice. Not yet aware that the friendship had expired its time limit, DeShante was surprised by the brute inquiry when Florence answered. "Why are you calling me . . . at my home . . . at this hour of the night?"

"Hello, Florence, this is DeShante," she responded.

"May I call you back tomorrow? I can't speak with you just now," Florence said.

"Okay. Sure." A return call was never made.

To the Wineglasses, their encircling, their watching, their hovering enabled them to assist. They did not pluck. They provided. They did not invest in deadbeats. The ruffling of their philanthropic wings scurried away the debts of each *ember* they had entrapped. Without an awareness of "The Buzzard Lope" slave song or its Ashanti origins, they saw themselves as "messengers of God" and their pecuniary dance among their community members as one of freedom and of hope.

Unknown to Florence, however, Chadwick's selection of her first *ember* had been made in hopes that she would learn through her time with Laverne that he was unlike Laverne's husband, Medicus. That he cared for aged family members. That he did not engage in perversities. That he would be her rock. In time, however, Florence's rock began to splinter in other areas.

Just like his father's unforgettable words, lessons learned from his schoolteachers at times reverberated in Chadwick's mind, springing to memory without provocation. A fellow board member of the Gardens at River Bend spoke with him and others during a board retreat about expanding their investment opportunities. Chadwick, in turn, recalled the South Carolina motto his civics teacher had drilled into him and his classmates: "While I breathe, I hope."

Sixty-five-year-old board member Agnes Cottonseed spoke about her novel, first-year anniversary gift to her only son and new daughter-in-law. She'd taken out a life insurance policy on herself and listed her son as her sole beneficiary so that upon her death, he'd be able to pay off his recently acquired home mortgage.

"Money works in mysterious ways," she'd stated boastfully, and added, "Now I can recommend an insurance agent to anyone who is interested—if you know what I mean. I'm in fairly good health, but if I go tomorrow, I don't want my son to be burdened with a mortgage that'll take him close to three decades to retire. The right attorney can make things beneficial for clients who may think things could never be beneficial for them."

On the return drive to his modest modular home, Chadwick began to reach for hope. Hope for trying for another child once Florence healed physically and emotionally. Hope for advancing Wineglass French Drain Installation as well as his and Florence's plans for helping others. And hope to provide for his ill and recovering grandfather-in-law who recently had temporarily moved in.

In consideration of Agnes Cottonseed's claim, he thought first to have Florence inquire if Emanuel Tucker had sufficient life insurance to cover his end-of-life expenses. If not, then perhaps they should consider purchasing a supplemental policy to preclude financial entanglement for any immediate surviving Tucker family member. His mind then became a honeybee, gathering pollen at different intellectual petals and feeding on it to stimulate other thoughts.

Bzzz. What amount would be sufficient to funeralize a community icon? A relatively healthy senior citizen who never smoked, had no medical challenges, and only drank homemade scuppernong wine at Christmastime?

Bzzz. If no policy was in effect, how much debt would he and his Florence, Tucker's eldest grandchild, be expected to incur? Except for Adam, none of his other children seemed financially capable or without major family health challenges.

Bzzz. Did Emanuel have a will that earmarked what would become of the home he'd built for himself, Blessing, and their children?

Bzzz. What did Emanuel hope to leave behind for his children, his children's children, and so on?

At that, his mind began to forage and feast on a different pollinator: Agnes Cottonseed's revelation. A different and more enriched question was birthed.

Bzzzzzz. Could money work in mysterious ways for him and Florence?

His father's familiar voice murmuring, *Be like God and help people, son,* steered Chadwick's thoughts as he spoke with his wife. At his urging, she'd learned that Emanuel had been paying twenty per month for forty-nine years on a $2,500 term life policy that was now worth less than its payoff value. Funeral arrangements for her mother had cost about eight thousand, and she, fortunately, had had an insurance policy through the SC Department of Education. The old fisherman and revered elder deacon deserved a more respectful homegoing service than that of a pauper with no family, despite his recent revelations. On this Florence and Chadwick agreed.

Their compromised agreement was to pursue the possibility of securing a ten- to fifteen-thousand-dollar life insurance policy for Emanuel, which, coupled with his primary policy, would leave five hundred to one thousand dollars in legacy funds to bequeath to each of his eight great-grandchildren. Florence offered to attempt a return to the workforce in about three to six months to pay for the monthly premium. By that time, it was believed, Emanuel would have long been back at home in Mausaville.

On the day following their discussion, however, and without alerting Florence, Chadwick contacted Agnes Cottonseed, who, in turn, recommended that he speak with Diamond Wasilewski. Their meeting occurred two days later. After listening to Chadwick's responses to a plethora of questions about his grandfather-in-law's health and assets and his and Florence's business interests and goals, Diamond pitched a proposal. Perhaps they should consider having Emanuel Tucker relocate with them permanently. Perhaps they could claim that expenses towards Tucker's care in their home be leveraged against Tucker's home ownership. Perhaps the monies they would receive as beneficiaries could fund the expansion and growth of Wineglass French Drain Installation and whatever other business objectives they longed to establish. These matters, however, could only be finalized with Emanuel's full approval and signature, she advised.

"Can you give an estimated monthly premium?" Chadwick asked in a hesitant tone.

Diamond provided estimates for life-insurance policies ranging from fifteen to $150,000. Each total was less than he'd anticipated, so Chadwick raised the stakes to $250,000. He filed her responses away in his mind, thanked Diamond for raising his awareness, and left with determination to share the information, or at least some of it, with Florence. He broached the topic during kitchen cleanup after dinner. Emanuel had retired to his bedroom.

"Florence, I spoke with an insurance agent about a policy on your grandfather. A fifteen-thousand-dollar policy, like we talked about, won't require too large a premium."

"Mm-hm," she said as she dried a saucer. "That's good! Granddaddy should be back to feeling like his old self real soon. I'll wait 'til then to talk to him about it. I don't want to be like the Angel of Death, having lots to say about dying while his head is still spinning from this vertigo. How much?"

Waiting for the slow stream to rinse away the suds and then handing her the accompanying cup, Chadwick breathed in deeply then stated, "Well, before I speak on that, there's some interesting twists and turns we could take on the matter that could be a blessing in disguise."

"Oi-ee," Florence uttered. "A could-be-blessing-in-disguise might mean it's not a blessing at all. Go on." She set the dried cup on the cabinet shelf near the stacked saucers and paused, looking at her husband in rapt attention.

"Well, if I understand right what I was told, and if Tucker agrees for us to be beneficiaries, a policy at a higher amount could help us to grow the company. Down the road. You know, no time soon."

"Grow? In what way, Chadwick?"

"I could hire a full-time worker and continue subcontracting for installing French drains, and branch into basement waterproofing and roof gutter installation. That could pave the way to becoming a general contractor and being made aware of more construction projects and more connections in the playing field."

"Mm-hmm. I've never heard you talk about expanding services. Only about finding more French drain work. Maybe in opening your service area a little wider."

"Well, with family plans for a Junior or a Juniorette, I've been brainstorming about ways to stay close to home."

His wife smiled. Some of the tension of their conversation seemed to relax, and Chadwick steeled himself to continue.

"What's the monthly payment for a ten- or fifteen-thousand-dollar policy?" Florence asked.

"Because his blood pressure is his only health concern—and maybe, now that I think of it, maybe that comes from being out on the saltwater every day since childhood—maybe that's why his blood pressure is high . . . well, that's not too bad of a problem for his age group. The premium could range from seventy-five bucks to one-twenty."

Florence braced her hips against the kitchen counter to soak in all the information. After a few quiet moments, she said, "I think that with his small policy and this new policy, if we reign in plans for having a homegoing service for Granddaddy that's unlike any other homegoing service ever in Mausaville . . . and if we 'build up Zion's wall' for him to leave legacy gifts for his young family members, like we discussed, then, if nothing too shocking happens between now and then . . . maybe a monthly premium for a twenty-thousand-dollar policy is something we can plan for. If Emanuel Tucker agrees, that is. What you say to that?"

Chadwick raised his head up and down, up and down, in faux agreement with her decision. He decided not to risk the mention of his thoughts about increasing the policy amount to enlarge their philanthropic funding pool. And not to divulge any business ideas about repurposing the Low Bottom Community Church's plan for low-income housing to appropriate its partial use for lodging relocated Jamaicans. He decided not to tread water with any such matters until he was more certain they wouldn't cause a tsunami wave that would beach his plans—plans for helping more community *embers* move out of debt and then help themselves and not rely on the Wineglasses for social or monetary contributions.

Blonde-haired Diamond Wasilewski met the Wineglasses and Emanuel Tucker in her Georgetown office overlooking the Sampit River.

"You're the first woman I ever met with that name," Emanuel told her as they sat. "Now, I know a Ruby, a Sapphire, and a Pearl. But fa sho I never met a Diamond before. It's good to make your acquaintance. Yes. Your mama or your daddy give you that name?"

"Oh, my daddy named me," Diamond answered. "My mama's birth name is Amber Citrine, and when I was born, Daddy said he was going to be surrounded with nothing but precious gems. I'm an only child."

"Names are important! Yes, indeed," Tucker continued. "They set you up for how you'll be treated and how you'll think about yourself throughout life. My wife made sure our daughters were named after things of beauty—the flowers she adored: jasmine, gardenia, and camellia."

"Those *are* adorable names," Diamond said, smiling with radiance. "And I love the fragrance of each of those flowers." She looked to Chadwick, readying to formally begin their appointment. "Speaking of names, well, first, it's a pleasure to meet each of you. Mrs. Wineglass and Mr. Tucker, your husband and son-in-law spoke about each of you when he met to discuss options. The name of the policy that would be best suited for your needs is 'Universal Life Lifetime Coverage.' Have you decided on an amount?"

Interested in maintaining the tenor of their conversation but not realizing that he was about to cut the proverbial hog, provoking a brutalized animal or a humiliated wife to turn on him, Chadwick spoke with candor. "Yes, the name of that policy has a sound of purpose: 'Universal Life Lifetime.' Just like my wife's name, Florence. I love that name. Florence means 'prosperous.' That's why I married her."

Florence's eyes blinked and widened. Simultaneously, her head flinched, and she turned toward her husband. The unspoken statements of her body language snarled, *Oh, that's the reason you married me? Because of my name? You for real? I prosper you? You see that as my only purpose in life? Well, then, why don't you consider my thoughts about the things I can do to prosper us? Lately, it seems that only YOUR thoughts count,* and *we will talk. Oh, yes. We will talk!*

It didn't matter that her actions afterward bore witness to the Gullah idiom. If you were born during hog-killing season, it meant that if you slice a hog's neck, you'd better be ready to bludgeon and kill it, or it will turn and kill you! Chadwick, innocent Chadwick, had no intention, no idea that he had sliced his bride. And those in the room who were oblivious to her three-second facial display had no idea that her pursuit of vengeance was only temporarily postponed. Four seconds later, her attitude pivoted with a beaming smile at Diamond and a look of caretaker's concern for her grandfather. She alone, without Chadwick's intervention, would speak about her grandfather's concerns.

"We're interested in a $20,000 policy," Florence stated with poise. "How should we proceed? Will we need to schedule a medical exam for Granddad? He's in agreement about this. Please inform us of any details we'll need to know."

Florence managed to look in the direction of, but never at, her husband during the forty-minute gathering. Emanuel signed and initialed all paperwork, designating the Wineglasses as joint beneficiaries. And Chadwick established a draft payment from his business bank account, pending approval of Emanuel's medical forms.

As they departed, Emanuel Tucker regaled Ms. Wasilewski with the elocution and discernment of an elderly A.M.E. deacon. Sitting with composure that commanded attention, he looked at her intently as he spoke, holding firmly to his cane that was planted onto the floor. He blinked his eyes with ease but did not look to the left or to the right, to avoid being overcome with dizziness.

"I'm gonna remember your name. Diamond," he said. "That's a thing some people will kill for. Uh huh. It shines just like a morning star. And that's what God called Lucifer. 'O morning star, son of the dawn.' Now, I hear that diamonds get made from all kinds of heat and pressure. More heat and pressure than people can imagine! You ever think about what kinda pressure made you the woman you is now? That's something to think about . . . ."

Diamond glanced with suspicion toward Chadwick. He shrugged his shoulders in response. Florence helped Tucker to rise and exit.

Like sentinel deities, silence and stillness filled the truck with their presence during the return ride to Black Duck Road. Each jockeyed for dominion. Silence prevailed. Chadwick attempted small talk and reached to rest his hand on Florence's left thigh. She did not engage. Rebuffed and with reluctance, his hand retreated to the steering wheel. In unspoken prayer as he rode in the cramped cab section, Tucker slayed the demons that were waging discord between his granddaughter and grandson-in-law.

His prayers continued after their arrival home. The quarreling from the master bedroom crescendoed like the outcome of Joshua at the Battle of Jericho. It sounded as though the walls would come a-tumblin' down! The din relaxed to a quieter rat-a-tat-tat. Florence asked the meaning of his remark about her name during their appointment. He explained, and she roiled. He apologized, but Florence was not yet ready to study war no more. After a while, Chadwick left their bedroom and then their home.

Emanuel remained in prayer like the Apostle Paul, determined to manifest that there was, indeed, a balm at Black Duck Road. Hours later, when Chadwick returned at dusk, silence and stillness no longer reigned. Emanuel could sense that there now was peace, though not like a river. Because he was still experiencing mild episodes of vertigo, he was not fully aware of the veil of darkness that had settled between the couple. For forty days afterward, Florence refused to enter her bedroom once she'd left it in the morning until she absolutely was ready to retire. She intended then to sleep without provocation. To dispel any thoughts to the contrary, for those forty nights she slept on the farthest edge of her side of the bed, on her side, facing outward, with her right leg and foot extended from below the covers—to step to another room if irritated.

Chadwick, in retaliation, began to stay longer at his part-time jobs, and to retire to their bedroom only after he unwound at home following hours in front of the TV, or after taking a prolonged shower.

Although both remained committed to each other, they spoke but did not hear. They loved but did not like. She cooked his meals and cleaned their home. He provided income so bills were paid on time. And with no interlocking connection between the two, a thought began to crouch at the door of Chadwick's reasoning. It took life and became gangrenous. To make Florence understand how they mutually prospered each other, how he appreciated all of her being and not just the meaning of her name but also her insights and independent ways of bringing in income, he had to act decisively to make money work in mysterious ways. For them. For their future.

The plan unraveled in the dark, and no detail, *no* detail, was brought to his wife's attention. Secretly, Chadwick asked Diamond—*O-morning-star-Diamond*, as Emanuel had prophesied—to amend the Universal Life Lifetime coverage with another zero, bringing the payoff to $200,000. For hush-hush recompense that followed a continual pattern with clients, she agreed to foster fraud and deceit for Chadwick. She risked covering her tracks and embodied the very heat and pressure that Emanuel had foretold about her name.

To secretly pay the additional premium, Chadwick, as he'd promised Florence for other circumstances, worked part-time jobs in addition to his self-employment, sacrificing time and energy for what he saw as a greater good. Spurred by the thought of making money work for him, Chadwick allowed his thoughts about new possibilities to morph as if on steroids. He assessed his cash flow and schemed a domino-effect plan that, surprisingly, worked. Contractual agreements for Wineglass French Drain Installation were doing well. His part-time jobs provided additional income. The homeowner of 496 Black Duck Road, a fellow Gardens at River Bend board member, was willing to sign a rent-to-own contract for a monthly mortgage payment that was only two hundred dollars higher than his current one. And he and Florence could maintain their modular home as rental property, raising the rent by two hundred to cover the mortgage at their new home.

Unknown to Florence, however, Chadwick blackmailed his grandfather-in-law to establish a small home equity loan, using his Mausauville property as collateral, so he could properly care for his growing family and Emanuel. In exchange, he promised Emanuel not to divulge to other family members his personal and unrevealed information that Florence had overheard. And he convinced himself to utilize the loan money only as default income if his family found itself in a pinch.

Toting Sheaves to the Plantation Yard

2000s

Following his meeting with Gregory Dunkin at the Georgetown Harborwalk, and his disillusionment about the altar of river rocks he'd constructed, Pastor Thunderbolt meditated on the account of Elijah and Obadiah in 1 Kings, Chapter 18. He repented for allowing self-control to master him and prayed for guidance concerning Eloise Nesbit's prophetic dream. He met with her in person at her home the next day and telephoned Gregory two days after their Harborwalk meeting. He wished to corroborate details Gregory had spoken with projected occurrences from Eloise's dream.

"Hello, Gregory Dunkin speaking. How may I help you?" were the words he heard when the phone ring stopped.

"Gregory, this is Pastor Thunderbolt," he stated. "I trust you're doing well. Is this a good time to talk?"

"Oh, yes, sir!" Gregory replied. "This is a surprise. I didn't expect you to—"

"Well, our meeting took some turns I didn't expect," Thunderbolt interjected. "But God works in mysterious ways . . . mysterious ways. How are things in the plant world?"

Gregory chuckled. "Funny you should ask. I've got some wingstem leaves in my hands as we speak. And I'm prayerful God will use them to help someone find their way."

Seeking to trail away from talk about leaves and plants and seeds, Thunderbolt made a U-turn in the conversation. "If you can recall," he said, "would you please repeat what you said about young folks in the community? What they need and don't need? God has laid it on my mind. And I want to make certain I don't leave out anything to think about."

"Oh, sure, sure," Gregory replied. "Just give me a minute or two to put my mind back there . . . ."

As he waited, Thunderbolt placed a notebook and pen nearby.

"Okay, this is it," Gregory began. "In this community, with all the oppression and violence that took place in Mausaville and Darcatia, there's an abundance of those who need help dealing with their inner ancestral child. They're within church congregations and outside the church walls. They are old, and they are young. And they need to know what it is they're dealing with. And how to overcome it!

"Those who are in this kind of bondage aren't helped by listening to screaming and yelling about what the Bible says for them to do. They need to be able to give voice to what they are experiencing, without condemnation and with assurance that they are being understood. They need to hear how they can apply God's words to their individual selves, in their unique circumstances, and not feel pigeon-holed with others. And above all, they need to feel loved and appreciated. Not castigated but loved. I think that's what I touched on, Pastor. Did I miss anything?"

"No, I think you repeated everything," Thunderbolt said with a smile in his voice. "Thank you very much."

"Oh, and Pastor," Gregory added, "here's another youth condition I've come across. It's not with anyone in your congregation. And it's not like what Barry is dealing with. But it's similar."

"I'm listening," Thunderbolt said, and Gregory continued.

"Well, there's a twelve-year-old girl who mirrors emotions that others are experiencing whenever they are in her presence. They may try to keep it stuffed down within themselves, but she senses it. And she then embodies what the others are dealing with. She picks up *stuff* from grownups, other children, teachers, strangers, parents even. It leaves her anxious, fearful, depressed, and sometimes frightened. Sometimes she faints or complains that her head hurts or she has a bad tummy ache. I think it's because she's been slammed with things, intense things, that she's not been prepared to deal with. Sometimes she just moans in a low, singsong, faraway wail. Maybe an ancestor in her lineage had been a Jalimuso who wasn't allowed during slavery to pass on the stories."

Pastor Thunderbolt paused the conversation with abruptness. "A jolly . . . what? You're losing me on this one, Gregory!"

"I've read that in West Africa, in the Mali Kingdom, Jaliyaa was the craft of storytelling, record-keeping. The Jali was the male storyteller, and the Jalimuso was the female storyteller. The Jalis documented the history of their village and the surrounding region. Births, deaths, marriages, battles, crimes, everything, through songs and stories."

"And what does this 'jolly'—or are you saying, 'jelly'—have to do with this twelve year old?" Pastor Thunderbolt asked.

Gregory paused, then answered. "'Jali,' Pastor. It's pronounced, 'JAH-lee.'"

After Thunderbolt repeated the word with accuracy, Gregory continued.

"Like I started to say. . . and it's just something I've been sitting with. Maybe an ancestor in this child's lineage had been a Jalimuso-in-training who wasn't allowed during slavery to practice her craft, to fulfill what she had been born to do . . . maybe the ups and the downs and the misery and the sickness on the slave ship fatigued her mind. Or the realization that she was now disconnected from the very people whose stories she had been learning, remembering since youth . . . maybe this realization caused her mind to snap. Her people could have been captured and enslaved from a large area of West Africa. From anywhere in modern-day Senegal, Mauritania, Mali, Burkina Faso, Niger, Gambia, Guinea-Bissau, the Ivory Coast, or Ghana.

"Maybe the ancestral spirit who is connecting with her just wants the child to know how to set boundaries around her own thoughts and to keep the thoughts of others in check until the proper time."

"What makes you consider this?" Thunderbolt asked.

"Well, so that she will live and not die and learn to pass on the stories . . . the good, the bad, the humorous, the unsettling ones . . . of her family. Because it's a necessary skill that isn't being passed on. Do you understand what I'm saying?"

Following a few moments of silence, Thunderbolt said, "Well, I must say, I've never heard history or pain or long-suffering expressed in this way. Thanks for sharing this with me. And I pray your day goes well and with God first in your heart, mind, and spirit."

Placing the phone on the hook, he looked at his notes. Arrows he'd sketched connected excerpts from Gregory's quotes to episodes from Eloise's dream.

"Oppression and violence in Darcatia and Mausaville" → *new slave masters at a new auction block.*

"Not helped by screaming and yelling" → *horror of church people to find themselves on the auction block.*

"They need to give voice to what they're experiencing without condemnation" → *felt preachers hadn't listened to anything they said.*

"With assurance of being understood" → *preachers purchased them then hauled them away and cast them in the fiery pit of hell.*

"Those who are in this kind of bondage" → *a buzzard hovering over the youths crowded in the holding stations; youths who were connected in some ways to an ancestral spirit; youths who are trying to connect with their inner ancestral child.*

"Feeling loved, not castigated" → *feeling preachers can't help them find freedom.*

"Need to hear how to apply God's words of life to their individual selves, in their own unique circumstances" → *don't care anymore about what preachers say or do to them when they are marched out to stand on the new auction block.*

Following the review of his notes and with the details that he'd connected ricocheting in his head, Pastor Thunderbolt lay prostrate on his office floor. His forehead, toes, and the palms of his outstretched hands became one with the carpet. He breathed in and out. Otherwise, he did not move. Not until he sensed a supernatural summons to get up. Finally, he rose from the floor and splashed water on his face at his bathroom sink. He patted himself dry with a paper towel, then brushed off, tucked in, and straightened his clothing. He asked Elizabeth to arrange an urgent 7:00 p.m. meeting for the following day with his church officers, staff, and prayer warriors, but to provide them with no details. He directed her to prompt them to be prayerful for God's guidance in an important matter.

Pastor and Mrs. Thunderbolt walked side by side into the sanctuary on the meeting date and awaited the arrival of the others. Each felt assured that meaningful changes would result from the meeting. Each underestimated the ferocity with which many cleave to their beliefs and shield themselves from adjustments or adaptations.

When all assembled, eighty-something Clarence B. Funnye, chairman of the deacon board, opened with prayer and lifted a song, which all joined to sing.

"I'm workin on de buildin
I'm workin on de buildin
I'm workin on de buildin
I'm workin fa my Lawd
Soon as I get finish wit workin on dis buildin
Goin home to Jesus and get my reward"

The polyrhythmic 1-2-3 Sea Island syncopation enveloped the room. Men beat 1-2, as women beat 1-2-3. Hands clapped. Feet pounded. Bodies swayed. Some stood. Some remained seated. All relinquished their fatigue from the day, their tensions about the meeting's purpose, the troubles of the world. Until, that is, some chose to pick them right up again after the song and carry them as swords and shields.

"Thank you, thank you, Deacon Funnye, for the inspiring prayer and song!" Pastor Thunderbolt said after standing and moving to the front of the first pew. "And thank you all for coming out on such short notice."

Church members nodded their heads, smiled, looked at him and then around to others, and waited to hear what he had to say.

"These are troubling times, but God is our rock!" he called.

"Yes, He is!" one member responded.

"Every minute, every hour!" another chimed in

"I've been wrestling with thoughts and concerns about our youth," the pastor continued. "And our adults. How to be supportive. How to be prepared to assist them . . . ."

"My, my, my, my!" an older woman voiced, as she lowered her head and raised and waved her right hand in the air.

"Now, this is not a formal business meeting. But I've called you together to express my thoughts to you, the leaders in this congregation. To listen to each other's thoughts. To consider how God wants us to move forward."

All eyes remained on him.

"First, our youth. I learned recently that Mother Eloise brought a troubling dream that she'd had to the attention of her prayer group. I've since spoken to her about it, and it seems as though it's a message from the Almighty."

Eyes turned to Mother Eloise who closed her own and bowed her head, then rocked her head gently up and down, up and down.

"And I heard a similar message from Brother Gregory Dunkin when we met about another matter."

Tension shifted the atmosphere in the room as soon as the name left the pastor's lips. It made him and Sibyl feel as though the first lines of verses to Ludie Pickett's hymn "Never Alone" became reality. "I've seen the lightning flashing and heard the thunder roll" was one line, and "The world's fierce winds are blowing" was another. The husband's and wife's supportive glances to each other steeled them both to trust in the meaning of the song's refrain:

"He promised never to leave me, never to leave me alone."

Among the gathered, murmuring began to buzz and facial expressions of understanding shape-shifted to scorn and revulsion.

"Pastor, I know you're not telling us to pay attention to the words of a—a root doctor!" a thirty-something year-old deacon opined. His eyes flashed in horror as he looked around to see the reactions of others.

"Told ya!" A woman two rows behind the deacon responded in a loud whisper. "Didn't I tell you that I heard that the two of them was struttin' around the Harborwalk like they thought they was Paul and Silas?" She folded her arms and looked at Pastor Thunderbolt with frowning lips.

Alarmed at how quickly the meeting had derailed, Pastor Thunderbolt began to respond to the first inquiry but turned left then right as individuals began to comment over each other.

"Orda! Orda!" Deacon Funnye bellowed, standing and then walking to the pastor's side. "Now, dis ain no business meeting. But we in de house ob de Lawd. And we listenin to a man of Gawd. We own man ob Gawd." He paused and eyed the audience, connecting with each and every one. "And, by Gawd, while we in dis place, we gonna show dis man ob Gawd . . . and each odda . . . wa?"

"Respect!" members began to respond quietly and slowly. Ruffled feathers began to lower, and a sweet, sweet spirit began again to pervade.

"Now, Pastah, if you so please, I'm stayin right yah by yo side," Funnye said as the two men locked eyes. "Dis ain no bizness meetin. But oona hab sompn fa say, sompn fa tell we. Sameso, seem like de membas have sompn fa say." He looked again at the congregation with eyes that mirrored a pillar of fire by night. "An orda ga rule!"

Thunderbolt nodded and looked to Sibyl, whose eyes said, "God's got this!"

Funnye pointed to an elderly man whose hand had remained raised. "Pastah, I ain know bout de son, but A been yeh tings bout de fada," he said about the Dunkins. "You a comeyah, an deh some tings oona might not know. A bleib een Gawd an A dohn bleib een no hoodoo. But peepul been say dat William Dunkin been make a spida crawl out a man belly button wa been cheat on e wife. An e been make a ooman git daid up wit cansa een one night afta e walk oba a sompn Dunkin gib a neighba wa been tel de worl de ooman been steal e money. Say ef ya drink e brew, e can make ya pee blood. Pontop e dah, A done been yeh plenty tings bout how Dunkin been leh some oomans pay fa de service e gii em wit...now, deh ain no betta way fa say em . . . wit . . . wit dey bohdy. Umf, umf, umf! All dah soun like ebil ta me. An we ain need no ebil een de chuch!"

Funnye looked to Thunderbolt to respond. Standing, the pastor first rocked his torso back and forth and opened and closed his eyes as he speedily translated the older man's words. *Pastor, I don't know about the son, but I've heard things about the father,* he'd said about the Dunkins. *You're a comeyah, and there may be so things you don't know. I believe in God, and I don't believe in hoodoo. But people have said that William Dunkin made a spider crawl out of a man's belly button who had cheated on his wife. And he made a woman get filled with cancer in one night after she'd walked over something Dunkin had given to a neighbor who had told the world that the woman had stolen his money. They say if you drink his brew, it can make you pee blood. On top of that, I've heard plenty things about how Dunkin let some women pay for the service he offered them . . . now, there's no other way to say . . . with their bodies. Umf, umf, umf! All that sounds like evil to me. And we don't need evil in the church.*

"Thank you for your courage to bring this concern to my attention," Thunderbolt stated.

"I, too, don't want to align with forces of evil, and I want to keep them far away from individuals in this church and outside the walls of this church," Thunderbolt said. He paused and inhaled, then continued. "I confess that I, too, had reservations about Gregory Dunkin based on my understanding of local lore and on the word of God. But to my surprise and by God's leading, I've changed my view of him as being a brother in Christ, a little different than what might be expected by others, but as a brother in Christ."

Low-volume responses of "Hmpf!" and "I don't know bout that!" and "The devil is a liar!" was a cacophony throughout the room until Funnye stated, "Orda! Qrda!" with quiet solemnity. He nodded to a woman, a business executive who was dressed in a tan pantsuit.

"Pastor," she said, "I trust that the Lord has given you vision and discernment. I, for one, would like to hear what you've brought us here to hear."

As she sat, a forty-something year-old stood, and without being recognized by Deacon Funnye blurted, "Mm-hmm. Some of these stories about the work of . . . Dr. Buzzard . . . have affected people in my own family. I trust you, too, Pastor, but remember, what's in somebody's bloodline doesn't wash out right away. It lingers."

Funnye moved toward the man with a stern expression on his face and outstretched palms that he flexed up and down, once, twice, three times. The speaker recognized the translation of Funnye's movements on the third down stroke, "Sit. Down. Now!" The head deacon nodded to Pastor Thunderbolt to speak among the members without fear of interruption. Each realized that at another outburst, the head deacon would usher the offending individual out.

Pastor Thunderbolt looked at his members and stroked his chin with his left-hand pointer and thumb. "Thank you for your honesty, for your openness," he said after dropping his hand to his side. "Let me address the last comment I heard before I move on." He smiled, shepherd-like, as he looked at the man dressed in a plaid shirt and blue jeans who sat near where Funnye stood. "I disagree with the sentiment that was spoken. Let us remember,

'Who the Son has freed is freed, indeed.' And 'If we confess our sins, he is faithful and just and will forgive us our sins and purify us from all unrighteousness.' And most importantly, 'You will know them by their fruits.'

"I had my doubts that God would reveal any fruit in Brother Dunkin, but God has. The Gilliards are not with us this evening, but some of you may be aware of their interaction with Brother Dunkin. Well, I have checked him out, and God has assured me that concerning any deep, dark, devilish connections with stories, true or false, about his father, I need not find fault in him."

Turning to all, he added, "And besides, some of us may have had grandmothers who were street walkers. Or great-grandfathers who were murderers. A generational curse does not have to linger. No, God. can. blot. it. out! If we let him, if we trust him, he. can. do. it!"

Having corralled their thoughts, Pastor Thunderbolt shared Mother Eloise's dream and the confirmation about it that he received from Gregory Dunkin's remarks.

"I believe that we—myself included—are making our youth feel hauled away to hell and disregarded because what they constantly hear from church leaders are messages that their differences don't make them fit for heaven. And this, in turn, makes them feel damned here on Earth.

"But our God is the Alpha, the I Am, and the Omega. And I'm sensing that we need to seek avenues to let our youth, our adults, and our seniors know that they don't have to *only* long to be in heaven. Because our God, our great God, can and will impact our presence and can unburden us from painful ties in our past."

Suddenly, the sound like the blowing of a violent wind filled the sanctuary where they were sitting, and members began to speak as the Spirit enabled them.

"Our youth are struggling with so much!" the plaid-shirted man said. "Drugs, depression, gender confusion, suicide, peer pressure, just to name a few."

The business executive in the tan pantsuit stated, "We don't have to sacrifice our individuality, which includes our afflictions, our bents, and our faults, to make us neglect knowing God."

Sibyl voiced, "We must learn to say, 'I will trust in the Lord with all of my heart'—even with thoughts of suicide, or gender confusion, or loneliness, depression, fear, or whatever . . . ."

The thirty-something year-old deacon, as if on cue, continued the scripture verse, "I will lean not on my own understanding; in all my ways . . . all—my—ways . . . I will acknowledge him."

And Mother Eloise concluded, "And he will direct my paths."

The woman who had scorned in a loud whisper about Pastor Thunderbolt being seen with Gregory Dunkin stated, "These concerns that our youth have, and the ones that our senior members have about living on fixed incomes, or living in homes that are deteriorating and falling down, or struggling to pay for high-costing medicines are like the Philistine giants that roamed the land."

Throughout the meeting, the church's ninety-four-year-old deacon emeritus sat silently. Deacon Funny walked to him, stooped, and spoke into his left ear. "Deacon Five Gratefuls, wa you haffa say? Wa de Lawd done tell ya?"

The wiry, dark-skinned elder turned his head to Funnye and looked at him through large thick-framed bifocals as his right hand trembled on his thigh. Ephesian Singleton had been called "Five Gratefuls" since his first year as chairman of the deacon board at age sixty. Because the office title marked him as the first church official to hear any—and sometimes every—negative accusation or rumor or account, he'd begun greeting those who wanted to divulge anything to him with, "Tell me fibe tings ya grateful fa!" His words would remove the sting and vitriol from whatever the accuser may have wanted to say and consequently, from what he was about to hear.

"Well, when Dabid gone fa kill Goliat," Singleton said, "de bigges ting him been fin out been dis: deh mo den one way fa kill a giant. Enty dah so?"

Well, when David went to kill Goliath, the biggest thing he learned was there's more than one way to kill a giant. Isn't that so? Thoughts about Deacon Singleton's grateful vision and the utterances by his members about dreams impacted Pastor Thunderbolt with a plan of action. Connecting the dots, he announced the proposal of a new church program, G.I.A.N.T.

"We will listen to our youths and adults and seniors," he said. "We will let them know that we hear them. We will help them to work on 'de buildin' just as we sang in our opening song tonight.

We will encourage all to realize that they don't have to 'go home to Jesus to get their only reward.' No, God has a reward for them not only in their future but also right now in the present. We will show love, God's love, to everyone, regardless of their conditions or hardships or faults. Because love embraces and offers more than criticism of wrongdoing, or instructions about avoiding it. We can shepherd, encourage, and guide, but we are not the masters of anyone's fate!"

The business executive, Belinda Manigault, raised her hand and commented, "Pastor Thunderbolt, I like the vision of this program, but I'm hopeful it won't be mostly for show like some church groups and denominations have demonstrated throughout history."

Pastor Thunderbolt cocked his head and asked, "Would you please explain?" Some members looked perplexed, while others who relied on the loudest voice of the moment to steer their thinking murmured, "Uh huh. That's right."

"Well, since the recent discovery of disturbed bones of former slaves on Hagley Plantation at what had been the cemetery at St. Mary's Chapel, I've been doing a lot of reading and researching. That building, built by former slave Renty Tucker, was so grand, so elegant . . . and it was built for enslaved people!"

"Enty Gawd good?" Mother Eloise shouted.

"Yes, God is," Belinda Manigault responded. "But people's motives must sometimes be questioned. "You see, planter Plowden C.J. Weston, an Episcopalian, had Tucker trained as a master carpenter in England and had him design and construct that magnificent place of worship that the Weston family financed."

"I'm not sure I understand where you're going," Pastor Thunderbolt interjected.

Manigault nodded and raised her right pointer to alert that it would all make sense in a moment. "Well, was this grand structure—that was built for slaves, now—was it built so that these rice plantation workers who were brought to this country to work against their will—"

"An rice plantation wok sho ain been easy. No, no, no!" the younger deacon muttered.

Manigault, unflustered, added, "Was this building just a distraction for them? So they could get dressed up one day out of the week and think about God and about going to heaven one day and not think about the plantation owner giants all around them? To not think about the people who didn't think they were worthy of being free? People who thought that they were human, but only enough to worship a God who would make them forget about the troubles of the world?"

"Ya cookin wit gas, now, sista!" someone exclaimed.

Manigault continued. "And other denominations did similar things during that same time period. Just so they could pat themselves on the back because of their missionary zeal."

The formerly scowling member said with a grunt, "Yeah, so they could say they treated *their* darkies better than others did!"

"That's right," Manigault affirmed with a point in the speaker's direction that declared, "I hear you!" Pastor Thunderbolt looked from face to face, and Manigault resumed her explanation. "A Methodist church elsewhere in the South had slaves to build a big fine church around the same time as St. Mary's Chapel. But the slaves had to sit in the basement, while the slave owners worshiped on ground level. And Baptist churches allowed slaves to attend, but they had to sit in the balconies. Behind railings so high they could not be seen by anyone below.

"I just hope that our church's 'G.I.A.N.T.' program *won't* just be about show and *won't* just be about distraction."

Thunderbolt walked to Bessie Manigault and laid hands on her left shoulder. "Thank you, sister," he said. "Thank you for those words about things we should be most mindful of!" He closed his eyes briefly then returned to the front of the sanctuary and raised both hands. "May God help us to remember that G.I.A.N.T. means God Is a Now-day Testimony. And every day that we have breath, we will praise the Lord. Because trusting in God shifts the burden from fearing that we won't make it to heaven or aren't worthy of heaven—and even from defending that we may not be interested in heaven. It allows God to guide us moment by moment to where He wants us to be." Paraphrasing Psalm 27:13, he concluded, "To be confident that we will see the Lord's goodness while we are here in the land of the living."

He thanked the group for attending the meeting and informed them that he would provide more details about the program soon. Deacon Funnye closed the meeting in prayer.

"Because you did what God told you to do, Tee, more blessings are coming," Sibyl told him when they arrived home. "You'll see." She nodded in affirmation and repeated her words. "You'll see."

Lying in bed, they chuckled as they recalled the evening meeting's rocky start, and embraced as they recounted the atmosphere's transition from stormy to spirit-filled. They melded their bodies together as one, filled with expectancy about what tomorrow would bring.

The "brrrringgg" of the phone on Pastor Thunderbolt's nightstand awakened them before the sunlight did. The news he received scattered away any remaining slumber he may have thought he had ahead, and after he hung up, his nudges on Sibyl's shoulder caused the same result for her. Struggling to believe what he'd just heard, Timothy sat up, rested his back on the headrest, and waited for her to join him. "Sibyl," he called in a stirring tone.

"What's going on, Tee?" she asked, covering a yawn with her right hand. "Is everything all right?"

"It is. It is, indeed! God's blessings are coming, just like you said . . . ."

She raised her eyebrows and waited.

"That was Deacon Five Gratefuls's youngest daughter, his caretaker. She said her father woke her up and wanted her to call me right then because God had laid it on his heart all through the night."

"What, Tee? What did she say?" Sibyl edged closer to her husband and watched every detail of his facial expressions.

"She said her father wants to donate five acres of undeveloped family property in Darcatia Plantation to Low Bottom Community Church, to develop low-income senior housing for the members. She said he has five more acres of adjoining property. But before that can be given to the church, his family will have to approve the progress of the project on the initial five-acre site."

Deacon Five Gratefuls's family had amassed thirty acres of Darcatia timberland over the years. His great-grandfather had been given fifteen acres by owner Andrew S. Singleton following the Emancipation Proclamation, and family members had teamed monies together to purchase more acreage as they were able.

"Come, Sibyl, let's get down on our knees in thanks right now. When I proposed this idea to the pastor search community, I . . . I had—"

"—no idea how or if any of my ideas could come about," she finished her husband's sentence. "But—"

"—look what God can do!" he said as he grabbed her hand, gently pulling her from under the covers and to the side of their bed where they knelt together in prayer.

Threshing and Milling

Flailing the Sheaves

2000s

The memory of meeting someone at a gas station and talking about the possibility of connecting with investors flooded Pastor Thunderbolt's mind as he drove to the church office. He searched his desk drawer upon arrival and smiled when he found Chadwick Wineglass's business card.

"What can you tell me about Chadwick Wineglass?" he called out to Elizabeth. "Is he someone you know?"

She walked to his office door. "Who doesn't know Chadwick Wineglass?" was her reply. "Some call him the 'Mayor of Georgetown,' the 'Black Mayor,' that is. Because he helps those who are in need. He's a member of Walking Up the King's Highway, an interdenominational church. He's a beenyah, from an upstanding Georgetown family. His wedding to my cousin Florence Tucker was the talk of the town. He started his own business, but from what I hear, he also has several part-time jobs. Trying to make ends meet, I guess. Anything else?"

Thunderbolt thanked her, and she returned to her desk. He made a mental checklist about Chadwick's character from her words. Christian-minded. Check. Businessman. Check. Good community standing. Check. Helpful. Check. Although all Wineglass's attributes seemed positive in his estimation, Thunderbolt remembered the error of his ways when he'd last scheduled a meeting with a community member. He decided he should pray first before arranging a get-together with Chadwick Wineglass. His phone buzzed as soon as he reached that conclusion, however.

Speak of the devil, Elizabeth thought, with humor, when she answered. She then relayed to her boss, "Pastor, you have a call from . . . Mr. Chadwick Wineglass."

"Please put him through," Thunderbolt responded. When connected, he said, "Mr. Wineglass, what a surprise that you should call. You were just on my mind."

"That so, Pastor Thunderbolt?" Chadwick said. "Well, this must be your lucky day! I hope you're doing well."

"Yes, I am. And how are you?"

"I'm doin," Chadwick replied with brightness. "I'll be heading to a work site in the Big Dam community early this afternoon. Would you like to grab lunch? Right now, I'm in Garden City."

"Why, yes. Why don't you call when you're a half-hour out, and my secretary will inform you where to meet. Does that sound okay?"

"Yes, it does. And that is what I'll do. See you soon."

"See you soon." This time, after hanging up, Pastor Thunderbolt did not forget to pray.

Chadwick looked forward to meeting with Timothy Thunderbolt but felt conflicted throughout his morning. On his drive from home to Garden City, he'd noticed Florence's lipstick imprint peeking at him on a piece of paper she'd tucked partially in the driver's sun visor. He pulled out the love-note Marcus Garvey quote. Smiling and bobbing his head, he read it as he drove.

"'The ends you serve that are selfish will take you no further than yourself but the ends you serve that are for all, in common, will take you into eternity.' Think B.I.G., my aqueduct-inspired hubby! - Florence"

Knowing that he'd need to respond soon to Otis Doyle about the investment opportunity, Chadwick performed mental gymnastics as he measured and fitted pavement for a drain installation. He wanted whatever project he supported to offer undeniable community benefits and began to hear two distinct voices of opposing thoughts, each clamoring in either ear for his attention.

If Gullah waiters spoke better, White tourists would tip them more, he heard in one ear, and *Jamaicans speak the way they do because that's their accent* in the other.

Lowcountry people are not punctual; they most always show up late and spend their hard-earned money on foolishness—and—*Jamaicans want a good job, will work for less pay, and will send their dollars home to support their families.*

Some Gullah people are just downright lazy—and—*Do you remember seeing even one lazy Jamaican down at the Market?*

As he hauled limestone, shells, chalk, other ingredients, a cement maker, and a metal grate from the truck's cabin, Chadwick battled the two inaudible voices while he worked, and the mental battle continued during his hour-long drive in the light rain, despite his efforts to silence them. He hoped the lunch meeting in Big Dam would help to resolve the dilemma of his "love-note quote vs. displacing others and being cutthroat."

The answer to Timothy Thunderbolt's prayer did not come through a small voice. It came through thoughtful, loving advice from his wife. He had telephoned her to recapture memories of the surprising outcomes from last night's meeting. When he casually mentioned Chadwick's morning call and asked for suggestions about where they should meet, she'd paused to think.

Mindful of her morning reading about English poet, literary critic, and theologian Samuel Taylor Coleridge, Sybil responded with a quote. "'Friendship is a sheltering tree,' Tee," she said. "This is a meeting about a potential church business project, not a meeting with a friend or even an acquaintance. So, meet at the church. Order take-out and have it dropped off or ask Elizabeth to pick it up. You don't yet know what kind of tree this Chadwick Wineglass is. Or what kind of shelter he can provide."

Following her advice, Wineglass and Thunderbolt lunched on pepperoni pizza, bread sticks, and soda in the church fellowship hall.

"I have a vision for a twenty- to thirty-unit, low-income, senior citizen apartment complex," Thunderbolt said, after resting his plastic cup of Coke on the table. "There are seniors in the church and in the community who are on fixed incomes, and their homes are falling down. I think the church should be able to assist them." He picked up another pizza slice.

Wineglass swallowed then responded. "That's a good-sized complex," he said. "Now, I parked in your gravel lot, and it's quite sloshy from just the light rain from a little while ago. Are you considering having the construction site somewhere near the church? Remember, now, this community is near a swamp. The septic tanks and plumbing concerns could be a nightmare!"

"Well, the project is just in the early stages," Thunderbolt said. He wiped his mouth with a tan paper napkin and continued. "I'm confident the deacons support it, but the matter has yet to be brought to the full church body, and then plans will have to be developed. But that's a good point you just raised. We've . . . not yet considered where the construction site could be located."

As he recalled his morning conversation with Deacon Five Gratefuls's daughter and wondered if he should share such vital information with a virtual stranger, Thunderbolt's head jerked, his eyes widened, and his movements froze.

"Pastor Thunderbolt, is everything all right?" Wineglass asked in panic. He moved his right hand back and forth in front of Thunderbolt's face and looked around to see if anyone else was nearby. "Pastor . . . Pastor Thunder!"

"Oh, yes, yes, I'm fine. I'm fine!" Thunderbolt said as he collected his thoughts and fluidity returned to his body. "I just remembered something, that's all."

Wineglass continued watching him with a guarded stare, still wondering if he should alert anyone.

"Well, there's a possibility . . ." Thunderbolt began. "I guess I can say 'a most certain possibility' of the church acquiring a tract of land for the project in Darcatia. And perhaps of acquiring more adjacent property, depending on the success of the first project."

"Well, the land is certainly higher in Darcatia than it is here," Wineglass said, glad to observe that Thunderbolt's movements and speech had returned to normal.

Thunderbolt smiled and determined it was time to bring the meeting to an end. He wondered if he had said too much but was confident that he had remained appropriately vague.

He did not yet know, however, that only intentional information should be expressed in a Lowcountry community. Vague ideas become elaborated on and expressed as authentic comments. Detailed ideas are shared nearby and beyond. Whatever the speaker may regard as private becomes public in no time at all!

Wineglass heard the words "tract of land for the project in Darcatia" and "a most certain possibility" and "acquiring more adjacent property" and was exceedingly, abundantly pleased that he had met with Pastor Thunderbolt. He met again with Otis Doyle at Calabash by the Sea a few days later.

Waiting for their table, Gregory Dunkin sensed a strange energy about Wineglass, as though he was deliberately posturing and ingratiating himself to Doyle and Calabash owner, Laurin Donald "L.D." Carpenter, who had joined them. An empty table set-up awaited a fourth diner.

As he walked to another table after serving their appetizers, Gregory overheard Doyle speak about him in a low voice. "Now our young waiter is one of the good ones, right?" Doyle asked. Gregory tried to hear more, but guests at the nearby table of six had many questions and the lunchtime crowd was growing.

"He takes your order but never hangs around the table," Doyle continued. "His nice white teeth look like piano keys against that dark skin. Maybe he should work on his Gullah, though. His English is a bit too proper. Tourists want the full Lowcountry experience, you know. And our friends from the small country across the water can well deliver on that. Their 'th's are pronounced as "d's" without a thought for correcting themselves. Sometimes their words that start with 'th's just drop the 'h's. Tourists will eat that up!"

Carpenter, a short White man with the keen eyes of a commercial fisherman, nodded to Doyle's comments but scanned the room with vigilance. As if to notice any disturbance on the horizon as though it was a school of fish or a flock of seagulls. "Dunkin is one of my best workers," he said. "He'd make a good manager if this plan comes about."

"Oh, it will. It will," Doyle said.

Gregory returned to the table as quickly as possible. To not only freshen their drinks and alert them that the meal would be ready soon, but more importantly to get a read on Chadwick Wineglass. "Is there anything else I can get for you, gentlemen? Mr. Doyle?"

"And how about you, Mr. Wineglass?" he continued. "How is the Mrs. doing? Please let her know I asked about her."

Chadwick's response seemed a bit stiff handed. "I most certainly will," he said. "And we are so looking forward to this meal. The sooner it comes, the better we'll feel!" His eyes never connected with Gregory's. His attention stayed focused on his tablemates.

"So, are you in the game with us, Chadwick?" Doyle asked when their plates arrived. Gregory tried to stall his delivery. To be seen but not heard. To learn more about this plan that was being plotted. But Chadwick seemed intent on not speaking in his presence. He sipped lemonade. He patted his lips with his white paper napkin. He lifted his right pointer finger and swallowed to alert the others that he would respond momentarily. He then looked directly at Gregory's face with a dismissive expression, a terse smile, a frozen stare, a tilt of the head that did not flinch, which stated, "You may leave now."

"How many other potential investors are there?" Chadwick asked after Gregory walked away.

"Well, in addition to me, there's Carpenter here," Doyle answered. "There's a silent partner, who doesn't want to be identified. There are two more who, like you, are slow in responding, and there's banker Bob Brittman, who I'd hoped we could pitch the idea to today. I don't know what's happened to him . . . ." He looked at the empty chair, then continued. "I find a group of ten partners too large to deal with, personally. Seven should be just right. Not too large, not too small. So, what do you say, Wineglass? Are you ready to do this?"

"If you're in, the other two who are floundering may jump in the boat with us," Carpenter chimed in.

Chadwick tapped his fingers on the table, then asked, "And where will this first wave of Jamaicans reside? How soon are you looking to kick things off? What's the rush? Can plans hold off awhile? Can monies be invested and allowed to grow until details are more fleshed out?"

Doyle listened with a paternalistic look of concern in his eyes. He then commented with a low-pitched, teacherly tone to his voice. "The plan has always been to have interested parties to invest . . . with a $2,500 buy in, as you've been asked to do, to make monthly five-hundred-dollar installments for the first year in order to let our investment grow, and to use a mere portion of the investment to get the plan rolling. We'll use the interest from our investment to roll out the relocation, travel, and lodging of fifteen to twenty Jamaican laborers during the first wave. Now, we've discussed this in detail before, Chadwick. If you just want to stay in the little leagues, we will understand." Doyle looked to Carpenter and patted his hand on the table next to Carpenter's place setting. "But it's those in the major leagues that will haul in the cash."

Pausing to allow his intimidation to sink in, Doyle smacked on a large bite of the fried chicken drumstick he'd lifted to his lips with both hands. When assured that his timing had modeled nonchalance and fortitude, he continued. "Out-of-season airfare from Jamaica to Myrtle Beach? Minimal. Or there are friends with private planes who make weekend jaunts there and can stow away one or two of them on their return. Lodging? Nominal. Three to five can huddle together in a Motel 6 room until other accommodations are found. They should feel right at home. It will be better than their crowded bungalow living in the hill country.

"Look, there's money to be made," Doyle concluded. "And the ones to make it will invest. And soon."

He picked up his glass of iced tea and swigged down a mouthful, looking at the few uneaten items left on his plate while keeping a peripheral, raptor-like watch on Chadwick. Carpenter looked around the room and smiled at repeat customers whose eyes he met.

Chadwick leaned forward and spoke softly, as though divulging classified information. "A Georgetown church will be building a low-income apartment complex soon," he said. "If investors can help them get started, maybe this complex could be a place, down the road, where some of the workers could be housed. And if the initial complex goes smoothly, there's adjacent property where more units can be added." He sat back and looked from face to face.

Unseen by Chadwick, at the mention of church property to be used for low-income housing and of potential usage of adjacent property, Doyle and Carpenter each began to have thoughts of hovering over potential prey. Plucking at their eyes, their organs. Ruffling their own feathers after devouring them. And, with their hunger satiated by filling their coffers, flying away. Far away.

On Chadwick's drive home, the battle of the two inaudible voices with opposing thoughts resumed. The one encouraging him to be more cutthroat in his decisions about the Jamaican investment loomed louder, snarkier. Its numerous sentiments became as prolific as the large, annoying black cluster flies that had gathered indoors on their living room windows at 496 Black Duck Road this warm fall day.

The frightful sight of flies, ominous to Florence, had caused her to alert her husband to return home early. *Where were they coming from?* she had wondered, as follow-up questions abounded. *Why were they flying as if in a stupor, landing on the windows, and peering outside? What darkness, what death were they foreshadowing or waiting to infest?*

She'd swatted, squashed, and smashed a few dozen before Chadwick's arrival, but more would soon appear. This perfect home that her husband had convinced her they needed, this life of largesse that they were leading, without fully acknowledging anyone's humanity, with encouraging strangers to depend on them and then detaching themselves when they did—was not so perfect after all, she thought. And the evidence was the carcasses of dead flies on their windows for all to see who looked upon the two of them as faultless!

The White next-door neighbor, a retiree, had been raking the oak leaves in his front yard when Chadwick parked in his own driveway. Surprised to see him home at such an early hour and alarmed about his quick dash from the parked vehicle, the neighbor asked if all was well as Chadwick raced to the door. After pausing to explain the reason for his wife's alarm, Chadwick listened to the man's neighborly advice.

"Large black flies on the window?" he'd asked. "That's nothing to be too worried about. We get them each year. They're cluster flies."

"Cluster flies?" Chadwick had replied.

"Yeah, that's what they do. They cluster." The man held the stationary rake upright in his left hand with the blades planted on the ground. "They develop inside earthworms living in your gardens in late summer. When they hatch, they fly into homes through any small opening and hibernate in attics, walls, or garages for the winter and lay their eggs. But on warm fall or winter days like today, they call their friends, who then gather and cluster on windows searching for sunlight in hopes of spreading their wings. Just call pest control. They'll take care of the problem."

"Thank you!" Chadwick said, "Thank you for this information. My wife was so worried! By the way, I'm Chadwick, Chadwick Wineglass. We moved in about three months ago." He extended his hand.

"Yes, I know. Welcome to the neighborhood, Chadwick. I'm Jeffrey, Jeffrey Newbern." They shook hands, and Chadwick turned to walk to the front door, purposely having not parked in the garage. He could not have imagined the dread he felt when he saw the large compound eyes of about fifty black flies looking back at him through the picture window, each eye an eerie mosaic of individual visual receptors.

Once inside, Chadwick and Florence engaged in combat and aptly expressed their actions to the tune of the old spiritual, "Goin' Shout All Over God's Heaven."

"I killed a fly
You killed a fly
Every Wineglass has killed a fly
An when a fly dies, we kill another fly
And we'll smash em til we see no flies, no flies
Flies on our window is a sight we can't handle
So, we'll smash em, smash em
And we'll smash em til we see no flies"

The exhilaration of their fly execution fostered a spirit of joy, accomplishment, and laughter among the couple. With his guard down, Chadwick began to speak about matters he usually would hold close to his chest.

"Now, that one was just moving on the windowsill real slow, real lazy-like!" Chadwick boasted after annihilating another cluster fly with a folded magazine. It left a spatter on the white wood, which he promptly cleaned with a paper towel.

"You go, man!" Florence cheered from the other living room window. "Watch me, now!" *Whap*! After making the kill, she threw her clenched fists in the air and bobbed her head from side to side. The decimated fly carcasses lay in a pile on the hardwood floor.

"Now, Otis Doyle thinks there are some Lowcountry Blacks who are lazy just like that slow scoundrel I just sent to fly heaven," Chadwick said with a titter. "He said—"

Florence looked at her husband in confoundment. "What? And just who is this Otis Doyle anyway?"

Chadwick realized that he had been too forthcoming. He turned to the window to hunt for flies that he knew had not landed, and also had not been seen heading toward the sunlight. He posed as though he were about to expunge one. "Oh, he's just an investor who's been talking about some project ideas," Chadwick said as a throwaway.

Florence, however, was not deterred. "That's a familiar name . . ." she said. "Is he the same Doyle who gave us the honeymoon cruise to Jamaica? No, this must be a family member."

"Yeah, he's the same one," Chadwick answered in a quiet voice.

"Well, he's not the kind of person you need to listen to, Chadwick. What new kinds of racist things has he been muddying your mind with?"

Never looking at her, Chadwick scanned the window, searching for nonexistent flies.

She hissed and then said, "No right-minded Black person would compare another Black person to some stinky black fly!" She began pointing her right index finger at her husband. "Doyle's statement was as godawful as that old buckra saying. You know, 'Niggers and flies. These two I despise. But the more I see of niggers, the more I like flies.' Umpf! Umpf! Umpf! Stay away from that one, Chadwick. When he comes your way, turn around and flee!" Her finger and hand gestured the suggested about-face movement. "And don't listen to nothing this one has to say! You hear me?"

Chadwick spoke no more about investments or Otis Doyle. He left around 6:00 p.m. for his evening part-time cleaning job.

A week to the day following their lunch meeting at Low Bottom Community Church of Big Dam, Chadwick telephoned Pastor

Thunderbolt. He knew the unlikelihood of the church project having advanced in any small degree in just seven days, but he wanted to pitch an idea—despite Florence's admonition to not involve himself with any ploy of Otis Doyle. And even though he had not developed any concrete plan or commitment with the proposed group of seven investors, he reasoned he was living large. After all, he was using business savvy. He soon would be making money work in mysterious ways.

"Pastor Thunderbolt," he said in his most professional business voice after Elizabeth had forwarded his call, "I'm just doubling back with you about our conversation last week. I hope all is well with you today."

"Good morning, Mr. Wineglass," Thunderbolt responded. "Yes, I am. Yourself?" Receiving an affirmative reply, he added with pastoral pomp, "'The Lord is in His holy temple. Let all the earth keep silent before him.'"

Keeping silent, however, was not Chadwick's preferred action. Not this day.

"The investors I've been speaking with may be able to expedite your construction plans," he stated matter-of-factly. "If they're able to partner with construction on Phase B, that is on the potential adjacent Darcatia tract, they may be able to assist you in securing loans for the church's low-income apartment complex in Phase A." He paused for effect. "Now, if you like, I'll be happy to arrange a meeting for you and your board to discuss the matter."

Had he seen Thunderbolt remove the phone receiver from his ear, hold it in his right hand, and stare at it in utter disbelief, Wineglass probably would've been prepared for the response he received. But he was not.

Changing the phone to his left ear, Pastor Thunderbolt rebuffed the offer. "It concerns me that you seem to have taken such a personal interest in this matter," he said. "I'm uncertain what has given you the impression that it is needed." With his right hand, he tapped the tip of his ballpoint pen on a notepad atop his desk. "Please forgive me if I am somehow to blame. This project, however, is in God's hands, and we have not yet received orders to bring anything about it to public notice. So, unless there's another concern that you wish to talk about, I believe this conversation has come to the end of its road." Thunderbolt did not wait long for a response before concluding, "Good day!" and hanging up.

Thunderbolt looked at the notes he'd jotted on the pad during the conversation. "A comes before B. B follows A. Does he think he's God? Well, he is not!" He ripped the paper in two and tossed the halves into the trash can.

As readily as Pastor Thunderbolt had extricated himself from Chadwick's conversation about the church project, Florence could not so easily detangle herself from Chadwick's conversation about Doyle's snub and snobbishness. She was revulsed at the thought of her husband having anything to do with such an individual, even one who had shown them a kindness, and she was determined to drill this awareness into his consciousness. Her breakfast, dinner time, and nighttime conversations for the next week were filled with examples of the work ethic, tenacity, and determination of Black Georgetonians.

"Don't forget that the majority of downtown businesses from Front Street to Prince Street used to be Black-owned or Black-run," Florence reminded Chadwick one morning. She spoke as she served him a plateful of pancakes, bacon, and eggs and stood with her left hand on the back of his chair as she continued. "Blacksmiths, cobblers, butchers, barbers, mom-and-pop grocers, all were workers who got up each morning and labored to feed their families and enjoy life."

She reminded him that Black business ownership commenced during Reconstruction and continued throughout the 1970s. That the community for a long time had been said by some to have looked like Little Africa after freedom was proclaimed and rice production was dethroned.

W.D. Morgan, a banker and Georgetown's first Mayor, opened the floodgate for Whites to move to Georgetown during his term of office from 1891 to 1906. He enticed northerners and Europeans with tracts of land to relocate there if they worked for the Atlantic Coast Lumber Company. Begun in 1899, the company built a hotel, sawmill, large general store, dry kilns, and a machine shop during its first years. In the West End of Georgetown, the company built row houses, single and duplex, for workers. These were years of Georgetown's largest building boom, and Black workers benefited.

Had Florence been aware, she would have told Chadwick that the Atlantic Coast Lumber plant was located on Goat Island in the bend of the Sampit River, and its property expanded to the mainland on property on which the steel mill now stands. That millions of tons of rock were moved to build jetties from the barrier island at the entrance to the harbor and ancillary businesses opened to benefit or support it.

According to a *Georgetown Times* newspaper report, a summer day in 1905 was described as bustling. "Front Street," it read, "all day long is filled with people, drays and wagons carrying merchandise; our merchants are busy; our banks are busy, our wholesale merchants are doing an immense business, our water front is alive with shipping of every description, as marked last week, when on one day, eleven large three- and four-masted schooners arrived, besides two steamships, two barges and the usual fleet of river steamers. There is hardly ten minutes any day but what your ear is greeted by the whistle of some ship, steamer or tug arriving or departing. It sounds sometimes as if you were in New York harbor."

Florence knew, however, that whether prosperous or low-income, some Georgetonians never considered themselves as "downtrodden," as they perceived Blacks in other Lowcountry communities to be. To celebrate their heritage and to get together, some coordinated and attended an annual Georgetonian ball. Beginning in the early 1940s, it was held in December in New York City, relocated to Washington, D.C. in 1975, and in 1999 was renamed Georgetonian Ball South and celebrated in Myrtle Beach. Attendees dressed lavishly, socialized, and feted themselves with "living high on the hog" pageantry.

When Chadwick dined on a Sunday-after-church meal of stewed chicken with okra and tomatoes over rice, sweet potatoes, and string beans, Florence did not allow his one day of no full-time or part-time job to rob her of the opportunity to inform him with more history. "Our community has preachers, teachers, civil service workers, funeral home directors, fishermen, even entrepreneurs who don't have a lazy bone in their bodies," she said. "Somehow, Chadwick, our people, even when we've worked cleaning hotels and working as cooks and waiters, have always embraced a thought that Marcus Garvey expressed when he said, 'Take advantage of every opportunity; where there is none, make for yourself.' So, don't let anyone make you think otherwise."

And one night, Florence emerged from the bathroom, beautified before they retired, and told him, "Chadwick, dear, guess what? A Black beautician did my hair." She ran her fingers smoothly over her relaxed 'do and behind her ears and smiled. "A brown-skinned store attendant sold me this nightie." Both hands caressed her uplifted breasts and moved downward, her right hand resting on her right hip and her right hand sliding down to her left thigh as she winked sensually. She leaned toward Chadwick as he sat on the bed. She moved her head and torso in a circular, flirtatious motion before his face and spoke softly, breathily. "This fragrance was suggested by a mocha-colored technician at the perfume counter. Do you like it?" When he nodded as though hypnotized, she pushed him lightly onto the bed, straddled his thighs, and crouched above him, so they were face to face. "Now if you and I do any work tonight," she whispered in his ear, "tell me who, if any one of us, is lazy."

A made-up mind, however, is not easily dissuaded by rejection, reason, quotations, or passion. And Chadwick's mind was no exception. He continued to consider connections that could cement Otis Doyle's investment opportunity with Timothy Thunderbolt's low-income apartment-complex-panacea. Only the thoughts of a high school classmate and an ill-considered meeting site would alter his frame of mind.

Following the autumn equinox and the end of daylight-saving time, cool weather chilled Lowcountry evenings and darkness crept over the landscape before 6:00 p.m. Doyle thought a late afternoon/early evening Saturday bonfire in the backyard at his grandparents' vacant plantation-style home in Darcatia would be the ideal site for the investors to finalize their commitment. Drinks flowed freely, smoke and embers wafted upward, and off-color jokes began to pollute the ambiance.

A nondrinker, Chadwick walked around sporting a new pair of black cargo pants and holding a can of Coke. Doyle greeted guests with a plastic cup of scotch on the rocks in his hand as he directed them to coolers filled with beer, soda, and ice. A nearby tree stump displayed a stockpile of liquor bottles. L.D. Carpenter, owner of Calabash by the Sea, sipped beer. Herman Greene, a light-skinned Black man with wavy hair, whom Chadwick had never seen before, chatted with others but seemed to look around and through Chadwick as though he was invisible. Holding a plastic cup and jiggling the ice every so often, Greene seemed at home in the setting. Chadwick, however, felt out of place. A fellow board of trustees member of the Gardens at River Bend mingled with him only briefly and meandered to others, joking, chatting, and refilling his cup at the tree stump.

When Bob Brittman arrived, Chadwick relaxed somewhat. The two had not interacted since high school but had kept up with each other's accomplishments through articles in the *Georgetown Times*. "Well, if it isn't the one and only banker, Bob Brittman," Chadwick proclaimed with excitement as Bob walked over to him. Smiling wildly, they shook hands and gave a brotherly embrace.

"And 'Entrepreneur of the Year' and 'Most Likely to Succeed' Chadwick Wineglass," Bob crowed when they released their hug. "It's good to see you here. I didn't know who to expect." Brittman looked around, and Chadwick walked with him to the coolers and bottles. Brittman pulled out a bottle of beer.

"Glad to see you too!" Chadwick said. "This is a . . . let's say. . . an interesting group. I was at the last meeting Doyle had at Calabash by the Sea, but you were a no-show. That's when, I understand, he was going to introduce the investment project to you. I was waiting to see you and to hear your banker ideas about it."

"Sorry not to be there too!" Brittman said. "I had to attend a call meeting of the Habitat for Humanity Foundation. Can you fill me in on what I missed?"

Doyle, seeing that all had arrived except for the one silent partner, asked the men to assemble closer. He addressed them with his back to the flames and smoke.

"You've had time to introduce yourselves to each other, but let's each give a brief introduction," he said, holding his cup outstretched as though he was about to make a toast. "I'll start off."

He lowered the cup to waist level. "All of you know me. I'm Otis Doyle, a man who makes things happen, and I thank you for responding to my invitation to be here! When we're done with the introductions, I'm going to make you aware of a business opportunity that will be a boon to local restaurateurs, the local economy, and, most importantly, the wallets of all who invest." With a smug smile, Doyle then pointed to the only other Black attendee, an invited guest whom Chadwick did not know, and added, "And this young buck was born almost next door in Kingstree and graduated from Clemson U."

The fair-skinned man with thin lips and hair that would never make waves or sport an afro spoke with bravado. His broad nose bridge and his teeth were the only two features that aligned him racially with Chadwick more so than with the others. The space between his two front teeth signified to Chadwick that the man might be a liar—not fact, but strong Lowcountry folklore. Chadwick would wait to see what might unfold.

"Thanks for the invitation, Otis," the gapped-toothed, light-complexioned man said. "I'm Herman Greene. I moved to the beach, coming back to the good ol' South from Delaware about two months ago as a partner with Armstrong Coastal Buick. And I've already become a Chanticleer admirer. Even though they can *never* compete with the Tigers!"

Chadwick listened to each introduction, smiled, nodded, and noticed with interest that when it was his turn to introduce himself, Greene left to refresh his drink. *I wonder if he's related to anyone here,* Chadwick thought. *I bet he'd never say . . . .*

Still backlit with the embers and flames, Doyle introduced to some, and re-informed others, about his plan to recruit and relocate Jamaican workers for the mostly upscale hotel restaurants in Myrtle Beach. He stressed the benefits their pay would provide for families they'd leave behind, the need for finding housing for the transplanted workers, the urgency of investing so planning could begin, and the increase, percentage-wise, that restaurateurs could gain by curtailing higher pay to the replaced workforce. He detailed the required investment from each of the group assembled and added, "I've got a commitment from one silent partner. I'll need to know where you stand in two weeks. Two weeks. After that, I'll connect with others. And I'm certain that by hook or by crook, the right investors will be found, and this plan will get the air beneath its wings." Some oak logs sizzled and popped and spit a flurry of embers into the night air. The men reacted with astonishment, and Doyle scurried closer to them to avoid being burned. Looking back, he concluded, "And money will be made! So, enjoy yourselves, please. I'll be here until the last guest leaves."

Chadwick noticed Doyle and Greene chumming together like two reunited buddies. Brittman walked toward Chadwick with a scowl of disbelief on his face. The two stepped away from the bonfire and from the others. Pleased that they'd disengaged from the group, Chadwick was eager to pitch a plea for loan assistance for the Low Bottom Community Church's low-income apartment complex.

"Bob," he said, "there's a church group that I'm not affiliated with that has an interesting construction project brewing. It's for a low-income apartment complex for senior citizens in the Low Bottom Community. I'm going to give your name to the pastor to speak to about possible loans from Rice Field Regional, if you don't mind."

"Of course, Chadwick," Brittman replied. "I'd be happy to speak with him. How soon are they thinking about breaking ground?"

Chadwick pursed his lips and folded his hands. "Well, I don't think breaking ground is even a close consideration for them," he said. "But they have a good business idea, I've heard. It could tie in with community projects you're interested in, like Habitat for Humanity. You think?"

Bob smiled and lay a hand on Chadwick's right shoulder. "Always business-minded, huh, Chadwick?" he stated. "I remember your plans for a French drain installation company back in business class. Seems like that idea has taken you a long way!"

"Yes, it has!" Chadwick agreed, smiling as Bob lowered his hand. He took a deep breath, then continued, looking Bob in the eyes. "And that idea would've died on the vine if you hadn't served up some good fertilizer with needed advice about tapping into the right revenue sources. I think you can really help this group to get off to a great start."

Replicating Bob's movements and placing his opposite hand on Bob's shoulder, Chadwick veered the conversation in a new direction. "Now, concerning Doyle's investment proposal," he said, "this same church could offer another opportunity to provide lodging for the Jamaicans if—"

Brittman's abrupt step back stalled the completion of his sentence and caused Chadwick's hand to disconnect from his shoulder. Wineglass watched his flopping hand and then saw the horror and indignation in Brittman's eyes.

"Please don't tell me you're thinking about going in with this cockamamie, racist endeavor, Chadwick!" he said. Chadwick stared at him blankly, until Brittman's head snapped back, and his eyes widened. "Where's the humanity in this business plan, Chadwick? Where? It's just about using dollars to make more dollars. Don't you see? Local Blacks who need all the money they can get will be replaced with Jamaicans who will make even less money but who can send some of this 'piece of money' back home to support their families. Right? What if they get sick while they're here? What if their families need them more back there? And who will get the lion's share of any profits that are made? Doyle's business idea is just a new kind of slavery. I will *not* support it. And if you can't see what's happening through the same lens as I just explained things, then please, tell me what it is that you see."

Brittman's words buffeted Chadwick with realization that he hadn't recognized before, despite his wife's pronouncements and words of encouragement. His gaze turned slowly to the embers and flames, the bodies laughing and scheming, the bottles of alcohol and cans of beer. In the distance, he saw a scene more real than imagined. Jamaican men and women hanging from nooses tied to tree branches. Their eyes staring into his. Their dying voices clamoring, "How you not see wha he been doin? Him tell ya wit him own teet. Now, wha dey do ta one, dey do ta all!"

As he watched, he recalled stories he'd heard about Georgetown's state legislator John Bolts, who was born across the water from Darcatia Plantation just as the Civil War began. His parents, who had been enslaved workers on nearby Sandy Island, had sacrificed to send him to Benedict College in Columbia, SC, to earn a teaching certificate so that he could return and teach newly freed young people of Georgetown County. He was elected twice to the South Carolina congress, becoming one of seven Black legislators in 1898. This occurred at a time when Jim Crow laws were established to eliminate Black representation; at a time when during his return home from congressional meetings he most probably witnessed scenes like Wineglass had just witnessed in his mind. Chadwick recalled seeing similar images in old *Ebony* and *Jet* magazines and hearing stories of members of the KKK burning crosses in fields, drinking liquor, chatting about wreaking violence and instilling oppression, and fueling thoughts about Manifest Destiny. Bob Brittman was right.

Together, Wineglass and Brittman walked to their vehicles, determined that they would not assist with Doyle's Jamaican debacle. And the spirit of the namesake of their high school Alma Mater, the Honorable Joseph Hayne Rainey, smiled on them both. Rainey, a son of Georgetown who had been born enslaved and was self-educated, rose in stature during Reconstruction to become the first Black person to serve in the United States House of Representatives. He championed legislation for voting rights and for the equal protection of everyone with the Ku Klux Klan Act of 1871.

"Tell me nothing of a constitution which fails to shelter beneath its rightful power the people of a country," Rainey had asserted on the House floor.

Bolstered by Rainey's impassioned declaration, the legislation empowered the Republican-led Federal government, to which he and numerous other newly freed Black Americans belonged, to take decisive action to protect the civil and political rights of *everyone*, including the newly freed people during Reconstruction. It in no way condoned the racist and dehumanizing posturing with which Wineglass and Brittman were severing ties.

Doyle eyed them walking away as he looked about during his private conversation with light-skinned Greene. "Hey, boys," he yelled to them, "no need to skedaddle away without saying good night!"

Chadwick and Bob continued walking.

"Don't be so sissified, now!" he snarled with increased volume as the other bonfire attendees began to take notice.

"Do not turn around!" Bob urged Chadwick. "We're almost there, and we can put this night, this nod to social and economic injustice, behind us."

"Hey, fellas," Doyle snickered to his cronies, "I guess they can't see we're just *real men* gathered here. Doing *real men's* business.

Business that'll improve *this community* and make us *tons a money* that'll improve our community standing and family connections." To Wineglass and Brittman, he yelled, "Don't you want that, boys? Now, don't walk away from this golden oppa-tu-nity. Cause once you out, ya can't get back in!"

The two continued walking. Chadwick slowed and stopped just as they reached their vehicles. Responding to his faltering movements and the pained expression in his eyes, Bob countered, "We are better than this, Chadwick! If we turn around, we will become just like them. Let's put this night behind us. If you have ideas about other business ventures, come talk to me."

As Chadwick reached into his right pants pocket for his keys, Bob added, "We need to build bigger and better prisons for people like them who build personal riches on the lives of others whom they don't regard as human."

"Um-hmm, um-hmm," Chadwick muttered nervously. He forced a hand into the left and right front pocket, pulled each out, then patted both pockets with both hands.

"What's wrong?" Bob asked. "Can't find your keys?"

"No," Chadwick said, looking on the ground around him and along the path they'd just walked. "I always keep them here in the right pocket. I don't know what happened to them."

"Hmpf. Let's retrace our steps," Bob said. "Maybe they fell out along the way. C'mon."

The two retreated in silence, looking to the left and right, planting their feet deliberately below and around them, but finding nothing. As they neared the bonfire, they overheard the group's continuing conversation, listened in stillness, and eyed each other with alarm.

To Greene, Doyle said, "There's nothing racist about this project. Let me tell you. It's similar to a program already in place in New England. There are apple orchards there that hire annual seasonal farm workers from Jamaica. It's a state-government-funded program. That means it's protected by law. And if something gets to be law, does anyone get hurt by it? No, no, no. Not to the left, not to the right, not up or down the law of supply and demand. Now, remember that! Grab another beer before you get out of here, Herman Greene. This project will start . . . . don't let those two losers spook you none!"

Bob's glance at Chadwick expressed, *See what I mean?!?*", while Chadwick's responding nod communicated, *Yeah, friend, you were right!* Thinking about Doyle's closing statement about the law of supply and demand, Chadwick began searching his pockets again. The left and right pockets up top and then the cargo pockets down below.

"Here they go!" he whispered, pulling the key ring out of the right pant leg. "I forgot I put them there. Let's get out of here."

Chadwick and Bob parted ways, the lights of their vehicles illuminated the darkness as they drove away, leaving the blazing flames behind them, as well as two men, Herman and Otis—one younger and the other older—whose profiles were quite similar.

Pounding the Grains with Mortars and Pestles

After Gregory boiled and drank the yellow wingstem that he'd gathered at Mourning Dove Cemetery, he reread the Bible verses that had been used to fulfill Florence's request. The two New Testament verses that he found were related to Chadwick, in his mind, and the two Old Testament verses that he found were related to Florence.

Florence had paid Gregory for his services and accepted that Chadwick had not contributed to her grandfather's death. But a fuller understanding of the other information that he'd freely dispersed to her only began to become evident at her Grandpa Tucker's homegoing.

The Saturday service had drawn an overflowing crowd. Deacons, church members, and community members lauded Emanuel Tucker as a family man, a lover of God, a servant to others. Family members paid tributes in word and song. All the while, Florence had wanted to shout, *Bless his soul but what you don't know is that he was also a liar. And an adulterer. And a cheat!* But leaning into her husband, she kept her thoughts to herself.

Bishop Jericho Bessellieu, the only human with whom Tucker had confessed his adultery, doused the fire of indignation that smoldered in Florence's thoughts with the closing lines of the eulogy. Emanuel had confided to him that his secret affair had been both his shame and salvation—that he'd failed his wife, his lover, and the children that he didn't acknowledge, yet memories of his dalliance enlivened him when moments with his wife were less than exciting. He confessed that he'd meant to take his secret to the grave, but that Blessing had sensed his wrongdoing by looking into the window of his soul.

"End it, Emanuel!" she'd told him one night as they lay in bed. And without explaining or asking forgiveness, he'd agreed. "Emanuel Tucker was not a perfect man," the bishop said. "And none of us is perfect. But I believe that one day he asked the God of Heaven to forgive him. One day, he told the Son of God he believed in Him. And the grace of God, that day, washed over him. And set Emanuel Tucker's soul on the course that he took to this day!"

"Pre-e-e-ach!" the congregants shouted. "Ya-a-a-s-s-s!" And then he implored further and prayed with the poetic decorum, staccato, and resonance of Black men of the cloth.

"Now . . . each of you . . . there's no need to hold onto things that'll keep you burdened . . . that'll keep you filled with guilt. Call those things out. At the sound of my voice . . . call them out . . . in your heart and in your mind . . . call them out . . . one by one."

He silenced his prayer, his vocal battle with the forces of darkness, as whispers, murmurs, and expulsions of identified bondages began to sound throughout the sanctuary. And walls began to come a-tumbling down as he continued.

"And now . . . Great God of Heaven . . . the keeper of our souls, I ask You to take the Knife of Sanc-ti-fi-cation . . . and cut and plug. To plug the gaping hole that is left . . . with Your amazing and sufficient grace and forgiveness. And to cast . . . whatever it may be that your people have confessed . . . to cast it . . . all of it . . . into the Sea of Forgetfulness. Where it will not rise again in this world. Or in the world to come! Amen. Amen. Amen." A dramatic pause followed, and the audience began to collect itself.

"I believe Brother Tucker has journeyed to that world that is to come," Bishop Bessellieu continued. "Some call it 'Sweet Canaan Land.' Some called it the 'Sweet By and By.' Whatever you know it as, some of you here can now say, 'I got a father . . . a grandfather . . . an uncle . . . a friend over there.' And so . . . my brothers and sisters . . . live lives that'll ensure you'll be rejoined with Emanuel Tucker. Where? In the sweet bosom of Jesus. When? Soon and very soon."

Afterward, the Friendfield A.M.E. choir started to sing and clap. The organ pumps began to pulsate, and the piano keys began to tingle. The ushers began to step forward. And the masses began the parade of the last viewing. It started with those seated in the balcony and then in the last rows downstairs. Soon and very soon, Florence saw the light—of one of the things Gregory had informed her.

She saw an almost identical version of herself—but older—walking toward the casket. The older self was wearing a black pantsuit. Florence was wearing a black dress. The elderly Tucker family women who resembled her older self all had the same slanted eyes, though hers seemed set deeply in their sockets. They had the same squared shoulders, though hers were not as erect; the same walnut complexion, though hers was somewhat sallow. Florence looked at her father Adam, then at other family members to see if they saw what she saw. All, however, were too caught up in their own grief.

Both arms of this older "self" fell straight by her sides as she walked. Her facial muscles seemed drawn. Following others, she turned left at the end of the church's right aisle. She looked only at the corpse in the coffin. Not at anyone in the front rows. Centered in front of it, she stared a while longer than others, as though she was seeing a face, a prone torso, not for the last time but for the very first. She rested both hands on her protruding belly as she gazed, and moved them inward and outward, up and down, as though she was conveying a detailed description of everything that she saw to the fetus within her womb. She stayed until an usher urged her and the younger person who accompanied her to move on and they then turned left onto the church's left aisle to proceed with others to the exit.

As mourners processed past the casket, Florence reflected on what Gregory had told her: *This is what the Spirit revealed. Your grandfather planted seedlings that became a low-lying vine. This vine was different from the high-blossoming bush that grew from the seedlings that your grandfather planted elsewhere. You, Florence, are a fruit from the high-blossoming bush. But fruit from the low-lying vine also have leafy boughs. Now, when those two fruits come together, there'll be healing.*

It wasn't until after Florence's second miscarriage that the meaning of Gregory's other words crystallized. "Chadwick has planted a thing that God did not ordain," Gregory had said. "It was a preference, but it was not aligned with principle. It will be pulled up by the roots. The blossom he planted that would give riches to others will scorch and wither. The beauty he hoped to produce will be destroyed. Unless his plans align with principle, they will fade away."

At the funeral repast, the older Florence lookalike lingered in the rear of the fellowship hall. Adam and Florence's siblings, aunts, and uncles eyed her from afar and assumed she must be a distant relative or cousin who would greet them once the immediate family had been comforted. But Florence was certain the stranger was the daughter of Rinda. Emanuel had accidentally voiced her name only once.

Rinda and Absalom must be here too, Florence reasoned, scanning the room for faces that she presumed she would recognize. How? She didn't know. Florence saw someone from Darcatia, a face she remembered from high school, standing near the older Florence lookalike.

"Hi," Florence said when she made her way through the crowd to greet them. She pulled the two visitors away from others. "I'm Florence. Thanks for being here." The look-alikes reached to shake hands, startled at their mirrored resemblances. "I believe you must be Lillie."

When Lillie heard Florence's greeting, she immediately placed both hands on her belly to calm the responding movement. Aware of some unexplained connection, the women stood motionless, their eyes surveying the other's face.

"She Easta," Lillie's companion said hurriedly. "Easta Middleton. E haad fa she fa taak. A Carrie Middleton. Huh cousin." Florence readily understood Carrie's musical and deep-voiced declaration that Easter Middleton found it difficult to speak.

Lillie coughed drily, then spoke slowly. Her teeth were yellow and jagged, signifying drug addiction. The pause after each word was a short eternity. "I was born Easter Lillie," she said, to her cousin's surprise. "Before my mother died, she told me to never use my middle name. To drop it. Said it would just connect me with sorrow."

Florence felt a gut-blow to her stomach.

"Dis e fus time down yah," Lillie's cousin Carrie explained. "E been sick an we gone an breng em frum New Yaark las mont. E a lee bit betta now. A breng em yah taday cuz e ain knoww who e daddy dah. A tell em e look like Manuel Tucker wa jes dead peepul. An looky, looky. Fa true, Lillie look jes like oona. Great Gawd!

Moreso dan anybody een Darcatia, where e Mama come frum." Carrie paused, noticing growing befuddlement in Florence's eyes, then continued. "We ain come fa make no nize bout wa we ain knoww nottin bout, dough. Jes fa see wa we see. We gone soon."

Florence responded to the crush of Carrie's words with movement. She told the women to stay put. That she'd be right back. Rushing to the kitchen, she reflected on what she'd been told. *This is her first time down here. She was sick and we traveled and brought her from New York last month. She's a little better now. I brought her here today because she doesn't know who her father is. I told her she looks like Manuel Tucker's people, Manuel Tucker who just died. And for true, Lillie looks just like you. Great God! Moreso than anybody in Darcatia, where her mother comes from. We didn't come to make a disruption about what we don't know anything about, though. Just to see what we saw. We'll be leaving soon.*

Florence returned with heaping to-go containers that were worthy of visiting clergy. She walked with the two women to the parking lot and made plans to meet with Easter Lillie on the upcoming Tuesday.

Up from the grave, the secrets of Emanuel Tucker's past arose on the third day following his burial. Florence met with Easter, Carrie, and Carrie's mother, Sophronia, at the Savory and Scrumptious Deli on Front Street. What she learned during their meeting was insipid and indigestible, the antithesis of the restaurant's name. Not only had her grandfather sired two illegitimate children while he was married, but he had also abandoned them. Her Uncle Absalom had died at age four, and her newfound Aunt Lillie, who was named after a thing of beauty like her also unknown half-sisters, had grown up without knowledge about any family heritage in Georgetown, in neither her father's nor mother's lineage.

Rinda had felt the need to flee. She birthed her second child on an Easter Sunday in March, six months following her Greyhound bus exodus. She named her "Easter" because they were starting a new life and "Lillie" regarding the naming practices of his other daughters that Emanuel had spoken about with pride to her. Each bore the name of a flower. Rinda had written to Emanuel once after Lillie was born, through a sealed letter she had mailed to Sophronia, with explicit instructions about where to leave it in her cabin in the woods, to not open or read it, and to check the cabin every two weeks to ensure its retrieval. She had written "Matthew 1:23" on the envelope, which was meant to identify who should read it, and to remind him of her/their plans for how his name would be fulfilled: "The virgin will conceive and give birth to a son, and they will call him Immanuel (which means 'God with us')."

Learning from Sophronia that the letter had been retrieved, she'd waited to hear from him. But Emanuel never responded. And each year she grew weary, embittered, and burdened that he was no longer with her, no longer with them.

In time, the no-man blues of the mom gave rise to heartache-induced cancer, and eventually, to the no-father pain and heartache for the daughter. Rinda erased Georgetown and Emanuel Tucker from her memory. And when Rinda died, sixteen-year-old Easter began living with whatever man took her in. Her soul, set on its course by abandonment and despair, began looking for love. Selling drugs. Doing drugs. Living low. From her teens to her forties. A life of trap houses, recovery centers, jail cells, and the streets.

Seven months before her trip south, Easter awoke in a hospital bed with no awareness of how she got there. Without a clue that she was pregnant or even who the father could be.

The missionary group from nearby Throw Out the Lifeline Church took an interest in her during their weekly hospital visits. Miraculously, Calvin and Annette Chenault, an elderly married couple from the church, received her into their home after she was discharged to a recovery center and from there to a dwelling. They loved her, nurtured her, renewed her. Coincidental natives of Georgetown, SC, the couple had no idea of her origins, and neither did she.

Calvin, having introduced Easter to the daily practice of morning devotions, completed the days with Round Table Thanksgiving. Easter had awoken not feeling well, with swollen feet and an elevated blood pressure. She rubbed her temples frequently to ease her headache.

"When you're feeling fair to middling or troubled or low, keep thinking of the good things that you know," he began. "Let's see . . .

I know Jesus loves me. He is good. And I am favored." He passed the torch. "What you know, 'Nette?"

Annette smiled and said, "I know Easter is healthier today than she was yesterday, or three months ago when we met her in her hospital bed. Not completely out of the storm she was in yet, but I know she's getting stronger. And her unborn child has a steady heartbeat. Boom-boom. Boom-boom. Now, that's a blessing!" She passed the torch. "What you know, Easter?"

She opened her mouth to answer but could only gasp, "Oh-h-h!" Her head jerked and her hands began to massage her abdomen where she'd been kicked or elbowed from within. "I know this one moves around like a wild donkey!" Easter said slowly when she recovered. "And a wild donkey is better than a . . . than a . . . a stinky skunk." They all chuckled and fanned an imaginary stench away from their nostrils.

"But this child has gotta know where he came from," Easter continued. "At least who my mother's people are. She never talked about anyone from her past. It's like the wind just picked her up one day and dropped her in Harlem."

"Umpf, umpf, umpf," Annette said, shaking her head. "I can't imagine! A life without knowing who your people are is like being lost in the wilderness."

Calvin quickly added, "Having no memories, no family stories, puts people in a barren land in a dry place without water to drink. Why, water is the connecting fluid of the universe!"

"Connection, connection, connection," Annette said, before standing and starting to pace the kitchen floor in prayer. "Troubling mind, Lord. She's got a troubling mind. Lord, we ask You right now to ease Easter's troubling mind!"

Calvin snatched the prayer torch and continued. "Easter needs a reunion, Heavenly Father, with her great cloud of witnesses. Wherever they may be. What she doesn't know, Lord, we know that You know. So, give her the wisdom. Give her the answers. Be with her and her unborn child on this new journey in her life. Hold her hand and help her to enter the chariot and travel along."

Like the appearance of an oasis in the desert, answered prayer emerged in a moment. In the twinkling of an eye. When the Chenaults ended their prayer, they looked up and saw Lillie thumping her left index finger to her forehead and patting her right palm on her belly. Opening her eyes in wonder, she said, "Georgetown . . . um . . . Mama was from Georgetown. I remember Mama saying that name to me, just once, when I was a little girl."

"Georgetown? In DC?" Annette asked. "You know a lot of Blacks came from there. It was a community that was once filled with free Blacks and with slaves who worked in the tobacco fields."

"Uh uh," Easter answered. She closed her eyes and pressed her temples with both hands. "No, she said Georgetown, um . . . South Carolina. That's right, Georgetown, South Carolina."

"Well, shut the door and shame the devil!" Calvin said. "Child, we were born and bred in Georgetown."

With growing excitement, Annette asked, "Easter, what was your Mama's name? Jesus is on the main line. Yes, indeed. We called Him up, told Him what we needed, and looky looky. A memory, like dust, dust and ashes, is now flying over the grave that held it down."

They promised to make some phone calls back home. To piece together Easter's roots. To help her to connect with her people.

Sunshiny skies sometimes change quickly to cloudiness. A few moments after her introduction to the possibility of connecting with her roots, Easter collapsed in her chair at the kitchen table.

1980s

Thelma stuffed all thoughts of marital discord within her psyche. She feared that if she talked about them to family, friends, or church members, her disclosure would authenticate them—would minimize her ability to control them or to make them disappear. Or to modify them to an outcome that she could manage. Her vow of silence ushered in shadows. The prayers of others kept her surrounded by light.

She recalled a tale told by one of her sorority sisters at Paine College, an AKA line sister from Georgetown whose personality had cemented her with the line name "Storyteller." During moments of hazing, Storyteller would regale them with antics about how, if she and her fellow pledgees could make a trip to see Dr. Buzzard, Dr. Buzzard would mix a concoction that would make their prophytes grow backsides as large as watermelons.

Thelma, coming from Seneca, had never heard of a "Dr. Buzzard."

Or black magic. Or Lowcountry lore. And Storyteller's yarns had made each speculation memorable! So memorable, during her and Melvin's first visit to Georgetown following their heated discussion when he had told her to "Haul ass!" that she secretly stole away from his company one morning. She asked questions of pedestrians on rural highways where large interlocking overhead branches from either side of the road made sunlight a stranger and queried strangers at convenience stores during her drive to the North Santee community. Her mission fulfilled, she found her way to Dr. Buzzard's front door.

She was unafraid when she knocked, though she had no idea what she would behold if and when the door opened. Because she did not see dead chickens hanging upside down in the yard to the stucco home or shrunken human heads decorating the front porch, or hairless green-eyed dogs or two-headed cats roaming about, she felt more at ease. The most peculiar sight that caught her attention were two large green succulent plants in black, urn-shaped flowerpots on either side of the front steps. Their long, pointed leaves bore prickly spines and spiraled up, out, down, left, and right, hydra-like from the soil. The base of the roots of each plant was thick and darker green, and the leaves seemed aware and prescient, giving Thelma the impression that these plants were sentinels who had guarded the entryway for a long time.

Hearing footsteps approaching from inside, she stepped back a bit. She breathed in, lifted her shoulders, braced herself, and widened her eyes to take everything in. To her surprise, a handsome, peanut butter-brown, slightly balding, mustached, middle-aged, five-foot, ten-inch tall Black man appeared. His smile inspired confidence, not fear. His voice was welcoming, not foreboding.

"Good morning, Miss," he said. "Can I help you? What brings you this way so early in the day?"

"I'm here to see . . . um . . . Dr. . . . Buzzard," Thelma stated in a low voice. He looked intently into her face, which remained wide-eyed, and then beyond her to the gold Ford Fairlane she'd parked below a magnolia tree. "I see . . . I see," he responded. "Well, come on in out this sun. E hot outcha, chile!"

What Thelma had not realized as she crossed the threshold was that William Dunkin, knowing that the human eye is the window to the soul, had already seen her past, present, and future. After she divulged her reason for being there, he'd politely responded, "Oh-h-h, I'm sorry, I can't help you with that."

Dumbfounded, Thelma had replied, "What? Oh, you don't understand. I heard you could—"

"Yes, I understand," he stated. "I understand, but . . ." His countenance mirrored the look Thelma had seen given by deacons at Cross Roads Baptist Church when they would charge distressed members with the statement and promise, "You'll understand it better by and by."

After offering to pay him whatever he asked to reunite her and Melvin's marital bond, Thelma left Dr. Buzzard's presence stymied, distressed. She did not know that Dr. Buzzard had seen her present—the two words her husband had hurled at her, which hid behind her eyelids, or her past; her machinations to control her husband and others, which hovered behind her eyeballs. Not even her future—her yet to be acknowledged embryo, which made itself manifest by her drooping eyelids and swollen veins in the corner of her eyes.

As a discouraged Thelma drove back to her in-laws' home, Melvin looked at the Black River from a field beyond his parents' backyard. It was a site where he'd come to fish or meditate throughout childhood. In the distance, he saw remnants of rice trunks, large handmade devices for flooding and draining, at numerous pathways on the water that led to former rice fields. The familiar scenery and the Lowcountry heat and humidity made him think about heritage. And the hovering clusters of pesky mosquitoes made him ponder his marital problems and the stinging words he and Thelma had expressed to each other. *Was their marriage grounded on something secure,* he wondered, *or should they dissolve it and move on?*

After checking the crab cage as his mother had asked him to do, Melvin purveyed the horizon. Flecks of sunlight on the water made him recall stories about his great grandfather Esau Marshel, who had been a trunk minder on Marshel Plantation in Mausaville. Trunk minders were the most respected enslaved workers on rice plantations. Because of their knowledge and skills about rice production, they ensured that the flap gates were opened at the precise moments to flood the rice fields with fresh water during high tides and opened during low tides to drain the stagnant water back into the freshwater creeks that flowed down to join the saltwater in Winyah Bay, which then emptied into the Atlantic Ocean. Without trunk minders and the other enslaved workforce, rice planters would not have risen to heights of aristocracy with Carolina Gold! They would not have cultivated and harvested and sold the bountiful crops from which only about one hundred grains were gleaned from each stalk.

He thought about Africans who had been transported to these shores. About their awareness of inserting hollow tree trunks into the mounds of dirt built around rice fields in their homelands to separate them from the surrounding freshwater waterways that at times teemed with saltwater. He thought about their tenacity when forced to clear cypress swamps in the Carolina Colony, to shovel earthen dikes around each rice field, and to build sturdy cylindrical boxes with six-foot tall flap gates out of cypress wood to replace the hollow tree trunks that had been a part of their history, their heritage.

Melvin sat down on the sandy creek shore. He swished his hat at annoying gnats and mosquitoes. The heat pulsated and throbbed in visible airwaves, registering higher than anything he'd become accustomed to over the past few years in Augusta, GA and Rock Hill, SC. With each sparkle of sunlight, he began to see Africans in the rice fields and on the water. Women wearing scarves on their heads were dropping rice seeds into the ground or hoeing weeds in the rows. Their long skirts, made from stout and unbleached fabric that was a cotton and wool blend known as slave cloth, were held lifted off the ground with a cord tied around their waists. Men, dressed in shirts and trousers made from coarse blue jean cloth, were hauling needed supplies in bateaux, or raising and lowering rice hooks. Several workers were toting sheaves of rice on their heads.

Catching sense, Melvin stood and walked from the direct sunlight to the shade below trees at the end of the clearing. He smacked and killed a large mosquito on his left arm. Its size surprised him as he flicked it off. The site of its bite began to hurt, reminding him of his recent spat with Thelma. Her words from an excerpt of their recent quarrel haunted him.

I never had to cook rice before I started cooking it for you, Mel, he remembered her saying. *And do you really want me to wheeze, itch, and feel like I'm going to die just to give you what you want? What about what I want?*

He realized that somehow, with the passing of time, he no longer knew what she wanted. And she seemed no longer to know what he wanted. What they each had wanted at one time was to live with, love, and cherish the other. *How could they get back to that?* he wondered. *Could they get back to that?*

Looking around, Melvin noticed cone-shaped cypress knees protruding out of the earth. In his frantic search for shade, he hadn't realized that he was standing below a cypress tree until he saw the triangular base of its trunk and the dull light green, needle-like and feathery leaves on its branches above. *Trunk minder Esau Marshel knew cypress trees,* he thought. *Every day that he raised and lowered the cypress flap gates to the cypress trunks, his soul grew strong like the cypress trees.*

As Melvin looked on the Black River, he continued to see the spirit-like images of Africans. Africans who had been brought to a new world without opportunities to bring family members or family keepsakes or mementos when they were ripped away from their homelands. Melvin had never thought about it before, but he began to wonder about the rituals, celebrations, and events that the Africans who toiled on the Black River had been forced to forget about. Or the rituals that had never been experienced by any of them. The creolized rituals that had to be re-created in this new world. Rituals that helped them to know who they were. Celebrations to attain religious beliefs, mark childbirth, adulthood, marriage, parenthood, harvest, old age, death and beyond. Markers that solidified them not only as individuals but as family, community, and a people.

"Yes, we *can* get back to what we had!" he heard himself saying aloud. "Thelma and I *can* re-learn to live with, love, and cherish each other. *That's* what I want! *That's* what these Africans are telling me."

He chuckled about his self-discovery and thought about returning to his parents' house. But then the memory of accusations he had hurled at Thelma stung his spirit as violently as the large mosquito that had at that moment impaled his arm. Would she be willing, or even able to meet him half-way?

And I ask you for more intimacy and for more opportunities to reach out and connect on a physical level, he remembered saying, *but all you want to do is talk about what you want and what you can do for others. Ways you can make your coworkers and my coworkers understand they're racists . . . I don't want to talk all the time about racists. No-o-o-o-o!*

You want to talk. So, I let you talk. I don't butt in. Do I? No, I listen. Even when I have something to say . . . or, should I say, when you allow me a moment to speak what's on my mind—I say it real quick . . . real quick, and then let you have center stage. That's what YOU love. And that's the love I make sure you get!

Finding himself in a state of indecisiveness, Melvin looked again on the water and saw the Africans looking dead at him. Startled, he threw his head back in disbelief. With frozen glances, they continued staring. Until he remembered his wedding vows. Remembered the ritual of his wedding ceremony. The love that he and Thelma had professed in the presence of God and their invited witnesses. When he smiled at the memory, the Africans returned to their toiling. Soon after, they disappeared!

Melvin checked the crab cage, dumped its contents into a bucket, and trekked back through the field to his childhood home.

Abraham and Precious Marshel snapped beans, seasoned fish, and joked between themselves like an old married couple in their kitchen. They were unaware of their guests' imminent return, their daughter-in-law Thelma by car or their son Melvin arriving by foot.

"Cyan hab no rice fa dinna taday, ennit?" Abraham asked, with lips frowning and eyes pouting.

"No, no, Abraham, man," Precious responded. "No rice dis day. Not wit Telma at de table. Gawd, hep me, no! A ga mek some good up macaroni and cheese. An some stick-ta-de-belly cornbread. Den we all can hab a seddown an talk bout dis tension wa seem da hang oba Melbin an Telma lokka daak cloud." She snapped several pole beans into a white Corning bowl that was decorated with an edging of blue roosters.

"Mm-hmm," Abraham said. "E a shame de chile cyan be roun no rice wa da cook, dough. Nottin but a cryin shame!" A look of disbelief spread across his face before he added, "But dat dohn mean no nebanomind . . . no, no, no, no. We ga eat good good taday!"

"Cornbread fa de mind," Precious began saying, with a chuckle. "Fush fa purify de blood, an macaroni an cheese fa tantalize de belly wen e trabble down de shroat an eben mo wen e git deh." She and her husband guffawed with joy and clapped their hands. "Wen ya done season de fush, Abraham, chop up dah okra an dem matas oba deh on de counta. Yuh? A been tell Melbin fa check de cage down ta de dock. Ef him come back wit a bucket a crab, oona haffa stew down dem matas an okra wit crabmeat de way dat only oona can do fa make me do my 'Great-Gawd-my-man-can-cook, enty?' dance!"

From her chair, Precious performed a jig. Swaying to the left, moving to the right. Hands in their air, palms flexing up and down. Fingers snapping, eyes smiling. Shoulders dipping, lips crinkling. Torso thrusting, feet thumping. And all her attention turned to her man.

Standing with his back to the kitchen sink, he basked in her admiration. "Now, yo macaroni and cheese, Precious Wigfall Marshel, e mek me bohdy do de same ting!" Abraham said as he raised his eyebrows and began stepping in rhythm toward his wife. He dropped a small sassafras tree root that he had just eyed and then grabbed onto the counter, stalling plans to boil it later for tea.

"Now, yo macaroni an cheese ain been tase DAH good wen we fus git married," he teased. "But A ain been mad! No. A jes been lob all ya da. An all ya do. An ebbytime oona been make macaroni, oona been add a leetle lob heh. An a leetle mo lob deh . . . ."

Precious batted her eyes at her lover man as he danced toward her. She stated in a sultry voice, "Til dah one day wen ya tase em and den turn ta me wit fiyah een ya eyes an say, 'Precious, oh, Precious, disya hit de spot!'"

"Fo dah day, ya been my Queen a Mos Ebbyting," Abraham crowed. "Bot eba sence dah day, Ooman-n-n, oona been me Macaroni an Cheese Queen . . . an me Queen a Ebbyting!"

He sustained a wink at her as he neared the table, holding his left eyelid closed and cocking his head at a devilish tilt. They connected by slowly slapping the raised palms of both of their hands together in the air. As Precious continued her chair-dance, Abraham two-stepped back to the counter. Turning to face her, the inner melody that he'd been listening to stopped abruptly, and he stated, "Too bad we cyan hab no rice, dough!"

"Anodda day, anodda time, Abraham," she said in a consoling tone. "We cyan mek de chile sick . . . Melbin lob em so. An we lob em so! Memba de way de two a dem beenna look at each odda on dey weddin day? Dah wa dis meal haffa git dem fa memba." She snapped more beans until they crowned the top of the bowl, then said, "Ya know wa A dream bout las night?"

"Wa?"

"Fush," she whispered. Precious eyed her husband and paused, to see if they shared the same thoughts about the meaning of dreaming about fish.

"Mm-m-m-m-m . . ." Abraham sighed, throwing his head back.

She described the dream in more depth. "E beenna school a fush da swim een de crick. A been see em and you been see em. But Melbin an Telma been deh, too, an needa one a dem chirren been see em. An de school a fush beenna look at dem scraight een de eye!" She halted her speech, keeping her gaze on him. "Tink dah a sign?"

Abraham moved back to the sink and picked up the sassafras root. Before he could answer, Thelma entered the house through the front door, greeted them in the kitchen but seemed to not feel well. With intoxicated smiles from their sing/dance/flirt/romance-encounter, both parents-in-law turned to her and noticed her clutching her stomach.

"Feelin bad?" Precious asked.

"Ef ya belly achy, chile, ya might need this," Abraham stated matter-of-factly as he held out the monstrous-looking root in his hand. Its twisted offshoots, and many tiny extending tendrils, some spiraling and some straight, commanded attention. Its green leaves were eerie, bobbing up and down from any air current in the room. And they looked supernatural; some were shaped like mittens, some looked like regular leaves, while others had three lobes.

Thelma's eyes bugged out! Queasiness, emanating from her stomach and enveloping her body, blurred her perception of reality. Her in-laws' facial expressions registered as impish. Their voices as hushed and deceptive. Their body movements as seductive. The object in Abraham's hand elicited fear. It was the type of apparition she'd expected to see in Dr. Buzzard's yard or home.

"Where did you get *that*?" she heard herself asking in a panic. She was so unsettled that she had no idea how she had mustered courage to speak.

"E a sassafras plant, Telma," Precious answered. "Ef ya find em een de woods, ya grab em up."

"Dis de root," Abraham chimed in with pride, cupping its lower end in his right palm and extending it toward her. "All ya haffa do is pull em up. A jes hice dis one frum de dut dis mawnin. Look at em. E smell good good. Enty?"

As he approached, Thelma stepped back. She looked at him face-to-face in horror. *Oh, no, everyone down here works roots,* she told herself. *I guess they're all connected. Maybe they already know where I've been. Maybe they knew before I got there. Maybe they've been waiting here for me with this thing. To make me sniff it and bow down to it . . . 'cause they think I haven't been treating their son right.*

Feeling a rumbling in her stomach, then chest, then throat, Thelma cupped her mouth with both hands, turned, and escaped quickly down the hallway. Precious and Abraham watched with concern as she bolted toward the bathroom. They followed her to ensure all was well. After the door slammed closed, they heard sounds of wrenching and regurgitating and looked at each other. Their mouths dropped open, their eyes enlarged, and they each cocked their heads to the side in affirmation.

They wondered if they should wait in the hallway for Thelma to exit or if they should return to the kitchen to avoid embarrassing her. At the same time, Melvin entered the house through the backdoor and walked toward the kitchen with a bucket filled with jumping crabs. He passed the hallway and stopped. The sight of his two parents standing motionless at the far end of the hall looking at him with speechless surprise concerned him.

"Is everything all right?" he asked, fearful to hear an answer. In a few moments, the doorknob to the bathroom door jiggled behind his parents. The door opened, and Thelma exited, shocked and flustered to see everyone looking at her.

Caught in the middle, Abraham and Precious looked from one adult child and then to the other. Several times.

"De two a you . . ." Precious began.

"hab anyting . . . fa tell we?" Abraham continued.

"Sompn . . . anyting . . . we need fa know bout?" they completed the thought in one voice.

The Marshel Lowcountry dinner menu was as magical as the ebb and flow of the tides, the seasonal beauty of Sea Island marsh grass, and the enchantment of a full moon sparkling on a waterway.

Satiated with food for thought, Precious shared her dream about seeing fish and its meaning. Abraham divulged that learning to love what you disliked about your spouse is an important ingredient for marital bliss.

"Ya cyan change nobohddy wa ain wanfa change," he explained. And his wife dovetailed his statement with, "An ef wa ya spouse do jes tarrygate but dohn hut ya, now, laarn fa lib wit wa dey do!"

Cleansed with an outpouring of family love and concern, Thelma confided that she had been feeling exhausted for a few weeks, her stomach had been queasy, and she'd been a bit jumpy, particularly with her husband.

Precious and Abraham observed their actions, said nothing, and shook their heads at each other across the table. Precious stretched her left arm to pat Thelma's right elbow that lay perched on the table with her arms crossed. "Wa ya say, chile, bout de way ya feel?" Precious asked, "Das de way us oomen feel wen we de mek foot fa socks. Wen ya git back home, Telma, go see ya docta. Ya jes might be pregnant. An call ya mama. A mama know wa fa do."

Abraham locked eyes with Melvin and, with parental concern, tapped him on the right shoulder and then detangled his rigidly crossed arms that lay against his chest as he sat back in his chair. Without speaking, the father gave his offspring a look that said, "Do right by this woman, son! No matter what the problem may be, work it out."

Nourished with the mesmerizing tastes of seasonings, vegetables, seafood, starches sans rice, and tingling sassafras tea, Melvin spoke about his dockside vision for a "cypress-kind-of-love, a long-lasting and enduring kind-of-love." He looked at Thelma with apologetic and forgiving eyes. Their spirits relaxed, and each seemed to lean into the other even as they sat across the table, realizing that deeper conversations and modifications in attitudes and behaviors would be in order.

And Abraham closed the meal with prayer that made their hearts dance. "Great Gawd Amighty," he began, "rula ob de eart, de heabens, an de unavus. Yeddy we, we pray. Lawd, we do wrong an we wan Oona fa hep we do right. We say tings we ain need fa say. Hep we fa breng laughta an joy ta peepul dem wa come we way. Cause we ain knoww wa oda peepul da goin shru. Lawd, Ya ax we fa trus Ya wit ebryting. So we ax Ya fa bless we chirren yah. Make em fa be one, de way Oona wan em fa be one. An ef nyew life done staart fa grow een em, bless de seed wa Ya put deh. Leh em grow een good good soil. Soil wa cry out to an say, 'Tenk ya, Lawd, fa ebbyting!', jes lok Ya say de rocks ga do ef peepul dohn praise Ya!

"We tenk Ya, Fahda. Fa de food we done nyam. Fa Ya lob wa mek we sing, an hope, an rejice. An fa Ya light wa mek peepul know 'we de chirren ob Gawd an ain nottin een dis worl can do we no haarm!' Wit ya fingas, Ya mek we. Jes lok Ya been mek de moon an de staars. Wit Ya lob, Ya tink bout we an cya fa we.

"So, full we up wit Ya wisdom. Wisdom dat none but de Lawd can splain. Leh we sleep with de res ob one wa da gadda unda de shada ob de Amighty. An, come dayclean, leh we find we sperit dress up een de finery ob Ya peace! Amen."

Winnowing Rice Grains with Fanner Baskets

2000s

"More money is needed to help Laverne," Florence informed Chadwick about her *ember*.

"More than the four hundred left for her in the kitty?"

"I gave that to her about a month ago," she stated matter-of-factly and smiled.

"You did? That's a surprise. About a month ago? You never said anything about that. How was I to know?"

"Well, you never asked."

Chadwick shook his head in confusion about the deviation of this transactional conversation. "Then, I guess it's time to move on to another *ember*," he said. "It took a while to wrap that one up, huh? Okay. Okay. Did you learn anything about yourself throughout the experience? I'm not yet settled on a new *ember* selection for you, but I can let you know tomorrow."

Florence looked at her husband in a new light. She shook her head, in defiance of the normalcy of what had become their transactional conversation. "I've come to consider Laverne a friend, Chadwick," she said. "She's now a friend in need, and we've got the money to meet that need. So, I've decided that I'm not going to leave her out in the cold like we've done with others."

"But we have a plan, Florence," Chadwick countered. "A plan to help others. And we've set ways to help others. Do you want to fund Laverne for a second go-round? I'm open to discussing that."

Florence dug in her heels before responding. "This plan of ours needs to be changed, Chadwick. Or scrapped. I can't continue to help people with unexpected gifts of money and then stop helping them at all or even connecting with them after an undisclosed time. I've found that this action plan of ours breeds contempt. And raises suspicions. And leaves people feeling used, bloodied, picked apart, and cast aside."

"I don't know what you're talking about. What we do gives people a breather to renew their hope—their faith in what they can accomplish if some of their debt is wiped out."

Florence breathed in deeply. Then released. "Chadwick, this is the very reason why the idea of getting Lowcountry people to lie about not knowing where a slave cemetery had been located, just to make thirty shckels of silver like Judas, while dishonoring their heritage, is something we don't need to be a part of! Now, we don't have to make any big decisions now. But can we agree on one thing?"

Chadwick looked into her eyes, then spread his hands open before her.

She continued, "Can we agree that I—not both of us—but I—cannot continue to make people feel as though I see them and then, without any knowledge on their part, refuse to see them or engage with them anymore?"

Florence awaited a response, but Chadwick looked utterly perplexed.

"And if I 'prosper' you . . . us, Chadwick," she continued, "you've got to start trying to see the things that I say, the things that you may disagree with, in a more favorable light. Can we agree on that too?"

Hoping to not end their conversation in a complete stalemate, she added, "Granddaddy's life insurance should arrive any day now. Laverne needs a brief separation from Medicus, and from his mother. I want to assist—with just twelve hundred from the policy payoff. Can we agree to talk about that tomorrow, please?"

Too many seconds tick-tocked in her mind before Chadwick responded. So, in frustration, she quickly added the rub. "This is the way of being 'prosperous,' as in the meaning of my name."

Chadwick had no problem with the amount she was requesting. He was baffled about why she wanted to modify their plans, however. And worried about her somehow becoming aware of his bank records for Tucker's life insurance—records of payments at twelve hundred dollars per month, not the 120 per month for a twenty-thousand-dollar policy that he'd led Florence to believe he'd taken out.

Surprised and elated to learn that her cousin Easter had been found, Sophronia Middleton, just like a rabbit scurrying across a field, "took her feet in her hand" to rescue her! She quickly began and maintained close touch with the Chenaults once they had connected with her, checking daily on Easter's status. She had learned about Easter's pregnancy and its complications because of her lifestyle choices and had sent money to compensate Calvin and Annette for their pledge to continue housing Easter until she could be relocated with family.

One month after her second hospitalization and one month before her due date, Easter traveled south with three newfound cousins who had made a thirty-hour round-trip journey to bring her back to the land where her life had begun. Their features and mannerisms resembled what she vaguely recalled about her mother Rinda, but much about her looks set her apart from them. Their love and concern for her and her unborn child, however, were undeniable. To her surprise, she felt at home, at peace among them.

Without complaint, her cousins Sophronia, Abraham, and Percy took an extra six hours on the return voyage. They kept Easter hydrated with fluids and made frequent restroom and rest stops so that she could rise from the back seat of the rented minivan, where she reclined with her feet atop a pillow, and stretch and take short walks. Still, her feet and legs were swollen when she arrived. Her blood pressure was slightly elevated, and she had a mild headache. The toxemia, however, did not deter Easter from marveling at the most alluring and enchanting sight she'd ever seen: bearded Spanish moss. It billowed in the breezes from tree limb to tree limb. And she alone heard whispering voices as she watched in fascination. *We've seen things,* she heard rustling. *We've got stories you need to know,* they called. *Welcome home, Easter Lillie, welcome home . . . .*

Diaspora, the scattering or dispersal of homogeneous groups or individuals, comes about in cultures, organizations, governments, families, and even marriages. Its causes are driven by lust. Lust for money, as in sugar, coffee, rum, rice. Lust for power, as seen with Adolph Hitler, Benito Mussolini, and Idi Amin. Lust for changing mindsets, as evidenced with Marcus Garvey's Back to Africa Movement; William Potter Gale's United States Posse Association, which endorsed and fomented White Nationalism; and Jim Jones' Peoples Temple occupation in Guyana. Sometimes, however, the scattering results from a lust for self-importance. Such was the lesson Thelma Thunderbolt Marshel learned from her mother.

Thelma followed her mother-in-law's advice to the letter. Upon receiving confirmation of her eight-week pregnancy from her ob-gyn soon after her return to Rock Hill, Thelma immediately called her mother—even before she informed her husband.

"Thelma!" Janie Thunderbolt screamed with delight when she heard her daughter's voice. "Baby Girl, you have been on my mind something strong for the past few days. Is everything all right? I called several times over the weekend."

"Mom . . ." Thelma said, in a voice moist with tears. She held the black phone receiver to her left ear as she sat on her bed. The push-button base lay on her nightstand, next to a gold-framed picture of her and Melvin. He was carrying her in his arms from the church to their car following their wedding reception. The joie-de-vivre on their faces was in juxtaposition with the somber expression that masked her face in the large rectangular mirror above her dresser.

"I'm here, Thelma," her mother said softly. "Take your time . . . my time is your time, so take all the time you need." Hearing only muffled sobs for a prolonged period, Janie stated, "I knew something was going on. Something . . . I could sense it."

"I'm pregnant," Thelma responded. "Eight weeks now. I just found out."

"Well, that's great news . . . right?" Hearing only silence, Janie asked. "What did Mr. Melvin have to say? He must be as excited as

I am. And as your father is going to be!"

Thelma breathed in slowly and exhaled quickly. "I haven't told him. Not yet. We visited his parents in Georgetown over the weekend. His mother told us she'd had a dream—something about seeing some fish. Which meant that somebody was expecting, and they thought it was me. I mean, us. How did you know something was going on?"

"Thelma," Janie answered with laughter in her voice, "I carried you and your brother deep down inside me for nine months, nine long months. Child, we are connected. Always will be!" She paused, then added, "So, what are you not saying that you want me to know? Are you happy about the baby? Scared? Angry? Come on, tell Mama."

Thelma relaxed into the light green ruffled pillow sham that lay atop the pillow encased in black linen. She sniffled and looked about the bedroom, noticing the many ways that her and Melvin's individual lives and preferences had merged.

"I'm . . . I guess I'm all three," she answered. "I'm happy and surprised about this baby." She placed her left hand on her stomach after transferring the phone receiver into her right hand. "I'm scared, 'cause everything I'm going through is new! And, yes, I'm angry too. But not at the baby." She looked at Melvin's socks cluttering the bedroom floor and she snapped, "I'm mad at this baby's daddy!"

"Oh, sweetie, pregnancy comes when pregnancy comes," her mother said, guessing the reasoning behind Thelma's exclamation. "Babies can't always be planned. They get started when people do what they do . . . and the two of you must've been doing *something*."

"We've been arguing recently, Mama. A lot! He told me I'm *controlling*! The nerve of him!"

"Is *that* what he said, now?" Janie asked. With feigned empathy, she added, "How could he have said *that* to *my child*? Not *controlling*?"

Feeling ensnared by the timing, tone, and delivery of her mother's words, Thelma said with a huff, "I know what you're doing. *You* can call me controlling. Since that's what you wrongly believe and have always falsely harped on, but *he* can't say that to me. And *not* in the *nasty* way he said it!"

"I'm so sorry he said that!" Janie spoke in a soft voice. "Now, tell me, was this your first get-real-ugly-as-husband-and-wife fight?

Couples say some real god-awful things to each other then. Then, if they can get past that gut-wrenching hurt and surprise, they can continue, more carefully, to *learn* each other. It takes a lifetime."

"That was not the most god-awful thing he said, Mama!"

"No?"

"No! He told me to H.A.!"

"H.A.? What's that mean? Hop away?"

Thelma held the phone away from her head and looked at it. "No, Mama," she said with exasperation. "He said . . ." and she paused to whisper, "*haul ass*."

"Oh, that was mean and hurtful!" Janie intoned.

"Yes, it was!" Thelma agreed. "And I keep hearing it. I keep seeing his lips move to say it. And the look in his eyes when he said it makes me back up when I get close to him. I'm scared it's going to jump out again from wherever it had been hiding."

"Oh, Thelma, I'm so sorry," Janie lamented.

Thelma had relaxed as the conversation continued, but her mother's next words brought her tension back. "What did he mean when he said it?" Janie asked.

"Mama," Thelma shouted, "what do you mean, 'What did he mean?' You know what he meant!"

"Baby Girl, all I'm saying is, you may think you know, but if you don't ask him, you really won't. People hear what they hear based on things that go on in their own minds, not necessarily in anyone else's."

Thelma was silent. Stilled. Sorry that she had started what had become an unsatisfying conversation.

"Let me tell you what I learned during my first year of marriage to your father." Thelma began to listen intently. "Your daddy, Henry Leroy Thunderbolt, told me, 'Now, don't ever dress up and sweeten yourself up like this in the morning on a weekday again. Please.' That man's words sliced through me like the paring knife I used to half the apples I put in his lunch pail! You see, when we got married his porter schedule on the railway had him leaving the station at 5:15 a.m. and returning four days later at the same time. If the trains stayed on schedule, that is. Two days off. Then back at it again.

"When he made it home, he'd rest up. I'd get up and dress to go to the White folks' home to pick up or deliver their laundry. And we'd get together and do what married people do when I came back home, or before he left on the next shift."

Thelma watched the image of herself listening to her mother in her dresser mirror. The image revealed that she had no idea where her mother's story was leading.

"Well, I decided, young-bride-me, to leave my husband feeling real good about his splendid wife he was about to leave for four days. While he slept, I got up, bathed, perfumed, dressed in a negligee, and fixed my hair and makeup to say, 'I am yours, and you will remember me!' How he slept through all this I do not know! But when I woke him up, the sandman left his eyes. And this was the first time he was later than usual in getting to the station.

"We kissed, starry-eyed, and then he walked out the front door, but he turned around fast and told me, 'Now, don't ever dress up and sweeten yourself up like this in the morning on a weekday again. Please.'" I was stunned.

"*What?* was the first question I wanted to scream, but he was running late. Other questions kept popping up in my mind for the four days he was away. *Did he not appreciate all I'd done to make that moment happen? Why were those words the last thing out of his mouth to me before he left? What, if anything, had displeased him? Does he want me to pleasure him only in the evening or nighttime, but not in the early morning?* Questions that need answers can make you evil-minded if you allow them.

"So, I was waiting up for him like a cocked pistol when he arrived back home."

"And did you ask him what he'd meant?" Thelma interrupted.

"Yes, I did!" Janie answered. "But not in such a pleasant manner as your question. And what he'd meant by those words left me ashamed for thinking he'd expressed anything like I'd imagined. He didn't want me going into those White people's homes presenting any portion of the passion that I'd just paraded for him, passion that was just for the two of us—not in my mind or on my person. He thought it would make the White women feel huffy about and intimidated by me as I walked about their houses. And if their men were home, it might make them consider having their former slave master ways with the women from slave row. And then your daddy would have to kill them dead!"

"Oh, Mama . . ." Thelma gasped.

"And he was right!" Janie stated. "And my mind had been filled with poisonous questions that left it too clouded with infection to see things any other way. So, Baby Girl, I'm going to say this one more time: you may think you know what Melvin meant, but if you don't ask him, you really won't. And even if what he meant was to be as mean and hurtful as those words sounded, you can't let the words or the memory of them freeze you in a death trap. No! Women can't let every hurt we feel, every injustice we know about, destroy us—or scatter us away from the people we love. Feeding on anger every minute of every day will leave us wallowing in worry. Negative thoughts will numb us. They'll bring on depression and sickness that'll sap you of your strength. You know what I mean—your strength to blossom into the beautiful woman and wife and mother. . . and everything else that makes you who you are. And remember, that baby inside you is feeding on everything that's in *your* body, *your* mind, and *your* spirit.

"Talk to him. You owe it to yourself to find out."

The rhythmic pounding of mortars and pestles used to be a mainstay on Lowcountry rice plantations. The process, which still is used daily in African villages, husked the outer shells from rice seeds that had been flailed off rice plants. Neither the crushing sound nor the up-and-down pestle movements were a part of Thelma's Seneca heritage. But the pummeling of questions and answers that she initiated and engaged in with her Gullah husband crushed and refined the seeds of their marital discord, fragmented the hard outer shell.

"Mortar and pestle
long time gone,
yet mortar and pestle
been deh, wit dem…
Pounding truth!
Poundling hope!
Pounding!"

Their living room, the space of their last quarrel, became their mortar. They agreed that the pulverizing of thoughts, feelings, and emotions should not occur in intimate spaces where they nurtured their innate appetites. Seated across from each other in two black leather armchairs, the pestle-pounding began.

"When you said those two horrible words, yelling at me about what I could do, you hurt me, Melvin!" Thelma began. Body stiff, with knees knit together and ankles crossed, Thelma looked at her husband with detachment, her hands clasped at the palms in her lap.

"I'm sorry I said those two words, Thelma," Melvin stated. "They should never have passed my lips."

"Which two words?" Thelma drilled.

A puzzled look spread across Melvin's face, but the intensity of Thelma's stare made it quickly vanish. Legs apart, he ground his feet into the floor, took a deep breath, and answered. "Haul ass!" were the words he expelled. "I told you to haul ass. And I'm sorry. I'm very sorry."

Thelma thought about her mother's revelation and continued, "What did you mean when you said those words, Melvin? Why did you hurl such a mean statement at me? I'm your wife. When I think about them, it feels as though spit is running down my face and over my body."

As Melvin watched, Thelma shuddered, then cupped her face in her hands, dragging her fingers down from her cheeks to her chin. He uncrossed his hands. Dropped his gaze. Shook his head. Closed his eyes. When he looked up at her, he spoke slowly.

"Sometimes, Thelma," he stated, "you don't let me talk—"

"What?" she snapped. "What do you mean I don't let you talk?"

He stared at her blank-faced, eye-to-eye, until his silence and lack of movement communicated the message that she should not interrupt. Thelma blinked, averted her gaze, breathed in. She relaxed her shoulders before returning her eyes to him, "I'm sorry," she said. "You were answering my question. I will listen."

Melvin leaned forward to continue, cupping his right hand into his left between his two legs, with his elbows on his thighs. "It's moments like that. That annoy me, irritate me, make my blood boil," he said. "I start to say something, and you take over! It makes me feel like you think I'm dumb or something—or that you think I'm not giving the answer that you think others need to hear.

Or that you *don't* want to hear."

Melvin's hands pushed on his knees as he elevated his posture. He turned his head and eyes away from Thelma and drummed his finger on his kneecaps, trying to think of how to express his next thought. "When you do things like that, Thelma, it's like you're trying to mold me into someone else, something else. And I don't like it! That's why I said those words. I meant, 'This is who I am.' He pointed both forefingers at himself. "So, love me just the way I am, the way I try to answer your questions or try to express my thoughts . . . or . . . or leave me."

"Is that what you want? I don't want to leave you, Melvin." Thelma massaged her temples and then her scalp with the fronts of fingers on both hands. With hair frizzed, she patted her right foot and quietly said, "That's the way I feel when you're slow in answering me . . . like maybe you'd answer more quickly if you were asked the same thing by someone else." She watched Melvin shake his head. "Or that maybe if someone else stated the same views or visions or plans that I express, you would offer feedback and just say something . . . anything."

When certain that Thelma was finished speaking, Melvin said, "You usually don't ask for my opinion, Thelma. You usually say, 'This is what you're going to do,' or 'This is what you think needs to happen,' and then you go on your way.'"

"But I always want to know what you want, Melvin."

"Well, you've got to be willing sometimes to wait until I express it. And not fight me when I begin to."

Husband and wife looked at each other. With new understanding. They held that gaze until the atmosphere in their living room, their mortar, began to feel renewed, recharged.

"Thanks for letting me know what you really meant to say," Thelma said with softened eyes. "I'm sorry about those times when my words or my actions have made you feel as though I'm trying to make you over into someone you're not. I'll try not to do that again."

Sporting a small smile, Melvin replied, "And thank you for listening, for listening and not interrupting. I accept that you really want to hear my views about matters and will try to respond to them more quickly. Forgive me?"

Thelma nodded her head. "Forgive me?" she asked.

Melvin pulled his armchair closer and reached for her hands. With the hard, outer shell of their discord now broken, Thelma looked lovingly at Melvin and whispered, "Your mother's dream was right, dear. How did she say it? 'We makin foot fa socks!'"

Florence could not believe her eyes! The life insurance check she'd pulled out of the envelope had one too many zeros. Instead of the anticipated twenty thousand, the payoff amount for Emanuel Tucker read two hundred thousand dollars. How could it be?

"Chadwick," she blurted into the phone when he answered and she launched into conversation, "the insurance check for Tucker has come in. It's the wrong amount. We've got to send it back! What are we gonna do? We've been waiting on this!"

The steeliness of his response alarmed her further. "I thought we'd agreed not to open it when it arrived, not until we were together," he stated.

"That's what *you* said," Florence responded when she got her wind back, "but we did not come to any agreement. What difference does it make? Both of our names are on this check, and it's for *my* grandfather."

"Florence, I—"

"And yesterday you seemed upset that the check was taking so long to get here. Said there were pressing bills that needed to be paid."

"That's right, but . . ."

"But nothing. If I deposited the check now that it's here, it would clear soon. And then bills would be paid. Am I right, or am I right?"

"Right, Florence. You're right!"

"Well, bills can't be paid any time soon, 'cause this check has got to be rewritten," Florence concluded. "That's what seems right to me."

"No, it's the right amount, Florence," Chadwick replied after a prolonged silence. "I'd hoped to talk about it before we opened the envelope. Together. It's the right amount. Can we talk about this when I get home? Please?"

Holding her mobile phone in her left hand, Florence stared at it in disbelief after the call ended. She eyed it up and down, up and down then up, as though it was her husband's face. When her feet pivoted, they launched her on a journey in her home that she had never walked, a lone reconnaissance regiment. She was on-mission to surveil information about which she had not been informed. She sat at Chadwick's desk in his new, in-home office and pulled out the checkbooks and ledgers of their personal bank account, from which she and Chadwick both paid bills. Five recent transactions had yet to be balanced, but nothing else seemed awry.

And then, as she'd never done before, Florence began to pore through Chadwick's business bank account. She noted deposits from his part-time jobs, transfers to their personal account for personal expenses, and hefty monthly draft payments to the insurance company that had mailed this sizable check. Monthly draft payments of $1,200. More money than she had been aware Chadwick had been raking in from his nighttime and weekend jobs—the work at which he'd toiled so that she could stay home as caretaker-in-chief. Rifling through his desk drawers, opening envelopes, Florence uncovered the copy of the home equity loan her grandfather had signed.

Her head began to boil!

Carrie Middleton drove her newfound cousin Easter deep into the backwoods of Darcatia Plantation, to the ruins near the shores of the Waccamaw River, where Rinda had once lived. To the cabin Tucker had visited on fishing jaunts away from Mausaville. To the site where Easter and Absalom had been conceived, close to a cypress swampland.

Billowing moss and whispering voices held Easter spellbound as soon as she stepped onto the soil. Standing outside the car, she saw visions. She saw the eyes of four alligators, the grins of three turkey buzzards.

She heard sounds. Her mother's eerie chanting of, "*Oh de possum laugh.*"

A male voice asking, "Wa e look like?" A sobbing, pregnant Rinda, dressed in black, watching in grief as a casket was lowered into the ground and then a man hiding behind others near the gravesite. She felt vibrations. Of a mist seeping up from the soil. Of the mist shackling her feet to the ground.

Captivated and alarmed, Easter set one hand akimbo and the other on her belly. The child within her womb had begun to bound about, unfettered. It darted left, then right, then down, then up.

As breezes tossed the bearded Spanish moss on the tree limbs, Easter heard gears shifting, tires rolling, and saw a Greyhound bus speeding north. Easter knew, as she watched, that she was inside the bus, not seated but nestled inside her mother, Rinda. And she knew that the pecan-brown man whom her mother had eyed at the gravesite had come out of hiding to catch sight of the retreating bus and then had turned around and walked away.

Carrie waited calmly as her cousin looked about the Darcatia Plantation scenery in silent revelry. When Easter began to thrash about, however, Carrie became concerned.

Easter had heard a slight pop, then felt a gush of fluid on her perineum. She had looked down and tried to spread her legs but couldn't. Seeing clear fluid trickle down Easter's leg, Carrie asked, "Gal, yo wata done broke. Enty?"

She watched Easter try unsuccessfully to lift her left leg then her right. *Had her paralysis returned?* Carrie wondered. She had no way of knowing that an invisible layer of mist had bound Easter immoveable so that she could see, hear, and know that the sins of her father and mother had left her and her brother shackled by a generational curse of death and despair.

Easter twisted and turned her torso and attempted to free her lower limbs from an unseen entanglement, but she fell backward onto the ground. She lay motionless. Her eyes did not open. And Carrie was concerned, deeply concerned. Fearing that Easter had suffered another stroke, Carrie knelt beside her, gently patting her face and calling, "Easta! Easta! Stay yah now. E ain time fa gone on wit de ancestas. Hep a comin. Hep a comin soon!"

She called 9-1-1, gave detailed directions about where to find them, phoned her mother Sophronia, and sat on the ground beside Easter. Holding Easter's limp hands, Carrie pleaded, "Hol on, now, Easta. Hol on."

At the moment Easter's head hit the ground at Darcatia Plantation, Florence was filling the kettle for tea. The water pressure at the kitchen sink constricted, reminding her of conditions at their modular home that had begun soon after her grandfather had moved in. At that time, Emanuel's past was being weighed on the scales of justice to restore balance within his family.

Florence began to ponder the thoughts that had motivated her to pursue Gregory's services. *Why had Chadwick wanted her to become caretaker of her elderly grandfather? Tucker could've returned to his own home and not remained in their at-home care. And why had Chadwick initiated plans for a twenty-thousand-dollar life insurance policy for Tucker? A ten-thousand-dollar policy in addition to Tucker's own $2,500 policy would've been sufficient.* The questions plagued Florence. *What other resources was Chadwick tapping into to secure all the upgrades they were enjoying? Why was Chadwick so overly invested with philanthropic zeal that allowed him to detach his care, concern, and humanity from those they had agreed he would help?*

She recalled why she'd selected Russell Porcher as Chadwick's *ember*. To connect him with a male who, like himself, was charitable; a male of about his same age who gave others a financial boost because he was aware of a need, as Porcher had done when he'd gifted them with twenty-five dollars upon learning they'd experienced a family death; he was an African American male who benefited another without looking for anything in return. Porcher, she was certain, had no idea of their economic status or community standing because he was a comeyah and had just met them. Aside from Chadwick's one fellow board member, none of their church or community members had ever shown them any financial favors. The standing perception was that the Wineglasses had no financial need.

Most men don't know how to connect with or realize the value of connecting with other like-minded men, she'd reasoned. *Each man thinks of himself as an island. Most hold stuff too tight to their chests.* She'd hoped Chadwick and Russell might develop a friendship, but when Russell's monetary allotment had been dispersed, Chadwick had been ready to move on to another *ember. What's he afraid of?* she wondered. *What voices is he listening to?*

"Florence," Sophronia stated with urgency when she'd answered the phone, "Easta Lillie on de way ta de hospital! Een de EMS. E been fallout wen e been out wit Carrie."

"Is the baby on the way?"

"Me ain de know. Me ain know if Easta been had anodda stroke. Me ain de know nottin!"

"Oh, Sophronia, I'm so sorry to hear! What can I do? What was going on when she fell out?"

"Keep huh een ya prayers, yah! Dah de only ting anybody can do now. Keep Easta an de baby een yah prayers."

"Listen," Florence said as she rushed to get her pocketbook and car keys, "I'm leaving the house in just a few minutes. I'll meet you at the hospital. Are you by yourself?"

"No, Carrie wit me. A een de passenga seat. Ebrybody else still at wok. Wen A wake up taday, A tell ya, A been yeddy a nightingale sing right outside ma winda. An a beenna know sompn been gon happen. E beenna sign, ya know. Umm-hmm. Sompn ga happen, Florence . . . ."

"Now, don't worry yourself into having an event, too! Calm down. Calm down. I'll be there soon. We'll all pray in agreement—that she and the baby will be okay, and all will be well."

Florence's call to Chadwick from the SUV went to voicemail. *Was this also a sign?* she wondered. *Shouldn't she, like Sophronia, have heard a nightingale singing outside her window this morning to prepare her for unsettling news?* Her voicemail message informed Chadwick where she was traveling and why.

As she drove, she reflected on the free words of advice Gregory had given her. *Your grandfather planted seedlings that became a low-lying vine,* he'd said. *This vine was different from the high-blossoming bush that grew from the seedlings that your grandfather planted elsewhere. You, Florence, are fruit from the high-blossoming bush. But fruit from the low-lying vine also have leafy boughs. When those two fruits come together, there'll be healing.*

When Chadwick arrived at the Greater Georgetown Community Hospital ER, he'd missed seeing the fullness of what was happening to Easter. Had missed witnessing the brunt of destruction wreaked by the gale winds of Emanuel Tucker's legacy that was launched when Emanuel's secret began—a secret launched years before Tucker realized the transformative richness of his blessing. Years before he had begun the rung-by-rung climb up Jacob's ladder to church and community eldership.

Yet Chadwick found himself in the eye of the hurricane. Florence's gaze, in response to their earlier conversation, tracked his walk toward her with longitudinal and latitudinal precision. With no awareness of where and when her accusations would land, he was rightfully fearful.

"Florence, I got here as fast as I could," he said, brushing up against her tepid, seated embrace. Attempting to deflect embarrassment, he quickly turned to the Middletons. "How do, ladies?" he asked. "Any news yet on how she's doing?"

Two doctors walked into the waiting room before they answered. Sophronia and Carrie stood to meet them and began to breathe heavily as they searched the doctors' eyes from face to face to assess their prolonged pause. The Middleton women clasped hands and moved their toes up and down to steady their knees from buckling. In a show of support, Florence stood and moved toward them, but kept a distance from her husband.

"I'm sorry to inform you . . ."

Sophronia gasped. Carrie's neck snapped upward and both hands moved to the sides of her face.

"We could not save her," the female doctor continued. "We sustained her vitals as long as possible, but she had lapsed into a coma before arrival."

"De baby . . . de baby gone, too?" Sophronia stammered.

"We successfully performed a Caesarian delivery of a baby girl," the male doctor answered. "The infant was rushed to the neonatal unit for a thorough examination, given the mother's medical records. There's evidence of some birth defects, but nothing is conclusive at this point."

Unsettled by the Middletons' despair, Florence stepped next to Chadwick and leaned on him. He wrapped an arm around her shoulder.

"Concerning the care of the newborn," the female physician stated, the Department of Social Services has been contacted to determine who is the immediate next of kin.

"Dere ain no fadah anybody know bout," Carrie said.

"Is anyone here the grandparent?"

All shook their heads. Sophronia looked at Carrie and Florence, then at the doctors, and said, "De baby we cousin."

After eyeing each other, the doctors answered alternately.

"Well, the social worker will come to speak with you soon about child custody and explain everything you and other family members will need to know."

"We'll give an update on the baby as soon as possible."

"When the mother is available for viewing, you'll be escorted to the room."

By the time the Middletons were escorted to view Easter Lillie's remains, Florence had retreated from her husband in the waiting room. The vortex of her emotions was spinning out of control. And the eyewall of her anger was awaiting the right conditions to land.

"Florence," Chadwick whispered. "I know I should've told you before today about the amended life insurance policy, but I can exp—"

"Explain?" she asked in a reciprocal whisper that raged. "The sizable premium payments?" The force of her questioning intensified. "The numerous part time jobs and hours away from home?" Her storm escalated to Category 4. "How about Tucker's home equity loan neatly tucked away in your desk drawer?"

Her questions stopped buffeting him, but Florence's gaze left Chadwick under the advisory that he was in the eye of her hurricane. He chose to remain silent and await conditions that were sure to unfold on the dirty side.

Certain that she had toppled his confidence about being in control of the situation, she imagined the scenes that her attitude was causing Chadwick to envision in his mind's eye. Power snapping. Automobiles standing underwater. Impressive houses ravaged.

"You can save all your explanations for another time," she said. "And I want to hear each and every one of them. But here's what's going to happen now." She paused and waited. "That newborn is my cousin. It has Tucker blood from limb to limb. We couldn't have any children before today. But today a child is born. A new life has been given. And I want to keep it. I want Easter's Lillie's child to be our child."

"Do we have to make a hasty decision about this?" Chadwick asked. "Shouldn't we get clarity on birth defects? On any other medical concerns? This could be a costly consideration."

"Costly?" Florence voiced coolly. Gale force winds had returned. "Why, the money we may need to cover our child's medical expenses arrived today in the mail. Didn't it? So, when the social worker arrives, let's become the parents we are meant to be. Please? Together, let's think big. About ourselves."

Bishop Bessellieu sensed the charred atmosphere in the hospital waiting room. After visiting with an esteemed hospitalized church member, he'd stopped there to await a colleague who was still in the room of a family member. Not wanting to interfere or to misjudge any known or imagined family drama, he began to pray. Silently. In intercession. Eyes closed. Requests ascending.

"Great God," he intoned. "You are the wheel in the middle of the wheel. Lord, Lord, I sense a wheel of confusion over here. A wheel of anger over there. There are numerous other wheels circling within this room that I can neither discern nor identify. But I know, oh, Lord, that You know and see them all. Nothing is hidden from You.

"So, Lord, Your humble servant asks in faith that now, at this very moment, that You take every disc and rim and axle hub, every spoke and wheel, rod and rim-rider of all the wheels in this very room, and charge each part to do Your will. Charge them to turn round and round for peace. Charge them to hover in the air like the wheel that prophet and priest Ezekiel saw for harmony. And charge them to journey to each heart and mind and spirit among me to inspire enduring connections between this place, where we deal with the troubles of the world, and Your kingdom, where life continues without end.

"Help us all who are waiting in this room to know Joy. The Joy that the world did not give, and that the world cannot take away. Hear my pleas, oh, Lord, I pray. Amen. Amen. Amen."

When The Right Reverend Bessellieu opened his eyes, a sweet spirit had cleansed the environment. And, unknown to him, an unheralded realization of the continuum of Gullah Geechee existence had done come on een de room. The realization that today's happenstance had occurred yesterday—and would occur tomorrow. That lessons learned are echoed. Indiscretions unacknowledged and unatoned for are repeated, in an infant's first breath and behavior, an elder's twitch and mannerism, an ancestor's whisper and intercession.

As Florence and Chadwick waited to speak with the hospital social worker, a forgotten memory floated into Florence's subconscious, relaxing the chains of disdain she had wrapped around her husband. Years ago, she recalled, soon after she'd begun cooking at Calabash by the Sea, she'd been surprised to see Gregory Dunkin looking at her side-eyed in the doorway to the restaurant kitchen.

Late 1990s

She'd arrived early to get the Chicken Bog underway before other workers arrived, and had begun humming, then singing, an old spiritual, "Ezekiel Saw the Wheel," that she'd heard her Grandma Blessing sing around her house.

> *"Wheel, oh, wheel*
> *Wheel in de middle of a wheel.*
> *Wheel, oh, wheel*
> *Wheel in de middle of a wheel"*

Florence had laid two chicken carcasses into a large pot of water and added a pinch of salt, black pepper, and garlic before bringing it to a boil for broth.

"'Zekiel saw de wheel of time.
Wheel in de middle of a wheel
Ev'ry spoke was humankind
Way in de middle of a wheel"

Entranced by the music in her head, Florence had chopped strips of smoked pork sausage into medium-sized chunks.

"Way up yonder on de mountain top
Wheel in de middle of a wheel
My Lord spoke an' de chariot stop
Way in de middle of a wheel"

She'd diced onions and carrots, then celery, and laid them in a bowl to stir-fry later.

"'Zekiel saw de wheel
Way up in de middle of de air
Zekiel saw de wheel
Way in de middle of de air"

Then Florence began to dance about the kitchen. She gathered two skillets: one to sear the sausage and the pulled chicken from quarter sections that she'd boiled and refrigerated the day before, and another for stir-frying. With a can of vegetable oil in her raised right hand, she lowered it slowly in tempo to the song, and poured enough to cover the skillet bottoms.

"Little wheel run by de grace of God
Wheel in a wheel
Way in de middle of de air
Wheel, oh, wheel"

Moving about as though she was shuffling in a ring shout, she laid a large bag of long-grain rice on the countertop close to the stove. She set seasonings nearby. Salt, chili powder, paprika, parsley, and several halved lemons to squeeze later. Her mind had drifted away, and with closed eyes, she envisioned the beauty of her cooked dish. The chicken and sausages had bogged down in the cooked rice. The rice, like Carolina Gold plants in the rice fields of yesteryear, had fluffed up after being reduced in the savory broth in which it had been submerged. Down in the broth like the rice seeds that had been plopped into the swampy, gumbo-like soil. To her, the dish that day had looked, oh, so delightful and welcoming, with flecks of orange, green, and yellow from the seasoned vegetables.

When she opened her eyes, Gregory was silently watching her, unamused, unengaged.

"I didn't hear you come in," she said, startled. "Been there long?"

His eyes were set on hers, and he did not respond.

"I know you know the song, Gregory. You should've joined me. Together, we would've made the spirits of every Black cook who ever worked in this kitchen sing new words to 'Adam in the garden pickin' up leaves.' You know, 'Chefs are in the kitchen cookin' up meals . . . .'"

Throwing her head back, Florence had laughed with abandon. Gregory, however, did not. She began to wonder if he was not well.

"Gregory?" she called to him in a low voice, looking around helplessly to see if any other worker had arrived.

Soon after, his eyes began to move, slowly, then his head, then his mouth. When he began to speak, it surprised her. "Don't let no preacher make you think that that song is just about crossing over into heaven," he'd said. "It's deeper than that, Florence. Way deeper! Do you remember when we learned about the atom in Mr. Deas's fifth grade science class?"

"Sure do," Florence had answered, pleased to know that Gregory was not experiencing a stroke. She breathed more deeply and rested her left hand on the counter.

"What did it look like?" he'd asked.

Pausing momentarily, she shrugged her shoulders, widened her eyes, and responded matter-of-factly and with childlike innocence, "An atom." Gregory's dumbfounded expression revealed that she had not provided the answer he'd expected. So, she continued, "Well, is there something particular that you were hoping I would say?"

His body language had mellowed, his stance had opened, and

he'd begun to speak with a sense of wonder. "When I first saw a picture of an atom, you know it looked like the song you were just singing," he'd said. "Like a wheel in the middle of a wheel."

"That's right! I remember seeing all the circles," Florence briefly hummed the first two lines of the chorus.

"And every cell in our bodies is made up of atoms," Gregory continued. "Every living thing is made up of atoms. Made up of little wheels in the middle of wheels. Electrons, or positive energy, circling around neurons and around protons, the negative energy. This is what keeps us alive!"

Florence nodded her head in slow, up-and-down motions to take everything in. She glanced quickly at the stove and lifted her nose to see and sniff that all was well with her meal preparation. Gregory continued revealing his recollections, and Florence returned her undivided attention toward him. With her back to the counter, she first used her palms and forearms to boost herself to sit on the counter.

"Daddy told me that too many people spend too much time worrying about getting into heaven," Gregory said. "And that many of them really don't want to get there, anyway. Uh uh! He said if they did, they wouldn't seek him out in secret, hoping for him to make bad things happen to those that they want bad things to happen to."

"Can he really do that?" Florence had asked sheepishly.

"Well, Daddy sometimes says things that make them think he can do such things—if that's what they want to believe. And if they follow through with his instructions and bad things happen to others, then just how do they think they're going to make it into this heaven that they say they want to get to?"

The water bubbled in the large pot, erupting scalding splashes onto the stove. Florence jumped onto the floor and scurried to lower the flame on the gas range. "That's a heavy-duty morning-time conversation!" She shifted gears. "Have you clocked in yet?"

She turned on the burners below the skillets and looked left and right to determine what action should be undertaken next. The past ten minutes had not unraveled as she'd planned upon her arrival. Yet, at that moment, her mind revealed a serendipity as magical as when she'd accidentally sprinkled basil and cilantro into a bowl of eggs she'd been about to scramble. It had become a sensation! And she and many Calabash by the Sea customers could not fathom how eggs could've been cooked without them before.

Florence had clapped her hands when she received the mental illumination. *Gregory's meanderings were for himself, not for her, not at that moment. But maybe, just maybe, one day, who knew when, his trip down memory lane would impact her just like the basil and cilantro chance discovery. Without his words, she perhaps one day would not be able to fathom the meaning of life without them.*

Gregory concluded his explanation before walking to the time clock at the far end of the kitchen. "God is divine energy," he'd said. "And light is energy. If we use our positive energy to circle around and around any negative energy, the negative energy won't thrive. Florence, we are each the wheel in the middle of the wheel. Like the song you were singing. That's the truth I want people to know. And people need to realize that casting negative energy on others will pull negative energy right back onto them.

"My dad, William Dunkin, wants me to study under him. Uh huh, and I'm going to study to help people to understand, to see the negative energy that they might be holding on to. When they do, then the wheel in the middle of the wheel, the many systems within their own bodies, can work to deliver them from any emotional, mental, or physical bondage." He stared into space and spoke as though he was teleporting a divine message. "Our circulatory system, nervous system, lymphatic system, musculoskeletal system, immune system, endocrine system, digestive system, excretory system, respiratory system, and reproductive system all circle throughout our bodies. We are the wheel in the middle of the wheel. And releasing negative energy is the way God sets us free!"

Late 2000s

Chadwick soaked in the scorn of Florence's words and realized that *he had, he had, he had, yes, been moved!* Budged from their vision as Benefactors in Generosity. Buffeted by enticements of personal gain camouflaged as community empowerment. Battered by flirtation with White supremacists. And busted up by framing success through the veil of White capitalism.

Of course, he could not support Doyle's scheme to disempower the local Gullah community workforce. He should not enable Gullah sacred sites to become sites of tourist construction. He ought not make others feel "a chill of terror" by "plucking out eyes and organs" and making "their debtors flee who'd been trying to devour them." Most importantly, he must reconcile with Florence.

Otherwise, his legacy would be like chaff. Worthless. The paper-like skin of rice seeds that have been pounded in handmade mortars and pestles. The refuse that blows away in the breeze as the grains of rice fall into fanner baskets. Winnowed, tossed up and down, up and down, Chadwick desired more.

Benjamin Neesmith, the hospital social worker, met the Wineglasses in the waiting room and escorted them to his office. They sat on the other side of his desk, which displayed several pamphlets about adoption and a set of forms to be signed.

Looking through black, heavy-framed glasses with round lenses, Neesmith rested both hands on his desktop and said, "If I understand correctly, you're interested in discussing the adoption of a newborn who is a relative and whose mother passed following childbirth."

"That's right!" Florence sat erect and stated. "We wish to adopt." She looked to her husband, who eyed her peripherally. He edged his chair closer to hers and nodded to Neesmith with a relaxed countenance.

"Wonderful," Neesmith said. "That's wonderful." His next statement was delivered as though it had been lifted directly from one of the pamphlets on his desk. "Adoption is a beautiful way to provide a family for a child in need. There are children of all ages in need of a forever home. Making sure children are in safe, loving, and permanent families is an important way DSS strengthens families in South Carolina."

Florence spoke calmly, looking to Chadwick to confirm any answers she offered. Chadwick was conciliatory and undefiant. "Yes, the infant is our cousin," Florence said, reaching with her left hand to grab Chadwick's right one. "Ours will be a forever home. It'll be safe. It'll be loving, and, yes, it'll be permanent."

Chadwick squeezed her hand, pleased that for now she had laid down her burden. He was hopeful that as they embarked on this commitment, Florence would "study war no more."

"It's of utmost importance," Neesmith explained, "that I review with you the medical report of the newborn. This was a high-risk childbirth." He lifted his glasses from his face to study the couple's composure. Each sighed softly, looked to each other, and then back to him. Their lips were pursed, their eyes steadfast but pained, their shoulders rigid.

"We're ready," Chadwick said with solemnity. "We're listening."

With his left hand, Neesmith returned the glasses to his face. He picked up the medical report with his right hand and began reading. The list of medical conditions was lengthy. The silence of the prospective parents as they listened was deafening.

"Thank you," Florence said. "How long will she be in the neonatal ICU?"

"What's the likelihood she'll outgrow any of these conditions, these challenges?" Chadwick inquired as soon as Florence's last word had been spoken.

Pausing a beat and grasping his chin with the thumb and forefinger of his right hand, Neesmith looked at them both with tenderness and compassion. "Those are good questions, very good questions," he stated. "Unfortunately, no definitive answer can be given to either one of them at this time. I can only say that the baby has a strong heartbeat. Her care is one for the long haul. Laboratory tests have begun and will continue for some time."

"Well, parenthood is for the long haul," Florence intoned. "Chadwick, are we in this for the long haul?"

"Yes, dear," Chadwick answered, and breathed a deep sigh. He placed his right arm around Florence's shoulder. "This child will be a Wineglass, and we're in for the long haul."

Florence's shoulders trembled, and a single tear cascaded down her left cheek. She opened her eyes and looked at her husband. Moving momentarily out of his embrace, she looked at his hands, and they were new. She looked inside him to his heart, and it was new too. Relieved, she nestled back below Chadwick's arm.

"Well, then," Neesmith stated, "have you had time to consider a name? It won't be needed at this moment, but for the birth certificate and the adoption papers, that's something that'll be needed sooner than later." He placed a form before them and began to read them the lines even as he looked at the form upside-down.

"Blessing!" Florence stated. She raised her head and then her hands. Chadwick and Neesmith looked at her in surprise. "I'm a name her Blessing. After my grandma. Bless her soul—for all she knew and did not know! And this birth today . . . this birthday of being a parent . . . is a gift from God Almighty. An outpouring from heaven. So, Blessing. Blessing Celeste Wineglass. That's her name. Write it down, now. Write it down. That's her name."

Poring through her pocketbook to find a Kleenex, she pulled out a love note, a Marcus Garvey quote that had been stuffed away: "If we as a people realized the greatness from which we came we would be less likely to disrespect ourselves." She passed it to Chadwick and moved her chair even closer to his.

Relishing the Savor

On a cool fall morning, three seemingly unconnected, yet intricately intertwined, couples found themselves walking around the grounds of Mourning Dove Cemetery in Mausaville. No couple had any awareness the others would be there, and upon their arrival were flabbergasted to see familiar automobiles parked at the trunk of the large live oak at the apex of the dirt road.

Each couple had been called there. One member of each pair had heard the sound of someone blowing into a conch shell—as plantation slave drivers had at one time made daily to call field workers to the rice fields. Each had sensed an inner prodding or a quiet voice telling them to invite the other individual to journey to the cemetery. There were no refusals.

Eloise walked with Sibyl to the left, near the Nesbit family graves from the 1800s. Hand-in-hand, Melvin led Thelma to the newer Marshel family graves on the right. And Pastor Timothy Thunderbolt, with patience, followed Gregory Dunkin to view the splendor of a field of yellow flowers, wingstem, a natural herb, God's abundant beauty.

"If Mobo ain been run way, e bohdy been gon res some wheh . . . right oba deh," Eloise said softly. "Dah wheh we peepul da."

The two newfound family members clasped their hands together and stood shoulder to shoulder. Breathing deeply, each looked in wonder at the mounds of dirt decorated with shells. Or broken glass. Or small sunken gravestones. Or old pieces of wood or board scraps shaped into crosses—not as the Christian symbol, but perhaps as an African Ankh, on which the teardrop-shaped loop may have been pillaged by those who had no understanding of its meaning as a symbol of unending life.

"Bot de sperit ob Gawd mek em fly way," Eloise continued. "Fly way . . ."

". . . to freedom," Sibyl whispered to complete Eloise's sentence. Her eyes closed in meditation of the words she'd spoken, and a rivulet of emotion began to cascade from each eyelid when she opened them.

"An de same sperit of Gawd breng Mobo sperit . . . back yah . . . shru you, chile," Eloise said, as she stood erect but with a heart that was knee-bent and body-bowed. "Back ta de lan e lef frum. Back ta e peepul wa e lef yah. Cause e nyame *Mobo*. An *Mobo* mean *freedom*, ya know. An we peepuls git free wen we memba de ones wa gone on. An tank em fa all dey gone shru."

The elder woman's shoulders began to droop. Her head fell forward and shook from side to side.

"Almighty God," Sibyl began to pray. With uplifted hands, head, and eyes, she intoned. "Thank you for connecting me with my roots. From across miles. Across waters. Across generations. Across tribes and lineages and history. I am now. I am past. I am future. I give thanks, oh, God, I give thanks!"

On the far and newer side of the cemetery, the no-longer estranged husband and wife walked among the graves of relatives and acquaintances that he'd not thought about since his childhood.

"That one, the one with the small cedar trees at each end," Melvin said, pointing when he saw the name on the gravestone. "You see it?"

"Uh huh," Thelma responded. "What about it?"

"Well, I don't want to talk bad about the dead, but that's the grave of No-Nose Mollie."

Thelma read the name "Mollie Ravenel" and waited with intrigue to hear what her husband had to say. She looked at him inquisitively, her head tilted and her eyes wide open.

"They say Miss Mollie had no nose," he began. "She came to church with gauze stretched from cheek to check and taped to her face with white surgical tape." He tapped the forefingers of each hand to his cheekbones three times for emphasis. "It was the scariest thing! The gauze above her top lip would flutter from time to time. From her breathing, I guess. Thelma, when I was a boy, I thought she was a mummy or something!"

Thelma shook her head and let Melvin continue.

"Miss Mollie was dark like burnt wood and had these large round eyes, with black eyeballs set in a pool of white. She always sat in the back of the church. She would look at those who looked at her for a brief moment and then look away. Now, we were told not to stare at her. But, you know me."

"You would stare," she answered, her eyes widening to parrot his childlike gaze before he nodded his head in solemn affirmation.

"Yeah, and that gauze above her top lip would flutter," he added. "And it'd make me think of that Bible story of the dry bones coming together. 'Bone to bone, the dry bones!'" he mimicked with the theatrics of a Baptist preacher. "It was like having a nightmare each Sunday. I'd look back again and again out of the corner of my eyes and would turn around to stare in front of me quickly if I felt like her head was turning to let those dead eyes rest on me again."

Melvin's body began to shudder from the memory, and Thelma moved close to rub her hands slowly down his shoulders and arms. To center him.

"That's a childhood memory you've never shared before," she said. "What'd happened to her?"

"Well, they say she had syphilis, and it ate away her nose," Melvin answered. "When I learned what syphilis was, that memory was the only thing I needed to keep myself protected if I ever was on the prowl!"

"You mean to say, the sight of Miss 'No-Nose Mollie' was your only moral takeaway from your childhood in the church?" Thelma asked. She stepped away from him, crossed her arms, and awaited his response.

"Now, there you go again—putting things I didn't say in my mouth." She watched Melvin's body tense but then relax as he listened to her soft chuckle, realizing that she had been joking and not arguing.

"Baby, don't fool around with me like that, please," he said, moving closer to hold her hands in his. "You know, making me feel like I've gotta be careful about the things I tell you."

Pulling him to her, she looked quietly into his eyes. "Mr. Marshel," she said, as she placed her palms on either side of his chin, "treat me always as your queen, and your stories will be my stories. Our stories will become our children's stories. Where you stay, I will stay. Where you die, I will die, and there I will be buried."

Their lips caressed, and the ancestors rejoiced. Husband and wife looked at each other with new resolve and affection.

Before their gaze fell on two familiar figures walking through a distant field of yellow flowers near the marshes overlooking the Black River, they began to sense a resonant pulsation throughout the graveyard.

"Well, it's a surprise to see my wife's car parked here at the entrance of this large cemetery," Rev. Thunderbolt said to Gregory as they opened the car doors and stepped outside. He peered in the distance to the left and to the right of the solitary oak, with his left hand shielding his eyes from the sunlight.

"I'm sure everything is all right," Gregory said in a calm voice. "Does she like to gather at sacred places?"

"Yes . . . yes, she does," Thunderbolt answered. "Her heritage is Chippewa and African American. So, seeking solace in the burial places of family members is in her blood and in her bones." He saw two couples, one to the left and the other to the right.

"There she is—over there," he said with relief as he recognized the colorful blouse she was wearing. "I didn't think she knew of this place, and she didn't say a word about traveling here. She was going to visit one of the church mothers today. That's all I know."

Gregory spread his hands, palms up, as he spoke. "Maybe an inner voice called her or whomever she's with to gather here." Tilting his head downward to the right, his eyes looked upward at Thunderbolt as he added, "And when the Spirit calls, those who hear must answer."

Thunderbolt chuckled and threw his head back. "Oh, yes," he said. "Yes, yes, yes. I awoke this morning to what I thought was the sound of the archangel Gabriel. You know, I thought I was hearing a calling of the Second Coming, and I sat up in bed with excitement. Sibyl said she hadn't heard anything, and when I thought about it, I told her that what I'd heard sure hadn't sounded like a trumpet."

He paused momentarily and nodded his head up and down, up and down. Gregory listened to what he said—and to what he did not say.

"It was alarming," Thunderbolt continued. "Just as I imagine it will be like in that Great Getting Up Morning! And right then a still, small voice told me to call you and find out more about this place you call home."

"Aha!" Gregory said in amazement, as he rested his chin on the two pointers of his folded hands. "That's interesting."

"And when I picked you up to go somewhere where we can talk," Thunderbolt continued, "you had me drive to, of all places, a graveyard—a graveyard that's located out beyond God's back, at that. And then I find my wife has come here too.

"I don't know what the Spirit is trying to tell me." He looked first to the heavens and then all around him. "But I'm open to hear what He wants me to know."

"Very interesting, indeed!" Gregory said. He looked intuitively and empathically at Thunderbolt with eyes to hear and ears to see. "Now, you said that the sound you heard wasn't that of a trumpet. What was it like? Can you describe it?"

Timothy Thunderbolt thought. Then he pressed his lips together, cupped his hands to his mouth, and blew a steady, low, resonant, ocean-like sound. "Like that," he said when he finished. "I don't think I've heard any sound like that before."

The outer corners of Gregory's eyes crinkled as he smiled. "Well, Pastor," he said, "the Spirit wanted you to learn about my homeland, all right! The sound that woke you up this morning was the slave driver's call to work in the rice fields. The call was made by blowing into a conch shell." With hands to his mouth, he echoed the sound Thunderbolt had made, and the two stared at each other.

"The slave drivers on rice plantations most times were Africans," Gregory said. "They assisted the overseer, who was the one that gave the daily tasks to each worker. The driver was responsible for directing each field hand where to work. And for punishing those who would not work. And those who didn't finish their work fast enough.

"Yeah, he looked like the others. Talked like the others. But the plantation owners pitted their drivers against all the others. Drivers were as mean as rattlesnakes! And you can guess why. The plantation owners would warn that if they didn't keep their dark brothers in line, the tide would change. And no driver wanted to end up as a field hand under a former field hand who remembered how he'd lashed them. A key to slavery's success was for one group of people, or an individual, to convince other human beings that they were better, worthier, greater than the others."

"*Black* slave drivers, you say?" Thunderbolt interrupted. "I never read that in any history book. I thought only White people were in charge on plantations. In fact, I thought most plantations in the South grew cotton. Or tobacco. I just heard about rice plantations when I came here to Georgetown. And I'm from the South Carolina Upcountry."

Gregory shook his head with the solemnity of a judge's gavel. "Well, ya don't know til ya know," he said. "And *we* need to know *ouah* story cause *his* story ain' bout us!"

Both men looked up at the sound of loud, shrilling alarm calls. A belted kingfisher squawked and rattled in a nearby tree to scare away an intruder, then poked its head out from a cluster of branches. With stealth, it flitted to a nearby branch to keep a watchful eye. Its large head, long, sharp, pointed bill, short legs, stubby tail, and colorful feathers made the bird readily identifiable to Gregory, and he regarded sighting it as a sign.

Without averting his eyes from the scene of the sounds, Gregory asked, "Do you know what this means?"

"Do I know what *what* means?" Thunderbolt responded.

"Seeing a kingfisher bird."

"Oh, is that what that is?" Thunderbolt said without excitement. He watched as Gregory nodded and then added tepidly, "No, I do not."

"It's a sign of freedom, of release." Gregory beamed as he locked eyes with the pastor. "To see a kingfisher means you should listen to your visions and dreams. You should overcome your fears of the unknown and plunge into something new." His eyes brightened with excitement.

Thunderbolt growled in a low voice, rolled his eyes, and took a step away. "Just sounds like Lowcountry hearsay to me," he chided. "Some kind of Gullah mumbo jumbo. The Bible doesn't say a thing about any kingfisher bird."

"That's true. That is true. But doesn't the Bible say, 'What God has planned for people who love him is more than eyes have seen or ears have heard'? 'It is more than what has never even entered their minds.'"

"Yes, it does," Thunderbolt conceded. "You are quoting a version of First Corinthians 2:9."

A moment of silence stilled their graveyard conversation before Gregory responded. "All I'm saying," he interjected, "is that you said the Spirit of God woke you up this morning and told you to call me. If it's the same Spirit of God that brought us here and allowed us to see birds of his creation take flight, then maybe that flight is something we should pay attention to. That's all."

Thunderbolt changed the conversation as his eyes followed the distant sight of his wife Sibyl and the woman walking with her. "What made these rice fields so productive?" he asked. "And why is no rice grown here anymore?"

Gregory looked to the other side of the Black River, pointed, and waited for Thunderbolt's gaze to follow. "See that line of trees over there?" he said. "They're growing on top of a long berm of dirt known as a dike." When Thunderbolt nodded, he continued. "There's a rice field on the other side of them. There are miles upon miles of dirt banks all around each former rice field in Georgetown County. And there are about forty-five thousand of those!"

Gregory's history lesson began to churn stories like the pounding of a mortar and pestle husking grains of rice. The rhythm of his words pounded. Up. And down. Up. And down.

"These Africans
Lying here
And their families
Transformed this earth
With dikes and fields
And ditches and paths
In forests that once
Were cypress swamps.
What they did
To this land

Was on the scale of construction
That can be seen
In Egypt
Of the pyramids!
God did this!
Through these people
Brought from shores
Far, far away.
They knew these fields.
Thousands died in these fields.
They grew this rice
That fed the world
With skills that were etched
On their DNA."

Caught up in a West African rhythmic, sermonic, storytelling stupor, Gregory did not notice the approach of Eloise and Sibyl, Melvin and Thelma. Each couple stood on either side of Timothy Thunderbolt, their common denominator, as they listened and learned.

Perspiration droplets began to dance down Gregory's face. He resumed his trance-like oration. Up. And down. Up. And down.

"No eye has seen,
No ear has heard,
No mind has conceived
What God has in store
For this people.
His African people
Brought to this land
Years ago
On ships,
Wrapped in chains,
Snatched from their homelands.
They brought their homelands
Within their memories
To this New World."

The pounding rhythm continued without words, momentarily, until they again were showered down upon him.

"Past is Present.
Present is Past.
Future is now!"

Gregory's eyes scanned the grave tops, the heavens, the branches of trees, as words reverberated within his mind and then were expelled from his lips. Pounding. Pounding. Pounding.

"All they accomplished
May be hidden from sight.
But it's all right there,
Right here,
Before our eyes—"

His knees buckled, he collapsed, and his fellow graveyard visitors rushed to revive him.

"Do you see it?" he asked when his eyes opened. Timothy Thunderbolt lifted his left hand from Gregory's forehead as he looked down upon him. Thunderbolt's right hand had been outstretched to heaven, and his eyes had been closed in prayer.

Mother Eloise began to sing-stomp the words of the spiritual, "What a Mighty God We Serve." Melvin Marshel, with hands still clasped in his wife's hands muttered, "We heard a rhythm, a pounding. Where was it coming from?"

Gregory's awakening released them all from whatever calling or spiritual enchantment had brought them, couple by couple, to Mourning Dove Cemetery. The three unconnected yet intricately intertwined couples had lost track of time or awareness of who else might be gathered there as they stepped toward an audible pounding of an unseen mortar and pestle.

"Tee, it's a surprise to see you here," Sibyl said, standing from her crouched position beside Gregory's prone body.

Timothy smiled and reached for her hand. Standing, he did a doubletake as he recognized his twin sister and brother-in-law. "Now, how in heaven did you two travel to Georgetown and not let us know you were coming?" he asked.

"Aww, please don't be upset, brother," Thelma said. "We didn't tell anyone we were coming. Not even Melvin's folks." She looked to her husband, who nodded in agreement.

"Uh, we're coming up from a rough patch in our marriage," Melvin said. He put his right arm around Thelma's shoulder and pulled her close. "We just took a drive . . . and shared stories, some old, some new. I wanted her to see where many in my family have been gathered."

Eloise interrupted. "Now, God is a wonder-working God! Dat fa true," she said. "And I wanted Sibyl to know where *our* family is gathered."

Puzzled, Timothy looked at Sibyl, who smiled. "And that's a new story I've got to share with you, dear," she began. "Remember my family's story of 'Mobo, the African,' my great grandfather?"

He nodded.

"Well, he came from here. From nearby Darcatia Plantation. Not from the 'Dark Continent,' as the story went. Well, yes, he did come from Africa. But he escaped from here. And Mobo was Mother Eloise's grand-uncle. She and I are related. I'm her great-grand-niece. Versions of that same Mobo story have been passed down in our families for generations. Now that we've filled in the missing pieces on both sides, the circle is unbroken."

More alert, Gregory began to move his arms and hands to push himself up into a sitting position. Timothy and Melvin rushed to assist.

"Do you see it?" he asked, repeating what he'd spoken when he'd regained consciousness. "All that our people accomplished? All that they endured?"

"Oh, we been comin a long time! Oh, yes," Eloise chanted. "But, like we ol peepul say, 'I come this far. Find no fault. An feel like journey on.'"

Timothy patted his right foot, trying to soak in all he'd experienced since he'd awakened. "But what I can't understand is this," he said. "Why don't they grow rice here anymore?"

"Hmpf," Eloise grumbled. "Chile, rice growin beenna slow down atta de war wa set we free. Wen de big guns been shoot, an we yeddy we ain haffa do da hard plantation wok no mo, tata done done, chile! Tata done! Mos ebbybohdy look fa betta tings fa do!"

Timothy chuckled at her poetic imagery of a cooked potato being done and nodded slowly.

"And when the hurricanes flooded these freshwater rivers and creeks with salt water from down in Winyah Bay," Melvin explained, "the rice fields were destroyed. My parents said their parents told them it was the storm of 1893. After that, hunting lodges opened up in and near many of the old plantation houses."

"But if these fields grew rice once, and big time at that, can't they grow rice again?" Timothy asked.

Gregory, listening intently, began to shake his head. "These fields are on private land, now," he said. "There's a new kind of rice production, maybe, that doesn't require as much labor as during slavery. But like Mother Eloise says, 'Who would want to do that backbreaking work again?' And the private landowners, in their lodges, and in their rice barns that have been converted to mancaves, do not want any farm workers traipsing across their well-manicured lawns. And the rice fields, after control-burns—enslaved Africans didn't call it that, but that's what they did each year after cleaning the trees from the dikes and then turning the ground before planting season. Well, after the burns and the new growth of rice plants, the rice fields become the place-to-be for migratory ducks and fowl. And that's how the hunting lodges thrive."

Sibyl tapped the fingers of her right hand on her right thigh as she listened to her husband. "What are you thinking about, Tee?" she asked. "Something's going through that mind of yours. I can feel it."

"Well, God brought us all here for a reason . . . and people need work. Work produces income. And income meets community needs. And above all that, I'm learning that there's a type of work in Georgetown that's of great historical significance."

Gregory began clapping in a slow roll, nodding in Timothy's direction, and smiling as though his soul was filled as the tempo increased.

"This is almost too much for one day," he said. "Most preachers I've come across are far too heaven-minded to be earthly concerned."

"Well, we got a pastor who is *dat* and *dat*," Eloise crowed. "Dat is why our church has started 'G.I.A.N.T'."

"It means God Is A Now-day Testimony," Sibyl added, swaying her shoulders and head in a triumphant bob.

Watching her brother's face and sensing a familiar fraternal-twin inkling from the furrow above his eyebrows, Thelma asked, "What's going on, Timothy? Are you getting a vision, a plan of action?"

Gregory's face opened up. He smiled at his twin and said, "Why, yes, sis, I am. It's always surprising how you know things I may be thinking before I even say anything." Glancing admiringly at Sibyl, he continued, "Since you got married, and I found Sibyl, only my bride has been able to connect with me like that."

Turning to face the group, he said, "Maybe, if the private landowners saw something in it for them, something more than just relinquishing their control of the land and the rice fields, maybe there can be a win-win situation for landowners and interested Black rice farmers."

"Uh huh," Melvin said. "What do you have in mind?"

"It seems to me," Thunderbolt began, "that if the landowners were inclined to rent the rice fields for rice production, say with planting in April and harvesting in August, the rice could be harvested, and then the fields could be flooded again, or burned, to be ready to attract birds for the hunting lodges. I think Carolina Gold could make a comeback, and this time Gullah people could reap the harvest!"

Melvin's mouth gaped open. "Now, why hasn't someone thought of that before?" he asked. "Daddy always said that the second crop of wild rice grows in the fields about four to six weeks after the first one has been harvested. Once the fields are re-flooded on the rice stalks that stand about a foot high, the wild rice will start to grow. And wild rice is what the ducks find when they migrate this way—not that first crop of rice that'll make Gullah people pat their bellies." As he tapped his tummy several times with both hands, he looked to Thelma with eyes of awkward affection that pleaded understanding. When she rolled her eyes then looked at him lovingly and smiled back, he continued with a flourish that revealed his deep Gullah heritage, "Den grea-a-a-t-t day een de maw-w-w-nin!" Thelma's body tightened.

"Well, that's the vision I've been given," Thunderbolt said. "And without a vision—"

"—the people perish!" all the others chimed in.

Pastor Thunderbolt looked from face to face. "Well, does it sound like something to move forward with?" he asked. "After a little more thought, of course."

"Well, I got a feeling everything is gonna be all right," Mother Eloise said.

"I think it's important that the *right* person make any initial inquiries about this to any community members, White or Black," Gregory said. "And it can't be you, Pastor. No matter what your church programs are."

Sibyl eyed Gregory with concern until Melvin agreed and offered further explanation. "That's right, Gregory Dunkin," he said. "I couldn't have expressed it *mo righta dan dat.*"

Thelma's body flinched at her husband's continued degradation of the English language, and she looked at him askance. Eloise's eyes smiled in understanding of Gregory's code-switching—aware of the couple's private disconnect.

"Regardless of good plans, ideas, or whatnot, Pastor Thunderbolt, here, is a comeyah," Melvin continued. "And beenyahs, White or Black, 'wohn yeddy nottin him haffa say.' That would be a *giant* faux pas!"

Eloise and Gregory guffawed their "Amens" of agreement, and Timothy, Sibyl, and Thelma, soon thereafter, deferred to their wisdom.

"All right, then," Timothy said. He thought for a few moments with his chin resting on the thumb of his right hand. His head began to nod slowly, and he asked, "Would you be interested in being point-person, Gregory?"

He began singing an answer to the tune of "Standing in the Need of Prayer," as he shook his head. "Not me, not me, not me, oh, no. I'm not the one to handle this . . ." and except for Timothy, all others chuckled at his solo. "To most, I'm just the son of a root doctor," he explained, with his eyes set on the pastor. "To others, I'm just some new kind of root doctor—carrying the weight of every kind of connotation people may have. I'm not the one you need, but—"

Here he paused, placed the fingers of his opened palms on either side of his head, closed his eyes, and remained silent. Others looked suspiciously among themselves. Without saying so, each was spooked by the thought of hearing pulsating rhythms throughout the graveyard again.

Gregory inhaled deeply and lowered his hands as he opened his eyes. All awaited his revelation. "There's someone you know, Pastor," he said. "A beenyah. A businessman who's well liked among community members and who knows investors who are associates of the very landowners you want to do business with. The Spirit says he's the one you should partner with because he has a legacy plan that's gotten off-rail and needs to be put back on track."

He closed his eyes again and lowered his head. When they reopened, he said, "Well, let all who have ears to hear, hear."

Barry's body rocked slowly on the sofa, nervously awaiting what would be the third weekly visit to his home by Pastor Thunderbolt. Today, he'd be accompanied by his wife. When the doorbell rang, his mother, Kendra Gilliard, set a pitcher of juice and a tray of fruit, crackers, and cheese onto the coffee table as her husband, Raymond, invited the guests in. The parents flanked their son on the couch. The Thunderbolts sat in armchairs angled towards the table's outer corners.

On the two previous visits, with the parents' approval, Thunderbolt had listened only as Barry shared his experiences, fears, confusions. At the conclusion of each meeting, he'd thanked Barry for his openness and promised to seek divine guidance. Unlike today's visit, just one parent had sat with them each time.

"Thanks for having us over, folks," Pastor Thunderbolt said. "I wanted Sibyl to join me this time just to emphasize that we, as a family, are prayerful for your family's peace throughout all you've been dealing with. Barry, the things you've shared with me are unlike things I've dealt with in my life, but I just want to assure you . . . I see God's hand in all of this."

Raymond and Kendra eyed each other and inched closer to their son. Barry's rocking slowed but didn't stop. Timothy looked to Sibyl, who nodded for him to continue.

"Well, Barry, I believe—with God guiding my thoughts, that is—that the taunts that you've received from people, the nightmares you're having about future experiences you'll encounter, and your body, mind, and heart's reaction to endure all of this each time you may feel like giving up, is a testament that God has got you!"

Barry stopped rocking. Hearing no unspoken criticism or demeaning voices from within, he relaxed. He smiled. He listened.

"My husband tells me God's preparing you for greatness!" Sibyl said.

"You've just *got* to stay close to God," Thunderbolt continued.

"When you lose your way—and if you do, you won't be the first person to do so—just find your way back to His care. He'll be waiting and He'll build you back up."

Glancing from Barry to his parents, Thunderbolt spoke about the biblical story of David, the shepherd boy who was anointed to be king. "His seven brothers were taller, better looking, older, and thought to be more accomplished," Thunderbolt said, "but God chose the shepherd boy, David, to be the second king of Israel. Not the brothers. It was David's experiences that skilled him. He learned to fight savage animals to protect the sheep. He learned to stay courageous when things didn't go well. And he learned to rejoice before God by playing his stringed instrument in the nighttime air.

"God has told me to tell you, Barry, that one day you'll share your story with many. And it's a story many will need to hear. The taunting is meant to strengthen you. It's okay to be different. Leaders are different. The nightmares about going through all kinds of unusual and unsavory experiences are to strengthen you. In each dream you've told me about, you've somehow gotten out of the pit you've found yourself in. People will need to hear how God brought you through. And all you've gone through so far, all of it has been to strengthen you. Maybe your parents have an inkling about what your story will be. Me? I don't have a clue. What I do know is this: God is raising you up to be a light. He is connecting things so that you can reveal to many the timelessness of a place, a place where the past morphs into future, and present into past. Seamlessly. Smoothly. A place where spiritual energy is felt. Ancestral echoes are heard. And melodies are sung in the speech of many and in the rustling of tree limbs."

Barry reclined his head on the sofa, lifted his feet, and wiggled them from side to side, as though they had been freshly washed. He sighed and continued listening.

"So, you must always remember to return to Him," Thunderbolt said. "And just as He is doing for you, at the right time you must tell others to return. To fetch and bring forward. To return to the wisdom, love, truth, strength, and heritage that sustains them. As a light, tell others to be enslaved to no one and nothing. Barry, Barry, Barry . . . until and when you know why you're being stretched and strengthened, don't dim your light. Don't allow it to fade. No, let your light shine!"

One week later

Laverne rose in surprise from her seat at Savory & Scrumptious Deli. Florence, responding to her invitation to have lunch and catch-up, entered carrying an infant car seat and holding a walnut-colored baby swaddled in a white blanket. *Now, she couldn't have been expecting when we last saw each other,* Laverne thought. *Not when she gave me the money to take a cruise to Jamaica to think things out. I know I was in a bad state, but I should've seen. I should've known!*

After Laverne grabbed the car seat, the women embraced, then sat. "I know this must be a shock for you," Florence said. "Well, it's still new for me. I'm a mom now! I didn't say anything about it when you called because the story is too long to tell over the phone. But every day is just filled with new surprises in the Wineglass home."

"What's the name?" Laverne asked.

"Blessing Celeste. Blessing after my grandmother. And Celeste because she's a gift from God. One day I wasn't a parent, and the next day I was!"

The ladies chatted, laughed, smiled, ate.

"Well, it's a new family scene for me too!" Laverne said. "Thank you so much, Florence, for your friendship, the advice, the money."

"Girl, it's when you're down and don't know you're down that you need a friend to help pull you up. How are things with Medicus . . . and your *beloved* mother-in-law?"

"Well, it was while I was sunning myself on the beach in Jamaica that I realized I had not felt the sun on my skin for a long time. I'd been too busy caring for Medicus, and making excuses for Medicus, and tolerating Hester, and I somehow forgot to care for me."

Thinking that Laverne's words parroted her own truth, Florence responded, "Oh, yes, sometimes that's what a lot of us do."

"But the one who knows to take care of herself, to let her life feel the warmth of the sunlight, is the one who will live," Laverne interrupted. "I'm a survivor, Florence. Thanks to you! Hester Grice is out of my home." She raised her hands and wiggled her fingers. "She's in a nursing home nearby and is getting adjusted. I returned to work two days ago after a three-week leave. And Medicus is working on his issues. All of them. How that goes will determine how the two of us stand, but right now, all I'm doing is just soaking in the sunshine as much as I can."

Heading home to Edisto Island early one Saturday morning, Porcher stopped for gas at a convenience store on the outskirts of Georgetown. He walked inside to purchase a cup of decaf and heard a familiar voice calling his.

"Well, if it ain't 'Mr. Grea-a-a-t-t day,'" Chadwick said with a chuckle from behind the register. "How's it going?"

Having not heard from him in a while and not certain of the reason, Russell responded with a greeting from his childhood, "I'm right here in mercy trus. I don't make no fuss." His tone had an air of indifference, and he looked at Wineglass indirectly. Indeed, making no fuss was his intent—that and leaving quickly. He had no concern for what may have led to Chadwick's disconnect.

"What's got you out before sunrise?" Chadwick asked, embarking upon a conversation.

"Headed to Edisto," Russell answered. "I couldn't leave last night, so I'm off to surprise Mignon before she wakes up, then to shuttle and sit at the kids' practices. You know, soccer with Eldridge this morning, jazz dance with Ethiopia in the early afternoon, then pizza night with the family."

"A busy day, Porcher. A very busy day!"

"Yeah-h-h-h," he answered. "Gotta get my quality time in."

The response seemed like the old Chadwick Wineglass Russell'd known. Before the new Chadwick Wineglass had begun ignoring him. Before Gary Windley had spooked him with cautionary tales. He decided to maintain distance, paid for the coffee, then smiled and nodded before extending a pleasant, "See ya later."

But a new and improved Chadwick Wineglass interrupted his salutation and altered his plans. "I know you're in a rush," he pleaded, "but if you can wait around for about ten more minutes, my shift will change, and I need someone to talk to . . . I mean . . . I need a friend. Could you do that? For me? Please?"

"Sure," Russell answered, taken aback. "I'll be outside." He pointed to the pump where he'd parked, then added, "I'll pull up to the front."

Wineglass seemed caught up in an emotional state that Russell had never encountered in him before. Russell extended a fist bump to Chadwick when he finally approached, ensuring there would be no handshake-exchange of folded dollar bills. Wineglass had nothing in his right palm when he opened it afterward, and his facial expression urged, *Can we talk?*

"Walk on around," Russell said, motioning his head to the passenger side and pushing the unlock button on the key fob. They sat for about forty-five minutes, delaying Russell's return to Edisto Island. He learned that this had been Chadwick's final part-time shift, and that he would be returning to only working at his full-time business, Wineglass French Drain Installation. Chadwick explained that in one surprising day he had become the father of a two-week-old daughter named Blessing Celeste. That his wife was a bit undone with him about, among other things, a practice of community giving that they'd been involved in—one that once had included Russell.

"Well, I hear my daddy's voice telling me to help people," Chadwick said. "I just want to honor him. I want a wife who'll help me, but she just wants to—"

"When we listen to the voices from our past, we've got to know exactly what those messages mean," Russell countered. "Sometimes we've got to fit their meanings from another time to our circumstances today. Seems like Florence wants to do the same thing as you, just in a different way. From what you're describing, what you want to do strangles people of hope, motivation, spark, and optimism."

"What do you mean?"

"I didn't want your money, Chadwick! Where did you get that story from? Friendship is good. Not friendship that must always tell me what to do. Not a friendship that always gives a handout, but a friendship that sometimes will just listen when I have something to say. That'll sit with me in sorrow. Laugh with me in times of joy. Help me to find my way home if I'm lost—

and allow me to do the same. That's what friendship is."

After a pause to let thoughts sink in, Russell asked Chadwick what kind of work his father had done.

"King Solomon Wineglass? Well, he was a clerk of court," Chadwick answered. "And he always cautioned us not to get tangled up in the court system."

"Ummm," Russell said. "I bet people who had family members in trouble with the law would try to curry favor with your father every day. Maybe they'd pretend to be friends until they got what they needed or wanted. Or maybe they'd turn their insincere friendship against him if they couldn't get the results they wanted."

Chadwick sat motionless without speaking for a few moments. "You know," he said, "I vaguely remember overhearing the conversations my parents would have late at night in their bedroom. Daddy would complain about going through another trial where the magistrate had contacted the same pool of downtown White business owners to serve as jurors for Black defendants. Mama would tell him he'd done all he could do for community members by always reminding them to stay out of the Georgetown legal system."

"Yeah?"

"Uh huh. Then he'd mumble about the jurors deciding before deliberation began just how long they would take to decide if the defendant was innocent or guilty. It was only a matter of how soon they wanted to get back to their businesses, never a matter how serious the charge might be. Wow, I haven't thought about that in some time."

Porcher responded, "Your understanding of your father's advice seems to have your mind all tied up in knots, Wineglass. We call that 'tanglyup' in Edisto. But, man, you betta bust loose from the story you've been telling yourself!" He pantomimed adult-like motions of the "Hokey Pokey" and sang, "You better turn yourself around. That's what it's all about!"

"Did your dad's words also make you wary of people offering you thanks?" he continued.

Chadwick rocked his head sideways several times, then nodded in surprise.

"Well, showing thanks is one of the things most parents start training children to do as soon as they can speak," Russell said. "'Say thank you,' we tell them. 'Give so-and-so a big hug for showing you some kindness,' we say. But after *you* bless someone, *you* tell them, 'Don't bless me back!' What's that? You think you're better than everyone?"

"No, it's not that," Chadwick answered. "I just don't want them to think they owe me, that they must outdo me."

"Now, how could anyone do that? Particularly when you've helped them out at a time when they're at a financial low point. Here's a story my father told me. There was an Island midwife who delivered more than two thousand babies. She'd charge six dollars for girls and seven for boys, but some of her patients never paid her—at least, not with money. When she was an old woman, Miss Maggie would joke, 'Some of the babies I delivered have died and gone to heaven, and the parents haven't paid me yet. Some parents were like the frog when the snake caught him. The frog say, "Turn me loose!" Then when the snake turned him loose, he forgot. That's how they did me.'

"But what Dad wanted me to realize was that they hadn't forgotten her. They hadn't turned her loose. Throughout her life, the Islanders would leave gifts at her door. Buckets of fish. Baskets of produce. Bags of pecans. They wanted to show thanks in the ways that they could. If you don't allow people to do that, you put a chokehold on an important part of a person's human decency.

"People who won't let you say 'thank you' in a way that's important to them to express thanks—not to pay you back, mind you, but to bless you in some small way because you've blessed them—well, people who do that have an arrogance in the pit of their heart that God despises."

"What?" Chadwick asked, and without awareness began to tighten his fists.

"They're selfish, Chadwick. Only thinking about themselves. And how God will bless them because they've blessed others."

"Porcher, you're talking loud but saying nothing," Chadwick stated. "God wants us to bless others. Nothing's wrong with that."

"Well, listen to this," Porcher said. "Here's what I know. The next time that person who has been blessed is blessed by someone else, that someone else who gives may do so from all of what they have, not from what they have in excess or abundance. Everybody doesn't give from excess or abundance. Some give only because they want to do what the Lord or the Spirit or the Universe has compelled them to do. And if the blessee of the second go-round has learned from the blesser of the first go-round not to express thankfulness in some small way, then the blesser of the second or subsequent go-round may not get the blessing that the Lord or the Spirit or Universe may want for him or her to receive."

Porcher tilted his head down to the right and raised it up, looking straight into Chadwick's face. "See what I mean?"

Chadwick bobbed his head back as though he'd been sucker-punched. "Blessees and blessers," he said. "You think you're a lawyer or something?" Then he chuckled. "So, what you're saying is like the words of one of the songs they sing at Walking Up the King's Highway."

Porcher waited for him to continue.

"You can't beat God's giving . . ."

Russell shook his head then joined him, ". . . no matter how hard you try."

They sat for a few minutes. Russell stared aimlessly at customers pumping gas and entering and exiting the store. Chadwick, lost in thought, patted a staccato rhythm on the dashboard with his right hand.

"Man, wha you not gon do is open dat can a beans an nyam em een my truck so early een de mawnin!" A man dressed in construction garb shouted to a co-rider after he'd placed the gas hose back on the pump. The culprit—muscular, about five-feet tall, midnight black, with a trimmed black beard and a thick set of eyebrows—pulled a plastic spoon out of the convenience store bag as he walked hurriedly back to the pickup truck. He'd already opened the can of baked beans.

"Oona pick me up a half ouah too early taday, Rufus," he responded. "Venesia ain had no time to fix me no breakfus. A hungry, man. Hungry hungry!" As he stepped from the running board into the front passenger seat, his hard hat grazed the top of the truck door opening.

Wineglass and Porcher turned to each other and chuckled at the ensuing Gullah conversation before the truck drove away. Each understood the driver's dilemma of having a farting co-rider in a crowded vehicle. The construction worker in the middle of the front seat and the two others in the cab section had lots to say.

"Oh, no! Yo beans-behine boonkus!"

"Him gon stink we up to high hebn!"

"Down de winda, yall! Down de winda an keep em down. Please!"

When their loud guffawing mellowed to more suppressed snickering, Russell stated, "Man, they so jokey!" and slapped his thigh with the palm of his right hand.

"Cracky is what you mean," Chadwick replied. "Cracky down!" Then he asked, "Porcher, how did you know Mignon was the one?"

"You know, my sister-in-law asked me that question two days before my wedding. My brother's family had just arrived in town, and we'd gone on an after-dinner stroll through the neighborhood. A brisk autumn breeze made me zip my sweater up to my neck. At that moment, out of the corner of my eye on the left, I saw an oak tree leaf pop off a limb and begin plummeting down. It swirled in the wind as it descended, showing off its discoloration along the way. And that's when I knew how to answer her question."

"Yeah?" Chadwick said. "What do you mean."

"I told her, 'See that? That's what Mignon would see. Now, I might not, and others might not. But she'd see it, and if we were walking together, she'd say, 'Vernon Russell, look at that! Isn't it beautiful? Magical?' Now, I don't like beautiful and magical to the degree she does. But I'm glad she wants to experience something that gives her joy—with me. That's right. Me! And she's the one who clasps my hand when I'm enjoying things she could care less about. It makes us partners for life.

"To stay ignorant of, or unconcerned about, what brings your lover joy will make the grains in your rice field dry up and wither. Even if the rice stalks rise above the floodwater, that stagnant water will breed heartbreak and stress and loneliness."

Code-switching, Porcher added, "Dah wa oona wan? Well den, ya belly won't get no rice een de mawnin or at dinnatime. Uh uh uh!" Then he concluded, "Let your wife be your friend, Chadwick! In that friendship, nurture and raise little Blessing Celeste."

"You're right, Porcher. You're right," Chadwick said. "She helps me to prosper, to think *big*!" He paused as he reflected on his and Florence's dream for B.I.G.—Benefactors in Generosity, his experience at Otis Doyle's bonfire, and the conversations he'd overheard about the disturbed bodies at the slave graveyard in Hagley Plantation. "Yeah, she's taught me that everyone who offers to help you is looking for something in return," he mused, "just like I'd been doing. Instead of helping others to prosper just because they're worthy of prospering in the best way they can."

Chadwick sat back and exhaled. Noticing the hurt behind his eyes, Porcher said, "Dats right, Wineglass. Sometimes the things we do that we think are good for others only leaves them feeling gutted and drained."

Chadwick gazed at the horizon. "I guess I better not hold you up any longer," he said to his friend. "I've slowed down your early reconnect with your family." He opened the door slightly, paused, and then pulled it closed. "Russell, you know what you've helped me to see?"

"What's that, Chadwick?"

"I think what Florence has been wanting me to realize is this: 'When we're connected, we know each other. And when we know our connections, we can best help each other!' She would always show me these writings of Marcus Garvey, a Jamaican hero we first heard about when we were on our honeymoon."

Glancing at his phone, Porcher sat erect when he saw the time. *I'd better call Mignon soon, to alert her I'll be arriving later than expected,* he thought. *Hearing about this morning's conversation will be a bigger surprise for her than the one I'd planned.*

"Wow, we've been here awhile," he said to Chadwick. "You wanna grab some breakfast somewhere?"

Chadwick's phone rang, and he motioned for Russell to wait a moment as he answered it. He sauntered behind the car, speaking in low, measured tones. "Yes, nice to speak with you too, Pastor," Porcher overheard him say. "This is a surprise. I thought you didn't wish to discuss any kind of business ideas with me."

"Next time, Porcher," Chadwick said when he walked back to the side window. "That was a call about a business idea that could change everything. It's just the kind of thing Florence and I had been planning for!" He turned and rushed to his SUV, calling out, "Next time, friend. There's some shrimp and gravy over rice waiting for me at home." He turned back, crouched at the car window, and said, "Thanks, man! Thanks for the talk. This won't be the last. Please forgive me for not being the friend you deserve. I've been confused about a lot of things. A lot of things. But 'when we know our connections, we can best help each other.' And I can't abuse others in any way in order to help them."

Chadwick expressed a thought with words that would've made

his mother Bernice believe someone had placed some of her hair inside a bird's nest to give her a splitting headache. Speaking in deep down Gullah Geechee he said, "Porcher, deres now a connection deep down een me sperit wit me wife, me famlee, me communatee, me peepuls, and me frien dem."

The sun was rising as Porcher headed south—much later than he'd planned but with an awareness that his time had been well-spent. Overhead, the shadows of two raptors, their pairs of large wings circling in flight, did not appear ominous, but majestic. In cemeteries and graveyards, the silent cities of the dead, the souls of settlers who'd scurried away the Cherokees before staking ownership to their homeland and establishing Owners Town recoiled in horror. The descendants of those they'd enslaved had reclaimed mastery of their culture, their beliefs, their economic destiny—without being returned to their African homelands, and without needing handouts. Instead, at times, they uplifted themselves or were uplifted by community members, Black, White, Gullah Geechee, American. Although the surnames of many linked their pasts, presents, and futures throughout centuries to the institution of slavery, changed mindsets unfettered them.

Realizing the depth of the pit of trouble, sorrow, and shame that his father's unquestioned words had hurled him into, Chadwick freed his mind and embraced friendship—with Florence, with others. And, like the wings of angels, the green fronds on the stately lone palmetto tree in Mourning Dove Cemetery moved up and down, up and down. The rustling branches proclaimed it as a tree in a community that was rooted in Wisdom, with heritage planted deep: fruitful and blossoming, remaining upright through times of trouble, prosperous from generation to generation.

Songbirds trilled and chattered, heralding the affirmations that abounded. All who listened without understanding could not comprehend. Yet the music, the messages, floated on the breezes. In the thermals of warm air or updrafts, the raptors in the ricelands soared, spreading the wisdom from lives lived and lessons learned.

THE END

Bibliography

Barksdale, Richard, and Keneth Kinnamon. "Oratory and Essays of Marcus Garvey." Essay. In *Black Writers of America: A Comprehensive Anthology*, 565–67. New York: Macmillan, 1985.

Beck, John J. "Root Doctors." https://www.ncpedia.org/root-doctors, 2006.

Blake, Tom. "Georgetown County, South Carolina, Largest Slaveholders From 1860 Slave Census Schedules and Surname Matches For African Americans On 1870 Census,." https://sites.rootsweb.com/~ajac/scgeorgetown.htm, August 2001.

Burt, Stephanie. "Natalie Daise on What We Call Holy." THE BITTER SOUTHERNER, February 16, 2021. https://bittersoutherner.com/feature/2021/natalie-daise-on-what-we-call-holy.

Cornelius, Janet Duitsman. "Slave Missions and the Black Church in the Antebellum South." Google Books. Accessed June 2, 2023. https://rb.gy/y17ty

Crawford, Eric Sean, and Bessie Foster Crawford. *Gullah Spirituals: The Sound of Freedom and Protest in the South Carolina Sea Islands*. Columbia, SC: the University of South Carolina Press, 2021.

Daise, Ron with Kemper, Sally. "Rice Field Creek Excursion, School Field Trip Revised Script," Brookgreen Gardens, 2019.

Daise, Ronald. *Gullah Branches, West African Roots*. Orangeburg, SC: Sandlapper Publ., 2007.

Daise, Ronald. *Little Muddy Waters, A Gullah Folk Tale*. Beaufort, SC: G.O.G. Enterprises, 1997.

Daise, Ronald. *Reminiscences of Sea Island Heritage, Legacy of Freedmen on St. Helena Island*. Orangeburg, SC: Sandlapper Publishing, Inc., 1986.

Daise, Sara Makeba. "Come On In The Room: Afrofuturism As a Path to Black Women's Retroactive Healing, A Creative Thesis," 2018.

Daise, Sara Makeba. "The South Is a Portal." Root Work Journal. Accessed June 2, 2023. https://www.rootworkjournal.org/daise.

"FROM WHENCE WE CAME: History of the Georgetonian Ball South." Georgetown, SC: Howard High School Alumni Association, 2019.

Garvey, Marcus Mosiah. "American Experience | Marcus Garvey | Primary Sources." PBS, Speech by Marcus Garvey, July 8, 1917. Accessed June 26, 2023. http://www.shoppbs.pbs.org/wgbh/amex/garvey/filmmore/ps_riots.html.

Google. Adoption - South Carolina Department of Social Services. Accessed June 2, 2023. https://dss.sc.gov/child-well-being/adoption/.

Google. "Ancestors Fingermarks Project." https://rb.gy/zmsnn

Google. "Chicken Bog Recipe: A Wholesome, Tasty, and Affordable Meal." Healthy Recipe 101, June 2, 2023. https://healthyrecipes101.com/chicken-bog-recipe/.

Google. "Cluster Fly." Google search. Accessed June 2, 2023. https://rb.gy/mu6b4

Google. Cross Roads Baptist Church (background-100s/2020/8/26/cross-roads-baptist-church), n.d. https://senecacitymuseums.org/background-100s/2020/8/26/cross-roads-baptist-church.

Google. "History of the Divine Nine Fraternities & Sororities, n.d." https://www.apsva.us/black-history-month/history-of-the-divine-nine-fraternities-sororities/.

Google. "Howard High School." https://greenbookofsc.com/locations/howard-school/, n.d. Accessed June 2, 2023.

Google. "It's Time to Stand against White Supremacy, Fort Mill." Medium, June 17, 2020. https://medium.com/@endwhitesupremacyfortmill/its-time-to-stand-against-white-supremacy-fort-mill-ac9d93a84e0e.

Google. "Maurisina Plantation – Sampit River – Georgetown County." Maurisina Plantation – Georgetown County, South Carolina SC. Accessed June 2, 2023. https://south-carolina-plantations.com/georgetown/maurisina.html.

Google. Museum around the corner: Lumber is big business | community ..., August 12, 2020. https://rb.gy/y17ty

Google. "Native American Quotes." Native American. Accessed June 2, 2023. https://www.xavier.edu/jesuitresource/online-resources/quote-archive1/native-american1.

Google. "Orangeburg Massacre." History.com. Accessed June 2, 2023. https://www.history.com/topics/1960s/orangeburg-massacre.

Google. "Rice Culture." www.gullahmuseum.com, n.d. https://rb.gy/wbqr0

Google. "Roman Aqueducts." Home - National Geographic Society. Accessed June 2, 2023. https://www.nationalgeographic.org/encyclopedia/roman-aqueducts/.

Google. "The 1968 Orangeburg Massacre in South Carolina." Orangeburg Massacre: South
Carolina State, 1968. Accessed June 2, 2023. https://www.sciway.net/afam/orangeburg-massacre.html.

Google. 29 Famous Marcus Garvey Quotes (Confidence, Race, God), n.d. https://blackalliance.org/marcus-garvey-quotes/.

Hanh, Thich Nhat. Healing the child within – mindful, April 5, 2011. https://www.mindful.org/healing-the-child-within/.

Huffman, Greg. "The Group behind Confederate Monuments Also Built a Memorial to the Klan." Facing South, June 8, 2018. https://www.facingsouth.org/2018/06/group-behind-confederate-monuments-also-built-memorial-klan.

Hux, Roger K. "The Ku Klux Klan and collective violence in Horry County, 1922-1925 – JSTOR." Accessed June 3, 2023. https://www.jstor.org/stable/27567857.

Hyman S. Rubin, III. "Ku Klux Klan." South Carolina Encyclopedia, August 9, 2022. https://www.scencyclopedia.org/sce/entries/ku-klux-klan/.

Kassadjikova, Kalina, Stevens, Williams, and Fehren-Schmitz, Lars. "Genetic Analysis From Hagley Plantation C. 1860, Preliminary Results and Future Plans." . Georgetown, SC: UC Santa Cruz (UCSC), 2021.

Lawrence, Demi. "'Georgetown Slave's Remains Laid to Rest 15 Years after Discovery.'" PostandCourier.com, May 22, 2021.

Livingston, Samuel T. "The Site of Memory: The 1526 Project and Why It Matters." Blog Posts: The Site of Memory: Morehouse College, November 22, 2021. https://facultyblog.morehouse.edu/blog-posts/link-to-article-25740-en.html.

Maffly-Kipp, Laurie F. "An Introduction to the Church in the Southern Black Community." The church in the Southern Black Community, May 2001. https://docsouth.unc.edu/church/.

Magazine, Smithsonian. "Meet Joseph Rainey, the First Black Congressman." Smithsonian.com, January 1, 2021. https://www.smithsonianmag.com/history/joseph-rainey-first-black-congressman-180976502/.

Morrow, Kylie. "The Top Traditional Jamaican Sayings and Phrases: Sandals Blog." Hello Paradise – The Official Sandals Resorts Travel & Lifestyle Blog, March 27, 2018. https://www.sandals.com/blog/jamaican-sayings-and-phrases/.

Quattlebaum, Donald, and Ron Daise. Rice Production in Georgetown County, SC. Personal, March 16, 2022.

Ronald Daise. "I Love You and the Sweet Spirit of Your Soul." Recorded 2001. Track 2 on*Sweet Surprises, Christ-Centered Inspirational Love Songs.* G.O.G. Enterprises, 2001, compact disc.

"Seen, Heard, Esteemed: Living History Narratives of Georgetown County, SC Audio Tour, John Bolts, Scenes B and C." Murrells Inlet, SC: Brookgreen Gardens, 2021.

Skutsch, Carl. "The History of White Supremacy in America." Rolling Stone, June 25, 2018. https://www.rollingstone.com/politics/politics-features/the-history-of-white-supremacy-in-america-205171/.

Smith, Noel. "'(God,) You Were in It after All', a Sermon." Pawleys Island, SC: House of God Church, February 19, 2023.

St. Ann Homecoming & Heritage Foundation, and St. Ann Parish Library Network. "A Lecture in Celebration of the Life of The Rt. Excellent Marcus Mosiah Garvey, National Hero," n.d. https://www.facebook.com/watch/live/?ref=watch_permalink&v=203994241580158.

Swindoll, Chuck. "Devotional library'" Chuck Swindoll's "Insight for Today" Devotional library - Insight for Living Ministries, August and September, 2021. https://www.insight.org/resources/daily-devotional.

West, Patricia, and Ron Daise. What 'de grains say: Multimedia Environments that Sustain Rice Heritage. Other, March 19, 2022.

Williams, Steve. *The Lost History of the Howard School: Howard's Hidden History.* Myrtle Beach, SC: Waccamaw Press (Waccamaw Press.com), 2022.

Glossary

Gullah Geechee, known formerly as "Gullah" in South Carolina and North Carolina, and "Geechee" in Georgia and Florida, is a creolized, English-based language spoken by residents and descendants of enslaved West Africans who were brought to plantations of the Carolina and Georgia Colonies during the 1700s and 1800s. Gullah Geechee also identifies a culture and a group of people. Many Gullah Geechee words, expressions, and its syntax, have roots in numerous West African languages and dialects. The creolization of these African languages was influenced by English, Portuguese, French, and other languages, beginning in slave prisons, on slave ships, and on isolated coastal communities that were surrounded by waterways and inhabited by few non-Africans. In recent years, the recognition of Gullah Geechee speech as one of many retentions of West African heritage has challenged the erroneous perceptions of the language as "broken English," "bad English," or "an indicator of low intelligence."

An oral language for centuries, Gullah Geechee has no established orthography. Spellings below and the nonuse of apostrophes to acknowledge the legitimacy of the speechway are based on my work as a charter member of the Sea Island Translation and Literacy Project, St. Helena Island, SC, which in the 1970s began translating the Bible, *De Nyew Testament*, into Gullah. Variations of Gullah Geechee words and expressions exist throughout the Gullah Geechee Cultural Heritage Corridor, however. Moreover, contemporary Gullah Geechee speakers utilize and will continue to develop different expressions and phonetic spellings.

A

A—I
Ama—I am
a—a (article) or of (preposition)
ain—isn'
ain de know—do not know
ainty—Isn't that so?
anodda—another
anyting—anything

B

beenyah—native resident of the Gullah Geechee community
been + verb—past tense of the verb
beenna—had been
beenna + verb—past participle of the verb
befo—before
behine—behind
bestes—best
beutaful—beautiful
bigges—biggest
bitem—bite him, her, it, or them
bizness—business
bohdy—body
boht—both
boi—boy
boonky or boonkus—behind
bout—about
bot—but
breakfus—breakfast
breng—bring
bun—bun (noun), burn (verb)

C

cause—because
Chaaston—Charleston
chirren—children
chuch—church
comeyah—someone who relocates to a Gullah Geechee community
communatee—community
conja—conjure
corona—coroner
cracky—addle minded
cracky down—very addle minded
crick—creek
cryin—crying
cya—care
cyan—can't

D

da—to be
da gadda—are/is gathering

Dabid—David
de—the
dem—them
dem (following a singular noun)—the plural noun
dey—they
dah or dat—that
daid—dead
dah or dat—that
das or dats—that's
dayclean—dawn
deh—there
den—then or than
dikty—uppity
dis—this
docta—doctor
dohn—don't
dough—though
down de winda—close the window
dum—dumb
dus—dust
dut—dirt

E

e—he, she, it, or they; his, hers, its, or theirs
eba—ever
ebbyting or ebryting—everything
een—in
ef—if
ennit—Isn't that so?
enty—Isn't that so?
enty dah so—Isn't that so?
em—it, him, her, them

F

fa kill—to kill
fa sho—for sure, certainly
fa true—really
famlee—family
fiyah—fire
fibe—five
flouah—flour
fo—for or before

fool up—very silly
frien dem—friends
frum—from
fus—first
fush—fish

G

gadda—gather
ga fullup—will fill up
Gawd—God
git bring—were brought
glad glad—very glad
Goliat—Goliath
gone—went
good good—very good
goofa—gopher

H

haard—hard
haarm—harm
haart—heart
haid—head
hab—have
hebn—heaven
hep—help
hice—life
hiney—behind, bottom
him—his
hoht—hot
hol—hold
holin station—holding station
huh—her
hungry hungry—very hungry
hunnah—you
hut—hurt

I

J

jes—just
jokey—full of jokes

K

kinda—kind of

L

listenin—listening
lob—love
looky looky—see something special or unexpected

M

make foot fa socks—to be with child, pregnant
masta—plantation owner
masta dem—plantation owners
matas—tomatoes
mawnin—morning
me—my
Melbin—Melvin
memba—member or remember
mine—mind
minnit—minute
mo—more
mo righta—better
mos—most
mout—mouth

N

nebanomind—never no mind or nothing to worry about
needa—neither
nize—noise
nyam—eat

O

ob—of
oda—other
ol—old
oona—you
ooman—woman
orda—order
ouah—our
outcha—out here
ownt—own
oysta—oyster

P

pastah—pastor
peepul—people

peepul dem—all the people
powdah—powder
put de mout—speak a curse or misfortune on someone

Q

quick-quick—very quickly

R

rejice—rejoice
ruff—rough

S

sameso—just as
scraight—straight
seddown—sit down
sence—since
shada—shadow
sho—sure or show
shroat—throat
shru—through
so—sore
sof—soft
sompn—something
sperit—spirit
speritual—spiritual
sto—store
sweetes—sweetest
swimps—shrimp

T

taak—talk
tanglyup—entangled
tase—taste
tata done—“The potato is cooked,” meaning an action is/was finished/completed/over.
teet—teeth
tek—take
tek ya foot een ya hand—hurry
Telma—Thelma
tief—thief
tiefin—thievery
tiefy—prone to steal
til—until
ting—thing

tote—carry on the head or in the arms
trabble—travel
trus—trust

U

unavus—universe

V

W

wa or wha—what
wancha—to want you
wanfa—want to
wata—water
we—our, us
wen—when
wheh—where
whyso—why
winda—window
wit—with
woice—voice
woice dem—voices
wok—work

X

Y

ya—you, yours, or you are
yah—here
yard children—children born out of wedlock
yaard chirren—children born out of wedlock
yasef—yourself
yosef—yourself
yeh—hear or listen
yeddy—hear or listen
yo—you, yours, or you are
yuh—hear

Z

About the Artist

Photo by Freda Funnye

Front cover art, "Oya in the Rice Field," by Natalie Daise. Used by permission of the artist.

Natalie Daise is a visual artist, storyteller, and creativity catalyst who resides in Georgetown, SC, with her husband, Ron Daise.

"*Oya in the Rice Field* was inspired by my friend, the textile artist Zenobia Harper, who embodies her Gullah Geechee ancestors. She started the Gullah Preservation Society of Georgetown to honor their story. Georgetown was the center of rice production in the United States, and thousands of Africans were brought here to establish and maintain the rice economy. Oya is the Orisha of the wind and storms, responsible for gentle winds as well as hurricanes. She is also the protector of women."

About the Author

Photo by Reese Moore

RON DAISE, a son of St. Helena Island, SC, is an author, performer, educator, and cultural interpreter. His books, productions, and recordings have documented and shaped Gullah Geechee heritage since 1986. Co-star of "Gullah Gullah Island," Nick Jr. TV's award-winning children's program of the 1990s, Ron also is a former chairman of the federal Gullah Geechee Cultural Heritage Corridor Commission, and is featured in exhibits at the International African American Museum, Charleston, SC; the Smithsonian National Museum of African American History and Culture, Washington, DC; and Brookgreen Gardens, Murrells Inlet, SC. When not writing and performing, Ron is a baker and owner of Mr. Ron's Gullahlicious Pound Cakes.

A graduate of Hampton Institute (now Hampton University), Ron and his wife Natalie reside in Georgetown, SC, and are parents of two adult children. He can be found online at www.rondaise.com, on Instagram @gullahron, and on Meta @rondaise.

www.ingramcontent.com/pod-product-compliance
Lightning Source LLC
Jackson TN
JSHW021059260125
77723JS00002B/8

9781958754825